THE WIZENARD SERIES

TRAINING CAMP

THE WIZENARD SERIES
TRAINING CAMP

RAIN

TWIG

CASH

PEÑO

LAB

CREATED BY
KOBE BRYANT

WRITTEN BY
WESLEY KING

GRANITY STUDIOS
COSTA MESA, CALIFORNIA

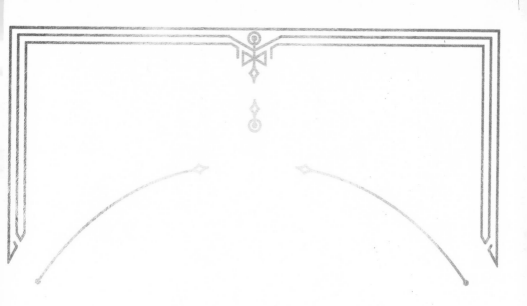

To my Wizenards—
Bill Russell, Tex Winter, Phil Jackson,
and Gregg Downer—who dedicated their time
to teaching athletes that magic comes from within.
Learning it just takes a little imagination.

—KOBE BRYANT

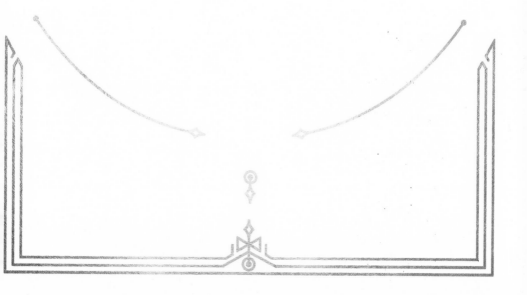

I, THE READER,
HEREBY AGREE
TO LEARN FROM

PROFESSOR
ROLABI WIZENARD

THE NATURE OF
ALL THINGS.

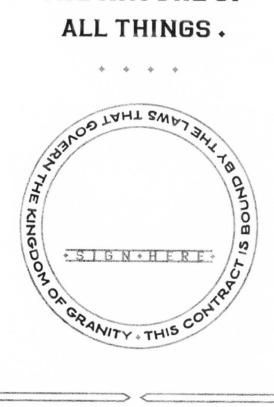

THE LAWS THAT GOVERN THE KINGDOM OF GRANITY · THIS CONTRACT IS BOUND BY

· SIGN · HERE ·

BOOK ONE

RAIN

THE PROFESSOR

Everyone has a choice every moment of the day.
Look, or look away.

✦ WIZENARD ⟨12⟩ PROVERB ✦

RAIN PULLED OPEN the doors and found darkness. He blinked until it became gray, then pale, then fluorescent. Shapes emerged like wraiths. Voices as faint whispers. Rain grinned.

It was good to be back.

Then Fairwood Community Center's sticky-hot air fell over him, thick with dust and the competing smells of mildew and dry rot. Rain sighed, his grin melting away with the first sheen of sweat. Fairwood was *old*. Seventy-five years of sweat had seeped into the hardwood and the yellowing walls and even the rafters that stretched overhead in creaking A-beam formations. No windows, no fans, no air-conditioning. The gym boiled in its own brine.

His eyes fell on the single line of fraying multicolored banners nailed into the concrete. Rain could recite the details on every one of them— the year, the team, and the title. When Rain was younger, his dad used to come to all of his practices and games, and afterward they stared at the banners together, and whispered, and dreamed of adding more. So as dilapidated as Fairwood Community Center was, the place was in Rain's bones. He knew every inch of the run-down gym. The stains and the smells and the forgotten glory.

"Not for long," he whispered, then headed for the bench to join the others.

"The Rain Maker!" Big John called out, cupping his mouth like a loudspeaker.

Rain laughed and exchanged props with the backup center.

"So, did Big John get any bigger?" Rain asked, sizing him up.

"All up here," Big John said, patting his biceps. "I've been hitting the gym."

"And the kitchen," Rain said.

Big John rubbed his belly. "You know my mama makes the best biscuits."

"We don't," Jerome said. "You always eat them before we can try any."

"Oh yeah," Big John replied thoughtfully.

"And what about you, Peño?" Rain said. "Grow any bigger yet?"

"Rain . . . you know I'm biggest up here," the Badgers' squat starting point guard said, tapping his head. "Making up for Big John and his little peanut brain."

Rain laughed and shook his head. If the team spent as much energy practicing as they did dissing one another, maybe they would win a few more games. But that was their problem. Rain was doing everything *he* could. He sat down on the end of the bench, and Peño grabbed his warped ball and stepped out onto the court, sending the first rhythmic dribbling through the gym.

In creaky Fairwood, the sound *resonated*. Rain felt it in the floors. In the bench. He could hear it echo in the rafters like the sounds of distant explosions. Basketball gave Fairwood its heartbeat.

"You got a rhyme for the season yet?" Jerome said.

Peño glanced back, grinning. "You ain't ready for it."

"No, we aren't," confirmed Lab—Peño's little brother. He was not a fan.

"Beats, please," Peño said, throwing the ball to Jerome and taking a bow.

Lab rubbed his forehead. "Please, no."

Big John jumped up, threatening to topple the bench on the way, and started beatboxing.

"Pugh, pugh, che, pugh, pugh, che, pugh, che, pugh, che—"

"Stop," Lab said.

Jerome started dribbling, adding a drum layer.

Boom, pugh, che, boom, pugh, che, boom, che, boom, che, boom, boom, che, boom . . .

"I should have stayed in bed," Lab moaned.

Peño swung his arm back and forth and started rhyming:

"The badgers are back
And yes, our gym is wack
But the boys are better
Down to the letter
We comin' for the win
Uppercut to the chin
Dren best watch for the badyers
Because we are... well..."

He paused.

"Mad... yers?"

Everyone broke out laughing. Peño had been trying to find a rhyme for *Badgers* for two years now. He had petitioned to change the name to Bears, Bobcats, or even Bats, but the team's owner, Freddy, was attached to the mythical creature for some reason. Most animals were mythical in the Bottom—Dren's poorest region didn't have many besides some wandering dogs and feral rats.

Rain turned to Twig, who was on the away bench ignoring everyone.

His long brown legs jutted out in front of him like sickly branches—an image that wasn't helped at all by the spindly fingers draped over his knees. Rain guessed he wasn't losing his nickname anytime soon.

"Twig," Rain said.

Twig gave him a quick wave. "Hey, Rain. Yo."

"You look the same."

Twig nervously scratched his arm. He seemed to be deciding if he should speak.

"I gained three pounds," he mumbled.

Big John broke out laughing. "Three pounds? What . . . in acne?"

"Ohhh," Jerome said, snickering. "That's cold, homie."

Twig looked down and fiddled with his hands.

"Boy says he put on three pounds," Big John continued. "This man kills me."

"I . . . I did," Twig said, sounding a bit defensive.

Rain could see Twig's discomfort, but he knew it wouldn't do Twig any good if he jumped in to help. Twig had to learn to stick up for himself, or he was never going to cut it in the tough world of the Elite Youth League . . . *especially* in the Bottom. No one survived here without a backbone.

"Three pounds!" Big John said. "I put on three pounds this morning! You need thirty to play down low. I'm not even sure why you're back. How much your dad pay Freddy to keep you on the team, huh? The rich boy out the burbs . . . We know how you got on the team."

"Yo, you ruthless," Jerome said, grinning. "This boy wake up just to get burned."

Twig looked away, his glassy eyes catching the light. Rain wondered if he would cry—a poor decision in front of this team. They were all twelve now, apart from Lab, who was a year younger, and in the Bottom that usually meant you had been through a lot. He felt bad for him, but Twig did need to toughen up, and so far he didn't seem to belong on the Badgers. He was so . . . soft. On cue, the first tears started to spill.

"You gon cry now—" Big John mocked.

Twig hurried to the bathroom, and Big John and Jerome cackled with laughter. Rain shifted, uncomfortable . . . maybe even guilty. But he pushed it aside. None of this was his job.

"Real nice," Reggie said quietly. "On day one."

Big John waved him away. "Boy should toughen up . . . or he shouldn't be here."

Reggie shook his head and went to warm up. On the way he glanced at Rain as if to say: *You the leader on this team?*

Rain scowled.

He opened his duffel bag and pulled out his shoes. His mama had packed a big lunch in there as always: two water bottles, a can of tuna, and a container full of brown rice, chicken, and green beans. It was always the same meal, and it represented a lot of suffering. His mom worked longer hours to afford it, drove to the nicer north district to find it, spent more hours to make it, and ate less to make sure he was full. All of this was because Freddy had told his mama that Rain needed to eat right if he was going to "make it big." She had taken that advice to heart and cooked only healthy food, even when his long-suffering brother, Larry, begged for something else.

Rain tightened his shoelaces, grabbed his ball, and started to warm up, draining one shot after another with practiced ease. He couldn't help but smile. Though he lived a few blocks away, Rain's home was here. Out there, he was just another Bottom beggar. On the court, he was a baller and a star, and the whole world was just two orange rims. No bills. No guilt. No memory.

He ignored the others as they filed in. He focused only on the ball and the rim. Nothing else mattered here. Jab step, shoot. Drop back, shoot. Fade, shoot. Spin, shoot. *Spin, shoot.*

He could almost hear the raspy voice. See the folded arms on a belly. Smell the smoke.

Watch me! Rain wanted to shout. *Watch me! Please!*

He checked the bleachers out of old habit, then shook his head, annoyed. He wasn't there. Hadn't been for four years. Rain pushed the memories away.

"My boys!" Freddy shouted, walking in. "All here? Come on over. Let me introduce Devon."

Rain turned to the front doors. The owner of the Badgers was dressed the same as ever: dark jeans, button-down shirt, gold chains, and a straight-brim ball cap pulled down past his eyebrows like a duck beak. He was in his thirties but might well have been seventeen.

"Rain, my man," Freddy said. "Here's the backup I told you about."

Curious, Rain tucked the ball under his arm and walked over. Freddy had called him a few nights earlier to talk about Devon and the new coach. Rain had been more curious about the coach—particularly how he was going to use Rain on offense—but he saw now that Freddy hadn't been bluffing when he said he had a "big" recruit: Devon was huge. He was about six feet tall and corded with muscle. His forearms were thicker than Rain's legs.

The team gathered around the recruit.

"What up, big man?" Rain said, impressed.

Devon kept his eyes down. His hands fidgeted at his sides. He toed the hardwood.

"Nothing," Devon murmured.

Rain glanced at Freddy, confused. Was this massive kid . . . *nervous?*

"He's quiet," Freddy said, patting Devon on the shoulder. "But a big boy."

"We can see that," Peño said. "He looks like a Clydesdale."

"Who's Clyde Dale?" A-Wall asked. "He a baller too?"

Rain scanned over Devon. Shy or not, he could be useful. If Devon could set some half-decent screens and box out, it would open up the driving lane and get Rain some better looks.

But what will you do for him?

Rain flinched and glanced around. The voice had been quiet, distant. Deep as thunder. He must have imagined it. He rubbed the bridge of his nose. Maybe he hadn't gotten enough sleep.

A-Wall eyed Rain, frowning. "You looking for something?"

"No," Rain said. "All good."

He shook it off and turned back to Freddy. Besides the name, Freddy hadn't given him a lot of information on the new coach. He just said he was very experienced, wasn't from the Bottom, and was holding a ten-day training camp to start the year. Actually, it had sounded like Freddy didn't know much about him either.

"Where's this new coach?" Rain asked. "Rolobo, or whatever you said his name was?"

Overhead, the lights crackled like eggs in a frying pan and began to flicker. Rain looked up as the bulbs pulsated, sizzled, and then returned to their normal dismal gray.

Freddy frowned. "I asked him to come at ten for the first day. I want us all to—"

He stopped, his eyes now fixed on the closest net. Rain followed his gaze.

Both ratty mesh nets were billowing around as if caught in a storm. Before anyone could question the source of the wind in a windowless gym, the nets fell still once again.

Looking even more befuddled, Freddy continued, "As I was saying, I wanted us all to catch up a bit first and—"

He never got the chance to finish.

The lights popped, plunging the gym into total darkness. The front doors flew inward and slammed into the walls on either side, propelled by a blast of frigid wind. The wind caught the banners and drove long-stagnant dust toward the team like a fuzzy tidal wave.

"Dust tsunami!" Peño shouted. "Run!"

Rain turned away from the onslaught, covering his eyes.

You cannot hide from the road.

"What?" he shouted over the howl.

"I said I should have brought a sweater!" A-Wall yelled.

The wind finally abated, and Rain turned back to the still-open doors. A silhouette blocked the sunlight.

The figure was enormous—tall enough that he had to duck to step through the doorway, which must have been near seven feet, and his salted black hair brushed against the frame. He wore a full three-piece suit and polished black leather shoes. Rain had never seen either apart from old movies, while a beautiful golden watch peeked out from his breast pocket, a gold chain dangling down beneath it. His skin was a warm light brown, marked with two white scars, thin as the edge of a knife, that ran from his cheeks to his chin. He held a leather medicine bag in one monstrous hand. As the man approached, his eyes moved over them—a fiery green wreathed in a yellow aura. His dark pupils, at first pinpricks, began to steadily grow. When Rolabi's gaze landed on Rain, he took an involuntary step backward. For just a moment, he thought he saw something there: two identical images of a snowcapped mountain rising from an island. Rain blinked. The image was gone.

"Oh," Freddy said, dropping his hand from Devon's shoulder. "You're early—"

"Being late or early is simply a matter of perspective."

Freddy paused. "Right. Team, this is Rolbi Wizen . . . umm, Wizaner . . . no . . ."

"You may call me Professor Rolabi, Professor Wizenard, or just Professor."

It sounded like *Role-ah-bee Whiz-an-Ard*. Freddy had been saying it wrong for days.

The new coach's eyes flicked again to Rain. The pupils grew and then shrank, refocusing.

What are you looking for? the voice asked. It was deep and distant.

Rain opened his mouth, caught himself, shrunk away.

It's not what you think, the voice continued.

"Professor . . ." Freddy murmured. "Sure, sure. Let me introduce the boys. This is Rain—"

"That will be all today, Frederick," Rolabi cut in.

His voice was smooth and deep, but there was steel in it. A crack of authority.

"I thought we'd talk about the upcoming season . . ." Freddy trailed off.

Rolabi didn't respond. He just stood there, staring down—*way down*—at the owner.

Freddy quailed and hurried out. The doors slammed shut behind him, and the sound seemed to search for a way out of the gym before finally fading. Fairwood grew eerily still.

Rolabi didn't speak or move or do anything at all. The silence dragged on until Rain could feel it sitting on his shoulders. It pressed down harder and harder with each passing second, and after a full minute, it was nearly unbearable.

Did you think that would make it easier? the voice asked.

Rain felt a queer sensation and glanced down. There was a hole in his chest. He grabbed at it, frantic, but his body was solid under his fingers. He tried to breathe, feeling his skin prickling. He must have been daydreaming. He had slept poorly. That was it. He tried to relax.

Finally, Rolabi removed a folded sheet of paper and a gold pen from an inner pocket of his suit. "I will need everyone to sign this before we can proceed," he said, unfolding the paper.

"What is it?" Big John asked warily.

"A contract," Rolabi replied. "Who wants to sign first?"

Rain tentatively stepped forward. He *was* the leader of the team, after all. Rolabi held the contract out for him in one hand, which was large enough to serve as a tray. A navy-blue *W* sat in the center of the letterhead, and a gold trim lined the edges.

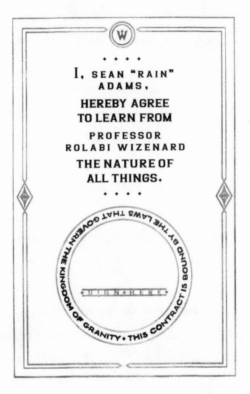

Rain stared at the contract, perplexed. It made no sense to him, but he couldn't see any harm in signing it, so long as the nature of all things included basketball. The professor was clearly a bit eccentric, but that didn't matter if he could coach. Rain reached out to take the sheet.

"Should I sign it on the floor or . . ."

"No need," Rolabi said.

Rain took it and frowned. The paper was as rigid as steel, despite having been folded. He accepted the pen as well, which was inscribed *Rolabi Wizenard* along one side, and signed his name as always:

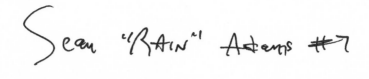

"Thank you," Rolabi said. "Next?"

Big John stepped forward, looking somewhat emboldened again. He reached for the contract, but Rain paused. The contract was written for Rain alone; it was of no use to Big John.

"We need another contract, right?" Rain said.

"Why?"

Rain gestured to the sheet. "Well, it says my name . . ."

He stopped.

The contract didn't say his name at all. It now said *I, Jonathon "Big John" Renly.* It was also unsigned, despite the fact Rain had just put his signature there. Without another word, Rain handed it to Big John and backed away.

He was daydreaming. That was it. He hadn't slept well last night. He needed sleep.

No. You need to wake up, the voice said.

Rain rubbed his forehead. *What is wrong with me?* he thought.

Rolabi was looking through his bag.

"Here we are," Rolabi said finally. "One for everyone."

He abruptly threw a ball at Big John, and it ricocheted off his cheek. Balls came flying out of the bag to each player in rapid-fire succession, though Rolabi never once looked up.

"We get to keep them?" Reggie asked excitedly.

Only four guys on the team owned a ball of their own: Twig, Peño (he shared with Lab), Vin, and Rain. Twig and Vin came from wealthier families, and Peño had managed to find an old misshapen one at a yard sale. Rain's was a gift from Freddy—brand-new two years ago but now worn nearly to the core, the pebbling smoothed out, the grip like a bowl-ing ball's.

"They are yours," Rolabi confirmed, still throwing the balls.

Reggie grabbed his and clutched it to his chest, grinning. Then his eyes went wide.

Rain caught a flash of orange and put his hands up just in time. The instant the ball touched his fingers, Rain felt a chill. Everything around him had changed. The gym was completely empty.

"Guys?" he whispered. "Guys? Is anyone there?"

His voice echoed through the gym, searching under the bleachers and through the locker rooms before returning to him with the same question. Rain hugged the ball without thinking. How could everyone have left so suddenly? And what was that draft? It snuck into his bones.

You wanted this.

"Who's there?" he shouted, whirling around.

Questions pounded through his head, though Rain didn't want to acknowledge them: *Why did he leave me? What did I do?*

"Stop it!"

Rain turned for the front doors, but they too were gone. He was trapped in Fairwood.

"Let me out!"

Are you ready for the road?

Rain started to panic. His heart was beating so loud, it echoed in the rafters.

"Peño?" he said. "John? Mama! Let me out!"

The walls seemed to close in. Impassable. A prison.

"Help me!" Rain screamed.

He suddenly had the distinct sense that something was watching him, and he whirled around and realized it was a *someone*. Rolabi was there, his hands clasped behind his back.

"What is this—" Rain started.

"Hmm," Rolabi said. "Interesting. That will be all today. I will see you here tomorrow."

With that, the team reappeared, all of them looking queasy. Rolabi closed his medicine bag and started for the doors, which swung open to greet him with another gust of frozen wind.

"What time?" Peño asked, rubbing a trembling hand over his head.

The doors slammed shut, and Peño chased after him.

"Do we keep the balls?" he shouted, pushing the doors open again. "What . . . Professor?"

Rolabi was already gone.

A SINKING FEELING

Give your fear a face or you will see it everywhere.

WIZENARD 2 PROVERB

RAIN SAT ON the curb in the corner of Fairwood's parking lot where two crumbling wooden fences met beneath an ancient, gnarled oak. He had come early that morning, but he'd been hesitant to go inside. He just sat there unnoticed as Peño and Lab went in, and then Vin and A-Wall. No one checked the corner, and the branches of the oak hung down like curtains even if they did. It was one of the last living trees in the Bottom. He'd always loved it, though he had no idea how it continued to grow.

The Bottom used to be greener, according to Rain's grandma. But the rest of Dren clogged the Bottom with factories until its air was choked, its soil poison. The trees had mostly died out in the inner city, and there were no gardens, no grass. Garbage clogged the rivers. Litter surrounded Rain's shoes even now. The air was thick with the smell of rot.

Some days, Rain felt like he was trash too. He knew the wealthier parts of Dren dumped everything they didn't want here, including people. His mom worked as a server in an old diner and struggled to keep the house. His younger brother was in school, flunking mostly, his prospects dire. His grandma lived alone nearby in a run-down nursing home infested with roaches. They were all discarded. All lost . . . his dad most of all. Only ball could bring them back.

And, of course, that was waiting inside. He stood up and eased one of the front doors of the gym open, his breath catching in his throat. He was ready to bolt if the gym was empty.

But a few of the guys were already shooting around, and Rain relaxed, trying to look casual in case anyone had spotted him. *You were just tired,* he told himself for the hundredth time.

It's easy to get tired of lying.

Rain stiffened at the sound of the deep voice that had haunted him yesterday. It sounded an awful lot like Rolabi's. He looked around, but he was alone at the doorway.

"Yo, Rain!" Peño called, tucking the ball under his arm. "What you doing, bro?"

Rain forced a smile. "Nothing, man. What up?"

"Working on my game," Peño said. "Even perfection needs practice."

Rain snorted. Lab was shooting around next to Peño, yawning as usual, while Vin and A-Wall played one-on-one beside them. At the far end of the court, Twig and Reggie were quietly working on their free throws. Devon sat alone on the home bench, lacing up his sneakers.

Everything seemed normal enough, so Rain plunked onto the bench beside Devon. He was exhausted. He'd slept terribly, waking every hour with a vision of an empty gym. He had enough nightmares already, or bad memories, or whatever they were. He didn't need more.

Rain stretched his calves out and sighed as the bench wobbled precariously.

It was embarrassing to host games in Fairwood. The visiting teams constantly made fun of the Badgers—especially the ones from the nicer regions of Dren. The kids from Argen were the worst: they called them the West Bottom Broke Boys. Teams *always* visited the Bottom; it was illegal for Bottom residents to leave the region. Apparently, the government was afraid they wouldn't go back. Basketball was one of the few exceptions, but only for national championships, scholarships, or a job in the professional league. No team from the Bottom had ever made the nationals. Fewer than ten had gotten a scholarship. Two had played in the Dren Basketball League . . . and neither had been close to a star. But Rain would be different.

Rain was born for it. It was all he thought about some days. The magazine covers, the trophies, but more than that, a new house for his mama, a nurse for his gran, a future for his brother. He saw it when he went to sleep. It was waiting for him first thing in the morning. He saw the house. It was white siding, green grass, a new roof that didn't leak. It was his mama relaxing in a recliner on the porch. Larry shooting around out front. His dad in a new car.

It was his sole purpose in life: to get out of the Bottom and take his family with him. His *whole* family. He would put them back together again with money for masking tape.

Rain opened his bag and spotted the folded note he kept in there. The slip of paper was so crinkled, it was nearly silken. Rain knew every word. He recited it in bed before he went to sleep, or when he was shooting jumpers, or tying his shoes in the morning. It had turned into a prayer.

"Dear Rain," he would say, watching for tears, "I hope you find this first . . ."

Rain started stretching as Big John and Jerome walked in. No one had really spoken after Rolabi's departure yesterday—they had all just packed up and headed for home, walking or catching buses or calling for rides from confused parents. Rain's mama worked long hours, so he always walked home, but when he told her about the early finish, she was furious.

"Tell that new coach we have no time to waste," she said. "This your year, baby. We can't mess around with no silliness. Don't make me pay him a visit. You know he doesn't want that."

His mama was infamous for her "visits." Freddy was petrified of her.

Rain reluctantly turned back to his bag. His new ball was sitting there, staring back at him. He had wanted to leave it behind, but somehow he felt like Rolabi was expecting them to bring the balls *he* had provided. Rain prodded it with his index finger and looked around.

Nobody disappeared, and he rubbed his forehead, exasperated. Of course nobody disappeared. Rain scooped up the ball, dribbled it once through his legs to test its weight, and then made his way onto the court. He had to admit: the ball was nice. He pulled up and took a three, the ball rolling smoothly off his splayed fingers. His wrist flicked as if chasing after it.

Swish.

"There he is," Peño said approvingly. "You got that fire going already?"

"Always."

Rain glanced at the dusty clock that hung over the doors. Rolabi was running late.

"I guess this Rolabi guy isn't worried about being on time," he said.

"Maybe he isn't coming," Lab suggested, almost hopefully.

"Or maybe he's already here."

The voice burst through the gym like a thunderbolt. Rain spun around. Rolabi was sitting casually on the bleachers, eating a polished apple. He stood up, took a last, savoring bite, and then, without even looking, tossed the core twenty yards into the gym's garbage can.

"Whoa," Jerome murmured.

Rolabi strode to the middle of the court, polished shoes as rhythmic as the clock.

"Put the balls away," he said.

Rain found himself sprinting to the bench and back without thinking, joining the others in a loose semicircle. The entire team seemed wary. They shifted on the balls of their feet or wrung their hands and pointedly avoided eye contact with Rolabi, who was looking them over. His eyes flashed and refocused. Rain stared at the far wall, feeling his heavy gaze.

"Umm . . . Professor Rolabi?" Twig said.

His voice was a near whimper.

"Yes?"

"My . . . uh . . . my dad was wondering when the parents can come meet you?"

Rain looked up at that. His mom had asked the same question last night.

"Following the tryout, I will meet with parents," Rolabi said.

There was a moment of silence.

"Did you say tryout?" Peño said. "This *is* the team."

"This *was* the team," Rolabi corrected. "Everyone *earns* a place on my team."

Rain smirked. That was fine by him. Maybe Rolabi could replace a few weak links: Twig for starters, though A-Wall was useless on offense, and Jerome was basically a human-size pylon.

"So our parents have to wait ten days to talk to you?" Vin said, frowning.

"If there is pressing business, they can call 76522494936273."

Rain tried to keep track of the number and failed instantly.

Twig was looking for a pen. "So . . . seven . . . eight . . . ? Can you repeat that?"

"I'm sure Daddy will figure it out for you," Big John said, and Twig flushed.

"We are going to start with a scrimmage," Rolabi said.

That was a surprise. Scrimmages were always at the *end* of practice. Rain figured coaches put them there so their teams would work to get through the drills quickly. But it was his favorite part of practice, so he wasn't about to complain. Maybe Rolabi had promise after all—he could deal with a little weirdness as long as the guy let them scrimmage and work on Rain's offense.

"We are going to use a different ball today," Rolabi continued. "Last year's starters versus the bench players. Devon will play for the latter for the moment."

Rain waited as the starters gathered around him: Peño, Lab, Twig, and A-Wall.

Big John and Twig stepped up for the jump ball, and Rain crouched behind Twig, ready to spring on the ball if it came his way. Rolabi tossed it up, and Big John ignored the ball and hip-checked Twig, using his round midsection like a battering ram. Twig doubled over, gasping for air, and Big John easily tipped the ball back to Vin.

"Foul!" Rain said.

Freddy *always* followed Rain's lead, but Rolabi didn't. He simply walked to the sideline and turned to watch. Clearly, he didn't know who the star of this team was. It was about time Rain showed him.

Rain and Reggie were paired on defense as always, and Rain tracked Reggie to the wing.

"You got moves for me this year?" Rain asked.

Reggie snorted. "I had moves last year. You kept blocking them."

"So, step your game up," Rain said. "Throw something new at me."

Reggie received a pass and surveyed the court. Rain stayed low and tight, one arm tracking the ball and the other blocking the lane. Reggie cocked the ball over his head for a two-handed pass to the post, but his intention was far too obvious, and Rain intercepted it and dribbled past him with a sudden burst of speed.

Rain was all alone—just him and the waiting net.

He glanced back to see if any defenders were close, debating a dunk attempt. Then he stopped, gathering the ball to his chest. The starters were gone. He could see the bench team: Reggie chasing him, and Vin and Jerome and Big John, and even the new kid, Devon, sprinting back from the block. But the entire starting lineup had vanished. Rain looked around, completely bewildered. They had been there only a second ago. He was sure of it.

"Where are they?" he murmured.

Right where you wanted them.

He turned to Rolabi on the sideline. His eyes flashed, locked on Rain like searchlights.

Rain didn't know what to do. His team was gone, and he had lost his dribble, so he had only one choice: he turned to the basket and took the shot.

He was too far out. The ball sailed well short of the rim and careened out-of-bounds, bouncing off the wall with an unceremonious *thud*. As soon as it did, Rain's team reappeared.

Lab scowled at him. "A bit far out, don't you think, Rain?"

Rain rubbed his eyes, disbelieving. "Yeah . . . sorry."

The bench players attacked again, and they began to move the ball rapidly around the perimeter while Devon and Big John ran screens down low. After Devon mysteriously passed up a wide-open layup, Jerome took the ball to the hoop, driving past Lab and Twig to score.

Rain scowled. They were losing to the *bench*.

He jogged up the court, getting into his usual position—the wing on the right. From there, he usually cut to the point for the ball and then drove hard to the net, either sticking with his left hand or crossing over quickly to his right for a layup or pull-up jumper. It was an almost unstoppable move for most Elite Youth League defenders. But this time the ball didn't come.

He turned back just in time to see Vin laying the ball in for a 4–0 lead.

"What are you doing, Peño?" Lab snarled, running back to collect the ball.

"Nothing," Peño said. "Just lost the ball. Get back and set a pick, why don't you?"

Rain scowled. He would have to do it himself.

But every time Rain touched the ball, his team vanished. He was forced to take bad shots or try to drive to the basket without even a fake pass or screen, which allowed the defense to double- or triple-team him.

Rain was soon forced to rely on fadeaway jumpers and threes, and he felt his temper rising with every miss. After almost an hour, it was only 28–24, a positively dreadful score line. More important, the bench was winning. It was preposterous.

Something weird was going on, but Rain was *not* going to lose to the bench.

As Twig finally managed to grab a defensive rebound, Rain broke for half-court.

"Twig! Here!"

Twig immediately lobbed the ball up the court, looking strangely eager to get rid of it. Rain caught the arcing pass and turned away from his team so he wouldn't see them disappear.

I don't need them anyway, he thought. *I am the team.*

His right sneaker suddenly stuck to the ground. He looked down and realized it wasn't just stuck: his shoe had sunk into the hardwood up to his laces. He stared at his submerged foot, dumbfounded. The floorboards had taken on the consistency of quicksand.

"How . . . ?" Rain said, yanking his sneaker free with a wet, suctioning *plop*.

He somehow kept his dribble, trying to make it to the net, but his feet sank deeper and deeper into the floor with every step. Soon they were submerged to his ankles, and he slogged forward, fixated on scoring and winning and showing the coach that he was the star of the team.

But as his shins sank farther into the strange bog, he imagined the rest of him slipping below the surface. Fear bubbled up in his belly, and without thinking, he took a desperate shot from way beyond the three-point line. As before, it sailed well short and thudded against the far wall.

The floor instantly returned to normal, and Rain spun around, looking for his teammates. They were all there. The fear that had flared through his stomach like a red-hot geyser receded and cooled to stone, heavy and nauseating. He took a deep breath, trying to hold back the bile.

It is so easy to sink into ourselves.

Rolabi stepped out onto the court, his hands still clasped behind his back.

"That will be all for today," he announced.

Peño turned to him, frowning. "We aren't going to do any drills?"

Rolabi didn't seem to hear him. He waited patiently as the ball rolled back to his feet as if it were tethered. Then he scooped it up, dropped it into his medicine bag with a distant-sounding bounce, and made his way back to the bleachers, where he sat down with his hands folded on top of his bag. As soon as he did, the locker room door slammed open with a gust of freezing wind. Rain turned, facing the gale.

"Where . . . How did . . . ?" Big John said.

Rain glanced back at the bleachers. Once again, Rolabi Wizenard had vanished.

"This ain't cool," Peño muttered.

"So . . . we're pretty set on our coach being a witch, right?" Big John said.

Lab scowled. "What are you, six? There's no such thing as witches."

"Aren't witches usually female?" Jerome asked.

"Yeah," A-Wall said. "Men are mitches."

Lab rubbed his forehead. "You are dumb as a post, homie."

Rain walked away from the ensuing argument. He sat down and turned to the banners.

He didn't have time for this. Even if what Rolabi was doing was magic—impossible as it all seemed—it didn't matter. Rain had one job: to put his family back together. Rolabi didn't understand that. No one here did. This wasn't a game.

He slipped his shoes off and went to put them away, then frowned. A business card was resting on top of his duffel bag. He checked the other bags and saw cards placed on each of them. The front of the card was mostly white with a blue *W*, like a simple logo, and a number:

76522494936273. The other players wandered over and found their cards as well.

"When did he put these here?" Big John said. "Who's got a cell? Vin, call it up."

Rain tucked his card away and hurried out. He didn't need to call Rolabi—his mama did. She would set him straight. Rain needed to get back to training. He had to be ready for the season.

As he approached the door, he saw something written across the old, dull metal in flowing cursive silver ink.

How does a leader open a door?

Rain stared at it, confused, as the silver ink faded away.

He pushed open the door and hurried into the morning alone.

A FORGOTTEN VOICE

The past is a gift.
It reminds you there is a future.

◆ WIZENARD ◈ PROVERB ◆

THE NEXT MORNING, Rain shuffled into Fairwood, dejected. The entire team was already there, sitting on the benches and talking quietly among themselves. He plunked down beside them.

"Did your mom—" Big John started.

"Yes," said Rain.

"And—"

"No." Rain scowled. As soon as his mama had gotten home from work he'd given her the card. It'd been almost ten p.m., but she had punched in the string of numbers anyway—informing him the whole time it was a fake area code—and then she had suddenly gone quiet. She had managed an "Oh," and an "I see," fiddling all the while with her stained waitressing uniform, and then hung up, stared at Rain, and slowly walked upstairs. For once, she didn't take off her shoes.

"What happened?" Rain had shouted after her.

"You got yourself a new coach," she said quietly.

He didn't get another word out of her on the subject for the rest of the night. He had been tempted to talk to Larry, but he didn't want him getting worried. Larry was nine, shy, and not very popular at school. Rain was protective of him, and he didn't want Larry to think there was trouble with Rain's career. Rain told him every day he was "going to get them up out the Bottom," and he had to keep Larry thinking that at all costs. It was easy to lose hope in this place.

"If Ms. Adams can't do something, we in trouble." Jerome shook his head. "It wasn't even a real phone number," he muttered. "I don't know how—"

"You didn't figure it out?" Reggie asked.

"What?" Peño said.

"The number. Didn't you spell it out on your dial pad?"

Rain frowned. He hadn't. His mama hadn't said anything either.

"No," Peño said.

"It spells Rolabi Wizenard," Reggie said.

There was a long silence, and then Peño whistled.

"He's got his own phone number," he said. "That's baller."

"So, our parents are out," Vin said. "Any other bright ideas?"

"We can talk to Freddy," Jerome suggested. "Get Rolabi fired."

Rain perked up. *Of course.* Freddy could fire the new coach.

"We're talking like this is normal," Big John said. "It ain't normal. It was magic, man."

"He's a mitch," A-Wall agreed.

Lab rolled his eyes. "There's no such thing as magic."

"Is that so?" someone asked from behind them.

The effect was like a perfect strike in bowling. The entire team yelped and spilled off the benches in a tangle of limbs. Rain took an elbow to the ribs. Grimacing, he turned and saw Rolabi standing behind the bench. The coach stared down at them, still wearing the same clothes.

"If you don't believe in magic," Rolabi said, "you need to get out more."

Rain watched—still lying speechless on the floor—as Rolabi

strode onto the court. He thought back to his mama's phone call last night and the dazed look on her face afterward.

"Did you hypnotize my *mama*?" Rain said indignantly.

Rolabi stopped at center court. "The truth is hypnotizing. I fielded calls from seven parents last night. I believe they are appeased. If any others would like, they can call as well."

"About the whole . . . tryout thing . . ." Peño said.

"We will start with laps."

The team unfurled themselves, groaning and muttering and falling into a broken line. Rain was last to start running, sparing a quick glance at the professor. Rolabi's eyes found his—with a noticeable twinkle—and Rain took off.

There are two types of runners. Some run toward. Some run away. Only one wins.

How about you run away? Rain thought angrily.

Freddy had them run laps once in a while, though usually just one or two as a quick warm-up. They had traveled five times around the gym— and many of them were already sweating profusely—when Rolabi spoke again. His voice seemed to chase them and nip at their heels.

"We will take free throws," he said. "One at a time. As soon as someone scores, you will stop running for the day. If you miss, the entire team runs five more laps."

"I got this," Peño said, gasping for air.

Rain was about to argue that it should be *him* shooting, but Peño proceeded right to the free-throw line with a hand perched on his thigh like an elderly man with a hip replacement.

"What . . . How am I supposed to . . . ?"

"Shoot it, please," Rolabi said.

Peño frowned, his thick black eyebrows forming a V that peaked at the top of his nose.

Then, with a strange, jerking motion, he heaved the ball upward like he was doing shot put. The basketball sailed over the backboard and struck the wall before pinballing its way down between the two and finally rolling away into the corner in an oddly dejected manner.

The entire team slumped.

"Five more laps," Rolabi said, his voice maddeningly calm.

Rain was furious with himself. He should have insisted on taking the shot. It was always his job in games to make the big shot. It had been since day one. He had to drag the team with him.

To where?

Rain ignored that one. They had finished 3 and 12 last season—last place in the league. He turned to start running again and froze. His eyes widened. The floor—the entire gym, in fact—was now slanted *uphill*, nearly at a 45-degree angle. Rain began to slide backward.

"Begin," Rolabi said.

"You are not crazy, you are not crazy," Peño whispered.

"Professor," Vin said, crouching to keep his position, "the floor—"

"When we are tired, the court can feel like a mountain," Rolabi said.

"It *is* a mountain!" Peño protested.

Rain got low as well, his fingers grasping at the hardwood. He barely held his footing, his mind reeling, feeling almost nauseous at the sight of his familiar Fairwood tilted up on its head.

"Just run," Reggie said. "We can get up there."

The line started, and Rain climbed after them, glancing at the cinder-block wall behind him and waiting for someone to take an unfortunate spill. He gulped and kept moving, almost crawling with wide frog steps. When he finally scrambled to the baseline, the gym shifted again.

Now they had to go *downward*.

"Never mind," Peño said. "I am definitely going crazy."

"Join the club," Rain muttered.

"So, about that magic that doesn't exist—" Big John said.

"Shut up," Lab cut in.

There was no break. At the next turn, the floor formed a steep stair-case. Next it slid like a treadmill. Then divots. Then hurdles. The floor changed with every single turn, and soon Rain's thighs were throbbing, his sides stitched with cramps. He suspected the only reason they made it was that Rolabi allowed them to set the pace. Big John was huffing like a steam engine.

When the five laps were done, the floor straightened back to normal, and everyone slowed and turned to Rain, their best free-throw shooter and surest bet for escape. He nodded.

"I don't want to know what's next," Vin managed through gasping breaths.

"Me passing out," Big John said.

Rain retrieved the ball from the corner and proceeded to the free-throw line, taking a slow, deep breath to calm himself. He dribbled exactly three times, same as ever, getting a feel for the ball and focusing. Shoulders to the hoop. Feet comfortably set with toes pointed. Wrists and fingers loose.

Then he narrowed his eyes, breathed out slowly, and lifted the ball, bringing his right elbow in line with the net and bending his fingers just slightly like primed pistons ready to erupt.

"It's all up to you, Rain."

The unmistakable voice whispered in his ear just as the ball was being released, and Rain flinched like he'd been struck. The shot careened off the side of the rim to a chorus of dejected sighs from the team, but Rain barely noticed. He spun around, looking for the source of the voice. But Rain was alone. The voice had no body. It *couldn't* have a body. That man was long gone.

Rain grabbed the ball and ran back to the free-throw line, lifting it for a desperate second shot. He felt his heart pounding madly in his chest, wishing and hoping, but for what, he wasn't even sure. Still there was no voice.

"Do it again!" Rain pleaded, turning to Rolabi. "Please!"

"I did nothing," Rolabi said.

Rain hurried over to him, fists clenched at his sides. His whole body trembled.

"Make it come back."

"I did nothing," he repeated.

"What is it, Rain?" Peño asked from the line, sounding worried.

Rain stared at Rolabi for a moment. He'd imagined the voice. He *must* have.

"Can I use the bathroom?" Rain murmured.

Rolabi nodded. "Certainly. Everyone, grab a drink. Laps will continue shortly."

Rain hurried to the locker room. He threw open the door to the biggest bathroom stall, locked it behind him, and gripped the sink with trembling hands. He had gone completely mad. That was the only explanation. The voice was a painful memory and nothing more. Rain had the note to prove it.

He looked into the mirror, cracked and splintered so that in some places his reflection broke into a hundred fragments. He realized his eyes were glistening, and seeing that made everything worse. Soon his nose was leaking too, and he roughly wiped his face with the back of his hand, furious that he was crying after so many dry months.

Rain stared at himself, trying to calm down.

Rain looked like his father. Everyone said it. He had the same hair—an understated one-inch cut—the same pointed nose, the blue-brown skin and copper eyes, the narrow face and sharp chin. He had his height and his lean, wiry build. His father was *in* him. He was staring at him even now. Even here.

More tears spilled down Rain's face. He gripped the sink so hard, he thought it might shatter.

"Why did you leave?" he whispered.

The reflection stared back. "You know."

Rain yelped and backed away, almost tripping over the toilet. He pressed his back to the wall, staring at the mirror. For a moment, the face in the mirror had looked exactly like his father's. He waited, watching it. But it was just a crying boy.

Slowly, reluctantly, Rain stepped to the sink and splashed some cold water on his face. He stopped shaking, took another deep breath, and wiped his face with his sleeve. Then he walked out, joining the team as they started running. He ignored their questioning looks.

"You good, bro?" Peño asked, hurrying to fall in line beside him.

"Yeah," Rain said. "It was nothing."

But he barely registered the changing floor and missed shots for the rest of the drill, which stopped only when Reggie hit a free throw. The team managed a croaking, feeble cheer.

"Water break," Rolabi said. "Bring your bottles over here."

Rain glanced at Rolabi as he walked by. What was happening? Was Rolabi doing this to him? How? How could he know about his father? How could he summon his father's voice?

Or was Rain doing this to himself?

"Sit in a circle," Rolabi said, moving to center court.

Everyone complied, plopping down like wet rags. Rolabi pulled out a daisy in a small clay pot—it was the first one Rain had ever seen outside of photos or TV shows. It was stark white with a yellow heart. Rolabi gently set it down and stepped back, staring in near rapture.

"What are we supposed to do with the flower?" Peño asked.

"We are going to watch it grow."

Rain waited for the professor to laugh or smile. To admit that this was an elaborate prank or a test of their patience. But Rolabi kept his eyes on the flower and stood still, apparently entranced.

"Why?" Lab asked, already fidgeting.

"Small, nearly imperceptible things make the difference between victory and defeat."

"In a flower?" A-Wall said.

"In everything. Don't overthink. Don't assume. Just watch. When your focus wanders, return it to the flower."

Jerome scratched his forehead. "How long we doing this for?"

Rolabi didn't answer, and finally, everyone turned to the flower. Rain tried to get comfortable on the old floorboards, which gave a surly groan. The flower stared back at him.

Rain glanced at the clock. The minutes ticked by as long as hours. Then the seconds felt like hours too.

At half an hour, Rain felt like he was ready to smash the pot and head home.

"What part of the body moves first?" Rolabi asked suddenly. "If you are defending someone, and they are approaching, what part of their body will move before the rest?"

Rain considered the question, trying to think back to their last game. He had never really thought about where movement began. Defending someone was a natural reaction. When they moved, he moved. That was all.

Rain pictured a player closing in on him. "I always try to watch their stomach."

"An admirable plan," Rolabi agreed. "But a perfect one only for the fastest player alive."

Rolabi stepped over Peño and stood next to the daisy. "The first thing to move is the mind. The opposing player must decide what he is going to do."

Rain rubbed his head. Why was everything a riddle? The game was simple.

Only for those who choose not to see.

How do I see, then? he thought sourly.

"You need more time," Rolabi said aloud.

"And how are we supposed to get more time?" Rain asked.

"By watching the flower grow. Water bottles away. We have one more lesson today."

As Rain started for his bag, Rolabi began setting up an obstacle course. Reaching into his medicine bag, he withdrew cones, upright poles that stood on end like stalks of corn, and a vertical ring on a metal stand that was bigger than his entire bag. Finally, he placed three basketballs together on the sideline at half-court.

Rain took a last drink of water and jogged over to the three balls to start the line. The rest of the team fell in behind him, while Rolabi positioned himself right in the center of the court.

"You will complete the circuit," he said. "A layup on the first hoop and a shot from the elbow on the other. When you return, pass the ball to the player who is first in line. You may begin."

Rain went to pick up his ball and screamed. His right hand was gone.

He gripped his now-vacant wrist with his other hand, staring down at it in horror. His right arm appeared to have been sliced perfectly clean, just past his wrist bone. The skin covering the end of the limb was as smooth and flat as a kitchen counter. Rain whirled around and saw that the rest of the team was shouting in panic as well, grabbing their own wrists, but none of them had lost their hands. Everyone but Rain still had them. Why were *they* screaming?

"Where is my hand?" Big John shouted. "What's happening?"

"An exercise in balance," Rolabi replied. "Proceed."

Rain stared at his wrist. He saw the end of his dreams and grand plans. No riches. No escape from the Bottom. No house with the porch and the net and the new car. No family gathered together on the weekends. It all vanished with his hand. He felt his knees buckling.

"This isn't possible," Lab said.

"Possibility is notoriously subjective," Rolabi replied. "Shall we begin?"

Everyone turned to Rain, including Rolabi. The team's eyes bored into him, but he couldn't start the drill. Not without his dominant hand.

You have two, don't you?

But, he thought, *my hand—*

Can be earned back.

Rain stared at Rolabi, furious and confused and scared. Still, what else could he do?

He awkwardly picked up the ball with his left hand and started the circuit. He made his initial layup, but proceeded to lose the ball through the dribbling segment and missed the pass through the ring by a mile. While he was collecting his ball, Big John pegged him in the back with his own misfired pass attempt, and the whole court descended into chaos. There were shouts and stumbles and the constant *clank, clank, clank* of missed shots and desperate warnings:

"Sorry, man!" Vin shouted after hitting Jerome with an errant pass.

"Watch your head!"

"Well, if you had just ducked—"

At one point, Devon attempted a pass to the front of the line and clocked an unprepared Vin so hard that he toppled to the ground. As he lay there, dazed, Rolabi called a halt to the drill.

"That will be all for today," he said. "Balls, please."

The balls were handed back to him, and he dropped them in his bag.

"Can we have our hands back now?" Rain asked hopefully.

"Tomorrow we will be working on our defense," Rolabi said. "They will be helpful then."

With that, he picked up his bag and started walking directly toward the nearest wall.

The lights flashed a blinding white, and a gust of wind whipped in violently from nowhere. Rain shielded his face with his arms as the lights blinked out, then flashed on again, dim and gray as ever. The wind died, and Rain knew before he even looked that the professor would be gone. Rolabi had just walked through a wall.

"Okay," Peño said, "I think maybe we should talk to Freddy. Rain?"

Everyone turned to him. Rain knew exactly what Peño was suggesting: getting rid of Rolabi. Considering this, Rain remembered the moment he heard the familiar voice. He tried and failed to stamp out the fierce, ridiculous hope that he might hear it again. But the magic and the visions and the drills were too much. The distractions were preventing him from practicing real ball. Getting in the way of his plan. His future. He couldn't afford that.

Rain nodded. "It's time to fire Rolabi," he said.

He started for the bench, ignoring the flood of conversations that followed. He thought he even caught a few players arguing against the decision, but it didn't matter. They didn't get it. It was his call. Maybe some of the other guys thought they could get their families out of the Bottom too. But it was just a dream for them. It wasn't *expected*. Planned for. It was for Rain. Basketball was his one chance to fix everything.

He sat down and turned to the banners.

"Just you watch, Pops," he whispered, "I'll get us back on track."

THE TIGER

Suffering is our greatest chance for strength.

❖ WIZENARD ⑦ PROVERB ❖

RAIN WALKED INTO Fairwood with Freddy trailing a few steps behind him. Freddy was clearly nervous. He had offered Rain a ride—well, Rain had insisted on it, to make sure Freddy showed up—and had kept shooting Rain leery half smiles throughout the drive. Even now he seemed to be moving with exaggerated slowness, like a prisoner debating an escape attempt. Rain had spent almost an hour on the phone convincing him to come.

Freddy was here, and this misadventure was over.

Rain still had only one hand. His mama and brother never said a word about it, despite Rain's attempts to bring attention to it. Larry was shy at school, but he was a motormouth at home, and even *he* didn't ask about it. Rain even waved it in front of his face, to which Larry said: "How do you give yourself a nickname? I was hoping for Maelstrom. Cool, right? Or maybe Downpour?" Rain had just sighed and given up. Clearly, it was some sort of illusion. But for him, his right hand simply wasn't there. He couldn't see it or feel it. He'd eaten dinner with his left hand, brushed his teeth with his left hand, gotten dressed with his left hand . . . All of it clumsy and awkward and frustrating. He needed his stronger hand back. Now.

So make one.

Stay out of my head! Rain thought, striding toward the benches.

When the rest of the team saw Freddy, they fell silent.

"Morning, team," Freddy said. "How are we?"

"Bad," someone muttered.

Rain checked the clock and the doors. It was nearly nine—the doors would be blowing open shortly. Would Freddy hold his nerve? Would the team? He steeled his own resolve. If he held, then Freddy would definitely fire Rolabi. But Rain's breath was short, his heart pounding. Rolabi was clearly some kind of magician. Maybe a sorcerer. Whatever you called him, he was doing things nobody should be able to do. How would he react when they tried to fire him?

Rain turned back to the team, tuning in to the conversation.

"Well, he seemed really good . . ." Freddy was saying.

"He probably hypnotized you," Peño cut in. "He already got Rain's mama."

Freddy stiffened and looked at the doors. "Rain, is . . . your mama coming today?"

"None of our parents are," Vin said. "He scared them all away somehow."

"We want him gone," Jerome agreed. "Everyone does."

Freddy sighed. "Okay, okay. Rain, you sure?"

"I'm sure," Rain said firmly.

Freddy checked his cell phone. "All right, well, he should be here soon—"

"Were you on any of these teams, Frederick?"

Rain whirled toward the voice and saw Rolabi standing beneath the old banners. He was looking up at them, hands clasped at his back. His presence was disconcerting enough. But that wasn't all.

Rain squinted, disbelieving. The banners looked . . . new. The fraying edges were straight and neat. The faded colors re-stained. The missing letters resewn. They could have all been won yesterday.

"Impossible," he breathed.

Rain stared at them every single day. He focused on one in particular: a District Runners-Up from sixteen years earlier. His father had been on that team—considered the best in the history of the Bottom. They had lost in the finals, which his father blamed on his teammates.

"Let me down in the end," he'd said. "But we were close, man. Right there."

And still Rain's father had never made the Dren Basketball League. He never saw his dreams realized. No wonder his father hated living in the Bottom. Rain felt a lump in his throat and choked it back. *He* would be different.

"What . . . Where did . . . ?" Freddy said.

"I suppose you were too young," Rolabi said thoughtfully. "It's been so long."

Rain caught his meaning—the Bottom hadn't seen a winning team in decades.

"Can I help you?" Rolabi asked.

Freddy paused and glanced at Rain, who nodded, gesturing for him to continue.

"Yes," Freddy said. "Can I speak to you privately?"

Rolabi walked over and fixed his gaze on Freddy. "No need. Go ahead."

Rain tensed. Freddy was going to have to do it *here*? In front of everyone?

The green eyes turned to Rain, pupils large, the color forming a thin ring around them like a solar eclipse. He saw it again—a lone mountain on an island. Snow had crept far down, right to the base and out toward the beach and the sea. The image seemed to grow larger.

Will you be ready when the time comes?

Freddy scratched his neck, snapping Rain back to attention.

"Okay," Freddy said. "Well . . . um . . . we have decided, that is, *I* have decided, that even though I'm sure you are a good coach, it's just . . . well . . . not a right fit for the Badgers."

"Ah," Rolabi said. "So, you would like to let me go?"

"Well . . . yeah . . . Yes," Freddy said, craning his neck to look up at the towering figure.

Rolabi nodded. His eyes began to dart around the team, falling on one face after another. He didn't look upset, but Rain still turned away, afraid to meet his eyes. He saw most of the other players do the same, finding sudden interest in their shoes or hands or anything at all.

If we encircle ourselves with fears, which direction will we turn?

Rolabi stuck out a hand, his unnerving gaze now fixed on Freddy.

"I understand," Rolabi said. "Good day."

Freddy cleared his throat. "Thanks, Rolabi. I will take over for the time—"

Their hands met, Rolabi's enveloping Freddy's like an oven mitt, and Freddy stopped speaking. His back straightened. His mouth fell open. His eyes went wide and stopped blinking.

Freddy looked around—at the bleachers, the banners, the walls, and finally, at the faces of the team. His eyes began to glisten, and a tear loosened and slipped down his cheek, beading on the edge of his mustache. Rolabi released Freddy's hand, eyes still locked on his face. Freddy stood frozen with his arm outstretched, then slowly pulled it back, nodding.

"Rolabi will remain the coach," he said. "I . . . I look forward to the season. See you then."

Without another word, Freddy walked out of the gym. Rain was speechless.

"He did it again," Vin whispered.

Rolabi set down his bag and turned to the team. Rain wondered if he would punish them—if they would have to run laps or do push-ups until they vomited. At the very least, Rolabi would certainly yell and lecture them about how they should never question their coach.

But as usual, Rolabi surprised him.

"Today we will be working on defense," he said calmly. "Before I can teach you proper zones and strategies, I must teach each of you how to be a defender. They are not the same lessons."

There was suddenly a low, scratching noise. Rain looked around, frowning.

"What must a defender always be?" Rolabi asked.

There was another deep scratch. Rain looked around nervously. Had Rolabi brought something dangerous into the gym? Was he going to get his revenge? Did he know the decision had been Rain's? He barely heard the others guessing answers to Rolabi's question. Every raking scratch seemed to travel up and down his spine. A shudder raced through him. What would he do? Could he run?

Always running. Ahead and behind and nowhere all at once.

Rain looked at Rolabi and felt himself shrink back. The gym seemed to grow black behind the coach, turning to shadow until only Rain and the professor remained. The big man stepped aside.

"Look," he said softly. "Do you see it?"

Rain frowned and peered past him. Images took shape in the darkness. Game-winning shots. A trophy, a gleaming car, a house with carpets in every room. His own face, a little older, flashing white teeth in a toothpaste commercial. A family of four sitting together on a soft sofa . . .

Rolabi stared at the visions. "Is that what you are chasing?"

Rain surged ahead, wanting, needing to get to the visions. His father was there. His family was reunited. Larry and his mom were smiling, and they had money, and he *needed* it.

A sharp pull at his waist stopped his advance. Rain looked down. A belt was wrapped around him, connected to a chain, and the chain led to an enormous lead ball nearly the size of a car. He tugged on the chain, and it moved, but an inch at most. He looked again into the darkness where he had seen his family.

The images were fading. The silhouette of a man was there, waiting.

"No!" Rain said. "I'm coming. Wait!"

He ran, fighting, pushing his legs ahead, nearly clawing at the ground. His whole body strained until he thought his body might pop from the pressure. Still he kept driving forward.

Then the image faded into blackness, and Rain sank to his knees.

"No," he whispered. "Please."

"It was always a long run," Rolabi said. "But harder when you bring all that weight with you."

"I don't understand—"

"You will."

The scratching returned, terribly loud. It echoed in the blackness a thousand times and shook the ground. Rain covered his ears, still staring out at the place where his family had been whole.

"What is that sound?" Rain shouted.

"Can someone open the locker room door?" Rolabi asked calmly.

The blackness grew brilliant white, then gray, dusty, and fluorescent. Shapes took form.

Rain was back in Fairwood, and the entire team had turned to the locker room door. Rain realized the noise was coming from *inside*. Something was in there. Something with large claws. He backed away.

Is it real this time? he thought.

It's all real. The sooner you realize that, the sooner you can start walking.

Rain blinked. Twig was standing at the door, trembling, but with his fingers wrapped around the steel handle. He pulled it open, revealing darkness, and then a flash of rippling orange fur.

Rain watched in disbelief as a tiger strolled out of the locker room. Tigers were long extinct, mythical really, and yet it walked right over to Rolabi and sat down, shooting the boys a toothy grin.

"Meet Kallo," Rolabi said. "She has graciously volunteered to help us today."

The tiger appeared to look them over. Her thick orange fur faded to white at her stomach as though she had waded through clean snow. Her purple eyes were flecked with gold like stars. But Rain was focused on her glistening fangs and the black claws partially sheathed in each massive paw.

"Rain," Rolabi said. "Step forward."

Rain looked at him, alarmed. So it was revenge, as he'd suspected. The tiger was here to maul him.

The rest of the team turned to him. He knew they were watching to see what he would do. He wanted to refuse. He wanted to quit and go home. No one could blame him if he did—Rolabi had basically threatened his life. There were teeth and claws waiting on the court. But he remained.

Rolabi had made it clear that if anyone left, they wouldn't be allowed back on the team. Period. He was obviously in charge now, so if Rain left, the entire season was over before it started.

There was no way he was leaving Elite Youth ball—and his plans—behind.

Rain stepped forward, his eyes on the tiger. "Yes?"

Rolabi set a ball on the floor and pushed it toward center court, where it stopped on the dot as if magnetized.

"The drill is simple," Rolabi said calmly. "Get the ball. Kallo will play defense. We will take turns and go one at a time. I want everyone else to watch and take note of what happens."

Kallo smiled, revealing two rows of scimitar teeth. Her tongue traced the tips of them.

"What?" Rain said incredulously. "I'm not going near that thing."

Kallo shifted, looking offended, and he took a step back.

"Maybe don't call her a *thing*," Peño suggested.

Kallo began to pace back and forth in front of the ball. She stayed low, her muscles poised, her stripes rippling, bending, sucking him in. Rain felt like he was being hypnotized.

But the fact of the matter remained: she was going to eat him.

"Okay, I get it," Rain said in a rush of breath. "I'm sorry we asked Freddy to fire you."

"This is not a punishment. It is a drill. Now get the ball."

"But . . ." Rain said.

"A true defender *must* be a tiger. The first one to get the ball gets their hand back."

Rain looked down at his stump of a wrist. He wanted his hand back—desperately. It wasn't just his future at stake. So he tried to quell his trembling and took a slow step to the right, testing the tiger's reactions. Kallo followed languidly like flowing water. Rain tried the left, and she matched him with the same easy grace.

Okay, he thought numbly. *I can do this.*

Rain suddenly faked left and went right, moving as fast as he could. He didn't have a chance. As soon as he changed directions, Kallo pounced on him, knocking him to the floor with surprising gentleness. He stared up at her open jaws, felt her breath wash over him. He gulped, waiting for the end. Instead, she licked his face with a sandpaper tongue and stepped off.

Rain lay there, too shocked to move.

"She killed him!" Peño cried.

"I'm fine," Rain said, climbing back to his feet. "She didn't hurt me."

"Devon," Rolabi said.

There is courage in you. Harness it.

How? Rain thought.

You know how.

Rain glared at Rolabi. Why couldn't he give straight answers? Why did he have to speak in riddles? Rain had planned for Rolabi to be gone today, and instead here he was, unleashing tigers and watching his team's star drag lead weights around. Rain steamed with frustration as one player after another approached Kallo, trying to figure out what Rolabi meant.

How could Rain harness his courage when he felt so afraid?

Nobody got through. Kallo knocked each player down and gave him a lick, eliciting squeals or giggles or disgusted *blech*s. Big John was last, and he folded his arms and outright refused to go. Despite teasing, despite Rolabi's veiled warnings, he was obstinate.

Kallo settled down on the hardwood and partially closed her eyes as though she could tell her opponent wasn't ready to play. Even resting, she still managed to look ferocious.

"It's not that bad," Twig said. "She's really gentle."

"You don't talk to me," Big John growled.

"I'm just trying to help—"

Big John whirled around, his cheeks quivering. "I don't need your help."

"Easy, man," Peño said. "You guys are on the same team, remember?"

"I didn't mean anything by it," Twig replied. "You looked like you could use a hand."

Rain flinched. That wasn't a wise thing to say to Big John.

Big John lurched forward and shoved Twig, who went down hard on his tailbone. Peño took a running jump onto Big John's back, wrapping his arms and legs around him in a bear hug.

"Down, boy!" Peño shouted.

Big John ignored him and started forward. His entire body was trembling with rage.

"I don't need your help!" he said. "You think you got the answers, huh? Rich boy out the burbs. New shoes. New cell phone. You don't belong here. You didn't *earn* it."

Rain glanced at Twig. What Big John said was true enough. Twig was from the wealthier northern district, where the houses had grass and the cars worked and the streetlights turned on at night. In the Bottom, the northern district was where the most affluent people lived—the ones who wanted to get out of the Bottom but were trapped by the boundary. Rain's dad used to call them the "Before Bottoms"—the ones who didn't quite belong.

Rain stared enviously at Twig's shoes—crisp white, high-top, self-tying, the newest ones on the market. Of course he had them. He had everything he wanted. Rain's were already scuffed, the soles worn, the laces thinning and threadbare. Part of him agreed with Big John.

Twig didn't belong here.

Big John was still advancing, carrying Peño on his back. A-Wall and Jerome grabbed his arms as he reached for Twig. Big John strained against all three of them, raging.

Twig climbed back to his feet. "What are you talking about?"

"You know where I go after practice?" Big John said, spitting. "To work. Two jobs. And we still can't pay all the bills. You ever spent a week in the dark 'cause you can't pay for no lights? You ever pick the mold off your food 'cause you got nothing else? You ever hold your mama in blankets 'cause you can't afford no doctor?"

"I . . ."

"This is all I got!" Big John shouted. "And you took it from me!"

Rain heard Big John's voice cracking, threatening tears.

Twig hesitated. "Freddy decided on who starts. It's just a strategy thing—"

That set Big John off again. He surged forward, his left hand balled into a fist.

He didn't make it. A massive hand landed on his shoulder, lifting Big John off the floor with incredible ease. Not just Big John. A-Wall, Jerome, and Peño came up too, clinging to Big John's arms and back. A-Wall and Jerome quickly let go, but Peño held on as Rolabi spun Big John to face him.

"Do you know why you are angry?" Rolabi asked.

Big John stared at him, lips quivering, limbs dangling down like an unused puppet.

"Do you?"

"Because he got into my business!" Big John snarled.

"Because you are afraid," Rolabi said.

He lowered Big John to the ground, and Peño hopped off.

"Fear breeds anger and violence," Rolabi continued. "It has made your choice for you. Fear of not being enough. But I value honesty. I will forgive the violence *once*."

"I'm done here," Big John said. "I'm done with this stupid training."

There were tears streaming down his cheeks now. Rain had never seen him cry before. He always played the tough act—had since his brother died. His father had left long before that.

Now he stood there, trembling, shoulders moving with sobs, and Rain saw a little kid.

If you find the child in the people around you, you find the truth.

How?

Look.

Big John started for the bench, fuming. He glared at Twig on the way. "You can all stay with this wack coach and this garbage gym and this spoiled brat. I don't need this. I got the real world waiting."

"Ten minutes in the locker room." Rolabi's voice was deep and commanding—enough so that Big John froze in his tracks.

He looked back at the professor. "What?"

"Go look at your reflection for ten minutes. Ask yourself carefully. Then decide."

Big John hesitated, then stormed into the locker room. He slammed the door so hard that most of the remaining gray paint flaked off.

Rain watched the fragments drift to the ground.

He looked around him. Did he know *anything* about his teammates?

Rolabi turned and rubbed Kallo's head. She let out a purr like an enormous house cat.

"None of you got the ball. But you all showed real courage. That is a good start."

Rain's right hand abruptly reappeared. He laughed without thinking, flexing his fingers and rolling his wrist to test it—there was no stiffness, no ache. It was as if he had been using it all along. The team broke into cheers and high-fived one another, but Rain just clasped his hands together, staring down at the meshed fingers. He had his future back.

Everything else was forgotten. It didn't matter now. He just had to play his game.

"What is that?" Jerome asked.

Rain followed his gaze. A black orb was floating in the middle of the gym. It fluctuated constantly, like a glob of oil suspended in water. For some reason, it made the hairs on Rain's arms stand on end, and he took a big step away. The gym felt cold. Deep and dark.

As Rain stared at the orb, he heard a voice whisper in his ear, quieter than Rolabi's . . . almost sinister:

What are you looking for?

"Ah," Rolabi said. "Just in time."

"What . . . what is it?" Peño asked, sounding as nervous as Rain felt.

"That is something you all will want to catch," Rolabi said. His voice was unusually hushed. "No, it is something you all *must* catch. Whoever catches it will become a far better player. But it won't last forever. And if no one catches it, we run laps." He nodded to it. "Go!"

The word was like the crack of a starting gun. Rain sprang forward without thinking, pulling out in front of the mad dash. He was so intent on being the first one to catch the orb that he forgot to consider if he actually wanted to. It didn't matter. The orb was not easily caught.

He reached for it, but the black shape zoomed past, moving in a blur. It weaved in between the team, dancing from side to side, almost taunting them. Several times Rain thought he had finally grabbed it, when the orb zigzagged past him again, just inches from his fingers. Players ran into each other, Vin rolled an ankle, there were shouts and warnings, but still no one could catch it.

Finally, the orb strayed too close to Kallo. She leapt up like a missile and swallowed it.

"A true defender," Rolabi said admiringly. "Get some water. Laps and free throws."

A groan went up through the group, and they trudged to the benches. Big John rejoined them, but Rain ignored the quiet conversations. He thought about the orb. The whispered voice.

He had heard that question the first day as well. It seemed almost silly.

It was no secret what he was looking for. *Who* he was looking for.

He caught a whiff of aftershave, tinged with smoke, and he breathed it in deeply. It was a memory, of course, but it filled his lungs anyway. Not pleasant, maybe. But the smell meant he was there. He used to wake to it, run down, wave as their rusted old car sputtered down the road.

How heavy weighs the past.

Rain glanced at Rolabi and turned away. The big man didn't understand. How could he?

The laps began, and once again the floors changed at every turn. Hills rose, and holes and pits formed. Once again, no one seemed to be able to hit a free throw—including Rain. This time no voice interrupted his attempt, but Rain waited for it, and he couldn't focus. An hour went by. Taking some pity, perhaps, Rolabi had the team study the daisy for thirty minutes while they drank their water. Then they ran again. Finally, Twig hit his free throw, and everyone doubled over.

"It's a start," Rolabi said, patting Kallo's head.

"A start?" Lab muttered. "I'm about to keel over."

"Tomorrow we will work on team defense," Rolabi said. "Get some rest tonight."

He scooped up his bag and started for the front doors with Kallo walking beside him.

"Are . . . are you taking the tiger?" Peño said.

The doors billowed open, and Rolabi and Kallo strolled into the daylight.

"He should really learn how to say goodbye," Peño said.

Rain shuffled to the bench, barely able to lift his feet. The team plunked themselves down. The bench teetered and held.

"We practiced with a tiger today," Peño said dully.

Someone started to laugh, and it spread down the line, turning into a roar. Rain couldn't help but join in. Their training was so ridiculous, so impossible, that it seemed like it was all Rain could do.

"Drop some lines, Peño," Jerome said, wiping laughter tears from his eyes.

Peño paused, and then began to bob to some unheard beat.

"We came to play ball
but that ain't all
We got a coach who's crazy
don't know this team is lazy
Big John don't run laps
now he's about to collapse
We got tigers chilling

Twig's the villain
and through it all
Peño the man keeps his eye on the north wall."

He finished with a dramatic point to the line of old banners.

"Maybe Peño should stop looking at the old banners and try to add a new one," Lab said.

"This year, baby," Peño said. "We'll just ask Rolabi to mess with the other teams."

Rain thought about that. Part of him still wondered if this was only Rolabi's doing—he was part of it, to be sure, but Rain couldn't shake the fact that he kept seeing all the things *he* wanted. The house with the big porch. His father. How could Rolabi know about those things?

He turned to the banners himself. He looked at the old dates, and the old teams, and he thought of sitting there with his father, his strong arm slung over Rain as he spoke.

"I didn't get a chance," he'd always said. "But you'll put one up there, son. I know it."

Son. He missed that word. The weight of it. The comfort that it implied.

Rain felt the shadow of an arm on his shoulder. He smelled pine again, and smoke, and this time he leaned into the scent, almost expecting a strong chest and the tickle of stubble on his forehead. He barely caught himself, sticking out an arm to steady himself on the bench. The pine faded into nothing, and the shadow was gone.

There was no father to look out for him. Only broken promises. Rain felt hot tears come on without warning. He couldn't let the guys see that. He was supposed to be the composed one.

He roughly wiped his face with his arm and hurried to the locker room.

There was a boy in the mirror in there, and they needed to tell each other to be stronger.

DEFEND THE KEEP

A champion is like the tide.
Controlled, powerful, and most of all, consistent.
◆ WIZENARD ㊶ PROVERB ◆

THE NEXT MORNING, there was a castle in the middle of the gym. Rain had just stepped through the double doors, thinking that he was ready for whatever Rolabi was going to bring to practice today. But he wasn't prepared for this.

The base of the structure was square, and the walls of smooth gray stone looked like they had been washed out by centuries of rain and snow. Four ramps climbed to a second story—each cut out from the exterior wall—and from there a final ramp led to the pinnacle. Perched atop the entire pyramidal structure was a large granite-and-gold trophy engraved on all sides.

Rain's knees buckled. He recognized it instantly.

It stood three feet tall and was adorned with a golden basketball, shining even in the gray fluorescent lights. The Elite Youth national trophy. To win that trophy meant fame. Sponsorship money. College. *Hope.* In the ninety-two years of Elite Youth ball, no team from the Bottom had ever won it. Yet there it was, sitting in their dilapidated gym. On top of a castle.

Rain blinked, trying to resist the urge to pinch himself. He turned to the bench and saw that it was empty. The whole gym was. He thought back to his vision, and his hands fumbled at the door behind him, ready to escape.

"What is basketball to you, Rain?"

He turned to find Rolabi standing beside the doors. The professor showed no signs of having built the huge structure—his pin-striped suit was spotless, his shoes polished, his face clean of dust or sweat. In fact, not a single hair on his head had shifted these last five days. He either was extraordinarily meticulous or simply didn't change or bathe or sleep or exist outside the gym.

"Where is everyone?" Rain muttered.

Rolabi didn't respond, his eyes locked on the fortress.

Rain realized that the professor was waiting for an answer. He considered the question for a moment, turning back to the beautiful elevated trophy and fighting a sudden urge to run over there and caress it. He had dreamed of doing that for as long as he could remember.

"It's an opportunity," Rain said finally.

"For what?" Rolabi asked.

Rain glanced at him. "For more, obviously."

"Ah. *More.* And what happens when you have it all?"

"What do you mean?"

"If you had that trophy up there. And the DBL championship one too. If you were an all-star or even the greatest player of all time. If you had taken your family out of the Bottom like you so desperately crave. Reunited them. Saved them from themselves. If somehow everything in your life was perfect. What would basketball mean then?"

"What do you know about my family?" Rain whispered.

"What would it mean?"

Rain paused. He'd never really thought about that. There was always more. Wasn't there?

"Well . . . I . . . I don't know. I guess I'll worry about that when I get there."

"How will you get there?"

"By being the best," Rain said.

He didn't need to think about *that* answer. He'd been chasing it since he could walk.

"I see," Rolabi said.

Somehow, Rain sensed that Rolabi was disappointed, but he wasn't sure why.

"Where is the team?" Rain asked again.

Rolabi lifted one of his salt-and-pepper eyebrows. "Getting ready."

Rain turned and saw that most of the team was indeed there, sitting on the benches or stretching and warming up. Peño was dribbling a ball on the far end, watching Rain curiously.

"Who are you?" Rain asked, turning back to the professor. "Really?"

"I am Rolabi Wizenard."

"How are you doing all this?" Rain persisted.

Rolabi allowed the shadow of a smile. "The same way you are."

Rain shook his head and hurried to the bench. As he approached, Vin leaned over to give him props.

"What were you guys talking about?" Vin asked, almost at a whisper.

"I have no idea."

Vin snorted. "Yeah . . . I hear you. He talked to me too. I . . . Well . . . Who knows."

Rain turned back to the bizarre structure dominating the center of the court. It was easily thirty feet tall, and the gilded top of the trophy was nearly scraping against the rafters. Rain figured the castle weighed many tons. It was a wonder that the floors hadn't been crushed to a pulp.

"Did he say anything about . . . that?" Rain asked.

"Nope," Vin said. "Because it's perfectly normal to have a castle show up on the court."

Rain snorted and pulled his shoes on. "I told my mama about the tiger."

"And?"

"She told me to trust Rolabi."

Vin turned to him incredulously. "Has everyone lost their minds?"

"I don't know," Rain said, sighing. "Maybe just us."

The team soon assembled in front of the castle. Now that he was up close, Rain could see that though the castle *looked* like real stone, it was in fact smooth and rubbery, like a balding tire.

"Today we are working on team defense," Rolabi said.

"Like . . . zone defense?" Peño asked, staring up at the fortress.

"In time," he said. "First you have to learn the fundamentals."

"Like how to pillage a castle?" Peño mused, running his fingers along the wall.

Rolabi ignored him and turned his bag over, dumping items onto the floor. They came out like a multicolored waterfall, and Rain heard something squawk in protest from inside.

The flow of items continued. First were padded helmets like the kind amateur boxers wore—half of them red, and half blue. Next came large plush pads that unfurled as soon as they hit the ground. Each was about the size of a classroom desk, with two thick straps on the back. When he had spilled the entire tangled heap onto the floor, Rolabi closed his bag and set it down beside him, muting a last annoyed squawk. No one moved, so Rolabi gestured to the pile.

"Take one of each, please."

Rain scooped up a blue helmet and put it on. It fit perfectly. He grabbed a blue pad and found it was heavier than it looked and nearly as firm as his bed—practically a slab of concrete. The others sorted themselves out, and soon there were five players with red helmets and five with blue. Rain examined his team: Peño, Big John, Twig, and Jerome. Definitely the smaller of the two teams, and given the pads and helmets, he suspected that was a bad thing.

"The game is simple," Rolabi said, gesturing to the castle that was looming over the team. "One team will attack the castle, and the other will defend it. The team to get the trophy in the least amount of time wins. The losing team will run laps while the winners shoot around."

"How did you get the national championship trophy?" Peño asked longingly.

"I borrowed it," Rolabi replied. "Blue team will defend first."

Rain eyed the castle. So he was on defense—it seemed simple enough. He hurried up the ramp, his team following. As he went, he examined the structure, trying to come up with a plan.

The walls were too high and smooth to climb, so the only way to get inside was to use the four ramps. Each of those was about three feet wide—identical to the width of their pads, so a single defender could block them. It all seemed simple enough. The blue team gathered around him.

"Obviously, we need to block the four lower ramps," Rain said. "One man on each, and two on whatever ramp they double up on. Big John, you need to try and match up with Devon if you can. Everyone else just take a ramp. I will play safety and go wherever the double-team is."

"What happens if they start switching and I get Devon or something?" Peño asked.

"We got to talk," Rain said. "Make sure you call it out if someone is getting past you. Got it?"

They all nodded.

"I don't feel like running laps for another two hours, so let's win this," Rain said.

"Let's rock it, boys!" Peño whooped.

They split up and hurried to the ramps. Rain followed Peño—he was the smallest and likeliest target for a double-team. From there, he could see where the red team would focus their attack and move accordingly. The red team had broken their huddle as well, and Devon was rolling his broad shoulders. Rain knew he was going to be tough to stop, even for Big John.

Rain frowned as he looked the team over. He realized now that his plan to match defenders against the attacking team was useless. The *attackers* got to pick their targets. The defense could never switch in time. He pushed the thought aside. He would just have to be faster with backup. He could do that. He could win this game alone.

"This is going to be madness," Peño muttered. "But it's kind of awesome."

"Agreed," he murmured. "We're defending a castle."

"We just need some armor and this will be really legit."

"Begin."

Even though Rolabi wasn't shouting, his voice blasted through the gym. At the sound of it, the dusty floorboards around the castle caved into a steep trench. Water spilled out through the cracks and created a brackish moat, green and brown with algae and sediment. The hardwood warped again and leapt across the moat in four narrow bridges, each leading to one of the ramps.

The castle changed too: its walls turned to actual stone, while forked blue flags began to billow from the corners. Rain felt his clothing grow bulkier and realized he was now dressed like the knights from the history books: he wore steel armor with navy-blue trim on the shoulders and collar, and his pad was now worn leather.

"Peño . . ." he murmured.

"Yeah, I see it," he said. "I had to open my big mouth."

"Charge!" Lab shouted, pointing his arm like a sword, and the red team broke into a chaotic dash toward the fortress. Like the blue team, each attacking player was dressed in steel armor, except trimmed with crimson.

Their boots clattered on the hardwood, and they formed a phalanx that immediately split apart. Vin charged right at Peño and Rain, shouting a war cry, and Rain spotted Reggie and Lab running for a bridge on the other side. They were doing exactly what he had expected—doubling up and trying to overwhelm a single defender. Someone weak. *Twig*. Rain had to move quickly.

"Help!" Twig called, confirming Rain's hunch.

"Good luck!" Rain said to Peño, and then took off just as Vin and Peño slammed into each other.

He sprinted up onto the first level—the armor was heavy but not over-whelming—and then he plunged down another ramp, where Twig was being steadily bowled backward under the combined assault of Reggie and Lab. Rain joined the fray, using the high ground to drive them all back down the ramp. Reggie broke off and hurried across the moat to attack elsewhere.

Rain's plan was working perfectly.

"Keep pushing, Twig!" he said.

Rain headed back up the ramp, sprinting around the castle to see where Reggie would re-emerge. Big John and Peño were still locked in one-on-one combat with A-Wall and Vin, both holding their ground, but Rain caught a glimpse of Jerome sliding up his ramp at an alarming pace. Jerome was facing the muscular Devon, and he was clearly outmatched. Rain hesitated, still not spotting Reggie.

"A little help!" Jerome called, peeking over his shoulder.

Rain realized he had no choice. Devon was almost through. Rain plunged down the ramp, halting the steady backward slide. Even with both of them *and* the higher ground, they were locked in an almost-even struggle. Devon was incredibly strong, driving his feet like the treads of an excavator.

"Where was this on the court?" Rain said, but Devon just ignored him and pushed on.

"I got two!" Peño cried. "I can't hold them!"

"Rain," Jerome said, straining, "I need help . . ."

But once again, Rain had no choice. He had to help Peño with the double-team.

"Hold him, Jerome! You can do it!" Rain said, and then took off.

Rain turned down Peño's ramp. He didn't have to go far. The two attackers—Vin and Reggie—were nearly through, and Peño's feet were sliding as if he were on ice skates. Rain plowed into him, sandwiching the squat point guard, and together, they held their ground.

"Push!" Rain shouted.

"A-Wall just took off!" Big John said.

"So did Lab!" Twig added.

Reggie looked up, smiling.

"Guys," Jerome whimpered.

Rain heard a pronounced *thump* and ran back up just in time to see Devon, A-Wall, and Lab stepping over Jerome, who was now lying flat on his back, dazed. The three red attackers broke for the final ramp . . . and only Rain was left to stop them. Devon took the lead, charging wildly.

"Help me!" Rain said.

He tried to block them. He set his legs, raised the pad, and closed his eyes. He knew what was coming. Devon was moving at full speed. It was like being hit by a locomotive.

The impact sent him flying, and he slammed into a stone wall and crumpled. The red team hurried up the last ramp, and Devon hoisted the trophy to a chorus of cheers. Rain slowly stood up, his back aching, and scowled as the rest of the blue team gathered around him, quiet and sullen.

"Don't worry," Rain muttered. "We'll beat their time."

On cue, Rolabi's voice cut over the cheering.

"One minute and forty-seven seconds. Blue team, you will now attack."

"Let's go," Rain said.

He led them across the moat, trying to understand how they had been defeated so easily.

"That was tough," Big John said.

"Well, it'll be the same for them," Rain said. "If they want to play tricks, so can we."

He glanced back at the castle. The flags had all turned to crimson now, flapping in the same nonexistent wind. The blue team huddled together, and once again, Rain created the plan.

He understood enough—the attackers got to choose. It was a game of offense.

"All right, we have the advantage. We saw how it works. We can pick our matchups, so we'll overpower them right away. Big John and I will go for Vin—easy prey. Twig, Jerome, and Peño will fake splitting up and then go at Reggie, unless he has help. Try and avoid Devon, A-Wall, and Lab. We'll drive right through their weak spots and get that trophy."

Peño laughed. "We'll have it in thirty seconds!"

"What if they double both the entrances we attack?" Jerome asked.

"Then another one is free!" Rain said. "This game is a trick. It's impossible to defend the trophy."

They broke up and spread out into a line, waiting for the red team to take their places. None of them appeared at the ramps—clearly, they were still trying to organize a defense. Rain didn't blame them. How could you possibly cover four ramps when the attackers could adjust and hit wherever it was going to hurt most?

Rolabi is saying the offense drives the game, Rain thought.

He could agree with that.

"Begin!" Rolabi said.

"They're not set up yet!" Rain said. "Follow me in!"

The blue team charged, and Rain grinned as they ran up the closest ramp unopposed. It was going to be an easy victory. He turned the corner, ready to head right for the trophy, and then stopped when he saw Devon waiting for them. The rest of Rain's team plowed into his back.

"What the—" Peño said.

Devon was standing right at the base of the final ramp. The whole red team was lined up behind him, their pads pressed against one another like the links of a chain. They were blocking the last ramp as one unit. There was no way to reach the trophy. Rain had been totally outsmarted.

But he wouldn't admit defeat.

"Push!" he shouted.

His team collided with Devon, and though the red team slid back a little at first, the progress stopped almost immediately. Rain pushed with everything he had, but thanks to both Devon and the higher ground, the red team easily held the attackers back. The muscles in Rain's legs burned. His body trembled. He clenched his teeth until he could feel pain in his jaw. But still he kept going.

"It's useless!" Big John said.

"Keep pushing!" Rain cried. He slammed into Devon's pad again, but the defense was as solid as the fortress itself.

"Just leave it," Big John said, letting off pressure. "We lost."

"No!" Rain said. "Harder!"

"My legs—" Peño said.

"Harder!" Rain demanded. He pushed with everything he had. Pain flared all across his body. It didn't matter.

After an agonizing minute or so, Devon and the rest of the red team *pushed*. Rain and his team fell backward into a tangle of limbs and angry shouts. Rain lay on the ground, gasping and defeated.

"The time is beat," Rolabi said. "The red team wins."

The red team cheered and hoisted the trophy. The flags disappeared, and the castle walls turned back to rubber. Even Rain's glittering armor melted into plain polyester gym attire—secondhand shorts, his father's tee. Both were ratty. The tee was moth-eaten. It was a reminder.

Rain was always looking up. Always at the bottom.

"The red team may grab some balls and shoot around," Rolabi said. "Blue team, laps."

Rain climbed to his feet, refusing to look at his teammates. *He* had made the strategy . . . and it failed. Lately, it seemed he was failing at everything. A leader couldn't lose to his own teammates—he had to be the best player. He had to control everything. He had to be above the others. And now he was watching from far below as half of his team hoisted a trophy.

The blue team shuffled dejectedly down the ramp, stripped off their helmets, and started running. It was well over an hour before Twig hit a free throw, and by then, Rain was sopping wet and annoyed. He had insisted on taking three attempts . . . and then proceeded to miss them all.

It was Twig who ended it. *Twig.*

Rain couldn't understand what was happening.

He shuffled to the bench and chugged a full bottle of water. It had been even more infuriating watching the red team shoot around and work on their game. Running laps for this long was a waste of his time and talent. It was a cruel joke. He sat down and miserably rubbed the sweat from his eyes.

"What was this drill about?" Rolabi asked.

Both teams had gathered on the benches now, and the red team still looked smug. Rain glared at them. It should have been him with the trophy. It wasn't his plan that let his blue teammates down . . . it was his teammates themselves. They didn't push hard enough. They quit.

"Team defense," Peño muttered.

"Yes. They played as a team," Rolabi said calmly. "You did not."

Rain stood up, scowling. "So, what? You want us to stand in a group on the court?"

"I want you to play as a unit, yes," Rolabi said. "What are you protecting on defense?"

"The net," Reggie said immediately.

Rolabi nodded and started for the fortress, his shoes rapping against the hardwood.

"The blue team tried to protect the entire court. Team defense is about working together. You all must be tigers. You must be strong and fast and have great reflexes. That is how you stop your man. But if you do not work together to protect the net, you will be scored on regardless. The net *is* the trophy. Protect it."

Rolabi reached down to a small black cap set into the castle wall, grabbed it between thumb and index finger, and pulled it out. Cold air started to whistle out of the fortress so forcefully that Rain felt it on his face, even from twenty feet away. The air began to rush out more and more through the penny-size hole, and the entire towering structure began to fold in on itself. In moments, it had shrunk to the size of a basketball, and Rolabi dropped it in his bag.

"What must a defender always be?" Rolabi asked.

"*Ready,*" Reggie said.

Rolabi nodded.

Rain turned his attention to Reggie. Why was this guy taking the lead? Rain's *backup*.

If there is a void of leadership, it must be filled.

I am the leader! Rain thought.

Are you?

"The same goes for the entire team," Rolabi said, starting for the doors. "If you are not ready, we are wasting our time."

"Are we done for today?" Peño called after him.

"That is up to you."

The doors burst open with a gust of cold wind, and the professor was gone.

"What does that mean?" Jerome asked.

"It means we can stay. We have balls," Rain said. He figured he could at least get some shooting practice today. "Want to scrimmage?"

"Look!" Lab shouted, pointing with a trembling finger.

They all turned. The orb was floating in the middle of the court. As before, it seemed to warp in midair. The temperature cooled. The black orb changed again, forming a perfect oval.

He saw something in it. A face. His own?

What are you looking for?

"What do we do?" Peño whispered.

"Rolabi said we had to catch it," A-Wall said, though he didn't sound convinced. "He said we would be better basketball players if we did, remember?"

Without warning, Twig made a dash for the orb. It zipped out of his way, and the spell was broken again. The whole team chased after it, waving their hands and shouting. Rain dove face-first for it and landed hard on his hip. Beside him, Lab and Peño ran right into each other.

"Watch out!" Lab shouted.

"You watch it!" Peño snapped in reply.

The orb weaved around them for ten minutes in a dizzying pattern, taunting them. Then it flew like a cannonball toward the nearest wall and disappeared. Rain rubbed his sore right hip, scowling yet again. It felt like it was already bruising. He limped back to the bench.

"Still up for that scrimmage?" Peño asked.

Rain glowered and sat down. The failures had begun to sour his mood. "Nah. Let's just get out of here."

"You all right?" Jerome asked Big John, who plopped onto the bench, massaging his ankle.

"Rolled it," Big John said. "Chasing some stupid orb."

"What do you think we're going to do tomorrow?" Jerome asked. "Go to space?"

"I have no idea," Rain said. "Today was a total waste of time."

"A waste of time?" Reggie asked suddenly. "Why?"

"Because he lost," A-Wall said, grinning.

The smirk was enough to put Rain's temper over the edge. Did they all forget that he was the star of this team? Did they think it was easy? He had to take the big shots. Everyone was relying on Rain. *Everything.* He felt sudden pressure welling behind his eyes.

It made him angrier.

"Who cares!" Rain snapped. "What did that game have to do with basketball?"

"Everything," Reggie said. "It was about playing defense the right way. As a team."

"It was a stupid game. You play D by stopping the ball. And you win by scoring." Rain tucked his shoes in his bag and stood up, staring down at Reggie. "By *me* scoring. And we aren't getting any closer to winning by me not working on my shot. This is a big year for me."

"You mean for *us*," Lab said quietly.

Rain started for the doors, bag over his shoulder.

"Yeah," he said. "Rain Adams and the West Bottom Badgers."

He stormed out of the gym and let the doors slam behind him. He was halfway across the parking lot before he felt guilty. And stupid. But he couldn't go back and apologize. This was the Bottom. There was no magic, no apologies, no forgiveness. Only the tough could survive.

He remembered who had told him that, and the tears spilled down after all.

6

THE SECOND SIGHT

The lone wolf will soon starve.
◆ WIZENARD (34) PROVERB ◆

IT HAD BEEN a long night. Rain had stared at old family pictures and spun his basketball on one finger like a top. He had never felt more alone. He'd wished for the millionth time that he had a computer or a cell phone or a working TV and thought constantly about what he'd said. It had been harsh, but it was true. If they couldn't see that, it wasn't his fault.

On the walk to Fairwood, Rain wondered what they were saying about him. Were they calling him selfish? Arrogant? Did it matter? How could anyone know what it was like to have his responsibilities? To need, to be expected, to get his family out of the Bottom? To bring them together? How could the other guys know the weight of that? They didn't have to see Larry looking at photos of their dad when no one was looking. They didn't have to see his mama struggling to work and pay the bills and take care of them alone. They didn't have to see his dad walk out the door because it all wasn't good enough. Rain got to the front doors and scowled.

He didn't need his teammates. Loneliness was fine. It led to greatness.

He grabbed the doors, then paused. They were freshly painted . . . a clean emerald green. He pulled them open. There wasn't a squeal or groan. They swung smoothly on brand-new hinges. And the gym was full.

The scene was almost—blurred. Just at the edges, like a photo left out in the rain. The bleachers were packed, and a game was going on. The players looked different. Longer hair, smaller shorts. Fairwood was cleaner, newer. Rain noticed his favorite banner was missing.

He stepped inside, watching the game. He made his way to the bleachers and sat down among the crowd. No one seemed to notice him. As he watched, he realized it was an old West Bottom team—the Braves. The team from his favorite banner. His father's team.

And there was a star out there.

One boy was clearly dominant. He moved with purpose on the court, always a step ahead, his eyes tracking everything. Crisp passes. Tight handles. He hit one shot after another. As he drained a third jumper in a row, he turned to the crowd and pumped a fist. His eyes . . .

"Dad?" Rain whispered.

The boy turned away. Rain stood up, watching as the boy dominated. He was incredible.

Rain couldn't take it any longer. He walked onto the court and tried to grab hold of his father, but his hand passed right through his shoulder. The boy's features blurred, and the whole scene turned into mist. Rain spun around, trying to find the familiar face. He waded through the fog.

"Dad!" Rain said.

But it was all gone. The current-day Badgers sat on the benches, not even noticing him.

Rain took a last look around. Why had he seen that game? Was that really the way his father played? He had been amazing. Rain's equal. Maybe even better. He'd never told Rain that he was *that* good. Why? And if he was so good, why hadn't he made it anywhere?

Rain sat down on the away bench for the first time in his life. It wobbled beneath him, threatening to tip. Twig nodded at him, and he heard a few muttered comments from the others.

"Look who it is . . ." someone said.

Rain glared at them and put his shoes on in silence. They could say what they wanted. He was the star here. Everyone knew it. Rain took the ball out of his duffel. The crumpled note was lying beneath it, and for some reason, he was tempted to read it for the first time in weeks. But not here—not in front of Twig. He left it at the bottom of his bag.

"How you feeling today?" Twig asked suddenly.

Rain looked at him in surprise. "Fine. You?"

"Nervous, I guess," Twig said. "Don't know what to expect."

Rain snorted. "Yeah, it's been crazy, all right. Since when do you talk?"

"I always talked," he said defensively. "Just nobody wants to listen."

Rain thought about that for a moment. Had they ever really given Twig a chance to join in the conversation? Or even asked him a simple question about his life outside of ball? Rain couldn't think of even one example . . . and Twig had played with them for a full year already.

"Okay, okay," Rain said. "So why aren't you avoiding me like the rest of the team?"

Twig managed a smile and stretched out his legs.

"I don't think they're avoiding you. You got upset yesterday. That's all right. We all do sometimes. I do . . . well . . . a lot of times."

"I basically said I was the team," Rain reminded him.

Twig shrugged and took out his ball. "Who can blame you? It's what you've been told."

Twig walked out onto the court. Rain followed him, thinking of his mama and Freddy. Twig was right: it was all they ever told him. His mama said it at least three times a day. But Rain had never argued with them. He'd believed everything they said. He thought he was special.

Did Dad think I was too? he wondered.

"Gather around," a deep voice announced. "Put the balls away."

Rain turned and saw Rolabi standing at center court, checking his pocket watch.

He and Twig hurried over with the rest of the team. A-Wall and Lab were pointedly avoiding Rain's gaze, so he did the same to them. An uneasy silence settled over the group.

"Today we are going to work on offense," Rolabi said.

"Finally," Rain murmured.

"We'll start with passing," Rolabi continued. "The foundation of all offense. What do all the great passers have?"

Rain stayed quiet. Passing wasn't exactly his strong suit.

Why pass when you were the number one option?

"Vision," Peño said suddenly.

"Very good. A great passer must be quick and agile and bold. But mostly, they must have vision. Both of what is and what will soon come. They must see *everything* on the floor."

Lab frowned. "So . . . we just have to practice seeing more . . . ?"

"Yes," Rolabi said. "And the best way to start is by seeing nothing at all."

The light suddenly blinked out. Not just the ceiling panels—even the sunlight that crept in through cracks around the door frame. It was so dark that Rain couldn't see the tip of his nose.

"Not cool," A-Wall muttered.

"Hey, watch it," Peño said sharply. "That's my toe!"

Rain closed his eyes, opened them, realized it made no difference. He wasn't afraid of the dark, but this was enveloping. It almost had a presence. It stifled him. His breathing quickened.

"*Vision* is an interesting term for it," Rolabi said. His voice was even more commanding in the darkness. "In this case, it isn't only reliant on eyesight. We can hear what is happening. We can feel it. We can predict it. If you can do that, your eyes are just an added bonus."

The sound of a ball dribbling broke the quiet. Rain relaxed as it bounced methodically: *boom, boom, boom.* The floorboards vibrated beneath him, and the noise was calming and familiar—the only nursery rhyme he had ever liked. His father used to play it for him almost every day.

"The game is simple," Rolabi said. "The attacking team will start on one end, and the other team will wait in the middle. The attacking team will pass the ball up the court. They cannot dribble: only pass. If they get to the far side, they win. If they lose the ball, then the other team gets a turn. We will go until one team wins. The losing team will run."

"You really like making us run," Big John muttered.

"Never underestimate the value of sweat," Rolabi said. "It can forge the greatest change."

Rain tried to focus. He bounced on his toes, feeling the floor bounce with him.

He knew this floor.

"Starters versus last year's bench," Rolabi said. "Starters will go first. Find the ball."

It took them five minutes just to do that. Rain waved his arms around, crouching low and flinching as he slapped shins or the walls. The starters eventually tracked the ball down, and it took another few minutes to get themselves organized beneath the net—they found the far wall and then turned and took a step away from it. There was much bumping and jostling and cursing.

Finally, both sides decided that they were in the right positions.

"Okay, I'm going!" Peño shouted.

"Here!" Rain said, moving toward his voice.

He turned his head away, worried about getting a pass right in the nose, but Peño wisely bounce-passed it, and Rain managed to block the ball and catch it on the second bounce. He heard shoes squeaking as the other players slowly advanced past him, taking timid little steps.

Rain looked around, lifting the ball to his chest. "Who's next?"

"Here!" Lab said, sounding like he was only a few feet away. "Pass it."

Rain bounced it as well, but he heard a low grunt.

"A little higher," Lab said weakly. "Keep moving!"

They continued up the floor. Progress was slow and awkward, but they managed to get the ball to half. When the two teams merged, however, chaos broke out. The voices began to jumble together, and Rain found it hard to listen for bounces. In seconds, the ball was lost again.

After a long search, the bench team took a turn. They didn't even make it to half before someone threw a wild pass, and the ball bounced into the bleachers with a disheartening clank.

"Hmm," Rolabi said. "Perhaps we will work up to complete darkness."

The ball suddenly turned a brilliant, crimson red, like a fire had been lit within it. Yet it cast no additional light, so that all Rain could see was the ball itself—like a night sky with one star. The red shape bobbed and started floating across the gym.

"This is weird," said Peño, who was presumably carrying the ball back to the starting position. The ball bounced back and forth between two unseen hands. "You guys ready? Go!"

"Can anyone see me?" A-Wall said. "I'm lost."

"Are you serious right now?" Peño said. "Just stay there. Rain, where are you?"

"Here! Pass!"

They moved faster now. It was still tough to make a pass without seeing the target, but at least the glow made catching the ball a little easier. Rain focused intently on the voices and the squeaking shoes, and the starters proceeded quickly to the halfway line. Then things fell apart again.

As the two teams merged, the shouts became one riotous mass of noise, the squeaks only adding to the confusion, and the ball was picked off by a whooping Jerome.

"Switch sides," Rolabi said.

He sounded amused.

They went back and forth until Rain was so drenched with sweat that he could taste salt on his tongue. He still couldn't see a thing, but he was feeling more and more comfortable in the darkness. On what must have been the thirtieth attempt at least, he sprinted right past the line of scattered defenders, waving to avoid a collision, and then turned back again.

"I'm open! Toss it up!"

Someone heaved the ball up in the air, and it sped toward him like a blazing comet. He caught the pass and heard frantic squeaking as both attackers and defenders sprinted toward him.

One voice rose up above the noise.

"Here! Rain!" Peño called. "I'm open . . . probably!"

It was coming from farther down the court. Guessing at the direction, Rain lobbed the ball up in the air with one arm. It seemed to move in slow motion, and he heard more squeaks and cries and curses and jumps. Then the ball abruptly stopped about four feet from the floor.

"Got it!" Peño said. "Who's next—"

The lights blinked on again, and Rain saw that Peño was standing right beside the net.

"The starting team wins," Rolabi said. "Water break."

Peño and the other starters exchanged high fives, but Rain didn't join them. He doubted they wanted to talk to him, anyway. That was fine. He headed to the away bench alone, satisfied that he'd won *something*. He pulled out his bottle and took a thirsty gulp as Twig joined him.

"That was crazy," Twig said, chugging so much water that it streamed down his chin.

"Yeah," Rain said. "Though compared to the tiger, that drill was nothing."

Twig laughed. "True."

Rolabi turned to them, his enormous hands clasped behind his back.

"The losing team will run at the end of practice. The winning team can decide then if they want to join them."

Rain had to stop himself from snorting. They had won. Why would they want to join in?

"So, clearly, on offense we must learn to listen," Rolabi said. "What else?"

"Score?" Rain suggested, hoping they might get to work on their shots.

"Yes, eventually," Rolabi agreed. "But more fundamentally."

"Talk?" Twig said.

"Exactly. We talk on defense but forget to do it on offense. Twig, come up here, please."

Twig flushed and put his bottle down. He nervously took a spot beside Rolabi, who loomed over even him. The top of Twig's head only reached Rolabi's chin, and Twig was six five.

"I want you to tell the team one thing you would like to say to them. One *honest* thing."

Twig glanced up at Rolabi. "What sort of thing?"

"It could be anything. If you cannot be honest with each other, you cannot be a team."

Twig fidgeted for a moment. "Umm . . . well . . . I don't have anything."

"Yes, you do," Rolabi said. "I am sure you have many things. Just pick one for starters."

"But . . ."

"Anything at all."

Twig scratched his arm, leaving white marks. Rain frowned. There were tons of them. He had always noticed Twig's cheeks—pockmarked and scarred. He'd never really thought about it, but now he wondered. Was he scratching at his cheeks too? Had Twig created the scars himself?

Rain shook the thought away. Twig was fine. He lived in a nice house with a nice family.

It was a birthmark probably. An accident.

Twig shifted uncomfortably. "Okay . . . well . . . I have been working really hard," he said. "You know, in the off-season. And I am trying
really hard to be better. I know maybe you guys didn't want me back this
season, but I really am trying to help the team. I want you guys to know
that, I guess."

He quickly scurried back to the bench. Rain watched him, thinking
back to his behavior. He hadn't really wanted Twig back this season . . .
none of them had. They hadn't hid that fact either. And for all that, what
did Twig do? He spent the entire off-season trying to get stronger and
become a better player so that it wouldn't happen again. And the first
thing Rain did was tell him he looked the exact same. No wonder Twig
had been upset that first day. Heat crept up Rain's neck as he remembered
how little he had done to stop Big John's mean comments. He was as
guilty as Big John and Jerome. Rain had tried to justify it, but he looked
again at the scars, and he wondered, and he felt ashamed.

"Jerome," Rolabi said.

They went through the team one at a time. Some of the things the
players shared were surprising, others obvious. There were personal goals
and team ones and fiery words from Peño about how they were going to
win the national championship trophy. Finally, when everyone else had
gone, Rolabi turned to Rain and nodded. Rain hesitated. He knew what
he needed to say . . . but he was embarrassed to say it.

The easy things to say are rarely worth saying.

Rain flinched. He stepped up beside the professor, faced the team,
and took a deep breath.

"I'm sorry," he said. "About yesterday. I shouldn't have said I was the
team like that."

"Do you believe it?" Vin asked.

"Of course not. It's a team sport." He paused. "But I am the top scorer
and the leader."

"Do they mean the same thing, I wonder?" Rolabi said.

Rain frowned. "Of course they do."

"No, they don't," Vin snapped. "The leader is supposed to push the entire team."

"I do push you to be better!" Rain said.

Lab shook his head. "No, you just try to score enough to pull us along with you."

Rain's fists tightened at his sides. It was true that he scored a lot of points. That was what the team needed him to do. "Well, what do you want from me?" he asked.

"To be a part of the Badgers," Lab said. "Not Rain Adams and the Badgers."

Rain saw the anger on Lab's face spread to others in the group. It was clear he had offended them all even worse than he had thought. That realization cooled his temper. He was still the one headed to the DBL. He was the reason the West Bottom Badgers existed in the first place. But these were his teammates, so he nodded. There was no need to alienate everyone.

"I will be," Rain said. "For real. Are we good?"

The team was silent for a moment, and Rain wondered if they would reject his apology. Would they refuse to play with him this season? What then? Could they kick him off the team?

And then Peño stepped out and gave him props. "We're good, bro. Let's forget it."

They tapped fists, and there was a general murmur of assent. Rain noticed that Rolabi was still watching him, and for just a moment, he saw a flicker of disappointment in his bright green eyes. But the professor soon turned back to the court.

"Let's scrimmage for an hour."

"No tricks?" Peño asked warily.

"Just working on our vision. Rain, Vin, Lab, A-Wall, and Devon versus the rest."

Rolabi pulled out a ball. He extended it with one hand, staring down at it thoughtfully.

"Humans are easily distracted. We focus on one actor and miss the others in the background. We watch one card as the dealer palms a second. We watch the ball but miss the game." He looked at the players and then back at the ball. "We can see so much, and yet we choose not to. It is an odd decision."

Then Rain's vision abruptly changed. It was as if he had put his fingers in front of his eyes, completely blocking his field of view except for the very periphery. He cried out and heard the others shouting, confirming that he wasn't the only one affected. Rain spun around, shook his head, and rubbed his eyes, doing everything he could to remove the strange new obstacle.

But nothing worked. Only his peripheral vision remained.

"Not cool!" Lab shouted. Rain caught a glimpse of him whirling around like a top.

"I can't see!" Big John cried. "Well . . . sort of!"

Rain tried to calm down. It was another illusion, the same as his missing right hand. There was no point in panicking. He breathed and tilted his head slightly, getting his bearings.

"Ready to play?" Rolabi asked.

"Just to clarify, does everyone else feel like they're talking to the hand?" Peño asked.

Rolabi tossed the ball up. Rain cocked his head, trying vainly to track the action with his limited vision. It should have been a bit easier than in the complete darkness, but he almost felt *more* disoriented using only his peripheral vision, because he was relying only on that. It seemed like his other senses had dulled again. Finally, he saw Vin scoop up the ball and start to dribble.

"Keep talking!" Vin shouted. "Tell me where you are!"

"Getting into my spot!" Rain called.

Rain moved slowly down the court, waving his hands back and forth. He reached the corner and saw Vin dribbling to the top of the key, but he couldn't see the defense or the net.

It doesn't matter until you have the ball, he told himself.

Vin passed him the ball, and Rain managed to catch it. He turned to the net, surveying the rest of the court. Rain dribbled to the left, trying to catch a glimpse of Reggie. When he saw him trailing a step behind, Rain cut toward the net, moving right past Peño and Jerome on the perimeter.

He was now alone with the big guys. He suspected that Twig or Big John would now be stepping up to block the lane. Normally, he would drive right past them and go for the layup, but it was impossible. He couldn't see where they were coming from. He needed another option.

Rain spotted Lab standing alone in the corner and passed him the ball.

"I can see!" Lab shouted. He lined up the shot and drained it. "Nice pass, Rain!"

Rain frowned and ran back to stay ahead of Reggie. He rarely made that pass out of the lane. Today it had been the only possible option. As they hurried back, he called out with the rest of his team to try to coordinate. It was like they had all become play-by-play announcers:

"I'm at the top of the key!"

"Play a three-two zone; Devon and A-Wall down low!"

"I've got the right wing . . . Peño has the ball . . . who's got him?"

"I see him . . . Stepping up! Fill in behind me!"

"Reggie just ran past me—who's got him?"

"I see him! He's dropping back for the pass. Watch for cuts!"

Rain defended Reggie on his wing, using a free hand to track him. His head was on a constant swivel. When an attacker ran past, visible in the corner of his eye, he had to figure out where they were headed and call out warnings. It was a game of strategy—slower and more methodical. But as the scrimmage continued, Rain felt increasingly attuned to his team. He relied on them on both ends of the court. It was only possible to get a sense of the game when *every* player talked. If one player went quiet, that part of the court went dark. It was a missing piece.

He also realized that whenever there was an open shot, the block in his vision lifted. If he was driving into a crowd, it remained. Same for fadeaway jumpers or long threes. But if he had a truly good look, he could fully see. To get those looks, he had to move, rub screens, change pace.

Usually he just demanded the ball and worked from there. Today he had to get open.

Finally, when the stitches had taken root in Rain's side and he was breathing heavily, Rolabi called the game to a stop and stepped onto the court. Rain turned his head to watch him.

Rolabi almost looked . . . pleased. It was an expression Rain hadn't seen on him before.

"Grab your bottles and join me in the center," he said.

In a blink, Rain's vision returned to normal again, and he sighed in relief. The team grabbed their bottles and hurried to join Rolabi at half-court. Many of them were sporting grins.

"Who won?" Peño asked, taking a drink. "I kind of lost track."

"Neither," Rolabi said. "And both. Was that how you normally play?"

"Of course not," Lab said. "We were moving in slow motion."

"Speed is relative. To the fastest, everyone moves in slow motion. What else?"

Twig wiped the drips from his chin. "We . . . we talked a lot. More than ever."

"True. Anything else?"

"We spread the floor on offense," Peño said. "More passes around the lane. Kick outs and stuff."

Rolabi nodded. "A natural choice when one cannot see his own path. And lastly?"

There was a long silence.

Rain took another drink, thinking back to the drill. One thing had stood out to him.

"We had to think about where everyone would be . . . and should be. We had to predict the game."

"Indeed," Rolabi said. "We had to see more than our eyes allow. Now, I am owed some laps."

The bench players grumbled and got into a line, Vin at the lead. The starters watched them, a few glancing at Rain, but he stayed where he was, arms folded. He had won a drill, finally. He didn't have to run. And so the bench team took off, and the starters remained, watching. Rolabi was watching too—but his bright green eyes seemed to focus more on the starters. Rain refused to meet his gaze. He could almost sense the big man's disapproval.

The bench wasn't running for long; Reggie hit a free throw after just five laps, and they joined the team at the center circle again.

Rolabi opened his bag. "You all have your full eyesight again. But are you really looking? We must relearn to see."

He withdrew the daisy from his bag and set it in the middle of the circle.

"Not again," Peño muttered.

"Many times more," Rolabi said. "If you wish to win, you *must* slow down time."

The front doors billowed open before Rolabi, crashing into either wall.

"How long do you want us to stare at it?" Rain asked.

Rolabi walked out into the sunlight. "Until you have seen something new."

The doors slammed shut, and the howling wind was silenced. Rain sighed. Just when he thought they were making progress, Rolabi brought back the daisy. Big John started for the bench.

"Where you going?" Jerome asked.

"I'm not staring at a stupid flower if I don't have to," Big John sneered. "I'm out."

"Everything all right with you?" Peño asked.

Big John turned back. "No, Peño. This is the Bottom. Things aren't just *all right*. You can go along with that weirdo all you want and play his games. But it's not a game out there. Remember where you are." He scowled at Twig. "I'm going to catch some extra time at work."

He grabbed his bag and walked out. Rain glanced at the flower, hesitated, and then started for the bench. Big John was right: staring at the flower was a waste of time. He took out his ball and went to shoot around. He needed to work on his game. Rolabi could have his drills.

When it came down to it, if Rain could score, he was going to make it big.

Peño, Lab, A-Wall, Vin, and Jerome followed Rain, but Devon, Twig, and Reggie remained seated.

"They're all stupid," Lab muttered. "Waste of time."

Rain shrugged. "They can do what they want. I'll work on my shot."

"I wonder if we're ever going to do any actual drills—" Lab said.

Peño cut him off. "Look!"

The black orb was hovering right over Devon's head. Everyone froze. Devon kept his eyes on the flower, not moving. Nobody called out to him to warn him. They all seemed transfixed, and Rain sensed that Devon knew it was there. The seconds ticked by slowly, until it seemed like the clock had stopped. Then, without warning, Devon reached up and closed his hand on the orb, the black matter slipping through his fingers like tar. Devon broke into a grin.

And then he disappeared.

7

MAKE IT RAIN

*Stare at the sky and choose if you will be a mouse
or a mountain. Either way, you are right.*

❖ WIZENARD ㊱ PROVERB ❖

RAIN SIGHED AND glanced at the doors. It was probably nine o'clock.
He had been waiting under the old oak again, and he had seen everyone
arrive but Reggie, Twig, and Devon. Rain assumed Reggie and Twig had
gotten there before him, and Devon . . . Well, it was tough to say if he was
coming to practice at all.

Yesterday, Devon had reappeared less than a minute after his disappearance, just as the team was deciding whether or not to call for help. A
couple of the guys tried to ask if he was okay, but Devon simply grabbed
his duffel bag and left the gym without a word. Rain had rolled around all
night thinking about it. The disappearance. The fear in his gut.

He was afraid to come back to Fairwood. He was afraid of the orb.
Of Rolabi. Of the whispered voice. A part of him wanted to quit. Even
now. But he couldn't give up on ball. He couldn't give up on his future. His
family. He would never quit.

Then you have taken the first step.

Rain flinched. So Rolabi could talk inside his head when he was outside of the gym after all. Rain rubbed his head, letting his fingers trail

over his eyes and cheeks. He almost felt like he was sliding on a mask. He walked inside and started for the bench to change.

"Ready for another day?" Peño called, shooting around at the near net.

Rain snorted. "I doubt it."

As he pulled his shoes on, he stared up at the banners. His gaze fell on his father's.

"Did your father ever tell you about his playing days?" Rolabi asked.

Rain barely managed to avoid spilling off the bench. The professor was sitting beside him, eating another waxy apple. He looked ridiculous sitting on the low bench with his knees bent up as high as Rain's chin, but he seemed quite comfortable. He took another thoughtful bite, staring at the line of banners.

Rain scowled and tightened his laces. "Just that they were runners-up that one year."

"What did he say about himself?"

Rain paused. "Just that he was good. But he was better than good. He was amazing."

"He was."

"You knew him?"

"I saw him play just as you did," Rolabi said. "A star. All the talent he needed."

Rain glanced at him, watching as he chewed on the apple.

"So why didn't he make it?" Rain asked.

"Arrogance. He expected rewards to come. He didn't *earn* them."

"But he always said I had to work harder than everyone else."

"A lesson he learned in retrospect," he said, nodding. "And one he shared with you."

"I work hard—"

"On *your* game. Your shot. Your future."

"So what am I supposed to work on?"

"The real goal. But first you must find it."

Rolabi stood up and absently tossed the apple core across the court, where once again it fell perfectly into the lone garbage can. Then he turned back to Rain, his emerald eyes narrowed.

"Are you ready to be a leader on this team, Rain?" he asked.

Rain looked up at him, hesitating. "I *am* the leader on this team," he said, though his voice faltered.

"No, you're not. But you could be."

Rolabi walked onto the court and addressed the team. "Gather around. Today we work on your shots."

Rain considered his words, remembering Lab's angry expression after Rain's apology. He wasn't the leader. Not really. Despite it all, they didn't want to follow him. They didn't respect him. Why? He pushed harder than anyone. He took the big shots. He fought on defense.

The team was gathering, and Rain jogged out to join them.

"How'd you sleep?" Peño asked quietly.

"I didn't."

He snorted. "Me either. Kept thinking I might go poof and disappear."

The professor pulled out a ball and examined the team, one player at a time.

"One of you has faced the darkness," he said. "The grana grows stronger."

With that, he passed the ball to Devon, and everything changed.

Rain stepped back in horror. They were no longer in Fairwood Community Center. The team was now standing on top of a barren stone pinnacle, so tall that the base was invisible, fading into haze. It looked like a once-great mountain had been carved by millennia of wind and ice into a narrow tower, cracked and jagged and standing easily a mile high. A basketball hoop was fixed to an even more precarious stone tower ten feet away, with open air between the two peaks fading to mist far below.

No, not mist, Rain realized numbly. *Clouds.*

He felt his stomach roil and took another step back. The plateau they were standing on was about the size of half a basketball court, and the air was *cold*. Rain was already shivering, despite the lack of a breeze. The air was deathly still. He looked for Rolabi, but it was only the team and the open skies.

Somehow, he knew this place. The mountain. The peak on the island he had glimpsed in Rolabi's eyes.

He heard the team arguing, but he couldn't focus. He looked around, reeling. It couldn't be. This tower of stone was too narrow. Skeletal. Broken. And yet he felt like it was the same one.

An earsplitting crack burst through Rain's thoughts. He whirled around and saw a piece of rock the size of his mother's car split from the mountainside and tumble into the clouds. The team backed away as new cracks snaked across the edges of the now-shrunken plateau.

"We need to do something," Twig said, cutting over the arguments.

"Like what?" Vin asked.

"We're supposed to be practicing shooting, right? Maybe we need to shoot the ball."

Rain yelped as another chunk of the mountain gave way. The noise was terrible: like dynamite blasting into the cliffside. The boulder bounced once with a second jarring crack and then spun into the clouds. Rain peeked over the edge and felt his stomach creep into his throat with a slow dredging of acid. If they fell, they would have a *long* time to think about the impact.

He thought about his mom and brother and gran and felt sicker still. He was supposed to be the one to save them all. If he died here, that was over. His dad . . . Would he ever even know?

"Take the shot, Rain," Reggie urged, his voice hoarse.

Devon tossed him the ball. Rain caught it and immediately felt the trembling. His fingers slid on the pebbling. Normally he would insist that he be the one to take the big shot, but it was impossible to focus. Still, Rain knew he couldn't trust anyone else to take it. They might get only one chance.

This was the ultimate buzzer-beater. The very last shot.

He stopped a few yards from the cliff edge, not daring to go any closer. He brought the ball into his usual position—elbow and shoulders pointed at the rim, fingers relaxed, feet shoulder-width apart—took a halting breath, and fired. It was the trembling that got him.

His fingers were clammy and shaking, and the ball rolled on release. It clanked off the front of the rim and tumbled into the abyss beyond the boulder. Rain watched it disappear, stunned. He had let his team down yet again. They had only the one ball. It was over.

He was just turning to face the group when the ball came rocketing back up again and landed in Vin's hands. Vin looked at it, eyes wide. And then a third boulder split from the mountainside.

"Keep shooting!" Twig shouted.

The team started to shoot. Two more missed, and then the ball came to Twig. He took a deep breath, stepped forward, and drained it.

"Yes!" Vin said. "Now we can get out of here and . . . Oh."

The ball came flying up and landed in A-Wall's hands.

"Looks like we all have to make it," Twig muttered.

"Perfect," Vin said.

And so it continued. Whether or not a shot went through the hoop, the ball would immediately catapult back up over the side of the mountain and straight into the next person's hands. Most shots missed. Devon airballed his attempt, as did Peño. The summit was shrinking steadily, becoming ever more precarious and jagged. Every minute or so, another piece of the mountain tumbled into the clouds, and the team was forced to bunch closer together.

When everyone had taken a shot, the ball flew back to Rain.

He tried to calm himself, but every short, uneven breath seemed to stoke the fire even more. The tremors bested him again. The ball rolled on his quivering fingers, and he missed the shot badly to the right. The mountain cracked and shed another boulder. The fall was coming.

Am I doing this? he wondered, looking around. *Are we here because of my failures?*

The word kept coming back to him. *Failure*. It was glory or that. There was nothing else.

And he saw now what failure looked like. A long fall into the mist. His stomach roiled.

"Faster!" Peño shouted.

Vin made his basket and stepped back, wiping his sopping face. Soon it was Vin, Twig, Jerome, and A-Wall who had made their attempts—two bench players and two low-scoring big men. There were still six to go. Lab went next and missed for a second time, flinching at another loud crack.

"Try to focus!" Jerome pleaded.

The ball came to Reggie. He stepped closer to the edge, the toes of his shoes nearly hanging in midair. Reggie took a few deep breaths, rolled his shoulders, and made the shot.

The ball flew to Devon, who missed badly.

"We're dead," A-Wall murmured.

Another massive boulder sheared away. The mountaintop had shrunk so much that the players were forced to stand shoulder to shoulder. Rain could hear their shallow breathing and chattering teeth and feel their trembling. Big John hit a shot, then Peño's went wide, and the ball came back to Rain.

He missed again. He stared at the ball as it fell, incredulous, disgusted. Another crack.

"Come on, Rain!" Vin shouted.

Rain's whole body was trembling now, though he didn't know if it was from terror or frustration. He could feel pressure in his limbs like a slowly tightening vise. Devon missed. Lab missed. Peño drained his attempt and pumped his fist. But the mountain was shedding faster now, and the three remaining players squeezed to the front of the huddle: Lab, Devon, and Rain. The ball came to Rain, and he missed yet again.

"Come on!" he shouted, his voice echoing a thousand times down the mountain.

He couldn't understand it. How were the others hitting their shots?

Devon missed, but Lab hit his and slumped in relief. The plateau was so small that Rain was being pushed toward the edge. He tried to stop the shaking but couldn't. He missed again.

"No!" Vin cried.

Devon caught the ball and lifted it to shoot, pausing for some advice from Twig.

Twig is coaching him to shoot, Rain thought numbly. *What is happening?*

Devon hit his free throw. There was only one player left to score.

He was the last. Rain. He felt smaller suddenly. Something inside broke, even as the mountain did the same. Another chunk of rock fell, bigger this time. There was almost nothing left to give.

His teammates were forced to grab on to backs and shoulders and arms for balance.

Rain had to push against the crowd or risk falling.

"What do we do now?" A-Wall whispered.

"We watch," Twig said.

Rain shrunk more. Because of his failures, they were facing death.

The moment comes, a familiar voice said, *when success doesn't. What then?*

The ball catapulted through the air and landed in his hands again. He heard splintering rocks. The last ones. The ones beneath them. The team cried out. Lab and Peño were holding each other's hands. A-Wall started to cry. Vin was shouting for someone, but it was all jumbled together in his brain. Then one voice came through above the others.

"Make it, Rain!" Peño shouted.

Peño used to shout that all the time when Rain was scoring.

There was another deep crack. It sounded like the last. If he missed this attempt, the team would fall. He tried to steady his hands and slow his breathing. He dribbled the ball between his legs on the tiny patch of stone beneath him, focusing on the bumps and the feel of the pebbling.

"Hurry!" Jerome screamed.

The ground beneath him shifted, and he realized the whole mountain was toppling.

"Shoot it!" A-Wall said.

Rain took the shot. The ground cracked. The ball traveled away from his fingers, and the team screamed as the entire monolithic stone tower teetered. Rain watched with wide eyes as the ball spun toward the hoop. He felt gravity tug at him, his limbs seeming to rise of their own accord. He was falling, and still he watched the spinning shot. And then the ball swished through the hoop.

Instantly, the Badgers were standing back in Fairwood, and Rain slumped over in relief. The whole team shouted and cheered, and Peño dropped down and kissed the dusty old hardwood.

"It's so disgusting, yet so beautiful," he said between kisses, wiping his tongue on the back of his hand.

Rolabi was standing there as calmly as if they had been practicing free throws in the gym.

"Welcome back," he said. "What makes a great shooter?"

Rain was too stunned to think. It didn't matter that he'd made the last shot. He had been the final one to hit his shot. He had been the reason they were in danger. He had almost cost them everything. Because he was afraid. Of failing. Of falling. Of something he couldn't quite place.

You're getting closer.

"Think about the *heart* of a great shooter," Rolabi said. "What does he lack?"

Rain looked up. He thought he had the heart of a shooter. What did he lack?

"Fear," Devon said finally. "He lacks fear."

Rain thought back to the mountain. To his panic. His shaking knees. Rolabi nodded.

"All great shooters are fearless. If they fear missing, or being blocked, or losing, then they will not shoot. Even if they do, they will rush it. They will allow fear to move their elbows and turn their fingers to stone. They will never be great. And how do we get rid of our fears?"

"We face them," Devon said.

"Yes, and one thing we all fear is letting down our friends," Rolabi replied. "Basketball is about confronting fear. If you won't face it, you will lose. We will practice a thousand shots. Ten thousand. Twenty. If you take them *all* from a crumbling mountain, you will become great shooters."

"You are gross," Lab said to his brother, who was still kissing the floor.

"That will do for today," the professor said. "Tomorrow should be an interesting day."

"What was today?" Lab asked incredulously. "Boring?"

Rolabi ignored him and started for the nearest wall.

"Not again," Big John murmured.

The lights flared and died. When they reignited again, Rolabi was gone. Rain stared at the bare patch of wall, and his eyes went back to the banner. He thought of his promises to his dad.

"I'll put one up there too," Rain had said. "A national championship."

But how? He had never done anything for the team. It was Rain. Always Rain. His mind was spinning. He was never going to win like that. He walked to the bench and grabbed his ball.

"What are you doing, Rain?" Peño said.

Rain didn't look at him. He just went directly to the free-throw line and lifted the ball.

"Shooting," Rain said simply.

First things first. He would never be the last one to score again.

Somewhere, from someone, he felt a flash of approval.

8

THE
DARK ROOM

If your nights feel empty,
then your day can still be filled.
◆ WIZENARD ◇18◇ PROVERB ◆

RAIN DASHED INTO the gym and doubled over, gulping down the humid Fairwood air. He had a minute to spare. His night had been riddled with dreams of falling mountains and lonely islands and missed free throws. He had finally fallen into a dreamless sleep at dawn and slept through his alarm. He had awoken fifteen minutes ago and been forced to run the whole way to Fairwood with his duffel bag slapping across his back like a riding crop.

"Sleep in?" Peño asked.

"How'd you guess?" Rain replied.

He hurried to the bench. He had just pulled on his shoes when the front doors blasted open. Wind howled in, as usual, but this time a gust of snow spiraled along the current of cold air. Rain watched as the snow curled and formed into vague shapes—frenzied players and fans and a giant snowball arcing toward midcourt. With a sharp sound like an exhalation, the shapes all burst into a puff of flakes that disappeared the instant they touched the hardwood. Rolabi came in a moment later, dusting fresh snow from the shoulders of his suit, and walked to the middle of the court.

"Am I still dreaming?" Lab muttered.

"Dreams are fleeting," Rolabi said, stopping in the center circle. "A wisp of smoke and they're gone. The question is whether you can find their heart."

Big John rubbed his temple. "It's too early for the philosophy, Coach."

"I got dreams," Peño said. "You need dreams. They keep you going sometimes."

"A dream is nothing without vision," Rolabi countered. "Don't dream— aspire. Find the rungs of the ladder and climb. And choose correctly. If a dream can be achieved without work, without sacrifice, then it is meaning- less. It will bring you no joy. You didn't earn it, and so you do not own it. Don't wish for fleeting dreams. The road to your dreams is paved with hardship."

Rain stood up and jumped on the balls of his feet. He was ready to work for his dreams.

But are you ready to suffer?

Rain frowned. A chill came over him, and he looked around for the orb. It wasn't there.

Be ready.

"Line up facing me," Rolabi said. "Three of you have caught the orb so far. I can see some changes. The rest must stay vigilant. They must be ready when the moment comes."

Rain glanced at the others. *Three?* He thought only Devon had caught it. Yet again, he was falling behind.

Rolabi started to pace, his hands clasped behind his back. "Today we will be focusing on team offense. You have worked on your passing and vision. You have worked on your shot. But this is not a game of one. It is a game of many." He turned to Rain. "Even the greatest players cannot win this game alone."

Rain met Rolabi's eyes. He knew that now. That thought had been stripped away on the mountain.

"It is good to recognize who is defending us at all times. To use size and speed advantages where they exist. But before that, we must understand what it means to attack as a team. And so, we remove those advantages and create fully equal defenders."

Half the lights in the gym suddenly blinked out. The only ones remaining were those facing the team, and they were now shining with a strange intensity. Rain turned around and saw shadows stretching out behind the group, spindly and dark as night. He frowned and faced Rolabi, bewildered. What was he talking about now? How could any defenders be perfectly matched to the attacking team?

"We will learn to attack as one. But first, we need defenders."

Rain felt a chill creep up his neck. He rubbed it, shivering despite the gym's always-stifling heat, and then absently glanced behind him. He wished he hadn't.

His shadow was *standing up*. And it was not alone.

"Look out!" he shouted.

Ten shadows climbed to their feet, shaking out their limbs and jogging on the spot like they were waking from a long nap. As they stretched, they filled out into perfect three-dimensional replicas of their creators—except black as tar and terrifyingly faceless. It was as if Rain had been perfectly cut out of the world and left a Rain-size void. The thought disturbed him even more.

"That . . . Are those . . . ?" Vin murmured.

"Meet today's defenders," Rolabi said. "You should know them well."

Rain's shadow stepped forward, extending its hand—slender and eerily familiar. Rain hesitated, then shook it, grimacing at the dry, cold sensation that sent tingles racing up his arm. The shadow gave him a curt nod and then proceeded to sling an arm over its chest and stretch.

"Into position, defenders," Rolabi said.

The starters' shadows promptly formed into a loose 2-3 zone in front of the net.

"I think it's obvious who will be guarding you," Rolabi continued. "But it won't be a scrimmage; we will just be working on our offense. You will sub in as we go. Let's try a few as usual. Starters, go first."

Rolabi passed a ball to Peño, who looked at the waiting shadows and grimaced.

"Line it up," he muttered.

Rain, Lab, Twig, and A-Wall stepped forward, moving with obvious reluctance. As Rain walked to his usual spot, his shadow followed, staying low and shuffling like an enormous crab.

"This is messed up," Rain said, glancing at it . . . him . . . whatever it was. "Are you . . . alive?"

His shadow shrugged.

"Right," Rain said. "Stupid question."

"Rain!" Peño called, and threw him the ball.

Rain caught the pass, and his shadow closed in, playing tight. Rain started dribbling, keeping his body between the jockeying shadow and the ball, hoping to draw an overreach. But his shadow kept its arms spread wide and moved with him, wisely blocking him from the lane.

Rain faked a quick step to the left and then drove right, but his shadow was ready. It didn't go for the fake and stepped right into his driving line, pushing Rain back. Rain tried the opposite side with the same result, and he realized that his shadow would know his game perfectly and be ready for his usual moves. Rain frowned and passed the ball back to Peño.

Peño tried the left wing, but Lab couldn't get open either. Finally, Peño got it down low to Twig, who attempted a rare turnaround jumper and was promptly stuffed by his long shadow.

"Switch it up," Rolabi said.

They went back and forth for an hour. Rain was blocked twice and then had the ball stolen right out of his hands. It was incredibly frustrating:

his shadow was quick and aggressive, and worst of all, it knew his tendencies. Rain had never been guarded so well before. He couldn't get an inch.

The bench players were no better. As Rain watched them struggle, he realized what was happening. The ball would go to each player in turn, and that player would try to win his one-on-one battle. It was the way they'd always played. Sometimes there were screens, but mostly it was about moving the ball around until the team found an *advantage*. Except today there wasn't one.

Rain downed his water and went out again. He needed more creativity. He tried fadeaways and quick pivots. But it did nothing. Again and again he was stopped. Soon he was pouring sweat, trying desperately to break through. But the shadow defenders were relentless.

They never spoke, of course, though some became mocking. Peño's shadow kept chest-bumping Lab's, and A-Wall's shadow put A-Wall into a headlock and gave him a noogie. But mostly, they just played doggedly tough defense. Rolabi called for a water break, and the shadows waited impatiently on the court while the team shuffled to their bottles.

"Why are you losing?" Rolabi asked.

Rain chugged half of another water bottle and let it dribble down his chin.

"We're all playing one-on-one," he said. "I guess I never really thought of it, but it's obvious. Our whole plan is to get it to the guy who has the best chance, but that's it. And it's tough because those . . . things know how we like to play."

He didn't mention that he was inevitably the "guy who had the best chance." He had never really thought about it because he could almost always score. But now he saw the problem.

What happened when he couldn't score? What did he do? How could they win?

Rolabi allowed a faint smile. "Precisely."

"But that's how you play basketball," Peño said. "You can pass and screen, but at the end of the day, you are just giving the ball to one person who has to shoot it. That's basketball. Even the pros."

"That is often true. But are we really no more than five individual players attacking five others? If that's the case, then why don't we all practice separately? Why even practice together at all?"

Peño scratched his arm. "Well, we still need to pass to each other and stuff . . ."

"The way you play offense is the way most people play offense. It is effective right until it is not. For the most skilled player in the world, and for him alone, there is always an advantage. For all the rest, they must create the advantage for themselves. And that can only be done with the help of their team."

"But—" Peño said.

"If we play defense as a team, we play offense as a team. We talk. We plan. We see the floor."

"But—" Peño tried again.

"We attack as one. And that starts with a simple spotlight."

Rain frowned. A *spotlight*? What was he talking about this time?

"Into your positions, please."

Rain jogged to the right wing, and his shadow stepped up to match him. The remaining lights abruptly dimmed. His shadow grew larger in the receding light, and more ominous. It was several inches taller now, and its arms and fingers had grown as well, the latter almost becoming clawlike. The gym grew darker still, and Rain took a step back.

Fears always grow in the darkness.

Peño threw him the ball. His shadow tried to intercept, but Rain shouldered it off and caught the ball with his left. A tangible darkness pressed into him, and he felt a flash of something—a memory and a familiar whispered voice.

Then a light fell on him, pushing the shadow back. The white glare, tinged yellow, formed a perfect circle around him. But as Rain surveyed his options, the darkness crept in, and it became difficult to see. His shadow grew taller again and swiped furiously for the ball.

"What's going on here?" Rain muttered.

Rolabi said nothing. The lights continued to fade, and Rain realized he didn't have much time until he would be swallowed by darkness. His shadow was still growing—nearly seven feet tall.

"Twig!" Rain said. He faked a bounce pass and lobbed it down to the center.

As soon as Rain made the pass, Twig flashed into life, illuminated by the same mysterious spotlight.

"The passing," Twig said. "It lights us up."

"Options light up a court," Rolabi agreed. "When everyone moves, the darkness lifts."

Rain thought about that. Options. That meant someone for Twig to pass to.

He cut to the corner, and white light flared around him. Twig hit him, and Rain dribbled for a moment, preparing to drive. But as he delayed, the light faded, and so did his team.

Peño cut toward the wing, and the spotlight fell on him. Rain threw him the ball.

This time, he didn't wait for the darkness.

Rain cut across the zone, lit up all the way, and Peño threw him the ball. Lab sprinted to the corner on the far side, and Rain passed to him. As one, all the starters began to move. They had no choice.

If they were stagnant, the darkness thickened, and they lost the ball. But as they began to move and cut and set screens, the court began to light up, and the shadows started to struggle.

At one point, Twig caught the ball on the left block, and Rain realized he wouldn't be able to see him on the right wing. Normally, Rain would call for the ball and wait for it to reset and come around from the point, but he didn't have time. The darkness was closing fast, and his shadow was looming over him like a nightmarish specter. So instead he cut hard through the key, shouting for the pass, and the blazing spotlight landed directly on him. Twig passed him the ball, and Rain put in an easy layup, his now-shrinking shadow unable to get close enough to block him.

"Nice pass, Twig," he said, getting a pleased flush out of the center.

"Again," Rolabi said.

They ran the drill for what seemed like hours—subbing in and out and chugging water and running what Rolabi called the Spotlight Offense. The rules were simple: if someone didn't get open, they were rapidly lost to darkness. As a result, everyone was involved in every play.

Rain set screens for the first time in his life. He cut into the zone. He crashed the boards. Rain's shadow was tireless, but it was constantly running into screens or shrinking from the glare. Rain scored again and again. Twig had never touched the ball so much. He was continuously moving in and out of the post and showing a surprising aptitude for passing. When Rain got a handoff from him and easily laid the ball up, Rolabi called the drill to a halt.

"Sit and watch," he said to the team, pulling the potted daisy out of his bag. To the shadows, he added, "Thank you, gentlemen."

The ceiling lights brightened, and the shadow team vanished. Rain grabbed his water bottle, wiping his face with a soaked sleeve, and sat in a circle with the others.

He ran through the drill in his mind. It had forced him to adapt. Adjust. Play together.

And it had been *easier*.

"What did you see during the drill?" Rolabi asked.

"Movement," Reggie said.

"And?"

"A team," Twig murmured.

Rain glanced at him. He could hear the pride and awe in Twig's voice. Twig had never felt like part of the team before—definitely not on offense. How could he? Rain did everything by himself.

Who was I leading? he thought.

Rolabi fell into silence, and Rain turned to the motionless daisy and took a drink of water. It already felt a little less strange to stare at it, if only because it was becoming part of the daily routine. Besides, his tired limbs needed the break. He tried to focus on the flower, but as usual, his mind wandered. He imagined chants of "Rain!" echoing through the building.

Then a stillness settled over the room—something deeper than silence.

Rain looked up and saw the orb floating above center court. Icy tendrils of cold followed, snaking down his body. Not from the orb itself, he realized, but from the *inside out.*

Finally, you know the source of the cold.

"Here we go again," Lab said quietly.

On cue, everyone apart from Devon, Twig, and Jerome sprang up to chase it. Rain couldn't believe Twig had caught the orb already. Rain felt a spark of competitiveness surge through him and ignite a fire. He prepared to join the hunt with the others.

Cold fire is better. It burns slowly, wisely. It is power with control.

Rain thought about the ends of games in the past, when he became nearly manic, fighting for the ball, screaming for it, driving into traffic to hoist up difficult shots. He had always played with fire, but maybe it had clouded his vision. Maybe *it* made his choices.

He took a breath and tracked the orb's movements. Then he approached like a wary tiger, watching for patterns. He made small movements only. A turn of the shoulders. A twist of the foot. He closed in, always repositioning to keep the orb in front of him. A tiny shift of angles.

The orb suddenly stopped in front of him, pulsating. But Rain sensed it wouldn't just let him take it. He needed to *earn* the orb. He took a last, deep breath, and then made his move.

He juked to the left and went right. As he expected, the orb zipped out of the way . . . reading his obvious fake and shooting like a bullet to his left side. Rain spun back, his right hand outstretched, and closed his fingers on the orb. Instantaneously, the gym was gone.

He found himself in a dark room.

The floor was a dull gray, like the concrete floors of the basement, and it stretched off forever into shadow. Everything around him was black. A terrible fear settled over him. It sat in his stomach and in his bones. It made his skin crawl. Every muscle in his body tensed. It was the starkest fear he had ever felt, and Rain shivered and hugged himself.

Why had the orb taken him here? What was he supposed to do?

A flicker of movement caught his eye—a shape in the darkness.

"Hello?" he called. "Who's there?"

The shape moved again. Rain's breath caught in his throat; his heart-beat filled the room.

A man began to form in the blackness.

"Dad?" Rain whispered.

His father stepped into the light. "Hello, Rain."

He was leaner than Rain remembered, with a patch of black curls drawn back into a widow's peak. His eyes, once almond-shaped, were now smaller and darker. But his features were the same—Rain knew them perfectly. He stared at old photos every day. He replayed memories of days they had spent together. He tried on faded jeans that his dad had left behind to see when he would finally fit into them.

He never let him go.

"Hi," Rain said softly.

He had dreamed of the reunion. Dreaded it. Planned it. He always thought he might run to him, embrace him. But now he felt reluctant. Wary. He stayed where he was, watching him.

"You're surprised to see me," his dad said. "Why?"

"I thought—" Rain felt his voice catch. "I thought you might be dead."

"Thought . . . or hoped?" his dad asked, raising a thin eyebrow.

Shame flooded through him. But it was hard to lie here. Impossible, maybe. It felt like all the darkness was a mirror now, and everywhere he looked he saw his fears. So he didn't bother.

"I . . . hoped, I guess," Rain admitted.

"Why?"

Rain looked away. "Because that would explain why you never came back."

"Ah." His dad spread his hands out. "Well, as you can see, I'm not dead. And you knew that, in your heart. That's why I'm here, isn't it? Because you were afraid that I was alive."

His dad stepped closer. His small eyes narrowed. His hands beckoned for Rain.

Rain didn't move.

"Even through that fear, you wanted to bring me back. That was your plan. That was why you drove yourself to be the best. Why you worked so hard." He searched Rain's face. "Something else frightened you too. What was it?"

Rain stared into the darkness, not daring to speak. The answer flashed before him.

"Tell me," his dad insisted.

"That you chose to stay away," Rain said. "That you abandoned me. Larry and Mama too."

He felt tears slip down his cheeks. He tasted them on his lips.

He was furious they were leaking now, after so many years of holding them in, but he couldn't stop them. The shame of it made them spill even faster. He didn't want to cry in front of his father. He didn't want to show how much it hurt. That it still hurt *every single day* that he had left. It hurt so bad, it was hard to breathe some days.

Rain wanted to be stronger and angrier, but still the tears fell until his mouth was full of them.

"I did," his dad replied. "I did abandon you. And your mother. And your brother."

He stepped closer. He was only a few inches away now. Rain could smell the aftershave. The smoke. The smells that had haunted him for four years.

"But that's still not it," his father said. "It's deeper. What is it, son?"

Rain felt his hands shaking. That word. That broken promise. More came flooding out now, pouring through broken walls. His dad was right. The scars went deeper still.

Rain turned to him, not bothering to wipe away the tears.

"Why?" Rain whispered. "Why did you leave?"

"I wasn't happy there," his father said. "At home. At work. I wanted to get away."

"But *why?*" Rain shrieked, losing all control, not caring in the least.

His father smiled. It was cold, though. A smirk more than a smile.

"Now I think I see it, but you tell me. Why did you really think I left?"

Rain didn't answer for a moment. He just breathed raggedly, staring at his father.

But the truth was flashing around him. It was in the nights awake. The hours spent in front of the mirror. It was in every desperate, last-minute shot. It was in his forced isolation.

"That I wasn't enough," Rain said finally. "I wasn't *worth* staying for."

More tears rushed out in a wave. The last dam had broken. It was the truth, of course. Rain had tried to cast it away. He had tried everything to change that. He had tried to be stronger and faster and a better player. He had tried to take it all on. But nothing had worked.

Because in the end, he felt like he had failed his father.

"Makes sense," his father said. "And so you isolate yourself. Your team can't let you down like I did. And you can't let them down either. So you play alone. You dream alone. You crave isolation."

"Do you have a new family?"

"Yes. A two-year-old boy. Strong. Going to be a baller, I would guess."

That struck deeply. Rain wiped his nose with his sleeve. Snot and tears came away.

"Are you ever coming back?" he asked, not sure what he wanted the answer to be.

"That depends."

"On what?" Rain asked.

He smiled. "On you."

Rain understood immediately. So his plans had been valid. If he became a professional baller, if he made money and left the Bottom, his father would come back. But is that really what he wanted? A father who was there for the money? That wasn't part of the family he had envisioned. But was it better than nothing? Why couldn't he just have the family that he wanted?

Rain stared at the man in front of him . . . the man that he had idolized for so long.

"You aren't real," Rain said. "But my father is alive, really . . . isn't he?"

"I have not lied," his father said. "No one can lie in this place."

Rain nodded, though it was painful to hear. His dad had left them and stayed away because he wanted to. He hadn't called or written once. He had simply abandoned them.

For a moment, Rain felt like he might fold up on himself. The air seemed to leak out of him. His shoulders slumped. His stomach hurt. But despite the weight of it all, he didn't collapse.

He had seen his fears, and he was still standing.

"You can go now," Rain whispered.

His dad stared at him for a long moment, and then he faded into the darkness. Rain broke into a sob, burying his face in his hands. Even now, after everything, he wanted to chase after him. He wanted him to come back. To watch one of Rain's games. To tell Rain he was worth it.

Rain dropped to his knees and wondered if he would ever leave this room.

"You will see him again. If you continue down this path, he *will* come back," a deep familiar voice said. Rolabi appeared beside him, and Rain felt strangely . . . relieved to see him.

"Why am I here?" Rain murmured. "What do you want from me?"

Rolabi was quiet for a moment. "A friend once asked me why, of all the things I could have done with my life, I chose to coach basketball. Why I spent my time focusing on a mere game, as she put it. I told her I don't. I focus on people. Sport brings us together like nothing else. It reveals our hearts. When the objective is simple, it's the people who make the difference."

"What are you saying?" Rain asked.

"I am saying that if you want to become a better basketball player, you have to become a better person. We all have dark rooms. We all have scars. A champion pushes on regardless."

"It's so hard."

"If it wasn't, it wouldn't be worth doing."

Rain thought about that for a long time. Then he pushed himself to his feet.

"Is my fear . . . Is it gone?"

"No," Rolabi said. "That is a much longer road. But today, you saw which way to walk."

The dark room vanished, and Rain was back in the gym, standing under the pale lights.

"You all right?" Peño asked, hurrying over.

Rain thought of how desperately he had missed his dad. Of the scars he had kept hidden for so long. They were revealed now, exposed. So many of his past choices made more sense to him. He was covered in scars. Rife with fear. And still he kept walking.

That made him stronger. That answered his question. He was worth staying for.

Rain nodded. "Yeah, I'm all right."

THE PYRAMID

There is always a deeper darkness.
Find it, face it, and know the night will pass.
✦ WIZENARD ㉕ PROVERB ✦

RAIN WALKED INTO the gym the next morning and felt lighter. It should have been the same. As always, the floorboards creaked and complained with every step. The air smelled of mold and sweat and rot. The lights were dim. But today, Fairwood was different. Maybe everything was different. Last night, Rain had taken the note out of his bag, crumpled it, and thrown it away.

"What up, brotha?" Big John said, gathering a rebound. "You look tired."

"I am," Rain replied. "Didn't sleep much. But . . . I don't know. I kind of feel awake too."

"That makes no sense."

Rain snorted. "What does these days?"

"Good point."

He sat down and put his shoes on. He didn't turn to the banners today. He was done reading them until he could add his own. He stared down at his bag. No note. No old memories.

Just a ball.

Rain stood up as Rolabi walked past the bench onto the court. The rest of the players hurried over. Rain noticed that for once Rolabi wasn't holding his familiar black medicine bag.

He stopped, hands clasped, green eyes sweeping over them. They fell on Rain.

The mountain stood in the pupils, whole again, snowcapped and beautiful.

"We have two days left of our training camp. And two left to catch the orb. After the camp, we will return to three evening practices a week until the start of the season. We will practice everything we have discussed here again and again until it becomes second nature. In your free time, you will focus on your mind. Read. Study. Learn to see. The mind and body are intertwined; if you neglect one, the other will fail."

Rain frowned as the professor turned and started for the front doors.

"There's no practice today?" Peño asked.

"Oh yes," Rolabi replied. "You just don't need me."

"What should we do?" Rain said.

Rolabi glanced back. "I leave that to you."

The doors blew open under a blast of wind, and Rolabi strode out into the morning sun. That was normal enough by now. What followed wasn't. The doors slammed shut behind him and then disappeared altogether into the wall, leaving only impassable cinder block. Rain shifted uneasily. The only doors in or *out* of Fairwood had just vanished. The team was trapped.

"Perfect," Peño muttered. "I guess he's making sure we don't go home early."

"I wouldn't be so sure," Twig whispered, looking around the gym.

The words were barely out of his mouth when a deep, grating rumble sounded from somewhere inside the walls, like a sleeping dragon roaring to life. The floors began to shake, and then the two longer walls flanking the court began to move. No. They began to close. The walls were sliding forward like a monstrous car wrecker, and the team was caught directly in the middle.

"Impossible," Vin breathed.

"Possibility is subjective," Lab said sarcastically. "Any ideas?"

The walls pushed on, sliding over the hardwood, tearing the banners from the walls.

Rain's eyes fell on the remaining door—the one for the locker room. He sprinted for it but as he approached, it faded into the cinder blocks. He cursed and slapped the wall. "Now what?"

"Maybe we need to score the ball again?" Vin suggested.

The team grabbed their balls and ran onto the court—taking an array of jumpers and layups and three-pointers until they were all drenched in sweat. The walls continued on relentlessly.

"This is useless," Lab said. "We did shooting two days ago. He wouldn't repeat it."

"What would he finish with?" Rain murmured.

There were no doors, no windows, no escape. What were they supposed to do?

"We need to stop the walls," Devon said.

Rain had barely heard him speak the entire camp, but his voice blasted across the gym now. He ran to the bleachers and heaved, but despite his strength, the bleachers hardly moved.

"Help!" he cried.

The team sprinted over. The bleachers were comprised of one large segment about thirty feet long and ten rows deep. It was made so long ago that they'd used steel, and it was incredibly heavy. Even with ten of them, it was backbreaking work, and they fought to turn the structure.

"Turn it sideways!" Rain shouted. "On three! One . . . two . . . pull!"

The team heaved again, crying out. Rain pushed with everything he had, driving his legs into the ground. They were just in time. The ends of the bleachers were only a foot from either encroaching wall when they slid them into place. Rain bent over, gasping, sweat pouring down.

He watched in morbid fascination as the walls finally reached the bleachers, almost gently making contact on either end. Then there was a terrible shriek of metal, and the enormous steel bleachers began to fold upward in the middle as if made of straw.

"Try the benches!" Twig shouted, heading for the away bench.

Rain grabbed the other, but even as he turned it sideways, he knew it would do nothing.

"Rolabi!" Peño called. "Help us! Someone!"

Peño started beating on the bricks where the front doors had once stood, but his fists barely made a sound. Rain knew that no one could possibly hear them outside—the walls were thick and solid. The team was trapped, and there was absolutely nothing they could do about it.

"He did all this training just to kill us?" Lab wondered aloud, almost in a daze.

Vin was trying his cell phone. "No reception!"

Rain turned around numbly, watching as Fairwood was torn apart and crushed. In a strange way, it almost felt fitting. The banners were gone. The benches. All of his old memories.

They were all destroyed. His whole world was coming together with him in the middle.

Maybe he had taken too long to find his scars. Rain stared down at his hands, numb, waiting for the end. For once, he didn't think about what he needed to do, or his future, or how to bring his family out of the Bottom. He thought about sitting down for a late dinner with his mama. He thought about playing ball out front with his brother. He thought about visiting his gran and how long it had been since he'd done that. He wanted those things, and nothing else really mattered.

"Look!" Devon shouted, pointing upward.

Rain followed his gaze hopefully . . . but that hope was quickly dashed. There, floating some twenty feet above the court, was the black orb. He could already feel its icy chill on his arms.

"Great timing," Peño snarled.

The walls had slid onto the court itself now. The team would be dead in minutes.

"Someone can get out of here!" Twig said. "You vanish, remember?"

"Only for people that haven't gotten the orb yet," Reggie said. "It will only work for them."

Lab and Peño looked at each other across the gym. Rain could see it in their faces: neither brother had caught it. One of them could still escape this—but only if he left his brother behind. He thought about Larry. Could he leave him? Of course not. How would the brothers choose?

"Get up on the bleachers!" Lab cried.

The team scrambled up onto the folding bleachers, which were reaching higher and higher as they were squeezed together into an inverted U, grinding and pushing together to form an almost-even surface. The team pulled and heaved themselves up onto the buckling steel.

Lab reached for the orb.

"It's too far!" he shouted.

The walls were getting close to each other now—chewing and pushing and crushing everything before them. The team looked around in desperation, and for a second, it seemed like they had failed again. Rain had no ideas. No inspiration. He stood there, frozen.

He was supposed to be the leader. He was supposed to tell them what to do. But he realized now that he couldn't. He didn't have all the answers. Sometimes he was afraid, and lost, and needed help. He needed his teammates to take the lead sometimes. But maybe he had never given them the chance. Maybe he had waited too long.

And then Devon climbed down onto all fours, bracing his arms and legs against the still-bending metal benches.

"Come on!" he shouted. "Make a pyramid!"

Twig, A-Wall, Big John, and Reggie immediately dropped down beside him. Rain stared at them, realized he was just a block, just a means to get Peño and Lab to the top. He was a part of the team and nothing more. He didn't think twice. He climbed on their backs, Jerome and Vin beside him. The base was wobbly and unsteady, and the human pyramid tottered but held. Rain grimaced as Peño climbed over him, digging his shoes in. Lab scurried up from the other side.

Rain couldn't see what they were doing. He was focusing on his hands, on his job. If he gave out, the whole pyramid would fall. He knew they were all hoping that if someone got the orb, the walls would stop. He wanted to believe that they would all be saved. But there was a distinct possibility that whoever disappeared would live and that everyone else would be crushed. It didn't matter. Not really. His part was here.

He looked out over the gym. The walls were only ten feet apart now. The bleachers were a ruined mass of steel. The nets had fallen, and their backboards had carpeted the floor with glass.

It's all gone, he thought. *The past is gone.*

He suddenly saw Rolabi crouching in front of him, eyes blazing.

"Look around you," Rolabi said. "What do you see?"

"The end," Rain whispered.

Rolabi smiled. "I see the beginning."

And then he vanished. The wall was so close that Rain could almost touch it. He closed his eyes.

"One . . . two . . . three!" Peño shouted. "Go!"

Rain felt a sharp pressure on his back and then no pressure at all. The walls abruptly ground to a halt, and with a deep rumble, they began to reverse.

"Badgers!" Peño shouted.

"Badgers!" Rain cried below him.

Peño scrambled down off their backs, and the whole pyramid disassembled in a tangle of laughs and cheers. As the walls retreated, the bleachers began to straighten and slide back into place. The banners resewed themselves in a flurry of twisting thread. The shattered glass flew into position and melded into two spotless backboards. Fairwood was being remade.

But it was different to Rain. It was all new.

The team exchanged high fives and props and relieved sighs. Rain looked around the gym, thinking about Rolabi's words. The beginning. It certainly looked like one now. Rain smiled.

"Anyone want to have a game?" Reggie asked. "We got this nice gym now."

"Let's do it!" Peño said, then slapped his chest. "Who wants to be on the champ's team?"

"Well, I can only take four," Big John said.

Lab returned, and the team split themselves into starters versus the bench and started to play. There were no tigers or visions or rules. It was street ball, and they ran trick plays and threw wild alley-oops or long threes, breaking into laughter at the flubbed attempts. But no one wanted to lose, so they ran, and hustled, and played hard defense.

For the first time, it felt like ten friends playing for fun.

When they had worn themselves out, Rain grabbed his bag and headed for home. He paused at the door, remembering the question that had been written there on the second day. He still wasn't sure.

"How does a leader open a door?" he whispered.

He shook his head and walked out. He still had no idea.

THE ROAD

You are stardust and light.
If they cannot see that, then you have chosen to hide it.

WIZENARD ❪45❫ PROVERB

WHEN HE GOT home after the scrimmage, Rain walked right up to Larry and hugged him. Larry had felt his brother's forehead for a fever, but he still giggled when Rain gave him a noogie. Rain hung out with him until his mama got home, and they even cooked dinner. His mama nearly cried when she saw it.

None of it made him better at basketball. None of it brought his dreams closer. None of it emptied the streets of garbage, or rebuilt his crumbling home, or made the Bottom any safer. But Rain looked at his street differently on the way to practice the next morning. He wondered what was beneath the litter. He wondered if the plants could grow, given a chance. If the people could start again too.

He stopped at the doors and pulled them open, relishing the quiet of greased hinges. He breathed in the scent of freshly polished cedar floors. The team was shooting around him, and he quickly changed his shirt and shoes and joined them, stepping out just as Rolabi walked inside.

The professor called them together. "All but one of you have caught the orb. Why?"

"Because . . . you told us to?" Vin said.

Rolabi turned to him. "But why? What did you find?"

"Our fears," Reggie murmured.

Rolabi nodded, turning to the row of banners that hung on the north wall. "If one thing will stop you in life, it is that. To win, we must defeat our fears. For basketball . . . For everything."

"But . . . we did, right?" Big John asked.

"Fear is not so easily beaten," Rolabi said. "It will return. You must be ready. We have much to work on before the season. For today, we will review what we have learned so far."

There was a sudden scratching.

"Twig . . . you know the drill," Rolabi said, reaching into his bag.

He began to walk around, tossing out scores of cones, rings, pads, and extra basketballs. The lights flickered, and the team's shadows crawled up off the ground behind them. Twig opened the locker room door, and Kallo walked out. Nine days of training took shape around them.

Rain looked at it all and saw more. He saw the future.

"In a line, please," Rolabi said.

Rain and the others walked to the center line.

"We'll start with the free-throw circuit. We will run laps until some-one hits. Once through that, we will watch the daisy for movement. We'll work on getting past Kallo and then strap up the pads for a defensive drill. After that, we will run the Spotlight Offense in the dark with a glowing ball, and then against our shadow defenders. Following that, we will run a circuit with our weaker hands. Finally, we will shoot to end the day and solve another little puzzle."

"Is there going to be weird stuff happening?" Vin asked.

Rolabi looked at him. "Weird stuff?"

"Never mind," Vin muttered.

The drill began. Rain slogged through quicksand. His team disappeared. His right hand vanished, and the shadows fought tenaciously on defense. He poured sweat out onto the floorboards and kept moving. The hours passed in a blur of endless running and drills and pouncing tigers. His heart pounded madly. And still they ran. He felt all his grief and pain pouring out of his skin. For the first time, his pain eased.

And when a familiar voice whispered in his ear, he didn't search for its source.

He watched the team work around him. All of them sweating. Trying. Fighting. How had he not seen them working before? Why did he think it was just him? He wondered suddenly what they had seen. Where had the orb taken them? Did they have their own dark rooms? What secrets and scars were they hiding? For a moment, he saw light in them. A gleaming silver, molten almost, flowing through and into the floors. He looked down and saw it in his own hands.

"Grana," he whispered, and the word hung there, and then the light was gone.

Rolabi finally ended the course and called them together. Everyone was exhausted, draining water bottles and letting ever more sweat pour out onto the greedy, polished floors.

The shadows vanished, Kallo walked into the locker room, and the team was alone again.

As the others talked, Rain went to grab his water and chugged it down. He felt fresh . . . like a weight had been lifted. It felt good to run and work and sweat. He heard laughter and joined the team again just as Rolabi started for the doors.

"I thought you said we had one last puzzle?" Rain called after him.

"You do," he said. "Each of you has one. And by the way, welcome to the Badgers."

A cheer went up as the doors closed behind him, and the whole team started for the benches. Rain walked among them, and when he sat down, he looked up and down the line.

"Anyone want to shoot some hoops tomorrow? We could hit up Hyde?"

"I'll play," Vin said.

"Same," Peño agreed. "Rain wants to chill . . . You feeling all right?"

Rain laughed. "Yeah. I feel good."

Rain changed slowly, reflecting on the last two years, and longer . . . All the time since his dad had left. He was tired of being an island. He was tired of wondering what he was worth and wanting the answer from a dad who had taken off. He had people here. Family. Teammates. Friends. It was time he proved his worth to all of them.

As each player finished, they zipped up their bag and waited for the rest. Rain did the same. There seemed to be an unspoken agreement. They would leave when they were all ready.

He thought about everything he had seen and done in the last ten days. He had lost a hand. His sight. Almost his life. He had gained more. And now he got to choose what to do next. That decision was easy enough, at least. He was going to play ball.

Lab was last to be ready to go. When he zipped his duffel bag and stood up, the team rose with him, and they all started for the doors together. Rain led the way, but then stopped for a moment. The question was written on one of the doors again in that silver, flowing ink.

How does a leader open a door?

Rain smiled and pushed the door open.

Then he stepped aside and held it for his teammates.

BOOK TWO

TWIG

THE POCKET WATCH

A person is the same as a tree.
Without a strong foundation, they cannot grow.

✧ WIZENARD ◈ PROVERB ✧

ALFIE WRAPPED HIS fingers around the cool metal handle, hesitated, and turned back to his father.

His car was already gone. The parking lot was empty, apart from scattered plastic bags rolling by like tumbleweeds. Alfie sighed, turned back to the doors, and nodded to himself.

"You can do this," he said. "You are going to go in there and rock it."

He rubbed his forehead.

"*Rock it?* What is wrong with me? Oh, now I'm talking to myself. This is going well."

He took a deep breath, jumping on his toes, letting his arms wobble loosely.

"Stop talking to yourself, go inside, and do your thing. Except, you know, better than usual."

He eased open one of the rusted doors and slipped inside like a shadow. The gym was deathly quiet, at least until the door clanged shut behind him. Reggie looked up from the bench.

Reggie was *always* the first one to arrive at practice. Alfie didn't know much about him, apart from the fact that his parents were gone, but he had overheard that Reggie took the city bus for over an hour to get here. Some of the guys lived within walking distance, and he still beat them all in.

They exchanged a quick nod, and Alfie shuffled to the far bench. He wrinkled his nose on the way. Fairwood smelled like malt vinegar. Alfie's grandpa used to douse his fries in the stuff, and it made Alfie sick to his stomach. He plunked himself onto the away bench. It teetered but held.

"Hey, Twig," Reggie said.

Alfie tried not to sigh. Even Reggie was calling him *Twig*. Alfie just couldn't shake the nickname. He didn't think Reggie meant much by it . . . He was the nicest one on the team by far. Reggie was lanky, though not nearly as thin as Alfie, with long arms and big hands. His skin was darker than Twig's, and he kept his hair cropped short, nearly shaved. A long white scar marked his chin.

"Morning, Reggie. How are you feeling? Or doing? You know. How are you?"

Alfie fought the urge to sigh. Why couldn't he just have a normal conversation?

Reggie snorted. "Good. Ready for some ball. You?"

"Yeah," Alfie murmured. "Can't wait."

Alfie slowly pulled his new shoes out of his bag. His dad had bought them for the season, and Alfie was a little self-conscious of them. They were self-tying and spotless—they had come out only a few weeks ago. Taking a quick peek to make sure Reggie was distracted, he slipped them on and pressed the little button on the side. Instantly they tightened perfectly to his foot.

"Whoa," Reggie said.

Alfie flushed and tucked his feet under the bench. "Just got 'em," he said awkwardly.

He knew the fact that he was from the wealthier, northern district of the Bottom was already a problem for some guys on the team. There were four sections of the Bottom: the industrial south, which was mostly a wasteland of packed dust and abandoned factories; the east and the west, which were both poor and plagued with violence; and the north, the suburban area. That was where Alfie's family lived. The West Bottom was probably the worst of the lot.

Reggie's shoes were ratty and worn, and it looked like he had glued the soles back on.

Reggie bent over to stare at Alfie's. "Those are sweet, man. You gonna fly this year."

"We'll see," Alfie said, forcing a smile. "Shoes don't put the ball in the net."

"Those will help," Reggie replied. "You know the kids from Argen will have them."

"No doubt," Alfie agreed. "You . . . practice much since the season ended?"

"Every day," Reggie said. "I got an old hoop up on the front of the house. Well, a tire rim. No backboard or mesh. Real official. But it does the job. At least, I think it did. We'll see."

"I'm sure it did," Twig said. He paused. "Like . . . the job is you being better, right?"

Reggie laughed. "Yeah. You practice much? You must have a nice setup in the burbs."

"Yeah," Alfie said awkwardly. "I got a hoop."

He desperately wanted to fit in on the team, but he had been painted as the rich outsider from day one. There was a North Bottom team in the Elite Youth League as well, the Blues, but Freddy had promised big things for the Badgers, and his dad had signed him up. The problem was, nobody else seemed to want him here. To make matters worse, he'd had an awful season.

"Been working on your game?" Reggie asked.

"Definitely," Alfie said. "Turnaround moves and stuff. Trying to get stronger as well."

"Nice! Gonna be a true big man this year."

Alfie looked away. He was far from a "big man." He was a pushover down low.

The front doors burst open and Peño walked inside, his younger brother, Lab, trailing reluctantly behind him, yawning and rubbing his sleep-encrusted eyes. Peño looked around the gym with a lopsided grin, even closing his eyes for a second. Maybe he was relishing the smells, disgusting as they were. Peño loved Fairwood Community Center, and he loved ball.

"Reggie," Peño said. "What up, brother?"

Alfie tried to make himself small on the other bench. At six foot five, that was difficult, though he weighed only about 120 pounds after a big meal. His spindly body had given him that nickname he hated so much. First Stick Man. Then just *Twig*. It meant the same thing. Skinny. Weak. Ugly.

Peño plopped himself onto the bench and turned to him. "Twig," he said. "Yo, dawg."

"Hey, Peño. Or . . . I mean . . . yo. Dog."

Alfie sighed inwardly and went back to staring at his hands.

I can do this, he told himself, trying to quell his rising nausea. *Just play the game.*

His dad had made him some bran cereal and toast that morning, and they were now sitting in his stomach like they had congealed into cement. He could still taste peanut butter on the back of his throat, and he wondered if it would turn into brittle soon in the heat. He looked at his ball. He was one of the few players to have one—and it was new as well. Was it showing off to go shoot around first? Would someone take it? Should he just sit there and be quiet?

The questions played through his mind, but when the door opened again, they were swiftly forgotten. Big John had arrived, Jerome behind him. That decided that, and he tried to get even smaller.

"What up, boys!" Big John said, putting his hand to his mouth like a loudspeaker.

Alfie looked at his shoes. *Please be nicer this year*, he thought. *Please be nicer this year.*

Big John and Jerome exchanged greetings with the group—a mixture of whoops and high fives—and then Big John turned right to Alfie, scowling.

"The Twig is back," he said in disbelief. "You didn't get enough last year or what?"

Alfie shook his head. *Please leave me alone . . . please, please, please,* he thought.

As usual, his wish wasn't granted.

"Well, I guess we need someone on the bench," Big John said. "New kid coming in down low, Freddy says. We're going to own the post this year, minus one Twig. The rich boy bust."

Alfie felt his cheeks burning. He was an only child, but he never felt more alone than he did right here, in this community center, surrounded by his team. He knew he wasn't wanted here. And why should he be? He sucked at basketball. He was a coward. He was useless.

The thoughts flew down like anchors, cast from his head to his feet, pinning him in place.

Rain walked in next, and Alfie looked at him enviously. Everyone loved Rain. It all came so easily to him—smooth shot, tight handles, and an almost lazy grace. He was the undisputed star of the team, and Freddy's showpiece. The ball *always* went through Rain's hands. Most of the time Alfie was just supposed to set a screen for Rain, block out a post player, or collect his rebounds. Alfie would have given anything to be like him. To have his life for just one day.

"You got a rhyme for the season yet?" Jerome asked Peño.

Big John dropped a beat, and Jerome dribbled a ball to add percussion.

Peño grinned and began rapping. There was something about their gym being wack and an uppercut to somebody's chin, and then he finished with:

"Dren best watch fur the badyers
Because we are... Well..."

He stopped.

"Mad... gers?"

Even Twig smiled at that one. Peño still hadn't figured out a rhyme. But Peño just shrugged off the laughter. He had Rain's swagger, if not his skills. Confidence seemed to be natural to everyone but Alfie. After Rain had greeted everyone else, he turned to the away bench.

"Twig," he said.

Alfie tried not to wince at the nickname. Everyone on the team followed Rain's lead, and obviously he too was sticking to the moniker that Big John had invented. It had stuck for a year now, so it was probably permanent. Alfie waved, then quickly put his hand down, feeling stupid.

"Hey, Rain. Yo," he said.

"You look the same."

The words stung. They brought weeks of hard work and nasty diets crashing in, all for nothing. Alfie scratched his arm—even though his dad had told him a hundred times not to do it. The gesture made Alfie look weak, he had said. Alfie tried to think of a response. He hesitated.

"I gained three pounds," he said at last.

He regretted the words instantly. They'd sounded ridiculous even on the way out. It was just the first thing that had come to mind, and in fairness, he *had* worked hard to gain even that. Big meals, weight lifting, buckets of avocados, carbohydrate gainers. Alfie had tried everything, and at least three pounds was *some* progress. But now it sounded so . . . pathetic. What a surprise.

Big John started to laugh. "Three pounds? What, in acne?"

Alfie looked at his shoes, trying to keep his hands busy in his lap so they wouldn't scratch anymore. So Big John had noticed his skin. Of course he had. The pimples practically covered his whole face. He wanted to rip them all off, and then he felt sick at the thought.

"Boy says he put on three pounds. This man kills me!"

Alfie wanted to leave. He wanted to go home and never come back.

"Three pounds!" Big John said. "I put on three pounds this morning!"

Alfie sank lower, willing himself not to cry. His shoulders stretched for his knees. He thought of Freddy telling his dad he had cried at practice. The shame made his eyes burn worse.

"You need thirty to play down low," Big John continued. "I'm not even sure why you're back. How much your dad pay Freddy to keep you on this team, huh? The rich boy out the burbs—we know how you got on the team."

Alfie's eyes started to well up. He knew he was in trouble.

"You gon cry now—" Big John said.

Alfie ran to the locker room without thinking. Laughter followed him all the way there.

The room was filthy, which was why the team always changed on the benches. Wedged in the back were a couple of bathroom stalls, one of which had a cracked sink with a tap that dripped constantly. Alfie faced the mirror, watching as the first tears slipped down his pockmarked cheeks. He put his hands under the tepid stream and ran them through his hair. Water leaked down his face, and he wiped it away, letting his fingers linger on his cheek. His eyes fell on the newest zit. Big and swollen and right on the cheekbone like a red button.

He was picking before he knew it. He saw a red bubble rise and quickly wiped the spot with some toilet paper. Tears filled his eyes again.

"You really are pathetic," he whispered to the skinny boy in the mirror. The boy said it back.

Alfie stood there, hands on the sink, staring at himself.

Just get through today, he thought.

Alfie shuffled out and saw that most of the team was warming up now, sharing one or two balls. He grabbed his and went to the far side of the court alone.

A-Wall and Vin came into the gym soon after, and Freddy with the new kid last of all. He'd mentioned him when he had phoned Alfie about the training camp, but Freddy hadn't said what position the recruit would play. It was pretty obvious now.

The boy was tall and muscular—he had a grown man's body. Alfie stared at him jealously. He would almost definitely take Alfie's starting position at center. Alfie couldn't compete with someone who looked like *that*. He slumped and looked away, ball forgotten.

His dad would be so disappointed.

"My boys!" Freddy called. "All here? Come on over. Let me introduce Devon."

Alfie walked over, letting everyone else gather first and then joining at the edge of the circle. He could look right over everyone's heads, so it didn't really matter. As he watched the introduction, he grew confused. He could see Devon's toes twisting on the hardwood, his eyes cast down, his shoulders bent. Alfie knew those signs. But could someone so strong really be *shy*? It seemed impossible. This guy had everything Twig wanted. Mainly, muscles.

Freddy slung an arm over Devon. "He ain't here to read poetry, boys. Devon is a power forward and a great defender. Well. He will be when we're done with him. He's going to play well with Twig."

Alfie tried to hide his surprise. Was Freddy still planning on keeping him on the starting lineup, even after his disastrous rookie season? *Dad will be happy*, he thought numbly. *If* Alfie didn't lose his spot before the season started.

"Where's this new coach?" Rain asked. "Rolobo, or whatever you said his name was?"

As soon as he said it, the fluorescent lights overhead began to flicker. They sputtered, blinked out, and then went back to normal—a pale gray color like sun through storm clouds. Alfie stared up at them, grimacing at the inch-thick layer of dust.

The doors suddenly burst open, and he jumped, nearly toppling over. Wind roared inside.

"Dust tsunami!" Peño shouted. "Run!"

Alfie squinted against the gale and made out a shape in the doorway. A man. He was huge—bigger than Alfie's dad, even. He must have been at least seven feet tall, since he had to duck to get inside. He was dressed immaculately: crisp suit, leather bag—he dressed like Alfie's grandpa, and he was somehow even taller. He drew out a pocket watch as he approached them.

His eyes fell on Alfie for just a moment, and Alfie felt a curious tingle on the back of his neck. The pocket watch seemed to grow louder, ticking very slowly, and Alfie caught a glimpse of something in the glass. A tall man with watery eyes. He frowned, and the image vanished.

The pocket watch was tucked back into his jacket, only the chain visible.

"Oh," Freddy said, sounding surprised. "You're early—"

"Being late or early is simply a matter of perspective," he answered calmly.

Alfie looked at him curiously. Was he a university professor? And why was he dressed like that? It was already hot both outside and inside the gym, and it would only get hotter. But Rolabi didn't even seem to be sweating, nor did he look remotely uncomfortable. He just stared at the team with bright green eyes, as though measuring each one of them, probing them.

When his gaze came to Alfie, Alfie took a step back.

How can a tree grow when the soil is poisoned?

Alfie whirled around. There was nobody behind him. Yet he'd a heard a voice there.

"Hello?" he whispered.

Reggie, who was standing near Alfie, glanced at him. "Hey."

Alfie forced a smile, humiliated. Was he losing his mind?

Rolabi dismissed Freddy, and when the doors crashed shut, silence fell over the gym. Everyone looked at Rolabi. His gaze darted from one player to another, and Alfie instinctively turned away when it fell on him, unnerved. He had never heard such a deep, thoughtful silence in Fairwood before. He imagined it was like floating in space.

Then, as if they had just gone around and introduced themselves, Rolabi pulled out a folded piece of paper from an inner pocket in his suit jacket, along with a magnificent gold pen.

"I will need everyone to sign this before we can proceed," Rolabi said.

They went one after another, all signing the same contract. There seemed to be some confusion, but Alfie couldn't hear what it was. He was last, and he took the sheet from Reggie.

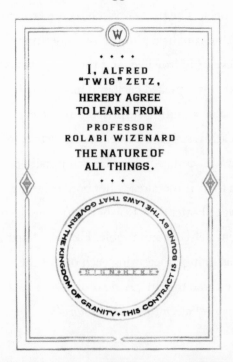

I, ALFRED "TWIG" ZETZ, HEREBY AGREE TO LEARN FROM PROFESSOR ROLABI WIZENARD THE NATURE OF ALL THINGS.

THE LAWS THAT GOVERN THE KINGDOM OF GRANITY · THIS CONTRACT IS BOUND BY THE LAWS THAT GOVERN

SIGN HERE

Alfie read it again. There was something familiar about . . . something tugging at his memory . . . The word *granity* in particular: where had he seen that before? He felt the stares of the others, though, and signed it, still trying to place that word. How did he know the word *granity*?

Rolabi took the contract back, read it over carefully, and nodded. Before Alfie could even step away, the contract disappeared with a watery *pop*, like a bubble bursting.

"What . . . Where did . . . How . . . ?" Alfie murmured.

The professor opened his medicine bag and stuck his arm in up to the shoulder. Alfie stared, bewildered—the bag was only a foot deep. Stranger still, he heard sliding, crashing, and a growl, low and unhappy. *I really am losing it*, he thought.

Losing what? the deep voice asked. He realized it sounded an awful lot like Rolabi.

Then, without any warning whatsoever, Rolabi took out a basketball and passed it to Big John. It collided with one of Big John's round cheeks, and Alfie had to bite back a laugh.

"That hurt," Big John complained.

Alfie caught a glimpse of something orange and just barely managed to catch the pass.

And then the gym changed. The team was gone.

Instead, he was surrounded by a dizzying collection of strange mirrors, as though he had been transported to a carnival fun house. Some of the reflections were short and squat and fat, others so tall and painfully thin that Alfie thought he might slip through the cracks in the hardwood. In one, his face was completely covered with acne, red and angry. He ran his fingers down it and saw that his nails were long, hooked, and razor sharp. Panic flooded through him.

Alfie whirled away, trying to find a way out, and then stopped.

There was another mirror. In this one, his shoulders and arms were lined with muscle, his face clear, his hair full and thick instead of hanging down in its usual greasy mop. The scars were gone. Alfie's gaunt face was handsome and stolid. He stepped toward the reflection, reaching out for that boy. That Alfie. Then he noticed Rolabi was standing among the mirrors, watching him.

"Hmm," Rolabi said. "Interesting. That will be all today. I will see you here tomorrow."

The mirrors were instantly replaced by the team, all of them looking uneasy. Rolabi was walking toward the doors. Alfie barely noticed them. He spun around, looking for the mirror that had shown him a better Alfie. The one his father wanted. His team wanted. The one he wanted.

"What time?" Peño asked.

Rolabi didn't answer. The doors swung shut, and Peño ran after him.

"Do we keep the balls?" Peño called, opening the doors. "What . . . Professor?"

Rolabi had vanished.

THE STICK MAN

Spectators can applaud or jeer.
Does it matter? Either way, the track remains.

WIZENARD 44 PROVERB

THE NEXT MORNING, Alfie stared at the old double doors, wondering if he could really bring himself to go inside. His father had been no help. He told Alfie that nervous minds could sometimes hallucinate, and that he just had to "man up." Alfie wasn't sure if that was true, or what it meant to man up, but he kept that to himself. He didn't question his dad . . . ever. That could only result in a lecture about respect, a grounding, or mostly just flat-out screaming.

His mom didn't believe him either, though she at least felt his forehead for a fever. He was almost hoping for one to explain his visions, but no such luck. She reminded him, as she always did, that he could quit ball if he wanted to. She said he shouldn't be on the team for another season just to please his father. But she didn't understand. Alfie wanted to play ball.

And that was why he was back today, despite the visions, despite the bullies.

Alfie opened the doors and went inside. As usual, Reggie was the only one there.

That was a relief, at least, even if it was only temporary. Alfie had left the teasing out of his recap of practice to his parents. His mom would have said she needed to contact Big John's mother. His dad would have said that real men weren't affected by words. Toughen up. Man up. That was his father's answer for everything. Real men were strong. Real men never got upset. Real men were made of stone and iron.

If that was true, then Alfie was even further from a real man than he thought.

"Morning," Alfie said, dropping his bag by the away bench.

"Morning, Alfie," Reggie replied. "Ready to try this again?"

Alfie forced a smile and started for the locker room. "Not really."

He locked the door of the biggest bathroom stall and stared in the mirror, taking deep breaths. His sallow chest rose and fell beneath his T-shirt. His eyes fell on his slender fingers. His thin neck. Hollowed cheeks. His dad said he had to get stronger, but his body wasn't built for it. He was overstretched, like a piece of gum being pulled off the bottom of a chair. Maybe that alone would have been fine. He could have dealt with that. But his skin was also beleaguered by acne—it was so unfair. Even that was bordered by scars and pockmarks from his constant picking.

He ran his hand over a new pimple on his cheek, wondering if Big John would say anything about it. Sometimes when he got a pimple, he felt like it took over his whole head. It was all that anyone could see, like a spotlight had fallen there. He was scratching before he knew it, and then holding scraps of toilet paper to the cut and wondering if anyone else could possibly be as broken as he was. He doubted it. He fought the urge to cry and flushed the red toilet paper.

"You can do this," he said, gripping the sink. "Today is going to be a better day."

When he felt like he could face the team, he walked out again and sat down.

"Hey, Twig," Lab said, blinking sleepily as he glanced over at him.

"Hi," Alfie replied.

Peño stood up and stretched, eyeing Alfie. "You sweating already?"

Alfie flushed. "No, just water. You know . . . to wake up a little."

"I hear you," Lab said.

"Well, I hope you got some rest," Peño said. "Who knows what this Rolabi dude has got going on today." He paused and then turned to Alfie. "Say, what did you think of him?"

Alfie wanted to talk about what he'd seen, but there was no way he was going to risk sounding like a weirdo. He had enough problems fitting into the team already. He shrugged.

"I don't know. A bit . . . odd, I guess."

Peño nodded, though it didn't seem like he'd gotten the answer he wanted.

"Yeah," he muttered. "*Odd* is one word for it."

Reggie was working on turnaround jumpers on the far end of the court. Alfie joined him and went to his familiar warm-up spot. He began to shoot one free throw after another, always promptly gathering his rebound and heading back to the line again, whether he scored or not.

Reggie stopped shooting for a moment, watching him.

"Really working on that free-throw game, huh?" Reggie said.

Alfie nodded. "Yeah. My dad said it was good for the mechanics."

"Yeah," Reggie said. "How many times you get to the line last year?"

"Once or twice a game . . ."

"Exactly. You can work on your free-throw shots, but you also got to get there."

"I know that," Alfie said defensively.

Reggie smiled. "I ain't getting on you, Twig. I'm just rooting for you."

"You . . . you are?"

"Of course."

He turned around and drained a jumper.

"Your shot looks good," Alfie said.

"Been practicing," Reggie said simply. "I guess that tire rim worked."

Alfie hesitated, and then he went down low to work on his back-to-the-basket moves. Pivot to layup, turnaround hooks, bank shots. When there was no defense around, no pressure, no eyes on him, he could hit them easily. Fake left, go right. Step back, fade out. Up, down, up.

He whispered the moves to himself, hearing his dad's voice.

"Fake the shot, drop the shoulder down, power up. Go!"

"There it is," Reggie said.

But the rest of the team arrived soon after, and when Alfie saw Big John sneering at him from the bench, he returned to the free-throw line. It was safer there. Easy shots. No judgment.

Reggie sighed and shook his head.

"Maybe he isn't coming," Lab said, his voice carrying from the far side of the court.

"Or maybe he's already here."

Alfie spun to the source of the voice. Rolabi Wizenard was sitting on the bleachers eating an apple. He climbed to his feet, took a final bite, and flicked the core aside. It sailed some twenty yards across the gym and plunked into the sole garbage can. Alfie stared in amazement. Rolabi hadn't even been looking.

"Nice shot," Reggie murmured.

Rolabi scooped up his bag and walked to the center of the court.

"Put the balls away."

Alfie ran back to the bench and stuffed his ball into his duffel bag. He noticed that everyone else was running too, which was odd because they'd never rushed to do anything in practice last year. Big John usually strutted around the gym like a peacock, and Rain listened only when he felt like it. But today even Rain was running. He was one of the first ones back to Rolabi.

The team formed a circle in front of the giant professor.

Alfie had never seen anything quite like Rolabi's eyes: a shifting shade of green, from electric to deep and dark. He wondered how Rolabi had gotten the thin white scars on his face—who would be crazy enough to try to fight *him*? Alfie bet not even his father would stand up to Rolabi, and Alfie had never seen his dad avoid an argument with anybody.

Alfie tried to summon his meager courage. His dad had been very specific: He wanted to meet Rolabi. Soon.

"Umm . . . Professor Rolabi?" Alfie said meekly.

He turned to him. "Yes?"

Alfie tried to clear his throat and made a strange, guttural noise like a sick cat.

"My . . . uh . . . my dad was wondering when the parents can come meet you?"

"Following the tryout, I will meet with parents."

Alfie opened his mouth, and then closed it again, confused. Did he just say *tryout*? Alfie could still be *cut*? His eyes went right to Devon. Was the new kid going to be his replacement?

"Did you say tryout?" Peño said, clearly having similar thoughts. "This *is* the team."

"This *was* the team. Everyone earns a place on my team."

Twig gulped. He was definitely going to be cut. Great. His dad would be furious.

He scratched his arm without thinking, then flinched when he saw the lines.

"So our parents have to wait ten days to talk to you?" Vin asked.

"If there is pressing business, they can call 76522494936273."

Twig patted his shorts, then frowned. Why would he have a pen? His shorts didn't even have pockets. He considered running to his bag for his cell phone, but he had already missed the number.

"So . . . seven . . . eight . . ." he said, trying to memorize it. "Can you repeat that?"

"I'm sure Daddy will figure it out for you," Big John said.

Twig stiffened and looked away, his cheeks burning. Why did he have to call attention to himself by asking questions? Talking never worked out for him. He needed to just be quiet and play. That was all anyone wanted from him.

"We are going to start with a scrimmage," Rolabi said.

Alfie tried to hide a grimace. He *hated* scrimmages. They meant that Big John got to shove him around while Rain took a thousand shots. Nobody played with any systems or zones—scrimmages were free-for-alls that devolved into one-on-one play. Thankfully, they usually only happened at the ends of practices, so Alfie could leave quickly afterward to hide any bruises or budding tears. But to start the day with a scrimmage? This was going to be an absolute nightmare. He wondered if it was too late to fake an injury.

"Last year's starters versus the bench players. Devon will play for the latter."

Alfie could almost hear the implied *for now*. And to make matters worse, he was playing against Big John. Alfie groaned inwardly as he squared off with him across the line.

The starters filled in around Alfie: Rain, Peño, Lab, and A-Wall.

"Ready to get stomped?" Big John asked, not even bothering to whisper.

Alfie felt a weight drop into his stomach. He wasn't cut out for this. A real man wouldn't want to cry over a stupid threat. But Alfie wasn't a man. He didn't know how to hide emotions. He didn't know how to be strong.

Hiding our emotions is not strength.

Alfie looked around for the source of the voice, but then stopped, considering.

It had almost sounded like the voice was inside his head.

Umm . . . hello? he thought.

Rolabi tossed up the ball. It was a perfect toss, and Alfie knew he was going to win the jump—he had almost six inches on Big John and a better vertical too. But Big John had other plans. He bodychecked Alfie in the stomach, knocking the wind out of him. Alfie bent over, wheezing, and Big John tapped the ball back to Vin. Alfie gasped, wondering if he would vomit.

He felt the air flood back into his lungs as he gathered himself, and a mixture of humiliation and anger and guilt flooded through him. Big John was wearing a lopsided grin as though he had done something clever. The worst part was that Alfie knew he wasn't going to do anything about it, despite his father's constant lectures and advice. He was a coward. A weakling.

Big John hurried to the low post, and Alfie followed him, still feeling the tightness in his stomach. Alfie moved behind him, keeping himself between Big John and the hoop, his arms waving like one of those ridiculous inflatable figures outside of car dealerships. Big John replied by lowering his shoulder and driving it into Alfie's chest, then cocking his elbow for a painful dig into Alfie's exposed stomach. Alfie bit back another shout.

"You gonna cry, Twig?" Big John taunted.

Alfie ignored him, trying to ward off the constant blows.

"Can't you speak?" Big John said. "Pathetic. Why you here, anyway?"

"To . . . play ball."

"You don't belong here, rich boy. Go back to the burbs with Daddy."

"Freddy asked me to come—"

"And now he's gone," Big John hissed. "Hey, new kid, switch!"

Big John lumbered over to the other post, and Alfie reluctantly went after him. Devon and A-Wall hurried by, and Twig noticed that Devon gently stepped around him, avoiding contact. He turned back, frowning.

Devon wasn't pushing or shoving down low at all. He just stood there, a lone arm up for the pass, and didn't say a word.

Why isn't he pushing A-Wall around? Twig thought, confused.

He saw that Reggie was trying to get a pass to Big John and remembered what his dad had said: try and get a hand in *front* of your man to block the entry pass. He fought to get in front.

"Here!" Big John said. "Let me snap this Twig!"

Reggie tried the pass, but Rain picked it off.

"C'mon!" Big John shouted. "What kind of a pass was that?"

Alfie tried to follow Rain on offense, but Big John stuck out a leg. Alfie toppled over, smacking his cheek into the floor, rattling his teeth. He lay there, stunned, checking his teeth with his tongue. Big John stepped beside him, staring down with a crooked grin, eyes gleaming.

"Stay down," he whispered.

Alfie wanted to, but he figured someone would step on him, so he scrambled up again and got to the block on defense. Big John deliberately overran it to collide with him, and Alfie gasped as the air flooded out of his lungs yet again. Jerome drove by him and laid up a basket.

"Nice D, Twig," Big John said. "Definitely living up to your namesake this season."

"Pick it up!" Peño snapped, thudding the inbound pass into Alfie's chest.

Alfie flushed and ran up the court. It was always *his* fault.

Before he could even get to the block he heard someone cry out. Confused, he looked back and saw Vin taking it to the hoop for a layup. They were now losing 4–0, and Peño looked bewildered. Peño very rarely turned over the ball—he told everyone he had glue on his hands.

"I thought you had mad handles?" Lab said. "You look like Twig dribbling."

"Thanks," Alfie mumbled.

Peño made it down the court this time, though just barely, and because

Rain seemed strangely uninterested in getting open, Alfie flashed across the key. To his surprise, he got the pass. He turned and faked the shot from the free-throw line, and Big John flew past, clearly trying to swat the ball into another stratosphere. Alfie smiled and prepared to dribble in for the now wide-open layup. Then he froze. There was a mirror beneath the net—just one this time.

Staring back was an almost skeletal little boy with a mop of unruly raven hair and big, watery brown eyes. It was Alfie as a second grader. He was holding the ball in the same position, getting ready to drive to the rim for a layup. But before he could move, other kids appeared around him.

"He's not gonna shoot it," one said. "He's scared."

"What a freak!"

"Sissy!"

Alfie knew the words by heart . . . he'd heard them all before. Then his dad walked up in the mirror, shooing the other kids away, and Alfie thought that maybe it was going to get better.

"No son of mine gets teased like that," he snarled. "You're embarrassing me."

A thousand memories flashed through his mind. His father driving him home from a game, telling him that Rain is a real player. His father telling him to be more like his cousin Gerald—burly, tough, and a complete jerk. Further back. His father taking away his stuffed hippo when he was four because "he wasn't a baby anymore." It all crashed together, and it was hard to see or think or do anything at all. Because for all of that, he was still an embarrassment.

Alfie passed the ball back to Peño, not even really hearing the tirade that followed. He shuffled down to the post, shaken. After that, he refused to get open for a pass. He didn't want to touch the ball. He didn't want to be Alfred Zetz.

He barely paid attention the rest of the scrimmage. He took elbows and shoves without complaint. Rain was clearly getting agitated, and when a lucky bounce brought a defensive rebound right into Alfie's outstretched and reluctant hands, Rain took off running, leaving Reggie hopelessly behind him. Alfie caught a glimpse of light reflecting off a pane of glass.

"Twig! Here!" Rain shouted.

Without thinking, Alfie lobbed the ball up the court, happy to get rid of it.

"Afraid to dribble?" Big John asked.

Alfie glanced at him and jogged after Rain.

"Nothing to say?" Big John said. "Always running, right? Always running scared."

Alfie felt his cheeks burning. Ahead of him, Rain was acting very bizarrely, moving in exaggerated slow motion. Then he stopped and heaved a long three that fell well short.

Rain didn't take shots like that. Something was happening.

What was Rain seeing? Alfie wondered.

Now you are asking the right questions.

Alfie flinched and turned to the professor just as he strode onto the court.

"That will be all for today."

"We aren't going to do any drills?" Peño asked.

As usual, Rolabi didn't respond. With an eerie precision, the ball rolled directly between his polished shoes and stopped there. Rolabi scooped it up and proceeded back to the bleachers, dropping it into his bag on the way. He sat down as casually as if he were waiting for a bus. As soon as he did, there was an earsplitting crash. The locker room door flew open at once, careening into the wall and causing everyone to whirl to the source of the noise. Icy cold wind rushed out from the locker room, and Alfie stared in wonder. There were no windows in there.

"Where . . . How did . . . ?" Big John said.

Alfie turned back. The bleachers were empty, and Rolabi Wizenard was gone.

Alfie continued staring as the others launched into an argument about magic and sorcerers and whether they were all going crazy. As he listened, a memory surfaced in Alfie's mind. It had been nagging him since yesterday. It was a story he'd read a long time ago, or perhaps had read to him . . . a children's story. It had been about magic, except it was called something else . . . grapa? He remembered a mountain, and an island . . . and something else. The Kingdom of Granity. His eyes widened. That's why the word *granity* had seemed familiar on the contract.

Alfie stepped back to his bag to put his shoes away and froze when he saw a business card on top of his duffel. The card was white and blue, inscribed with a *W* and the number 76522494936273. He picked it up, wondering when Rolabi had possibly placed it there. Alfie hurried out to the parking lot and dialed the strange number. To his surprise, it started ringing.

A deep voice answered. "This is Rolabi Wizenard—"

"Hi, Rol—"

The voice continued unabated. It sounded like a prerecorded message.

"This line is for parents only. Have a good evening, Twig."

Alfie flinched and hung up. He stared down at his phone, bewildered, and then another piece of the old children's story came back to him. A specific word. One he had long forgotten.

"*Wizenard*," he whispered.

It wasn't a last name. It was a title.

He called his mother for a ride, suddenly eager to get home. He had to go find that book.

THE
DISAPPEARING SWEAT

If you can't read minds,
put yourself in others and open your eyes.

✧ WIZENARD ❰29❱ PROVERB ✧

THE NEXT MORNING, Alfie sat alone in the locker room, the stink pushing its way up his nostrils like two festering slugs. He was perched on the wooden bench that wrapped around the room, attached by steel brackets and spotted black with mold. The walls, once white, were now stained yellow with coppery rings from water damage. A few remaining rust-colored hooks jutted out over the bench. Alfie wanted to be alone, and in here, loneliness was guaranteed.

He held the old, crinkled book in his hands. *The World of Grana.*

He'd found it buried at the bottom of his closet and read it at least ten times last night. It was about an island, a place far out in the ocean and marked with a single snowcapped mountain: the Kingdom of Granity. There were teachers there—women and men who traveled the world unlocking grana, moving in and out of societies like ghosts. They were called Wizenards. In the story, an orphan—a girl named Pana—lost at sea stumbled upon the island and was trained to be one of them. She wanted to stay on the island and forget her old life, but after she learned the secrets of grana she realized she couldn't. The last lines of the book were:

Pana realized grana had always been there. And she knew she had to go back to the world and share its lessons with them. And so Pana left the Kingdom, but now as a Wizenard.

Alfie chewed on his nails. He'd brought the book to show the others, but it was ridiculous to think they might take it seriously. It was a story for children. His mom used to read it to him before bedtime. He could picture Big John laughing hysterically. He ran his fingers over the painted pictures on each page. A beautiful golden cup. A white stone castle. A great, arching door cut into the mountain and a cavernous, round room inside.

He shut the book and put it back in his bag. It was a coincidence. It had to be.

And yet Rolabi was far from a normal coach. Alfie's father had phoned him last night, looking for answers about Alfie's playing time. He had made the call from his home office, and when he came out, he had looked a little . . . uneasy. He softly told Alfie that Rolabi seemed like a good coach. That was it. He didn't say another word. Alfie had never seen him so quiet.

Maybe that was grana too.

When Alfie pulled out his sneakers, a little folded note spilled out from one of them.

Dear Alfie,

You looked ill at dinner tonight. I know you said you were fine, but I am worried about you. Is everything okay at training camp? Are the other boys picking on you? You can come talk to me at any time.

Love always,
Mom

Alfie felt his eyes well up, and he wiped them gruffly with the palm of his hand, smearing the hot tears across his cheeks. He believed her. He could tell her about Rolabi, and she would listen. But then she would tell his father. He would find out, and he would yell, and he would tell Alfie that cowards never win. That he needed to focus on his game.

Alfie folded the note neatly and tucked it back into his duffel bag.

"I can't go out there," he said softly, his voice lingering in the empty room.

It felt like there were iron weights strapped onto his limbs, tying him to the bench. He knew he could sit there for the entire day and his teammates wouldn't care. They probably wouldn't even notice. Alfie leaned back, staring at the far wall, and then squinted.

Something was written on the cinder blocks.

He crossed the room and found a short message. Alfie wondered how he had missed it when he first sat down. The penmanship was surprisingly elegant, almost like calligraphy:

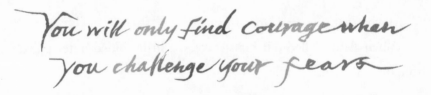

You will only find courage when you challenge your fears

Alfie ran his hands over the dried ink, considering the words. Then he nodded and went to get his shoes on. Hundreds or maybe even thousands of people had sat in this old locker room before, and some had probably been afraid. Maybe even whoever wrote that message. But they'd stood up anyway and went out there to play basketball.

Alfie could do that too. He could face another day.

When he walked out, most of the team was already there, and the home bench was full.

Alfie sat on the away one and waited for Big John's inevitable taunts.

They didn't come. In fact, no one was really talking at all. If they were speaking, it was only in whispers.

Alfie slipped the book out of his bag. Was their coach really a Wizenard? Was it all true?

"There's no such thing as magic," Lab snapped, rising above the whispers.

"Is that so?"

The voice came from behind them. Alfie twisted so sharply, he fell right off the bench. The rest of the team toppled over on the other bench and spilled into a tangle of limbs. Rolabi walked onto the court, his leather medicine bag in one hand, the other swinging rhythmically at his side like the pendulum of a grandfather clock. It was almost hypnotizing.

"If you don't believe in magic," Rolabi said, "you need to get out more."

His eyes flicked to Alfie, and as before, Alfie heard the ticking of the pocket watch.

There is always time for change.

Alfie didn't look away this time. He met Rolabi's eyes.

He was looking at a Wizenard.

The first to find the truth. But will you be the first to face it?

How do I face it? Alfie thought.

You work.

"We will start with laps," Rolabi said.

Alfie blinked and climbed to his feet. He noticed that the team was turning in his direction to run, so Alfie took off, finding himself in an uncomfortable lead. He set a slow pace, but five laps in, he was starting to sweat. A lot. It crept down his forehead and along his pointed nose, and he soon tasted wet salt on his lips.

"We will take free throws, one at a time," Rolabi announced. "As soon as someone scores, you will stop running for the day. If you miss, the entire team runs five more laps."

"I got this," Peño said, wheezing as he stepped out of the line.

Alfie doubled over, watching the sweat dribble down. It pooled on the floor for a second and then suddenly drained as though a plug had been pulled. He frowned. He had never seen the hardwood do that before. He looked around and saw the others gulping air beside him. Their sweat was dripping onto the floor and disappearing too. It was as if Fairwood was drinking it.

He knelt down and felt the floors. They were coarse now—most of the wax had been stripped away, and the wood had splintered in places. Alfie's fingers seemed to dry on contact.

"What kind of a shot was that?" Lab asked incredulously.

Alfie looked up. The ball was rolling away from a very dejected-looking Peño.

"Five more laps," Rolabi said.

Alfie stood up among the groans and prepared to start running again. His eyes widened.

"Does anyone else see this?" Jerome whispered.

The floor now veered upward at a 45-degree angle, as if the entire gym had been picked up on one end. Alfie felt his shoes slip backward, and he crouched, shifting his weight.

"Begin," Rolabi said.

A Wizenard, Alfie thought in awe.

Are you ready to find your grana?

I . . . I don't know, he thought.

Then run and find out.

Alfie took off. He was forced to widen his strides and lean forward, pushing himself up the incline with his arms ahead of him as a counter-balance. His legs pumped side to side like an ice-skater's, and his thighs were burning terribly when he finally reached the baseline and turned again. Alfie slid to a halt, feeling a pileup behind him. Now the floor slanted *downward.*

"Oh boy," Alfie murmured.

Climb high. Fall far. Go off in seek of truth.

Alfie leaned back and descended with little jab steps.

"If I die, tell my story," Big John said, gasping.

"From falling in a hole or dying of a heart attack?" Vin said.

"Either one."

When they had made it through five laps of constantly shifting obsta-cles, Rain stepped forward to shoot. Alfie was thoroughly drenched with sweat. He could have wrung out his shorts.

Thankfully, he knew the drill would end here. Rain never missed a foul shot.

Rain stepped up to the line, and Alfie anticipated his routine. Bounce, bounce, bounce. Deep breath. Everything as usual. But as he released, he jerked. The ball thudded away off the rim.

"No," Big John breathed.

"Everyone, grab a drink," Rolabi said. "The laps will continue shortly."

Alfie grabbed his bottle and watched as Rain slammed the locker room door behind him. Was he that upset over one miss? He didn't know much about Rain, other than that his life seemed pretty perfect. The best player, the coolest, the one with a real shot. Rain had it easy.

"What's that about?" A-Wall muttered.

"No clue," Peño said. "But I'm sure Rolly Weird-in-ard has something to do with it."

Twig took a gulp of water and glanced at the professor. He stood like a statue at center court, his eyes on the banners. Alfie thought of another part of the old book:

> *And they told Pana that Wizenards are old as stone. Some live*
> *for a thousand years. Theirs is the oldest and most important*
> *job . . . to remind the rest of the world what they really are.*

"The floors . . . They were moving, right?" a deep voice asked.

Alfie turned to Devon, surprised to hear him speak. "Yeah. Or . . . I think so."

Devon nodded. "Just checking."

They ran again. As before, the gym changed with every turn, and the missed shots began to add up: Lab, Vin, Big John. The team could barely keep running.

"Twig," Reggie said, gasping at the next stoppage. "You go."

Alfie glanced back and saw the rest of the team hunched over. No one volunteered, so he gulped and walked out onto the court. His legs felt stretched like old rubber bands. He took a deep breath.

Nice and easy, Alfie thought, dribbling the ball and wiping his sweaty hands on his shirt.

He copied Rain: bounce, bounce, bounce, deep breath. Then he prepared to shoot.

But as he went to lift the ball, it suddenly felt incredibly heavy. He saw that he was now holding a black lead sphere, like the ones prisoners used to have chained to their feet. He strained to lift it, spreading his feet to get better positioning. His whole body felt like it was being crushed into the floor. He gritted his teeth and kept pushing, lifting the ball overhead.

"He's so weak," Lab said.

He looked back at the team, but no one seemed to be talking.

"He can't even lift the ball," Big John said, laughing.

"It's . . . it's heavy," Alfie said.

"This is embarrassing," Rain replied. "His dad must be ashamed."

But their mouths weren't moving. Were they? Alfie turned away from them.

Again, he fought to lift the ball, shifting beneath it like he was doing a dead lift, and then heaved it forward. As soon as he let it go, the lead ball immediately turned back to a normal one. It flew in a straight line and crashed into the backboard, rebounding right back and almost hitting him in the forehead. Alfie heard groans of disbelief from his teammates, and his cheeks burned.

In a daze, he rejoined the group. They ran five more laps, facing more strange obstacles at every turn. Alfie was staggering now, his legs almost giving out. Mercifully, Reggie hit his attempt, and the team let out an exhausted cheer.

"Water break," Rolabi said as he strode to center court. "Bring your bottles over here."

Alfie grabbed his bottle, thinking about the weight of the ball. He hadn't just seen it. He'd felt it. It was tangible. Real. Again he thought about the book. Pana had learned that it wasn't the Wizenards creating magic—they were just using the grana that everyone possessed.

One of her main lessons was that *she* was creating her own world.

Aren't you?

Twig whirled around, dropping his bottle and scrambling to pick it up again.

Not used to that yet, he thought sheepishly. *Talking in my head like this . . . is this grana?*

Everything is.

He downed some water and joined the seated circle around Rolabi, who fished a potted flower out of his bag and set it down. It was a beautiful, stark white daisy—Alfie had only ever seen flowers like that in books.

Do you want to see grana?

Yes, Alfie thought excitedly.

Then watch the flower grow. Be aware of every detail. See the imperceptible.

Alfie frowned and stared at the flower. He refolded his legs beneath him and tried to focus. The first minute or two he actually tried to see something. But it remained a simple daisy.

Soon sounds disrupted his focus: the ticking clock, frustrated sighs, and the rustling of people shifting uncomfortably. He tried to see the flower growing, but nothing was happening.

Why are you rushing time?

I'm not, Alfie thought, glancing at Rolabi.

All you want is change. A new body. A new life. What have you done to build the one you already have?

Alfie looked away. When he turned back, the daisy had withered, and he was alone in the gym. A shiver ran down the nape of his neck. Was this scene real? He crawled over to the pot and reached out to touch the daisy. It collapsed into dust and ash. He stared at it, confused, strangely sad. It had been so beautiful.

"When we look for more, we forget what we have. What's ignored then withers away."

Alfie looked up and saw Rolabi looming over him.

"I'm trying to be better," Alfie protested.

"It is wise to grow what you are," he said. "Not to wish you are something else."

Alfie blinked, and he was sitting in the circle again, surrounded by his teammates. Rolabi was tucking the flower back into his bag. Alfie stared at him, unnerved.

"We have one more lesson today," Rolabi said.

His green eyes darted to Alfie.

It's time for the Twig to grow.

Alfie climbed to his feet with the others. Rolabi began to set up a training circuit around the gym. He threw the cones without looking, and they fell into perfect zigzag patterns. Reaching into his bag again, he withdrew ridiculously large objects: a hoop on a metal base, six-foot-tall poles, and ever more cones. It was enough equipment to fill the bed of a pickup truck. As if that weren't enough, he finally pulled out three more basketballs and placed them in a line.

"Am I seeing this correctly?" Reggie murmured.

"I don't know anymore," Alfie said.

When the team had gathered in front of the three basketballs, Rolabi turned to them.

"You will complete the circuit. A layup on the first hoop and a shot from the elbow on the other. When you return, pass the ball to the player who is first in line. Three may go at a time. You may begin."

Rain went to grab the first ball and unleashed a bloodcurdling shriek. He grabbed his wrist, dropping the ball, and Alfie watched in astonishment as he continued to scream madly. Frantic shouts went up from other players, and with something like grim reluctance, Alfie looked down.

His right hand was gone. His wrist ended in a flat, skin-colored wall of flesh. Alfie stared at the missing limb, dumbfounded. He poked it with his left fingers and felt nothing. He heard shouts and complaints and cursing, but he could barely process the sounds. His hand was *gone*.

"I'm the only one who lost it!" Lab was shouting.

"I don't have one anymore," Alfie said numbly.

Lab stared at him and then turned back to Rolabi. "This isn't possible."

"Possibility is notoriously subjective," Rolabi replied. "Shall we begin?"

No one said anything for a moment—there were just whimpers and muffled curses.

Then Rain picked up the ball with his left hand and started the circuit. Everyone reluctantly followed suit. Alfie missed his layup badly and barely made his way through the cones. He lost the ball twice, though he passed a frustrated A-Wall before subsequently being passed by Jerome. When Alfie tried to throw the ball through the vertical ring, he missed by ten feet, then took an absolutely terrible one-handed jump shot that sailed wide. As he grabbed the rebound, by now thoroughly embarrassed, another shot ricocheted hard off the back of his head.

"Sorry, man!" Lab said.

Apologies seemed to be a common theme around the gym.

"Watch out!" Peño bellowed, smacking Vin with an errant pass.

"This ain't dodgeball, bro!" Vin said, rubbing his cheek.

The circuit continued. Alfie was hit six more times, including once in the nose. He sank about a third of his left-handed layups and didn't make a single jumper or pass through the ring. It was humiliating. When Rolabi finally called an end to the practice, Alfie sank down, exhausted. He was sweating so much, his eyes stung with salt, and he could barely open them.

"Can we have our hands back now?" Rain asked.

"Tomorrow we will be working on our defense. They will be helpful then," said Rolabi.

With that, he scooped up his bag and began walking directly toward a brick wall.

"He knows there isn't a door there, right?" Peño said.

The lights flashed like mini supernovas, bathing the room in blinding white. Alfie heard something—waves, maybe. A howling alpine wind. He caught the whiff of a salty ocean breeze.

"The Kingdom of Granity," he whispered.

The lights flicked on and off. Rolabi was gone.

He slowly picked himself up, and the floor made a suctioning *plop*. He looked back and saw that it was already perfectly dry. It was impossible. Alfie knelt down again and felt the hardwood. The wide slats were slowly pushing apart, and he ran his finger along the spacing.

An image flashed in front of him. Thousands of silvery veins and arteries ran beneath his feet, snaking up the walls and over the ceiling. They were pulsating. Beating. Pumping sweat.

The gym looked *alive*.

"A heart," he whispered.

The image faded, and Alfie realized he had spilled backward onto his butt. He hadn't even noticed. The veins and arteries were gone, but he could almost hear the heartbeat.

"You okay?" Reggie said, sticking a hand out to help him up. "Besides the hand."

"Yeah," Alfie said, accepting gratefully. "Thanks."

"Crazy stuff, huh? You can see mine, right?"

"Yeah. It must just be an illusion for one person."

"I don't get any of this stuff," Reggie said. "I would love to know what's happening."

Alfie opened his mouth to mention the book, then hesitated. He didn't want to be laughed at, and even though Reggie was nice, it was a kids' book. So he just nodded and forced a smile.

"Same."

They started to the bench together, and Reggie glanced at him. "Where did you get those scars on your cheeks, anyway?" he asked. "Meant to ask you."

Alfie put a hand to his face. The skin picking had marked his cheeks with little white spots and divots where he had picked too much. It gave him a grizzled look, like an old soldier. He thought it was hideous, but he couldn't seem to stop.

"Born with it," he said.

"Oh. Just thought you were getting more of them lately—"

"No," Alfie snapped.

It came out sharper than he intended, and he looked away.

Reggie flushed. "Sorry. Just making sure you were good."

Reggie continued to the bench, obviously embarrassed. Alfie chewed his nails, thinking that he couldn't afford to lose his one friend on the team. He didn't want to talk about the scars . . . but he *could* tell him about the book. Maybe Reggie would see it as a sign of trust. Alfie chewed some more.

"Can I show you something?" he called after him.

Reggie turned back. "What?"

Alfie led him over to the bench, looked around to make sure everyone else was occupied, and then pulled out the book with his left hand and showed it to Reggie.

"*The World of Grana*," Reggie said slowly. He seemed to sound out each word with care. "I think my gran read this to me when I was little. It looks familiar. Why did you bring—"

"Just read it. You can borrow it tonight if you want."

Reggie frowned, and then opened the book, resting it on his lap and turning the pages gingerly with his weaker right hand. The first page was a painting of the island and mountain.

The book began:

Once, in the Kingdom of Granity, there were a great many Wizenards . . .

"Oh," Reggie said quietly. "I see."

THE LONG WALK

If you are afraid of loneliness,
spend more time alone.
✧ WIZENARD ㉓ PROVERB ✧

ALFIE CHECKED TO make sure no one was looking, then reached down with his left hand to press the button on either shoe—both of which sealed comfortably. The others were all struggling with their laces, and he didn't want to draw any more attention to himself. He could sympathize, anyway. Since yesterday's practice, he had almost swallowed his toothbrush, dropped a glass of milk, and completely given up on reading a book. It was shocking how useless he was with his left hand. It might as well have been a pirate hook.

His parents never said a word about it. They could see his hand. Alfie just had to try and tough it out. That's what his father always said. A cold? Tough it out. Bullies? Tough it out.

Tough it out. He didn't even know what that meant. Don't complain, or don't get sick in the first place? Don't cry about bullies, or don't let them pick on you? What was considered *tough*?

"Some night, huh?" Reggie said, plopping onto the away bench after a few quick laps around the gym. They were the first ones as usual, but a few guys had started arriving. "Oh, here."

He took the book out of his bag with his one hand and gave it back to Alfie.

"How many times you read it?" Alfie asked dryly.

"About twenty," he said. "Kind of identified with Pana, you know?"

Alfie almost smacked himself in the forehead. Of course. Reggie was an orphan too.

"I didn't even—"

"Don't worry about it," Reggie cut in. "The point is . . . it all looks pretty accurate now."

Alfie glanced at him. "Yeah. You mentioned anything to your gran?"

"Nah. She'd tell me I was nuts. She's pretty old-school, you know?"

"What do you mean?"

"No complaining. No talking back. She wouldn't believe in magic. Or grana."

Alfie nodded and tucked the book back in his bag. "Same with my dad. How long has your gran been watching you?"

"Seven years this October. Since I was six."

Alfie hesitated. He shouldn't ask. He knew he shouldn't. But he really, really wanted to.

He was never good with self-control.

"Your . . . parents?" he asked.

Reggie was silent for so long, Alfie was sure he had gone too far. He was already preparing an apology in his head. He was so *stupid* sometimes.

"I don't know," Reggie said finally.

"What do you mean?" Alfie asked, unable to stop himself. "They . . . left?"

"Not exactly."

Reggie sighed and looked down at his hands as if the answer were written there. "They were in a car accident."

"I'm sorry," Alfie murmured. He couldn't imagine losing his parents.

Reggie glanced at him. "That's what the police told me, anyway. But

I never saw their car. No pictures. Nothing." He paused. "They were both reporters. They spoke out about the president."

"I didn't know that," Alfie murmured.

He felt a tingle of nervous energy. What was Reggie saying? That the government killed his parents? He looked around the gym to make sure no one else was listening, but they were all warming up. It was dangerous to even think something like that.

"No one on the team does," Reggie said.

"But you told me."

"Yeah," Reggie said, nodding. "I trust you to keep it between us."

Alfie nodded. "Of course. And . . . I'm sorry."

"Me too," he whispered.

The doors swung open, and Rain walked in. Freddy trailed behind him, his eyes flicking nervously around the gym. Alfie guessed at once what was happening: Freddy was here to fire Rolabi Wizenard. Alfie had seen Rain talking in low voices with some of the other players before they left yesterday, but he hadn't been included. Clearly the decision was made.

"Might not have to think about Wizenards for much longer," Reggie said quietly.

"Did they ask your opinion?"

Reggie snorted. "Of course not."

Alfie listened in silence as the team complained to the owner. Freddy clearly didn't believe any of it—missing hands that everyone else could see, tilting gyms, voices. But he just fidgeted and listened and agreed to fire Rolabi. Ultimately, if Rain wanted something done, Freddy would do it.

Alfie wished he could argue for keeping Rolabi, but he didn't even try, and shame flooded through him. He really was a coward. His dad knew it. The team knew it. And worst of all, Alfie knew it. He stayed silent.

Freddy peeked at his phone. "All right, well, he should be here soon—"

"Were you on any of these teams, Frederick?"

Alfie spun to the voice. Rolabi Wizenard stood below the line of multicolored banners.

"What . . . Where did . . . ?" Freddy asked, stuttering.

Rolabi strode toward them. Freddy tried, to his credit. He even took the blame.

But Rolabi didn't move. A hush fell as he looked over the team, and when his eyes fell on Alfie, a single word seemed to pass between them: *Courage.* Alfie stared at his shoes. It didn't matter that he had wanted to argue. He hadn't. He'd kept his mouth shut, just like always. Alfie had no courage.

Wrong, the voice said. *It takes courage to know ourselves.*

Rolabi shook hands with Freddy, and the team owner went rigid. Alfie counted nearly sixty seconds slip by in utter silence. Then, without a word, Rolabi removed his hand from Freddy's.

"Rolabi will remain the coach," Freddy said softly. "I look forward to the season."

And with that, he left. Alfie watched, wondering what Freddy had just seen.

The future.

Rolabi waited until the doors shut, then turned to the team as if nothing had happened.

"Today we will be working on defense. Before I can teach you proper zones and strategies, I must teach each of you how to be a defender. They are not the same lessons."

He let the silence hang, but it didn't last long. Something was *scratching*. Alfie looked around, searching for the source. It was far too loud to be a mouse. An enormous rat maybe? A stray dog?

"What must a defender always be?" Rolabi asked.

Nobody answered—they were all listening to the scratching. Alfie's eyes fell on the closed locker room door and saw it rattling on the hinges. Something was inside. Something *big*.

He took a step back, thinking about the book. There had been animals on the island, living among the Wizenards: elephants, lions, dragons, gryphons. Had Rolabi brought something like that with him? Alfie hoped so. He would love to see a mythological creature.

"Well . . ." Peño said. "Umm . . . in position?"

"Before that."

"Talking?" Vin said.

Twig watched the door, entranced. What was back there? A lion? A basilisk? A hippo?

"Before that," Rolabi said.

Silence fell again. Or, at least, silence punctuated by a low, steady scratching.

"*Ready*," Rolabi said. "They must always be ready. A defender must be a step ahead of their opponents. They must outthink and out-strategize. They must always be ready to move."

There was another scratch. The door was rattling madly.

"Can someone open the locker room door?" Rolabi said.

Nobody moved. It was clear no one was going to open it. It was probably not a good idea. And yet . . . Alfie felt his hands twitching at his sides. He thought back to the message on the wall and his shame when Rolabi had looked at him earlier. He was a coward, but couldn't he change that? Even for a moment? The door began to shake. So did he. A voice told him to run and hide.

Courage only counts for the coward.

Alfie was sick of being afraid. He was afraid at practice, afraid at school, afraid at home. As the rest of the team backed away, he started forward. He was trembling. His stomach danced a fumbling jig.

But he kept walking.

"What are you doing?" Peño asked in disbelief.

"I want to see what it is," Alfie said.

The Twig sets its roots.

Alfie grabbed the door handle. The scratching stopped. For a moment, he heard only the pocket watch ticking away behind him—slow, strangely calming. He had time to take a breath.

Then he pulled open the door, and a tiger walked out.

It started right for Rolabi, moving with silky, quiet confidence. To Alfie's satisfaction, Big John fled to the bleachers. But Alfie found that he wasn't afraid at all. The tiger was beautiful.

"Meet Kallo. She has graciously volunteered to help us today."

Kallo turned and scanned the group. Her eyes were a rich purple.

"So he *is* a Wizenard," Reggie whispered.

"Yeah," Alfie said softly.

"Rain," Rolabi said. "Step forward."

Rain's eyes widened. He seemed to consider his options for a moment, and then reluctantly stepped out ahead of the group. His knees were wobbling so much that Alfie thought he might faint.

Rolabi rolled a ball right to the center of the court.

"The drill is simple," Rolabi explained. "Get the ball. Kallo will play defense. We will take turns and go one at a time. I want everyone to watch and take note of what happens."

Rain blanched. "What? I'm not going near that *thing*."

Kallo growled, her purple eyes narrowing.

"Kallo won't hurt you," Rolabi said, running a huge, calloused hand over her neck and scratching behind her ears. "She is the best defender I have ever seen. Relentless and quick."

Kallo began to pace. Alfie watched her easy, fluid movements, hypnotized.

"A true defender *must* be a tiger. The first one to get the ball gets their hand back."

Rain stood there, not moving. Alfie was sure he would refuse. He might even quit the team and walk out. If he did, the Badgers would likely fold, and the season would be over before it began.

The gym seemed to grow still with anticipation.

And then Rain made his move. He was fast, but not nearly fast enough.

Kallo pounced onto his chest and knocked him to the ground, pinning him. As he lay there, stunned, she licked his face and stepped off again, prowling back and forth in front of the ball.

"Devon," Rolabi said.

He didn't fare much better, but he did receive the same consolatory lick in the face.

"Twig," Rolabi said.

It suddenly occurred to Alfie that Rolabi was calling him *Twig*. He frowned. Didn't Rolabi know he hated that nickname? It was insulting. It meant he was skinny. A weakling.

Alfie stepped forward nervously. He had more immediate concerns.

Kallo's eyes followed his every movement. Her body rippled with countless muscles.

"You can do this," Alfie whispered.

He took a hard step right and then tried to spin to his left like he was pivoting on the post. It didn't work. Kallo was on him in an instant. He laughed as she licked the side of his head, her tongue dry and coarse. Then she strutted back over to Rolabi and paced again.

The players went one after another . . . and then it came to Big John.

He folded his arms and refused. "No. I ain't doing it. Pass."

"If we pass on the struggle, then we pass on the lesson," Rolabi said.

"Then that's what I'll do."

Alfie wasn't sure why he said anything. He didn't talk to Big John. It was a proven strategy. And he should have been greatly enjoying the fact that Big John was the coward today.

But Alfie's mouth rebelled against his much-wiser brain and decided to jump in.

"It's not that bad," he said. "She's really gentle."

"You don't talk to me," Big John snarled.

Alfie lifted his hand. "I'm just trying to help—"

Big John turned to face him. His eyes, already small and beady, had narrowed to slits, and there was a shocking amount of hatred in them. Alfie was taken aback. He knew Big John didn't like him. That was obvious. He had assumed it was because he was quiet and shy and they played the same position. Or because he was different: a kid from the wealthier suburbs playing here in Fairwood. But this was different than dislike. It was *hatred*, dark and deep.

Hate arises from fear, the voice said.

I'm afraid, Alfie thought.

Then you have a chance for courage.

Alfie took a deep breath. He had faced a tiger today. He could face this.

"I don't need your help," Big John said, his voice almost serpentine.

Alfie held Big John's eyes. Normally, he would look away. When confrontation came, he could find his shoes or his hands—anywhere but the source of the problem. Here. At school. At home. He always looked away. *Always*. And nothing ever changed.

"You think you're a big tough guy now or what?" Big John asked.

Alfie saw Big John's hand closing into a fist. It was the size of a softball, and it trembled, itching to punch something. Or more accurately, someone. Still, Alfie didn't move.

For a moment, he pictured his father, towering above him, filled with anger and frustration. Alfie would cower before him. Apologize.

Fold in on himself like a raisin. But today he met his father's eyes.

"I didn't mean anything by it," Alfie said. "You looked like you could use a hand."

Big John snapped. He shoved Alfie in the chest and sent him flying. Alfie gasped as his tailbone struck the ground and sent a lance of pain up his back. His eyes flooded with tears. He rolled onto his side, trying not to cry out.

Peño took a running jump onto Big John's back and wrapped his arms around his torso. "Down, boy!"

Big John continued toward Alfie, clearly ready to pound him. Jerome and A-Wall stepped in too, grabbing either one of his arms and trying to forcibly hold him back.

"I don't need your help!" Big John snapped. "You think you got the answers, huh? Rich boy out the burbs. New shoes. New cell phone. You don't belong here. You didn't *earn* it."

He was spitting each word, his whole body shaking. The three boys clung to him, one on either arm and Peño on his back, and still he fought to get closer.

Alfie stood up. Something stood out to him—that he didn't earn it.

"What are you talking about?" he asked.

"You know where I go after practice? To work. Two jobs, and we still can't pay all the bills. You ever spent a week in the dark 'cause you can't pay for no lights? You ever pick the mold off your food 'cause you got nothing else? You ever hold your mama in blankets 'cause you can't afford no doctor?"

"I . . ."

"This is all I got!" Big John screamed. "And you took it from me!"

Alfie realized Big John's eyes were watering, and he couldn't see his bully anymore. Suddenly he saw another kid. One who was holding in a whole lot of anger. And pain. And who could blame him for that? For everything Alfie went through, he had never had to work a job, let alone two. He had never had to worry about bills. Food. Clothing. He had never had to wonder about whether the lights would be on when he got home.

Big John did. Twig realized that he'd had it all wrong from the start. Big John *envied* him.

"Freddy decided on who starts," Alfie said quietly. "It's just a strategy thing—"

He was trying to make Big John feel better. To justify the situation. It didn't work. Big John charged him, fists raised, and Alfie knew he was about to be flattened.

Well, he thought, *at least I won't die a coward*.

And then Rolabi laid a massive hand on Big John's shoulder. His fingers gripped him like the jaws of an overhead crane and lifted Big John, Peño, A-Wall, and Jerome clean off the ground. A-Wall and Jerome hurriedly let go, but Peño held on as Rolabi spun Big John to face him. Rolabi didn't seem the least bit strained from the impossible feat of strength.

Alfie watched as Big John dangled there, flooded only with empathy.

Once, Alfie might have enjoyed the scene.

Rolabi put Big John down, and Peño hopped off. Everyone stared in wide-eyed awe.

"Fear hardens to anger and violence," Rolabi said. "It has made your choice for you. Fear of not being enough. Blame where it doesn't belong. But I value honesty. I will forgive this violence *once*."

"I'm done here," Big John hissed. "I'm done with this stupid training."

"You know the consequences."

Big John started for the bench, turning his back on the team. "I don't care."

"Ten minutes in the locker room," Rolabi said.

Big John paused and glanced back. "What?"

"Go look at your reflection for ten minutes. Ask the boy in there carefully. Then decide."

Big John hesitated, then stormed into the locker room and slammed the door.

"None of you got the ball," Rolabi said, patting Kallo's head. She purred so loudly, it seemed to shake the hardwood floors. "But you all showed real courage. That is a good start."

With that, their hands reappeared. Alfie flexed his fingers and smiled as the others cheered and high-fived and did secret handshakes. No one turned to him, though, and he just clasped his own hands together. Even though he was happy to have his hand back, he felt a little bit lonelier.

He kept glancing at the bathroom. He wondered if Big John was lonely in there too.

"Why couldn't you get past her?" Rolabi asked, cutting into his thoughts.

"Because she's a tiger," Peño said.

Rolabi smiled. "But what does that mean?"

"She's strong," Jerome said.

"And big," Vin added.

"Both true. We must work on our strength and always play big. What else?"

Alfie was still watching Kallo. "Her reflexes," he said. "She reacts so quickly."

"Indeed. How are your reflexes, Mr. Zetz?"

Alfie thought about that. It wasn't really something he'd ever considered.

"Well . . . I think they are good," he said.

The words were barely out of his mouth when Rolabi flicked his index finger. A circular black button came flying at Alfie and pinged right off his forehead before he could even move.

"Maybe not great," Alfie said sheepishly.

"Your reflexes can be honed," Rolabi said. "They are a direct, unthinking connection to your brain. A measure of nerves and awareness and alertness. Train them. Training tells your brain to stay prepared. Always."

Alfie felt a sudden chill. He checked the doors, but they were closed. It was so *cold*.

"What is that?" Jerome asked.

Alfie followed Jerome's gaze and stiffened. A black ball was floating in the middle of the gym, as dark as a blotch of ink. It seemed to be made of a liquid. It wobbled constantly, shifting.

What are you afraid of? a raspy voice whispered. Alfie shuddered involuntarily.

"That is something you all will want to catch," Rolabi said. "No, it is something you all *must* catch." He turned back to them, his eyes flashing. "Whoever catches it will become a far better player. But it won't last forever. If no one catches it, we run laps." He nodded to it. "Go!"

Alfie wasn't sure he wanted to catch the orb—in fact, all he wanted to do was run away from it—but without thinking, he was in the chase. He assumed it was a footrace. It wasn't.

As soon as the group closed in, the orb moved with lightning speed, weaving in and out between the players like a crazed bird. No one could get close. Devon and A-Wall collided with a thud, and then Jerome tripped over them both and went flying.

"I don't remember basketball being so painful," Jerome groaned from the floor.

At one point, the orb changed directions and flew directly at Alfie's head. He was so surprised that he threw himself *out* of the way—much to the rest of the team's amusement. He jumped up, embarrassed, and rejoined the chase. It was mindless, frantic, and impossible.

In the end, the orb wandered a bit too close to Kallo, and she swallowed it whole.

"A true defender," Rolabi said. "Get some water. Laps and free throws."

As the rest of the team shuffled or limped to get their bottles, Alfie slowly approached Kallo. He had figured out what was drawing him to her—she radiated confidence. It was infectious, and he wanted more. He gave her a nervous pat, and she purred and nuzzled his hand.

"Where is she from?" he asked Rolabi.

"Somewhere far from here. A place of snow and sand."

Alfie glanced up at the professor. "An island?"

He smiled. "Children's stories are so often the last reservoir of truth."

"I'd like to go there."

"You can. But the journey is not an easy road."

"I'm not afraid," Alfie said, though he wasn't sure he believed it.

"Of course you are. If you weren't afraid, it would be impossible to grow stronger."

Alfie looked away. "I'm not strong."

"We are all strong," Rolabi said. "Life is hard, so we must be. We just forget our strength sometimes."

Alfie managed a smile and went to get a drink. As he put his bottle away, the locker room door eased open, and Big John walked out. Alfie tensed, wondering if he would attack him again.

"What did the boy in the mirror say?" Rolabi asked.

Big John hesitated. "He said to stay."

"And?"

"And sorry," he said softly, glancing at Alfie.

The hatred had cooled, but it remained, etched into Big John's features. It didn't shock Alfie this time. He didn't know how to change it, but it felt like a start to know *why*.

"The boy in the mirror is often wiser than the one who stares at him," Rolabi said. "But it is hard to listen."

Big John grabbed his own right hand and kissed it.

"Laps," Rolabi said.

The laps began, and as before, everyone was missing their free throws.

The team was drenched by the time Alfie stepped up, the last one to shoot, apart from Devon. He walked to the free-throw line and saw the mirror below it. The nervous little boy was standing there again, surrounded by taunting peers. His dad was approaching in the background, looking stern and angry. But this time Alfie didn't wait for him to arrive. He rolled his shoulders and shot the ball.

Swish.

Alfie slumped with relief, watching his sweat disappear into the floor.

"Tomorrow we will work on team defense," Rolabi said. "Get some rest tonight."

He started for the front doors with Kallo.

"Are . . . are you taking the tiger home?" Peño called.

The doors flew open, and Rolabi and Kallo strolled outside.

"He should really learn how to say goodbye," Peño muttered.

Alfie shuffled to the bench, exhausted, and started to take off his sneakers.

"We practiced with a tiger today," Peño said.

Jerome was the first one to laugh. Then the sound started to roll down the benches, and when it reached Alfie, he couldn't hold it in either. It was all so ridiculous, he didn't know what else to do.

"Drop some lines, Peño!" Jerome said.

Peño stood up, bobbing and using his right hand as if conducting his own performance. He freestyled another verse and finished with a dramatic point to the north wall. Alfie laughed, then realized it was the first time he had ever laughed inside of Fairwood. He had been playing here for nearly a year. This place had always been about pressure and cruel words and failure. Today, for once, it was about strength.

He sent his mother a text for a ride and waited on the bench, sneaking looks at Big John, who said very little and then left in silence. Alfie wondered if he was off to one of his jobs.

After a few minutes, Alfie zipped up his bag and went outside. On the way, he felt a stirring of pride. He had faced a tiger . . . and something he feared far more. And he had not backed down. Alfie thought of his father and wondered if he could find that same courage at home. As he walked out, Reggie fell into step beside him, slinging his bag over his shoulder.

"So, what do you think about our Wizenard now?" Reggie asked.

Alfie glanced at him. "I think I'm glad he's here."

A WINNING STRATEGY

What you see in the mirror
comes from the mind, not the body.

❖ WIZENARD ㊼ PROVERB ❖

THE MORNING WAS already scorching hot when Alfie stopped at the front doors of Fairwood. Summer in the Bottom was notoriously fickle—waves of dead, dry heat could be replaced by blankets of humidity within hours, and both could be chased away at any time by cold rainfalls rolling in from the east. Alfie would have loved some of that rain right now. Today seemed like it was a dead heat kind of day. He sighed and stared at the doors, where waves of heat were rolling off the dented metal. Then he frowned.

The doors had always been dilapidated: the moss-green paint was patchwork, the metal beneath marked with the residue of a hundred different government posters from back before they gave up promoting anything in the Bottom. But today the doors had been freshly painted a sharp emerald green, and when Alfie pulled them open, they didn't make their usual complaints.

He stepped inside, still wondering at the paint, and saw a castle.

It was a pyramid-like structure with high stone walls, open passageways at all four corners, and a towering pinnacle at its center, upon which stood a huge trophy. Every youth baller in Dren knew it well: the national championship trophy. Alfie stared at it longingly.

Then he noticed that no one else was in the gym. Not even Reggie. He frowned.

"Why do you play this game?"

Alfie jumped, dropping his duffel. He turned around and saw Rolabi leaning against the wall beside the door, his eyes fixed on the stone castle.

"Did you build that?" Alfie asked.

"In a sense," he replied easily. "Well?"

"I . . . well . . . I like it." Alfie paused. "I love it, actually."

"Why?" Rolabi asked, glancing at him. "Your teammates are often cruel to you. Your dad lectures you and makes you feel small. You don't sleep before games. You are afraid."

Alfie was about to ask him how he knew all that, and then he remembered that Rolabi did a lot of things that didn't make sense. He tried to think. Everything Rolabi had said was true enough. Yet Alfie really did love playing basketball. Why? What did he love? The answer appeared and surprised him.

"I guess I like being on a team. Even if they don't want me."

"And you believe that—that they don't want you here?"

"Yeah," Alfie muttered. "I kind of got that impression from day one."

"How many games have you missed?" he asked.

Alfie frowned. "None."

"Practices?"

"None," he said, not sure where Rolabi was going with this.

Rolabi laid a strong hand on his shoulder, calloused and rough yet gentle.

"They will need your courage on this road, Alfred Zetz," he said gravely.

"I don't have much courage . . ."

"I think you do."

Alfie heard movement and turned to see Reggie stretching by the bench. He glanced at Rolabi, who was staring at the castle again as if deep in thought. Sensing their talk was over, Alfie wandered over to join Reggie, still thinking about his answer. It really was the team that mattered to him most—he could sense the truth in that—but he didn't know why.

Because you have a lot to give, the voice said.

For some reason that brought a lump to Alfie's throat, but he pushed it down again.

"Hey, man," Reggie said. "What did you and Rolabi talk about?"

"I think it was about basketball."

Reggie laughed. "Yeah . . . same."

Alfie stared at the castle in wonder—ramps and ramparts and heavy stone. There were no scuff marks on the hardwood, no tools, nor any other signs of how the structure had been built.

"Yeah, not sure about that either," Reggie said, gesturing toward the towering stone structure.

"Gonna make a scrimmage kind of tough."

"There was a castle in that book," Reggie pointed out.

"I remember. I just didn't know he was going to bring it."

Reggie laughed and pulled his ankle up, stretching his quads.

"Last night, my gran asked how training has been going," he said.

"And?"

"I told her it's been a little weird."

"A pretty big understatement," Alfie said. "What did she say to that?"

"She said things are only ever weird because we don't understand them."

Alfie snorted and started to pull on his sneakers. "She sounds like a smart lady."

"She is, I guess. Maybe a bit optimistic."

"What do you mean?"

Reggie hesitated, and then shook his head. "Nothing."

"What is it?"

Reggie scratched the back of his arm—a habit Alfie knew well.

"She thinks I can play in the DBL. Says I've got the heart." Reggie sighed. "Kind of funny, since I don't even start on the Badgers. I told her I'm trying, but it ain't gonna happen."

"Who says?"

Reggie gestured around them. "Just being real. We're in the Bottom. It takes a special kind of talent to get out of here. Rain talent. You don't get to the DBL being a bench player."

His voice cracked at the end, and he looked away.

"I think you have the heart too, Reggie," Alfie said. "That counts for a whole lot."

Reggie glanced at him, and Alfie saw that his big, dark eyes were like glass.

"Thanks, Alfie," he said hoarsely.

And then he took off, running faster than any normal warm-up would call for.

Alfie began to stretch, watching as the team came in one by one. Even Peño and Lab arrived separately. Each player jumped when Rolabi spoke, talked to him briefly, and then wandered over to the bench with the same bewildered look Alfie figured he'd been wearing after Rolabi questioned him. When everyone had arrived, they gathered in front of the castle.

Twig eyed the ramps, wondering what the drill could possibly be.

"Today we are working on team defense," Rolabi said.

He unceremoniously flipped his bag over and dumped a pile of helmets and pads onto the floor: five red and five blue of each. Something in his bag squawked.

Rolabi closed the bag. "Take one of each, please," he said, gesturing to the heap of equipment. "Fasten the helmets tightly."

There seemed to be no talk of starters versus the bench, so Alfie grabbed a blue helmet and matching pad at random. Belatedly, he checked to see whose team he was on: Peño, Rain, Jerome, and Big John, who glared at him with distaste, if not quite hatred.

Great, Alfie thought. *My own teammates will probably knock me off the fortress when I'm not looking.*

"The game is simple," Rolabi said. "One team will attack, and the other will defend. The team to get the trophy in the least amount of time wins. The losing team will run laps while the winners shoot around. Blue team will defend first."

Unsurprisingly, Rain took the lead. He led the blue team up the closest ramp, and Alfie felt the walls on the way: they weren't stone at all. They were rubbery and firm, like the mats his father kept in the garage. His defensive pad covered the ramp opening almost to the inch, so there was no way to squeeze past it. It seemed like it should be easy to stop the attacking team.

When they had climbed the ramp, Rain gathered them into a huddle and assigned a man to each of the lower ramps, with himself as the floater. The idea was to simply call out if you were doubled.

"What happens if they start switching and I get Devon or something?" Peño asked.

Alfie was thinking the same thing. In fact, the more he thought about it, the trickier the game became. While there were five defenders and only four initial ramps, the other team got to choose *where* they attacked. How could the defense stop them from doubling or even tripling up?

"We got to talk," Rain said. "Make sure you call it out if someone is getting past you."

Everyone nodded, but something about the plan was still nagging Alfie.

"Let's rock it, boys!" Peño shouted.

It was too late to argue now. Alfie ran to one of the ramps and raised his pad like a closing drawbridge, shifting anxiously behind it. His chosen ramp was at the back, facing the bleachers, so he couldn't see the red team. Standing there waiting was giving him butterflies.

What if Devon came to his ramp? He would run right over Alfie.

"Begin," Rolabi said.

The word seemed to echo around Alfie, bouncing off floors and walls and reverberating through the castle. Then the scene changed.

Alfie stepped back in amazement as the hardwood floors caved into a ditch surrounding the castle. Dark, brackish water sprang out and filled the moat instantly. The floor on the far side then stretched into a narrow bridge that led directly to Alfie's ramp. The fortress walls turned into blocks of real stone, and even his T-shirt and shorts changed into a suit of shimmering armor with blue trim.

Oh man, Alfie thought, shifting nervously. *Please don't give Big John a sword.*

"Charge!" Lab shouted from somewhere unseen.

It didn't take long for him to spot the attackers coming for his ramp . . . Reggie *and* Lab. They charged across the narrow wooden bridge, their armored boots clanking on the wood.

"Help!" Twig shouted.

He was almost bowled over, but he spread his feet wide and held, straining against the joint attack. Reggie was pushing into Lab's back, driving him forward, and with their feet churning, the two boys started to push Alfie back. His feet slid steadily up the ramp.

He glanced behind him, alarmed. In seconds, they would be through.

Then Alfie felt someone slam into him from behind, stopping the slide. Rain had joined the fight.

Together they pushed forward, using the downhill slope to their advantage, driving the attackers back toward the bridge and the swampy moat. Reggie abruptly broke off, abandoning Lab and sprinting back across the bridge. Reggie turned, heading for another ramp.

"Keep pushing, Twig!" Rain said, taking off again.

Alfie set his legs and drove into Lab, trying to keep his feet from sliding.

"Give up, Twig!" Lab said through gritted teeth.

"You give up!"

It wasn't much of a comeback, but in fairness, Alfie was kind of preoccupied.

"You can't hold me, Stick Man," Lab said, pushing again.

Alfie reddened. He hated that name even more than Twig.

"I'm doing . . . fine . . ."

"You sound tired."

"Nope," Alfie replied, trying to keep his voice steady.

He readied himself for another push, when Lab turned and ran across the bridge toward a different ramp. Alfie spilled forward, landing on his own pad and sliding down the ramp like a toboggan. He groaned.

So much for his valiant defense.

"A-Wall just took off!" Big John shouted.

"So did Lab!" Alfie said, picking himself up.

"Help me!" Rain said.

Alfie hurried up the ramp. He was too late.

Rain and Jerome were both lying on the floor, dazed, and the five red players were hoisting the trophy. Alfie realized what had happened. They had simply overwhelmed one defender and smashed through the weak outer perimeter. That left Rain to attempt to block the final ramp alone, but he had no chance against the entire red team. The attackers used their advantage.

They could find the weakness.

"Don't worry," Rain said, climbing back to his feet. "We'll beat their time."

"One minute and forty-seven seconds," Rolabi said, his disembodied voice still strangely amplified. "Blue team, you will now attack. You have two minutes to prepare."

"Let's go," Rain muttered.

Alfie followed the dejected group over the moat. He thought he saw something green swimming in the water and quickly hurried to the other side, making a note to watch his step when he crossed again. He heard something fluttering and glanced back. He stopped, astounded.

It was indeed a true castle: stone and mortar and wood, topped with crimson flags that billowed in some imagined wind. It looked like a miniature version of the castle in the old book, the one they had called the Castle of Granity. He imagined himself as Pana, seeing the real thing for the first time as she wandered up the debris-strewn beach. He found he *wanted* to see it.

The blue team formed a huddle near the benches, and once again, Rain took the lead and laid out the same approach as the red team: double up on some ramps and overwhelm the defender. Alfie couldn't argue with the logic of that. There was no way to stop the attack—the defense was spread too thin. Obviously, the defenders were realizing the same thing. No one appeared at any of the openings. Alfie spotted someone's head on the second level. Maybe more.

What are they doing up there? he wondered.

"Begin," Rolabi said.

"They're not set up yet!" Rain said. "Follow me in!"

The blue team charged in a single-file line behind Rain. Peño shouted war cries and hooted as he ran. As they ran up the closest ramp, Alfie fell into the rear, wondering how the defenders could be so unprepared. And then he ran directly into Big John's armored back plate.

"Watch it!" Big John shouted.

"Sorry," Alfie said, peeking around the group. "What did we . . . Oh."

He immediately saw the problem. Devon was standing at the entrance of the final ramp, and the rest of the red team was lined up behind him, stacking their pads on one another's backs. Alfie realized the genius of their plan. The red team was blocking the only ramp that mattered.

Rain didn't seem as impressed. "Push!"

They attacked as one, driving forward, and Alfie felt his boots sliding on the stone. It felt like pushing against a wall. The red team had the higher ground . . . and Devon was holding them there. Getting past them would be impossible.

"Keep pushing!" Rain shouted.

A painful minute slipped by. Rain refused to admit defeat. It was admirable, but foolish.

They had been outsmarted.

Finally, Devon and the rest of the red team stepped forward as one and sent them all flying. Four players landed on top of Alfie in a downpour of elbows and knees. He groaned and crawled out from under the ragged pile. Big John's big butt had landed right on his chest.

"The time is beat," Rolabi said. "The red team wins. Blue team, laps."

Alfie sighed, and the blue team trudged back down the ramps like a captured regiment. He stripped off his helmet, tossed it aside with the others, and started to run. It felt like an hour went by at least, and then Alfie finally made a free throw to end the misery. It was a small consolation, since they got to watch the red team shoot around and play games the whole time.

Alfie grabbed his water bottle and took a drink, plunking himself onto the bench. His feet felt like lead weights, and he struggled to even draw them in. Rolabi walked over to the benches.

You knew the plan was flawed.

Alfie glanced at him. Rolabi was right. He had suspected . . .

You have too much to give to stay silent.

No one will listen to me—

Because they know you won't listen to yourself. Confront the hidden darkness.

Alfie frowned. Not because he was confused. Because he felt it. A cold spot.

The road is coming.

Rolabi walked over to the castle and plucked something round from one stone. It looked like a small cap. As soon as he did, the structure began to deflate. Alfie watched in disbelief as the whole castle shrank into a shriveled ball of rubber. Rolabi scooped it up and dropped it into his bag. Then he turned to the team, eyes flashing.

"What must a defender always be?" Rolabi asked.

"*Ready*," Reggie said.

"The same goes for the entire team. If you are not ready, we are wasting our time."

With that, he abruptly started for the doors, not sparing them another glance.

"Are we done for today?" Peño asked.

"That is up to you."

The doors burst open, and Rolabi disappeared into the morning. Sunlight poured in for just a moment and then was wiped out by the doors. Alfie felt a familiar, unpleasant chill on his arms.

He looked up and froze. The orb had returned.

It was floating over center court like a miniature black hole, wobbling and wavering and unstable. Alfie couldn't look away. Like a real black hole, the orb seemed to be inexorably drawing him in.

Alfie took off, running for the orb like he was in the hundred-meter dash. He had just about grabbed it when the orb zoomed out of reach, and the rest of the team joined the chase. Once again, everything descended into chaos as the players scrambled and shouted and laughed. Rain ended up on the ground, Peño and Lab collided, and Big John tripped. The orb was too cunning.

It finally flew into a wall and vanished, and Alfie slumped, disappointed.

"Still up for that scrimmage?" Peño asked.

"Nah," Rain said grumpily. "Let's just get out of here."

No one argued. Alfie sat down and slipped off his shoes, wrinkling his nose at the sour smell. His mom was going to spray his bag with lavender again. He made a mental note to sit as far as possible from Big John tomorrow. He had an excellent nose when it came to lavender.

Alfie sighed, put his shoes away, and took out his cell phone to text his mom for a ride.

"A waste of time?" Reggie asked loudly. "Why?"

Alfie looked over, frowning. Reggie almost never raised his voice.

"Because he lost," A-Wall said.

"Who cares!" Rain snarled. "What did that game have to do with basketball?"

"Everything," Reggie replied. "It was about playing defense the right way. As a team."

Rain sprang to his feet. "It was a stupid game. You play D by stopping the ball. And you *win* by scoring. By *me* scoring. And we aren't getting any closer to winning by me not working on my shot. This is a big year for me."

"You mean for *us*," Lab said, sounding a little hurt.

"Yeah," Rain said. "Rain Adams and the West Bottom Badgers."

He stormed out, slamming the doors, and the rest of the team fell into a moody silence. Alfie was stunned. Rain rarely lost his cool. Alfie looked at Reggie, making sure he was okay, but he was just shaking his head. Alfie glanced at the doors again. Why was Rain so upset over a drill?

The team began to file out, and Reggie walked over to Alfie and extended a fist for props.

"See you tomorrow, Twig," he said.

Alfie met his fist, smiling. No one had ever given him props before.

"Yeah," he said. "Thanks."

"I guess you don't need heart to be the number one prospect, after all," Reggie said.

Alfie shrugged. "Maybe not. I bet you need it to be *more* than a prospect, though."

Reggie looked at him for a moment and then headed for the door, laughing.

"Twig the Sage."

Jerome and Big John were the last to leave. But just as they were walking for the exit, Big John hung back, letting Jerome go ahead. Alfie felt his heart pounding. He had never been alone with Big John. He grabbed his duffel bag and started for the door.

He was halfway there when Big John approached him.

"So you still think you starting, huh?" he said.

Alfie froze. Should he just run? No. That was the old Alfie. He turned to face Big John. "I don't know."

Big John walked toward him, eyes narrowed. "And you think you deserve that? To start over me? In this place? In the Bottom?"

"I don't know."

Big John stopped in front of him, eyeing him up and down, *measuring* him.

"That's your problem," he said. "You don't know anything."

"Why do you keep going after me?" Alfie asked. "You know it's not my choice whether I start or not."

"Because you don't belong here. You ain't a real Bottom kid."

Alfie had rehearsed this conversation a million times since yesterday. He wanted to connect with him. He wanted Big John to know that he was just here to play ball the same as him.

"I live in the Bottom too—" Alfie started.

"The burbs," Big John cut in. "The nice parts. The rich boy part. And here you are taking more stuff away. You know where I live, Twig? In the *real* Bottom."

Big John stepped so close that Alfie could feel his breath on his face.

"I got nothing there, man. Nothing. Just ball to get me out. And you came to take it."

"I came to play basketball," Alfie said. "I don't want to take anything."

"But you are. And until you prove you deserve to be here, you don't."

"Then I'll prove it," Alfie said quietly, holding Big John's eyes.

Big John seemed to reconsider him. He opened his mouth, closed it, then snorted.

"We'll see. Go put some meat on those bones, boy. You ain't doing nothing as a twig."

The doors slammed behind him, and the words stayed. Alfie suddenly felt tired. Weak. His courage was a distant dream. It had taken everything he had not to back away from Big John.

I thought I was getting stronger, he thought glumly. *I'm not. I'm just pretending.*

He started for the doors. His father would remind him of the same thing later.

He always did.

In a flash, the doors moved upward, out of Alfie's reach. The floor sloped and became pockmarked with hundreds of shallow grooves. Alfie yelped and threw himself down as the whole gym teetered and rotated, as though a giant had picked up the building and turned it on its side. Alfie started sliding and just managed to grab on to two of the handholds, clinging there.

The floor had become a cliffside.

"Help me!" he shouted. "Someone, help! Big John! Rolabi!"

There was no answer. Alfie clung to the floor and stared up at the door, which still stood upright, as if perched on the edge of the cliff. Then he glanced over his shoulder. The ground below was a hundred feet away, and solid brick. His eyes filled with tears, streaming down, clogging his throat.

"Please!" he screamed. "Somebody."

He clung there desperately. Seconds ticked by. His fingers began to ache and burn.

"Anyone!" he cried.

He knew he couldn't hold himself up for much longer. No one was coming. Just the fall.

He pressed his forehead to the hardwood. He had to get up there. He had to try. He swung his feet around until he found small grooves for his toes. And then he started to climb.

The grooves were loosely spread and shallow, so he had to stretch and grip with every ounce of strength he had. His muscles raged. His fingers shrieked. But he had no choice but to go on, and so he kept climbing. When he finally reached up and touched the doors, the gym straightened, and he found himself lying face-first on the ground. His whole body was throbbing, stretched, worn.

We are climbing every minute of the day. How can we be weak?

Alfie lay there, his cheek pressed against the floorboards, soaked with sweat and tears and snot and unable to even lift a finger. He smiled. For the first time in his life, he felt strong.

6

SOMETHING TO SAY

Even the loudest voices cannot fell a tree.
WIZENARD ⟨24⟩ PROVERB

ALFIE STARED AT the bathroom mirror—his reflection cracked and marked with stains. His face was gaunt and sallow as ever. Angry zits dotted his cheeks. He ran his fingers over them, considering.

He'd left the gym last night feeling strong, but it hadn't lasted. His father had made him walk through his "hall of accomplishments"—a room in their basement filled with trophies, ribbons, and medals. He had been a collegiate ball player and had lots of success, but he had never made it further. It was bad coaching. Bad teammates. Bad anybody but Alfie's dad.

His fingers fell on a zit, nail waiting above it. He wanted to pick. Not just to get rid of the zit. To get rid of something. To stare at his reflection and scream: "I am in control." He tried to fight it. Willed himself to stop. But the weakness was there. He reached for his cheeks.

He stopped as words began to appear in the mirror, written this time with silvery ink.

*Self control begins with
small difficult steps*

Alfie stared at the words and lowered his hand. Then he nodded and walked out.

He realized to his surprise that Rain was sitting on the away bench. Alfie sat down on the far end, watching Rain take out his shoes. Rain stared at something inside his bag for a moment, and his expression became . . . sad. Even guilty. Alfie wondered what was in the bag.

"How you feeling today?" he asked.

Rain turned to him, raising his eyebrows. "Fine. You?"

"Nervous, I guess. It's been a little crazy. Don't know what to expect."

Rain started to laugh. "Yeah . . . it's been crazy, all right. Since when do you talk?"

"I always talked," Alfie said defensively. "Just nobody wants to listen."

Rain seemed to consider that. "So why aren't you avoiding me like the rest of the team?"

Alfie stood up and stretched, glancing over at the others. "I don't think they're avoiding you. You got upset yesterday. That's all right. We all do sometimes. I do, well . . . a lot of times."

"I basically said I was the team."

Alfie grabbed his ball. "Who can blame you? It's what you've been told."

He started onto the court, taking an experimental dribble through his legs. He didn't dribble much during games—Freddy yelled at him whenever he tried. No threes! No dribbling!

His job was just to stand by the net and get rebounds. It always felt a bit . . . stifling.

He put up a three-pointer and hit it, smiling despite himself.

"So there, Freddy," he muttered.

"Gather around," a deep voice said. "Put the balls away."

Alfie glanced at the clock. Nine already. Rolabi had appeared.

Alfie and Rain joined the others, and he noticed a lot of dark looks directed at Rain. Strangely, Alfie felt defensive. Rain wasn't so bad. He was cocky, to be sure, but Alfie could use a little more of that himself. Alfie wondered if they could even become friends, given Rain's newfound lack of options. He found himself standing closer to Rain in a show of support.

"Today we are going to work on offense," Rolabi said. "We'll start with passing: the foundation of all offense. What do all the great passers have?"

Alfie had no idea. He considered himself a pretty good passer, but he wasn't sure what made him one. He just threw the ball where it needed to go and never really thought about it. It was likely part of his not wanting to shoot and get lectured—he was a pass-first kind of player.

"Vision," Peño said.

"Very good. A great passer must be quick and agile and bold. But mostly, they must have vision. Both of what is and what will soon come. They must see *everything* on the floor."

Lab looked confused. "So, we just have to practice seeing more?"

"Yes," Rolabi said. "And the best way to start is by seeing nothing at all."

It suddenly went dark. Not just nighttime dark, when streetlights and the moon turned the streets of Alfie's neighborhood to sullen shades of gray. This blackness was complete, as though there had never been light before and never would be again. Full. Close. Almost heavy. Alfie felt a tingle run down his neck and spun around warily.

In the dark, we only have our fears.

Alfie flinched. *I've never seen darkness like this*, he thought.

Then this is a good place to start.

Alfie tried to stay calm. He heard breathing and shuffling and whispered conversations as the others argued and panicked. They were still in the gym. Nothing had changed. But he was uneasy. He felt like someone was creeping up on him and he'd be attacked. Every muscle was tense.

If you feel like this in the dark, you feel it in the light too. You have buried the unease.

Suddenly the darkness diminished, interrupted by an orange, flickering light. Alfie stood in a long corridor of rough concrete and arched stone, the walls inset with countless black steel doors. The orange light came from the ends of the corridor, behind and in front of Alfie, but he couldn't see the source. He whirled around, his heart pounding.

"Professor Rolabi?" he called.

His voice echoed in either direction. Both paths were identical. Endless corridor and countless doors. The doors were unmarked and black as night, each with a simple ebony door handle. Alfie chose a direction and started walking, then running, then sprinting until he was dripping sweat.

He stopped, bent over, gasping.

"Risks are frightening things," a deep voice said.

Alfie looked up and saw Rolabi standing in front of him, his head brushing the ceiling.

"Where am I?" Alfie asked.

"So many doors, yet you didn't try a single one. Why?"

Alfie stood up, hand grasping at a cramp in his side. "Well, I don't know what's behind them."

"Exactly," Rolabi said. "When we fear the unknown, we avoid it. We let our fears define the possibilities around us. We imagine that this one leads to failure. Here loneliness. Here heartbreak. The world becomes cruel."

Alfie frowned, turning to the closest door. Unmarked. Ominous.

"Go on," Rolabi said. "Release another tiger."

In one motion, Alfie pulled open the door and stepped inside. The space surrounding him was black, but he smelled must and rot and heard his teammates shuffling around and, over that, Rolabi's deep voice explaining the drill.

Don't assume that darkness contains danger.

Alfie thought about that. About waiting for Big John to taunt him. Or for his dad to lecture him. For acne to form. For himself to pick. He was always waiting for something bad.

In a sense, he was always in the dark. How would he get out of it?

Open doors.

"We will go until one team wins," Rolabi said. "The losing team will run."

"You really like making us run," Big John complained.

"Never underestimate the value of sweat. It can forge the greatest change."

Alfie perked up at that. He had been thinking about the mystery of the disappearing sweat for two days now and about the image he had seen of the silvery beating heart. Was Fairwood somehow collecting their sweat? If so, gross. And more important . . . why?

"Starters versus last year's bench," Rolabi said. "Starters will go first. Find the ball."

That proved to be a challenge. Alfie walked around like a zombie with his arms in front of him, jerking every time he felt a wall or bleachers or another wandering player. Eventually, he kicked something, jumped about a foot in the air, and then listened to the ball bounce away.

"There it is! I just kicked it!" he shouted.

"I'm on it!" Lab said, followed by a flurry of activity. "Got it!"

"Now into position," Rolabi said. "Line up beneath the net."

That took another few minutes. Alfie heard the defenders getting into position at half. Everyone was talking and grumbling and thoroughly disoriented in the pitch-blackness. He sensed this was going to be a complete disaster. He felt around him and touched a shoulder.

"Who's touching me!" A-Wall shouted. "Stay away, ghost!"

Alfie almost apologized, but then leaned closer. "Boo!"

"Ah!" A-Wall shouted, and Alfie had to stifle a laugh.

"Okay, I'm going!" Peño said, though where he was moving, Alfie had no idea.

It was indeed a disaster. Not only did his team lose the ball, but Alfie ran straight into a very broad chest and ended up on his butt for the second time in three days. Fresh pain shot through his tailbone, which was still sore from his last unplanned trip to the floor. He rolled and groaned.

"Sorry," Devon said.

"No problem," Alfie wheezed, slowly climbing back up.

"Switch," Rolabi said.

The bench didn't make it to half.

"Hmm," Rolabi said. "Perhaps we will work up to complete darkness."

Out of nowhere, a glowing scarlet orb appeared, floating about six feet up in the air—or perhaps sitting on the bleachers. Someone picked it up, and the shape went bobbing off through the darkness.

The glowing helped. Alfie managed to catch the ball on the first try when it came to him, and he made a pass to Lab. But when they reached half-court and the other team, play broke down again. It was impossible to find his teammates, and he lobbed the ball right into the triumphant hands of Jerome—which he knew only because Jerome shouted: "Stolen!"

"Switch sides," Rolabi said.

Neither the bench nor the starters could get past the defenders. Alfie had tripped three times already, but he was getting better. His other senses had adapted somewhat, and he found he could focus on his teammates' individual voices and breathing. Everyone had their own tune: a mix of squeaks and huffs and short gasps of breath. It was the world's strangest orchestra.

Finally, Peño managed to break through and catch the ball on the far end. The fluorescent lights blinked back on, forcing Twig to squint and shield his eyes.

"The starting team wins," Rolabi announced. "Water break."

"That's it, boys!" Peño said.

He walked over and surprised Alfie with a high five.

"Thanks," Alfie said, flushing.

Rain was already heading for the away bench, and Alfie could tell that he was feeling lonely. Alfie knew all about that. He joined him and took a drink, finishing the bottle at once.

"That was crazy," he said, wiping his chin.

"Yeah," Rain replied. "Though compared to the tiger, it was nothing."

"True."

"The losing team will run at the end of practice," Rolabi said. "The winning team can decide then if they want to join them."

Alfie glanced over at the bench players. He knew what Rolabi was doing: giving the starters a chance to show some sportsmanship and build some team morale. Specifically Rain. But judging from the surly look on Rain's face, he wasn't going to take the opportunity.

"So, clearly, on offense we must learn to listen," Rolabi continued. "What else?"

"Score?" Rain said.

"Yes, eventually," Rolabi agreed. "But more fundamentally."

Alfie thought about the purpose of the drill. "Talk?"

"Exactly. We talk on defense but forget to do it on offense. Twig, come here, please."

Alfie felt his stomach drop. Why did he have to say anything? He put his water bottle down and shuffled over to Rolabi, feeling the eyes of the team on him, including Big John's glare.

"I want you to tell the team one thing you would like to say to them. One *honest* thing."

Alfie looked up at Rolabi. He had never been put on the spot like this at practice. "What sort of thing?"

"It could be anything. If you cannot be honest with each other, you cannot be a team."

Alfie looked away, biting his lip. He had a lot to say to them, of course. He wanted to tell them he didn't buy his way onto the team and that he didn't sleep some nights because he was so nervous about coming here.

He wanted to tell them that every time he walked into Fairwood last season his stomach was wound like a coil, and he felt like he might throw up. He wanted to say he was trying his best. But he couldn't say those things. Not to them.

"Umm . . . well . . . I don't have anything."

Courage requires vulnerability. Open a door.

"Yes, you do," Rolabi said. "I am sure you have many things. Just pick one for starters."

"But . . ." Alfie said, fidgeting.

Let them inside.

Alfie took a deep breath and decided to just say the first thing that came to mind.

"Okay, well, I have been working really hard," he said, trying not to scratch his arm. "In the off-season, I mean. And I am trying really hard to be better. I know maybe you guys didn't want me back this season, but I really am trying to help the team. I want you guys to know that."

He hurried back to the bench, not making eye contact with his teammates. He was sure someone would laugh or make a joke, especially Big John, but no one did. The gym was silent.

"Jerome," Rolabi said.

Jerome strolled up and pivoted: "I'd like to try and start some games this year."

A lot of them were like that—game-related—but a few stood out to Alfie.

Big John said, "I'm going to start this year and crush it."

He looked right at Alfie when he said it.

A-Wall's was promising: "I'm going to try and get kicked out of less games this year."

But most notable to Alfie was Reggie's: "I want to make some people proud, I guess. People who aren't here anymore, but who might be watching. And I'm working hard, even if I don't play that much. It's kind of stupid, I know, but well, I'd like to play ball for a living. You know?" He shifted uneasily, his cheeks flushing. "It's a pipe dream, but that's what I want."

Alfie smiled at him as he walked back to the bench.

Rain went last and apologized, and after a bit of a heated discussion, it seemed like everybody was fine again. He melded back into the group almost immediately, exchanging props with Peño, and Alfie was forgotten again on the outskirts. He smiled sadly. He'd kind of felt like he was becoming friends with Rain, if only for a day. Clearly it wasn't meant to last.

"Let's scrimmage for an hour," Rolabi said.

"No tricks?" Peño asked suspiciously.

"Just working on our vision. Rain, Vin, Lab, A-Wall, and Devon versus the rest."

It was an odd mix, and unfortunately it meant that Alfie was playing with Big John and *against* Rain. Worse still, he had to match up against Devon. He was going to be outmuscled for every rebound. Twig wondered if this was the new starting lineup, and if he had been removed, as he'd expected, or was close to being cut. He glanced at Rolabi, but the professor was facing the court.

Alfie pictured his father's reaction and shuddered.

"You didn't put on enough muscle!" he would shout. "I'll make you a shake."

He could almost taste the chalk on his lips.

"We focus on one actor and miss the others in the background," Rolabi said, holding out a ball. "We watch one card as the dealer palms a second. We watch the ball but miss the game."

Alfie faced Devon, sighing inwardly. This was going to hurt.

"We can see so much, and yet we choose not to," Rolabi mused. "It is an odd decision."

The words were barely out of his mouth when Alfie went blind again. No, not blind. There was something blocking *most* of his vision, but not the periphery. It was as if his fingers were laid across his eyes, and his eyes were forced to choose one side or the other. He heard the other players crying out in alarm and saw them rubbing their eyes and spinning around. They looked like little kids purposefully making themselves dizzy. Alfie tried to stay calm. It was a test, and spinning wasn't going to help.

He had two slivers of vision, and he had to use them.

You are becoming a master of fears. But when will you face your deepest?

Alfie felt the cold again. The darkness.

"Ready to play?" Rolabi asked.

"I can't see my nose," A-Wall said.

"That's your concern?" Vin muttered.

Alfie caught a flash of orange as Rolabi tossed the ball up. He leapt for it, waving his hands, but caught only air. He lost his footing and landed in an awkward crouch, swiping again for the ball when he heard it bounce off a shoe. Devon grunted as Alfie smacked him in the leg.

"Please don't hurt me," Alfie said, trying to get back up.

He turned, trying to spot the ball with his peripheral vision, and caught a glimpse of Vin scooping it up. Alfie realized he had to get back on defense. He slowly made his way down the court, sweeping his head back and forth to try to figure out where he was going. He saw Devon heading for the block and followed him. In a strange way, Alfie was far more aware of the players *around* him, mostly because he couldn't focus on where he was going. Finally, he stepped behind Devon, planting a tepid hand on his back to keep track of him.

"Is this okay?" he asked.

"Fine," Devon said. "I don't think you have to ask."

"Just being polite."

There was sudden shouting, and Alfie turned and saw Rain driving right for him. Alfie instinctively stepped into the lane to block him, and then Rain did something very unexpected: he *passed*. The ball sailed out to Lab in the corner. Lab took his time and drained a three.

Alfie spun around, looking for the ball.

"Let's get it back!" Peño said. "Twig, where you at? Throw me the ball!"

Alfie spotted the ball and inbounded it. He ran up the floor as fast as possible and tried to get open. Everyone was talking and shouting orders. Slowly a picture of the game was revealed.

It was like building a mental puzzle:

"Jerome is going left."

"I'm at the top of the key!"

"Rain just cut!"

Each piece was filed in Alfie's brain and then organized into a picture, one that he added to with his own flashes of vision. He slowed down and waited to act. He moved the picture along.

When the ball came to Alfie, he knew Reggie was on the right wing because Rain had called it. He knew that Peño was cutting and that Big John was trying to get open for a pass behind him. Everyone was moving much slower than usual—they had no choice. Alfie passed the ball to Reggie and ran to the other block, listening for clues. He had never focused on voices so attentively before—it seemed unnecessary when he could look. But there was another game in the words. Intentions were revealed. Strategies were made. Trouble was foreshadowed.

The ball reset to the point, and Big John lumbered to the top of the key for a screen. The play was moving so slowly. Alfie always felt a step behind in real games. Everything became a whir of motion, and he was breathing hard, and he felt like he couldn't do anything in the chaos.

Now it seemed like he just had to stop and *think*.

The next choice was easy. He set a screen on the wing for Jerome, and

Jerome rubbed off his shoulder and cut to the net. Peño went by his man and got the ball to Jerome, who laid it in.

"All day, baby!" Jerome said. "Nice screen, Twig! That's what I'm talking about."

Alfie grinned. Freddy always told him to stay on the block and be ready for rebounds. But it didn't make sense now. He had to follow the flow of the game. He had to predict it.

And that's how the scrimmage went. Everyone checked where they were going and checked again. Alfie did things on instinct: he knew Big John would set a screen, or that Jerome would drive and that he should therefore cut for the pass. When he caught the ball, he didn't immediately think about the safest way to get *rid* of it. He surveyed his options—both the ones he could see and the ones he heard. He remembered where his teammates had been running.

The game was 360 degrees. He had been playing with half that.

At one point, he pivoted and made a wide-open layup . . . and the blockage in his vision disappeared. His vision cleared again the next time he was open too, and he scored again. But for contested shots, bad shots, and bad angles, the blockage remained.

They played until they were drenched with sweat. Alfie had no idea how long it had been, and he didn't care. For once, he felt like he was playing on an actual *team*.

"That will do," Rolabi said. "Grab your bottles and join me in the center."

Alfie's vision returned to normal, and he couldn't help but smile. He had always thought that basketball was only about strength and athleticism and talent. But now he realized that understanding what was happening was more important than he thought. There was a mental chess game happening that he hadn't even noticed. Rolabi said they needed to slow down time.

It had seemed like a meaningless cliché. Now Alfie wasn't so sure.

"Who won?" Peño asked as they gathered in front of the professor. "I kind of lost track."

"Neither," Rolabi said. "And both. Was that how you normally play?"

"Of course not," Lab said. "We were moving in slow motion."

"Speed is relative. To the fastest, everyone moves in slow motion. What else?"

"We . . . we talked a lot. More than ever," Twig said.

Including me, he realized. He had been talking the whole time and hadn't even really thought about it. He almost never talked during games. But for this drill, he'd had no choice.

Rolabi nodded. "True. Anything else?"

"We spread the floor on offense," Peño said, stroking his wispy mustache. "More passes around the lane. Kick outs and stuff."

"A natural choice when one cannot see his own path," Rolabi agreed. "And lastly?"

"We had to think about where everyone should be," Rain said. "We had to predict the game."

"Indeed. We had to see more than our eyes allow. Now, I am owed some laps."

The bench team took off around the gym, and Alfie glanced at Rain, wondering if he would take his chance to prove he was a good teammate . . . but he didn't. Alfie wanted to join them, he felt that he should, but he didn't want to go alone. He just watched them run, dejected.

He really was a coward.

Thankfully, Reggie hit a free throw after just five laps, and they returned.

Rolabi took out the potted daisy and set it down.

"Not again," Peño muttered.

"Many times more," Rolabi said. "If you wish to win, you *must* slow down time. Begin."

He abruptly headed for the doors, bag in hand.

"You will take the daisy home tonight, Peño. Be careful with it, please. Water it."

Peño looked at the little flower like it might eat him in his sleep. As Rolabi walked toward the doors, they burst open, flooding the room with a frigid gust of alpine wind. And salt, Alfie realized. He could taste it on his lips. Alfie exchanged a knowing look with Reggie.

It smelled like a mountain by the sea. So that was where Rolabi was going.

Home.

"How long do you want us to stare at it?" Rain said.

Rolabi didn't look back. "Until you see something new."

The doors crashed shut, and Alfie shivered as the last of the wind receded. The others broke into conversation, and Alfie and Reggie plopped down next to the potted daisy.

"I don't think I'll ever get used to that," Reggie murmured.

"Do you think . . . he's going there?" Alfie said.

"If he is, I want to go with him."

Alfie laughed. "Same."

Peño's voice cut through their conversation. "Everything all right with you?" he called to someone.

Alfie turned and saw that Big John was already heading for the exit. He turned and sneered at Peño.

"No, Peño. This is the Bottom. Things aren't just *all right*. You can go along with that weirdo all you want and play his games. But it's not a game out there. Remember where you are."

Big John stared right at Alfie, his lip curling in derision.

"I'm gonna grab some extra time at *work*."

The doors slammed shut, and it fell silent. Alfie felt a weight settle into his stomach.

And then the players all started to walk away.

Rain, Vin, Lab, Jerome, A-Wall, and Peño grabbed their balls and went to shoot around. Normally, Alfie would have followed them. But not this time. Alfie finally understood the flower.

He had been missing the details. The way the petals curled gently downward at the tips. The haze of yellow emanating from the brightly colored center. When Alfie failed to slow down and make careful note of every part of the flower, he missed the bigger picture.

So he sat there with Reggie, and Devon remained as well. The three of them fell into a comfortable silence. Alfie could hear balls bouncing, the clank of the rim, shouts and laughs, but he let the sounds blur together in the background. He didn't see the flower grow, of course, but that didn't really matter. The daisy held his focus.

And now the roots spread.

Alfie had completely lost track of time when a flicker of movement caught his eye. He looked up. The orb had returned, and it was sitting right over Devon's head. The gym fell silent.

Devon remained perfectly still—not even glancing up.

Alfie wanted to say something, but he was afraid he might scare it off. Then, without warning, Devon grabbed it, grinning as the black liquid seeped between his fingers like tar.

Then he vanished. Alfie rocked backward, stunned, and the gym erupted with noise.

"I told you this would happen!" Lab shouted.

"Call the police!" someone said.

Alfie just sat there, staring at the now-empty spot.

Reggie leaned closer. "You saw that, right?"

"Yeah."

"What am I supposed to tell the cops?" Vin said. "My teammate vanished into thin air?"

Amid the shouting and exodus toward the benches, Twig and Reggie stayed put.

"You think he went to the island too?" Reggie asked.

"Maybe," Twig said. "But that thing seemed . . . bad. I don't think it would lead there."

"I hope he's okay."

"Yeah," Twig said. "Me too."

There was a pop, and Devon reappeared, standing upright at center court. His eyes were glassy, but he seemed fine otherwise. He grabbed his bag, slung it over his shoulder, and left without a word. Everyone watched, apparently too stunned to ask him questions, and then filed out after him, muttering and uneasy.

Peño hurried over and scooped up the daisy, grimaced at it, and left.

"Another fun day at training camp," he called over his shoulder.

Alfie and Reggie were alone now, and they climbed to their feet.

"That was weird," Reggie said finally.

"Yeah."

Reggie paused. "If the orb comes back tomorrow, you gonna try and get it?"

Alfie didn't hesitate. "Yeah."

"Same," Reggie said, laughing.

They went to change their shoes, plunking down onto the away bench. They both sat there in socked feet, staring out at the old hardwood and silent gym. It occurred to Alfie that no one was locking the place after practice. He wondered if it stayed open all night.

"Can I ask you something?" Reggie said.

Reggie was quiet for a moment, shifting, and then he glanced over.

"The other day, when I asked you about your cheeks. Were you angry at me?"

Alfie felt heat rise to his face. "No . . . of course not."

"I felt bad all night. I didn't mean to get personal—"

"I shouldn't have snapped like that," Alfie cut in. "It's . . . tough to talk about."

"I just wanted to make sure you were cool."

Alfie folded his hands in his lap, thinking. No one knew about the skin picking but his parents. His mom tried to talk to him about it, but his dad didn't get it. He said men didn't care about acne. He just told him to stop. To *toughen up.* Somehow that never seemed to help with anything. But Reggie had told Alfie a secret. He had trusted him. Maybe Alfie could trust him back.

"I . . . uh . . . did that to myself," he murmured.

"Oh," Reggie said. "But . . . why? When?"

Alfie took a deep breath. Those were good questions. He asked them himself all the time.

"I don't know when it started," he said. "It just kind of happened. I picked at my acne, and got rid of it, and even though it was bad, I kept doing it. It made me feel better, somehow."

"That's how you got the scars?"

"Yeah." Alfie looked away, embarrassed. "I don't know why I do it. I guess . . . I'm sick."

"Did you tell your parents?"

"They found me doing it one night. My dad told me that men didn't do that stuff."

"I've seen him at the games," Reggie said carefully. "He seems a little intense."

Alfie snorted. "That's an understatement. He wants me to be better. Stronger and stuff."

Reggie nodded and looked down at his hands. They twisted in his lap, fidgeting.

"I had some issues when my parents passed away. Well . . . I still do. Don't sleep much. Can't relax at night, you know? I get . . . sick a lot too. I think I do it to myself. Like I think so much about them and I get sad again and it turns my stomach. I end up throwing up."

"Why do you do it to yourself?" Twig asked.

"To feel pain . . . or suffer . . . I don't know. Maybe to make the outside feel like the inside."

He sighed and glanced at Alfie.

"Maybe we both feel like we deserve to be hurting, you know?"

Alfie ran his fingers over his cheeks. Felt the divots. The scars.

"You don't deserve it," he said.

"Neither do you," Reggie said. "Maybe we can remind each other of that sometimes."

Alfie felt a weight slip off his shoulders he didn't even know was there. "Deal."

They exchanged props, and Alfie smiled as he pulled on his shoes. He thought about his father, and Big John, and all the kids who had called him weak. He thought about his own internal voice, saying the same thing, telling him he would never be strong. His own voice was the worst. And maybe he had been listening to all of them for too long.

7

THE DARK ROOM

Never let your identity be written by another.
✦ WIZENARD ⑤ PROVERB ✦

ALFIE WAS BACK in the locker room. He liked it there now. It had been thoroughly cleaned in the last few days—who had done it, Alfie had no idea. The room was quiet, and it was *his* place, since all the others still got changed on the benches out of habit. He was thinking about the future. He did that a lot.

He usually thought about his dad. His dad said he wanted his son to surpass him, but Alfie thought he wanted another shot . . . through Alfie, maybe, but really for himself. Sometimes his dad stood alone in the basement for hours and stared at the old trophies and dusted them even though he never dusted anything else. He'd had so much success in high school, and it wasn't enough for him.

Alfie was afraid that he couldn't even get to that level. It often kept him up at night. It turned his stomach at dinner. His father was always there, hounding, criticizing, *pushing* him.

Alfie sighed and leaned against the brick wall, feeling the comforting warmth against his back. He realized he hadn't really been thinking about the future. He was thinking about failure.

That was what was behind all those doors—in his mind, anyway. Different ways to fail.

As Alfie zipped his bag up and headed for the door, a flash of movement caught his eye. He froze. The orb was back. And this time, it had come just for him. He knew that down in his bones.

He slowly turned and faced it.

The orb was floating in the corner of the locker room at about eye level. Alfie let his duffel bag fall to the floor. The orb didn't move. Neither did he. He took a deep, calming breath.

And then he made his move.

Alfie lunged straight at the orb and missed. He spun and chased it around the room, running and jumping and reaching wildly. He stepped off the bench that wrapped around the room and flung himself upward, trying to swoop down on top of it like an eagle. But the orb flitted around, always out of reach, taunting him. Alfie narrowed his eyes and kept chasing.

Soon sweat was snaking between his eyes. He was preparing to charge again when he thought back to yesterday. To the lack of vision. More so, to the way things had *slowed down.*

Buy yourself time.

He thought of the flower and took a deep breath, letting out some of the tension in his muscles. The orb shifted like a suspended raindrop. When Alfie moved again, he didn't rush. He thought about what the orb would do next, and how he would respond, and how it would play out. The orb avoided him, but he didn't put all his effort into a blind chase. He watched where it went, and slowly, meticulously, he discovered a pattern. If he charged, the orb dodged left, then left, then right. Left, left, right.

Left, left, right.

Alfie grinned. It had just gone right.

He charged, faking right, but shot his hand out to the left at the same time. The orb zoomed into his outstretched fingers, and the locker room turned to black.

Alfie was standing on a smooth concrete floor that stretched out into shadow all around him. There were no walls, no ceiling. Just floor and space and a chill that stuck in his lungs and crawled along his skin with probing, icy fingers. Where was he? Why was he here?

There were no doors. No corridor. This place felt deeper than that.

Alfie turned and found himself looking at a mirror. His reflection stared back at him: gangly and pale, with fiery red spots on his cheeks and a quivering bottom lip. His waxy hair was plastered to his forehead, making him look sickly. His shoulders were slumped and bent, his posture defeated. Words spontaneously looped across the mirror in silver ink:

Alfie's reflection began to scream the words at him.

He covered his ears on instinct, but he couldn't turn away. He was fixated on the mirror.

His reflection changed again. His body filled out with muscle and fat. His cheeks cleared and hardened. He grew facial hair and hard, dark eyes. This wasn't Alfie anymore. It was his father.

His face was lined with something Alfie recognized all too well: disappointment. He was always wearing it. It was in the eyes mostly, but also the hard line of his stubbled upper lip, the folded arms, the tilted head. The cool words in his throat. All of it ready to tell him he was *weak*.

"I'm trying," Alfie said, feeling himself shrink down before his father. "I'm trying."

"It was a powerful image for you. The mirror. I wondered why."

Alfie spun around. Rolabi was standing beside him.

"I don't like mirrors," Alfie said quietly.

"Why?"

Alfie turned back to the image of his father. He was still there but blurring, as if rain were running down the glass. Alfie realized his eyes were watering. He didn't even know when they had started.

"Because I don't like myself," he said.

"How strange not to like ourselves. We're the only person we've ever truly known."

Alfie frowned. "I can see other people. It's obvious how I compare. I'm a loser. I know you or the gym or the grana or whatever has been trying to help me, and I've had moments of feeling stronger. But it's a lost cause. Look at me. I'm still weak."

"You live in a world framed within your mind. You are the master of your perception."

"What is that supposed to mean?" Alfie asked, louder than he intended.

"It means you have decided you are a loser. You can change your mind."

Alfie gestured to the mirror, where his father's face was still barely visible. "It doesn't matter. I'm not like him."

"We are standing inside your fears. Is that your fear—that you won't be like him?"

"Of course," Alfie said. "I don't want to let him down."

"Look closer."

Alfie stared at the reflection, and as he did, the reflection began to shift again. His father's short hair grew longer and thinner, and his dark eyes softened. The belly melted away with the muscle, and his cheekbones morphed into ridges. Alfie took a step back. He was looking at himself, but the same age as his father. He looked *disappointed*. Alfie stared at himself, horrified and transfixed.

"Is—is that me?" he whispered.

"If you continue the way you are going, yes."

Alfie felt his eyes flood with fresh tears. These were tears of guilt. He saw the truth now.

"I'm not afraid I won't be like him," Alfie murmured.

"What, then?"

Alfie hesitated. It felt traitorous to say it. "I'm afraid I *will* be like him."

It was true. His father was stuck in the past. He was angry and full of regret. He shouted at Alfie and at his mom, and he went to work and hated it. Alfie had long ago stopped admiring his father. He had started to resent him. And, somehow, to *pity* him.

"You are your own person," Rolabi said. "If you spend all your time chasing someone else's shadow, how will you ever find your own light?"

Alfie watched the mirror shift again to reflect his own gangly body. He stared at it.

"I have high hopes for you, Alfred Zetz. You will need all of your courage."

"I'm still afraid," Alfie whispered.

"For now."

With that, the darkness was gone. Alfie was back in the locker room, staring at his empty hand. He knew he hadn't beaten his fear. But he'd seen it. And he realized now that he had been afraid of the wrong monster all along. No more. He had to face that deeper question:

Why didn't he like himself, and how could he start?

He grabbed his duffel bag and walked out to the gym. He noticed Rolabi standing beside the front door, and the professor nodded at him. Alfie nodded back, got his ball, and went to warm up. Rain was the last to arrive, and then Rolabi walked crisply to center court.

"Gather around," Rolabi said. "Today we work on your shots."

Rolabi reached into his bag and removed a ball with a *W*. Then his eyes fell on Devon.

"Hmm," Rolabi said. "This will be fascinating."

He tossed Devon the ball, and the second it touched his hands, Fairwood vanished.

This time Alfie wasn't thrust into a dark room. He was on top of a mountain, along with the rest of the team. Alfie looked around in wonder. The mountain was narrow, more like a stone tree, and it rose to such terrible heights that the clouds floated far below like distant tufts of cotton. Across from the mountaintop was a second stone tower with a lone hoop and backboard, and between the two, only cold, endless space. Rolabi was nowhere to be seen.

The others started arguing, but Alfie stepped toward the ledge. His heart was lodged in his throat like a cork, but he was trying to think. There was no place like this in all of Dren—he was sure of that. All around them clouds rolled off to the horizon, framed beneath a blue-black sky. The sun was pale enough that stars littered the sky. It felt like Alfie could reach out and grab one.

A tremendous *crack* like a thunderbolt split the air, and he nearly toppled over the side. Alfie turned just as a piece of rock split from the mountain and was swallowed eagerly by the clouds. He never heard it land. More deep cracks splintered the mountaintop, creeping toward the team like vines. Alfie looked between the cliff and the hoop.

"We need to do something," he said, cutting right over the other players' arguments.

Everyone looked at him.

"Like what?" Vin asked.

"I don't know," Twig replied.

He thought back to what Rolabi had said. Shooting. And there was a hoop . . .

"We're supposed to be practicing shooting, right? Maybe we need to shoot the ball."

There was another thunderous crack.

"Take the shot, Rain," Reggie said, and Devon quickly threw him the ball.

A huge chunk of stone split off, shrinking the plateau by another ten feet. The team closed in, forming a little U around Rain, who set up to shoot. He was trembling madly, and Alfie knew immediately he would miss. Rain's shot clanked off the rim and plummeted into the clouds.

Alfie peeked over the edge. "That's not good—"

The ball abruptly flew back up and landed in Vin's hands. He stared at it, wide-eyed.

"Keep shooting!" Twig urged.

Vin missed. Several more missed after him. No one could make the shot.

The ball came to Alfie.

Someone has to open the door.

He stepped forward, taking a deep breath. His hands were shaking, so he breathed again, trying to still them. He knew it was the fear making people miss. But he was always afraid when he was shooting . . . of missing or being blocked or getting yelled at. He knew that feeling well.

What was the difference, really? Fear was fear.

"Hurry up!" Peño urged as another crack split the mountain.

The old Alfie would have hoisted up a shot immediately. But he fought the urge and went through his routine. He dribbled it, took a last breath, and then rose up for the shot and drained it.

"Nice one, Twig!" Reggie said, clapping him on the back.

Alfie stepped back, shocked that he had been the first and hoping the mountain would vanish. But it wasn't enough. Nothing changed. It seemed that *everyone* had to score.

And the others were still struggling. Rain missed yet again, and the mountain was shrinking fast. It was about the size of Alfie's bedroom now. Devon missed badly once again. Then Lab. Then Rain.

"Come on, Rain!" Vin shouted.

Round by round they went. Soon it was only Rain, Lab, Peño, and Devon left. Peño made his shot and pumped his fist. More of the mountain collapsed. There wasn't much time now.

Alfie imagined falling into the distant clouds and felt dizzy. Rain missed again.

"Come on!" Rain shouted in disbelief.

Devon missed. Lab made his next shot, and his older brother pulled him into a hug. Another chunk of the mountain fell. Now Rain and Devon—the last ones to score—had to press their backs against the group while they shot to avoid falling. Rain took a shot and rimmed out.

"No!" Vin shouted.

The ball came to Devon. As he lifted it, Alfie realized that they weren't attacking this drill like a team. Watching and shouting and getting angry at one another wasn't helping.

This wasn't just about individual shooting. If it were, why were they all here?

He pushed his way through.

"Wait!" Alfie said, stepping up beside Devon.

Devon looked at him in surprise but lowered the ball.

"Just breathe," Alfie said, gently pushing down on his elbow. "Tuck your arm in. Yeah . . . perfect. And follow through toward the net. Your wrist will flick at the end." He showed him what it would look like. "Flick it like you are dropping it in there."

He could hardly believe *he* was coaching someone, but Devon listened carefully, watching Alfie's form, and then took the shot. The ball hit the rim, careened off the backboard, and dropped in. Devon laughed and gave him a clap on the shoulder . . . hard enough that he knocked Alfie toward the edge. His shoe slipped, and he felt empty air, flailing wildly.

Devon grabbed his shirt, pulling him back to safety.

"Sorry," Devon said.

Alfie managed a weak smile. "No problem."

Rain stepped forward just as another huge chunk split away. There was no more time. The next boulder would take the team with it. The ball flew up and landed softly in Rain's hands.

"Make it, Rain!" Peño shouted.

There was a deep crack beneath their feet. The mountain's bones were giving way.

"Hurry!" Vin said.

The ground shifted.

"Shoot it!" A-Wall said.

"Stay calm," Alfie whispered.

Rain took the shot just as the final crack split through the air. The mountain teetered and swung backward, and Alfie watched as the ball spun toward the net, wondering if they were all about to die. He grabbed Devon's arm and felt open air on his back. The ball continued.

Swish.

The net rippled, and the mountain was gone.

They were back in Fairwood Community Center. His teammates collapsed to the ground or cheered and laughed manically. Alfie did neither. He stood there, thinking that he might have accomplished more today than he had in his entire life. Rolabi was waiting calmly for them.

And now the tree stretches for the sky.

"Welcome back," he said. "What makes a great shooter?"

"You almost killed us!" Vin shouted.

"Twig, what do you think?" Rolabi asked, ignoring Vin's hysterics.

Alfie thought about that. "Good form?"

"A good shooter needs that, certainly. But more is needed for greatness."

You know the answer. What does a great shooter lack?

Alfie was confused. Why would a great shooter *lack* anything?

"Fear," Devon said. "He lacks fear."

Alfie almost laughed. Of course.

"All great shooters are fearless. If they fear missing, or being blocked, or losing, then they will not shoot. Even if they do, they will rush. They will allow fear to move their elbows or turn their fingers to stone. They will never be great. And how do we get rid of our fears?"

"We face them," Devon replied.

Rolabi nodded. "Yes . . . and one thing we all fear is letting down our friends. Basketball is about confronting fear. If you won't face it, you will lose. We will practice a thousand shots. Ten thousand. Twenty. If you take them *all* from a crumbling mountain, you will become great shooters."

Alfie thought about that. It was the heart of his entire game. Fear of losing. Of humiliation. It drove his decisions on the court. Without that fear, he could just *play*.

Rolabi strolled toward the wall, bag in hand. The lights flashed, and he vanished.

Alfie turned to Reggie. "That was close."

"Yeah," Reggie said. "It's crazy, you know . . . what you think of."

"What do you mean?"

He hesitated, lowering his voice. "When I was falling. I just thought: I ain't done yet."

"And here you are."

They started for the bench together. He realized, almost to his surprise, that they had become friends, real friends, almost without his knowing. He had spent so much time thinking about how to get a friend. Smart things to say. In the end, it was just about opening up.

"You caught it, didn't you?" Reggie asked suddenly. "You caught the orb."

Alfie glanced at him, frowning. "Why do you say that?"

"You were a different kid on that mountain," he said. "A leader."

"I'm not a leader."

"Could have fooled me," Reggie said.

Alfie flushed and looked away. He caught a glimpse of Rain heading for the closest hoop with his ball tucked under his arm. He was wearing a look of intense concentration, even anger.

"What are you doing, Rain?" Peño asked.

Rain stopped at the free-throw line. "Shooting."

He began to shoot, grabbing the ball and returning to the line after every hit or miss. Everyone got their balls and joined him, including Alfie. As he started shooting, he thought about the future.

His future.

8

SHADOW ALFIE

If you are unsure of your destination,
you might as well keep walking.
✦ WIZENARD ◈ PROVERB ✦

ALFIE LIFTED THE ball over his shoulder, jab-stepped left, and then pivoted for a jumper. He banked the shot in and grabbed the ball as it fell, feeling sweat leak out along with some disappointment.

He had wanted to stand up to his father last night. He had planned it and talked himself through it and been ready when the front door opened. But his resolve had melted the second he had faced him. So Alfie had walked through the trophies and talked about calorie-heavy diets and listened to his old stories. And as he did, he knew he still had a long way to go.

But it wasn't all bad. Accepting that he was afraid of ending up like his father was a start. He knew what he was fighting against. That gave him just a little bit of hope that he could beat it.

The front doors of Fairwood blew open, and Alfie looked on in wonder as a wave of snow rushed in and filled the court with blurry shapes of trophies and basketballs and mountains wreathed with clouds. A player made of snow dribbled past him, dodging a tiger, and then they, along with the rest, burst into snowflakes and evaporated. Rolabi walked through the doors, and they slammed shut behind him.

"Must be snowing in the Kingdom of Granity," Reggie said, eyes wide.

"Apparently."

"Still not going to tell the rest of the team what we learned from that book?" he asked.

Alfie considered that. "I think Rolabi probably has that covered."

"So he talks in your head too?"

"Yep."

"That's a relief," Reggie murmured.

The team assembled in front of Rolabi, and he looked them over.

"Three of you have caught the orb so far," Rolabi said—to Alfie's surprise. "I can see some changes. The rest must stay vigilant. They must be ready when the moment comes."

Alfie wondered who the other player was. He guessed that it had to be Rain.

"Today we will be focusing on team offense," he continued. "You have worked on your passing and vision. You have worked on your shot. But this is not a game of one. It is a game of many. Even the greatest players cannot win this game alone."

Rolabi looked up, and Alfie followed his gaze. He frowned.

The fluorescent light panels had been dusted, and the once-decrepit A-beam rafters were covered in a fresh coat of stain. Fairwood was looking better every day. Alfie knew there was no super janitor. No secret renovation team. It seemed ridiculous, but Fairwood was cleaning *itself*.

He had seen plenty of grana, of course, but this was different—concrete and permanent. Clearly, grana wasn't just capable of visions or bizarre drills. It could create real-world changes.

That part hadn't been in the book.

"It is good to recognize who is defending us at all times," Rolabi said, still staring up at the lights. "To use size and speed advantages. But before that, we must understand what it means to attack as a team. And so we remove those advantages and create fully equal defenders."

As soon as he said it, half of the overhead lights switched off. The remaining ones brightened, and Alfie squinted against the glare. Only the lights facing the team remained on, as though they were standing on a theater stage.

"We will learn to attack as one," Rolabi continued. "But first, we need defenders."

Alfie suddenly felt like he was being watched from behind, or like a feather was being dragged along the nape of his neck. He tensed, wondering what was happening now.

Rain shouted a warning, and Alfie turned around to one of the most terrifying sights he had ever witnessed. His shadow was standing up. It seemed to be waking from a long slumber, stretching its limbs and jumping on the spot. The shape was a perfect three-dimensional replica of him: tall and frail. It was flanked by a whole team of ominous shadow players. Alfie was speechless.

"Mommy," A-Wall whispered.

"Meet today's defenders," Rolabi said. "You should know them well."

Alfie's shadow stuck out its hand. Alfie looked down, bewildered, but he didn't want to be impolite. He tepidly reached out a hand.

"Nice to . . . uh . . . meet you . . . Shadow Alfie."

Shadow Alfie shook his hand. The grip was limp and weak . . . exactly like his own, but ice-cold. Everything was mirrored. The posture. The nervous energy. Shadow Alfie went back to its warm-up.

"Into position, defenders," Rolabi said.

Five of the shadows jogged over to the net and formed a loose zone, while the rest hurried to the sideline to wait, high-fiving one another. Alfie had never seen anything so bizarre in his life.

"I think it's obvious who will be guarding you. But it won't be a scrimmage; we will just be working on our offense. You will sub in as we go. Let's try a few as usual. Starters, go first."

I guess that's me, Alfie thought nervously.

"Line it up," Peño said.

As Alfie headed for the post, his shadow matched every step with an arm out to jockey him. The team worked the ball around but couldn't find an opening—even Rain was stymied. Eventually, Alfie caught a pass down low, turned to shoot, and was stuffed by his own shadow.

"Thanks," he said. "My own shadow is making me look like an idiot."

Shadow Alfie gave him a comforting pat on the back.

"Switch it up," Rolabi said.

The bench players were shut out as well. Both teams played against the shadows, taking turns for nearly an hour, and scored only a few buckets. Alfie had always relied on being taller than his defender, and without that advantage, he was lost. They all were.

"Take a break," Rolabi said as yet another pass was stolen by the shadow team.

Shadow Alfie tapped its wrist like it was wearing a watch.

"I guess you don't get tired, huh?" Alfie asked.

Shadow Alfie shook its head, and then started doing jumping jacks to prove its point.

"Show off," Alfie muttered.

He gulped some water down, feeling a splash drip into his already-sopping shirt.

"Our shadows are kicking our butts," Reggie said, finishing his own bottle.

"I know. I'm not sure if we get any credit for that."

Reggie laughed. "I doubt it."

Alfie tuned back in to the conversation. Peño was answering a question. "Well, we still need to pass to each other and stuff."

"For the most skilled player in the world, and for him alone, there is always an advantage," Rolabi said. "For all the rest of us, we must create the advantage for ourselves. And that can only be done with the help of our team."

"But—" Peño said.

"If we play defense as a team, we play offense as a team. We talk. We plan. We see the floor."

"But—" Peño persisted.

"We attack as one. And that starts with a simple spotlight. Into your positions, please."

Alfie jogged down to the post and put his arm up for the pass, trying to hold his position. He kept catching glimpses of a faceless head over his shoulder and shuddered. It soon got worse.

The remaining lights began to dim. As they faded, Shadow Alfie grew, and Alfie felt himself being driven away from the hoop as it became stronger. His teammates began to slip into darkness around him, until he found himself squinting. Alfie did not like where this was going.

"Peño, pass the ball to Rain," Rolabi said.

Peño hesitated. "I can barely see him. Can we turn some more lights on?"

"That is the hope. Pass the ball."

Peño sighed and passed the ball to Rain. As soon as Rain caught the pass, the darkness receded, but from Rain only. It was like a spotlight had been turned on him, and his defender stepped back. As Rain held the ball, clearly deciding how to attack, the spotlight dimmed again.

"Twig!" Rain said.

He faked a bounce pass and then lobbed it down to the block, and Alfie caught it, fighting to keep his shadow back. As soon as he caught the ball, the white spotlight fell on him.

As he held the ball, the lights began to dim again. He suddenly understood.

"The passing," Twig said. "It lights us up."

Rolabi nodded. "Options light up a court. When everyone moves, the darkness lifts."

Options, Alfie thought. That was a different thing entirely.

Rain sprinted to the corner, losing his defender, and though he didn't have the ball, a spotlight fell on him immediately. Alfie passed him the ball, and Rain began to dribble in one spot. The spotlight faded, so Peño made a quick cut for the ball and was suddenly illuminated.

You have to make yourself available, Alfie realized. *You light up if you get open too.*

Alfie moved for a screen and then rolled. A brilliant white light fell over him.

There was no choice: move or be swallowed by shadows. Alfie set countless screens, caught passes, and dished the ball. Even if he was out of the play, he searched for ways to get in.

At one point, Alfie got a pass down low. He saw a flash of blinding light as Rain cut behind him, which Alfie knew meant that Rain was the best option for a pass. He threw a no-look pass behind his back, and Rain scored easily.

"Nice pass, Twig," Rain said, sounding surprised.

Twig flushed. Rain had *never* complimented him before.

"Again," Rolabi said.

Alfie was soon drenched. But once again, he was enjoying the drill.

Not only was he part of the offense, he was *integral* to it. The ball was constantly coming down low. Before he knew it, he was hitting players on the cut with bounce passes, faking shots, and even tossing skip passes to the other side. His shadow was a tenacious defender, but it couldn't keep up with the sheer options he had on offense. As the drill continued, the advantage changed, and the attackers scored more often than not. Even though he was tired, Alfie was alert.

He was *useful*.

He handed the ball off to Rain for an easy layup, and Rolabi stepped forward again.

"That's enough for today," he said. "Sit and watch."

He pulled the daisy out of his bag and set it down, glancing at the shadows. "Thank you, gentlemen."

The darkened lights flashed, and the shadows vanished immediately. Alfie sat down in front of the daisy, stretching his legs. He was exhausted and sore, but he was smiling.

"What did you see during the drill?" Rolabi asked.

"Movement," Reggie said.

"And?"

"A team," Alfie said proudly.

He liked the sound of that. A lot.

"Yes. We are a team on *both* ends. If you use the Spotlight Offense, you will be more effective."

The professor fell quiet, and Alfie let his mind focus on the flower. He watched the leaves and the petals. He saw no movement, as usual, and the ticking of the clock seemed to slow. He didn't fidget. In fact, he welcomed the stillness. But Alfie soon noticed that the room was oddly silent. There were no sounds of shuffling or even breathing. He looked up and realized why. The orb had returned.

Alfie knew instantly that it wasn't here for him.

He had found his dark room, and it was up to the others to catch the orb now.

"Here we go again," Lab whispered.

The team charged, though three stayed seated: Alfie, Devon, and Jerome. The three of them exchanged a quick nod. Alfie wondered what they had found in their dark rooms. For the first time, it really clicked that they *all* had something they were afraid of. It felt like an obvious realization, but somehow, Alfie had almost assumed he was the only coward. The only one struggling.

Finally, after a clever pivot, Rain caught the orb and was gone. Alfie wondered what he would find. Surely Rain, at least, wasn't afraid of much. His life was perfect.

Everyone has their own battles. Wish for others' circumstances at your peril.

But don't some people have it worse than others? Alfie thought.

There is no scale apart from our own.

Rolabi left, but his words remained. Alfie thought about the previous season. He had spent so much time assuming he alone had all the problems that he had never asked anyone about theirs. Never looked to help. Reggie and his missing parents. Big John and his two jobs.

What else was staring at him, begging to be seen?

And that is the question that every leader must ask themselves.

THE
FIRST STONE

No one wins alone.
Those that forget this do not win.
✦ WIZENARD ⑨ PROVERB ✦

THE NEXT MORNING, Reggie and Alfie were sitting on the away bench. They had already been shooting around and had come back for a drink of water—Alfie from a store-bought bottle and Reggie from an old refillable, the logo long since worn off. They drank deeply and sat quietly.

The rest of the team was warming up, and they were alone there.

"Can I ask you something, Alfie?" Reggie asked.

"Sure."

"What did you see? In . . . that place?"

Alfie glanced at him. Reggie had said little during their warm-up, which was nothing new, but he looked different today. His hands were clasped in his lap, his eyes staring at something far away. They looked swollen. He had been crying.

"You caught the orb."

"This morning," Reggie said. "When I was alone."

Alfie took a moment. He wasn't ready to get into specifics. He wasn't sure if he ever would be. But that wasn't the point. If he was right, Reggie would have found the same thing.

"I saw my fears," he said at last. "I had to face them."

Reggie nodded slowly. "And . . . were there people there?"

"Yes," Alfie said. "One, anyway. You?"

Reggie's eyes were glistening. A tear wandered down his cheek, and he didn't wipe it.

"I wanted to stay there," he whispered.

So he had seen *them*. Alfie couldn't imagine the pain of that . . . of seeing his parents and hearing their voices and then having to say good-bye yet again. His father was difficult, and hard, but he was there. He felt a deep pang of sympathy. Pity.

No one needs pity. They need understanding.

"Are you sure you aren't already staying there?" Alfie asked. "I was living in mine."

Reggie closed his eyes for a moment. It was as if he was picturing them again.

"You're probably right," he said. "I guess . . . I just didn't want to admit the truth."

"Me either. Maybe nobody does."

Reggie wiped his eyes. "Think they're up there?" he asked. "Watching us?"

"I'm sure they are."

Reggie stuck a fist out, and Alfie met it—knuckle to knuckle.

"My brotha," Reggie said, smiling through the tears.

"And you are also . . . my brother," Alfie replied.

Reggie laughed and stood up, shaking his head. "You kill me, Twig."

They heard clacking shoes and turned to see Rolabi striding onto the court.

"We have two days left of our training camp," he said. "And two left to catch the orb."

Alfie looked around, wondering who still had to catch it. He looked at Big John, wondering what his dark room was. He blinked when he saw Rolabi turn and start for the doors.

Peño frowned. "There's no practice today?"

"Oh yes," Rolabi said, heading for the front doors. "You just don't need me."

"What should we do?" Rain said.

"I leave that to you."

He strode into the gale-force winds and was gone. The doors slammed shut again behind him, but this time, they vanished completely, leaving only yellowed cinder blocks in their wake.

The only way in, or out of, Fairwood was now gone.

"Perfect," Peño muttered. "I guess he's making sure we don't go home early."

"I wouldn't be so sure," Twig said warily.

A deep rumble filled the gym. It sounded as if some ancient engine had been restarted. Alfie thought of the silvery arteries running through the floors and ceiling. The pulsating heart. If the gym was actually alive . . . did that mean it could move as well?

And then the walls that ran alongside the court began to push forward, closing in.

"Impossible," Vin murmured.

"Possibility is subjective," Lab snarled. "Any ideas?"

Alfie was stumped. He stared slack-jawed as the walls approached, driving the bleachers and the locker room doors and everything else along with them with slow, unstoppable force. He tried to think. It was a test, surely . . . but of what? If they would panic?

If that was it, they promptly failed. Rain began to pound the walls. Vin grabbed his ball and tried to score. The team joined him, sinking layups and free-throw shots and threes, but nothing worked. The walls closed in with the slow inevitability of the tide. Alfie tried not to think about being crushed, and of course that was all he could think of. He racked his brain.

They had done team offense, team defense, shooting, passing, even cardio.

What else was there to basketball?

Devon suddenly ran to the massive steel bleachers and began to pull on one end.

"Help!" Devon called.

They all scrambled over and started to heave the mammoth, single-structure bleachers off the wall. The unit must have weighed three tons. It took all of them to get it moving—and Alfie felt his muscles pulling and straining until his body was on fire. He ran around and found himself shoulder to shoulder with Big John, driving one end forward.

"Turn it sideways!" Rain shouted. "On three. One . . . two . . . pull!"

They turned the bleachers with mere inches to spare on either side. The walls closed in, and everyone waited in silence, chewing nails, whispering prayers, or just watching them come.

With an awful, wrenching noise, the walls met the bleachers. They didn't even slow down. The middle of the steel bleachers began to rise up in an arch, squealing all the way.

"Try the benches!" Alfie said desperately.

Even as he said it, he knew it was useless, but he felt like he needed to do something. He and Rain repositioned the wooden benches, but they looked like toothpicks set against a giant vise. The bleachers were still folding, and they were far sturdier and stronger than the benches.

"Rolabi!" Peño shouted, pounding on the walls. "Help us! Someone!"

Vin was trying his cell phone, but he tossed it to the floor in frustration. "No reception!"

Alfie thought of his parents and felt sick that he might not see them again. For all of his dad's lectures and hard words, he was protective. Alfie was an only child, and he was the first person his dad sought out when he got home from work. His dad was always ready to take him shopping or work on his game or watch ball with him. And his mom didn't even want him to come here. She had been worried it was too much pressure. She had told him he could stay home. How would the police tell them . . . *this*? They would be devastated. What would they do?

"Look!" someone shouted.

Alfie spun around, searching for a hidden door. Instead, floating well overhead, was the orb. The walls had already slid onto the court. In minutes, the team would be crushed between them. The orb couldn't save them. Or . . . not all of them. But it might save one.

"Someone can get out of here!" Alfie said. "You vanish, remember?"

"Only for people that haven't gotten the orb yet," Reggie said. "It will only work for them."

Lab and Peño looked at each other, and Twig knew it was the brothers who were left.

"Get up on the bleachers!" Lab said.

They all began to climb. It was difficult with the bending metal, but soon they had hoisted themselves onto the archway in the middle. Alfie stood up and reached, but the orb was still far overhead. There was no way someone could reach it, even him, even from up here. Lab and Peño didn't have a chance. Alfie slumped. It was over. The orb had been their last chance.

But Devon wasn't ready to give up. He got down on all fours, bracing against the warping benches with his hands and feet and creating a relatively flat surface with his back.

"Come on!" he shouted, his deep voice carrying over the noise. "Make a pyramid!"

Alfie didn't even think about it. He dropped down beside Devon, and A-Wall, Big John, and Reggie did the same, forming a solid base. Rain, Jerome, and Vin climbed onto their backs, building a second level. The whole pyramid wavered, but Alfie clenched his teeth and held on with every ounce of strength he had. Finally, Lab and Peño climbed to the top, digging their shoes into their teammates and fighting to stay balanced. Alfie bit back a yelp as the weight increased even more.

He knew the rest of the pyramid—including him—might be doomed. Yet somehow, it still felt like the right decision. If they could save even a single teammate, then they had to try.

All he had ever seen in the mirror was a coward. Yet here he was, sacrificing himself.

And he didn't feel sad at all.

It was strange at the bottom of the pyramid. Silent. Alfie just felt a strange numbness. Calmness, maybe. The walls closed in.

"Hurry!" Rain shouted. "Get it!"

The walls had almost come together. Alfie closed his eyes.

"One . . . two . . . three!" Peño's voice suddenly broke over the noise.

Alfie heard someone cry out as if in pain. He opened his eyes just as the walls ground to a halt and began to slide back the way they'd come, revealing piles of crushed debris in their wake.

"Badgers!" Peño shouted from the top of the pile.

Suddenly the whole team was cheering and shouting madly.

"Badgers!" Alfie cried.

Guys spilled off his back, scrambling onto hands and knees and pulling the others up. He looked around and realized Lab had gotten the orb. He should have known that Peño would never go without him.

Soon everyone was hugging and laughing and high-fiving. No one was even bothering to hide their tears. As the walls slid back into place, the bleachers straightened, and the team climbed off easily. The crumpled rims joined a shower of glass shards to form nets once again, while the splintered wooden benches were rebuilt in a beautiful swirl of pulp and nails and stain. The banners were resewn and hung in perfect order. Soon everything was back as it was, even the front doors. But it was new, and rebuilt, and Alfie felt like he belonged in this Fairwood.

Alfie turned to Devon. "You saved us."

Devon smiled awkwardly. "I was just doing what I thought was best."

"No," Alfie said. "You kept your head. You knew you might not survive, and you did it anyway. That took a lot of heart, man. We're lucky to have you."

Devon glanced at him, biting his lip, then just nodded and turned away.

You opened a door for another. Keep working. You must get them ready.

For what? Alfie thought, frowning. *Training camp is almost over.*

And now the real game approaches.

THE BROKEN MIRROR

*We are made of a million questions
that only one person can answer.*

WIZENARD (47) PROVERB

ALFIE LOOKED OUT the passenger-side window. The sky was over-cast today—the last day of training camp. Part cloud, part smog. The sun-light filtered through almost brown, and there wasn't a whisper of wind. It had been silent for most of the ride.

Alfie's father glanced over at him. "You seem quiet lately."

"I guess so."

"Something up? You've been quiet a lot since training camp started."

They pulled up and parked in front of Fairwood's front doors.

Alfie paused. "I just feel different, I guess."

"Different in a good way?"

"Yeah," Alfie said. "I think it's going to be a good year."

"Hmm," his father said. "Well, you need to get out and assert yourself to the team—"

"I got it," Alfie said, stepping out of the car. "I'll see you tonight."

He closed the car door and started for Fairwood, smiling. Reggie was waiting inside as ever, shoes on, sitting alone on the far bench, staring out at the court. Alfie dropped down on the bench beside him.

"What up, brotha?" Reggie said, giving him props.

"Ready to play."

"Yeah," Reggie said. "Me too. I've been thinking. What do you think it's all for?"

"What?"

Reggie gestured to the gym. "All of it. Rolabi coming here. Why us? Why the Badgers?"

Alfie slipped his own shoes on, considering. That question had occurred to him too, of course. He'd gone back to the book, and he'd realized that they had sort of breezed over one of the key lines.

He glanced at Reggie, then pulled the book out and opened it to the page. There was a picture of a woman—tall and handsome, a leather bag at her side. She was walking into fire.

"Read it," Alfie muttered.

Reggie took the book. "'The Wizenards often go where the need is greatest and the hour is late.'" He frowned. "I missed that part, apparently. It doesn't sound very promising."

"No."

Reggie ran his fingers over the picture. "So you think something bad is coming?"

"The rest of the book seems pretty spot-on," Twig said. "Rolabi said something . . ."

"And now the real game approaches," Reggie murmured.

Twig snorted. "Yeah. I guess we got the same memo."

Reggie handed the book back, checked the door, and leaned in, lowering his voice.

"There's a reason we had never heard of grana before Rolabi got here," he whispered.

"What do you mean?"

"Who do you think got rid of all the Wizenards in Dren?" Reggie asked.

The rest of the team was arriving, but they were getting ready and ignoring the away bench. It felt hushed on that side of the gym. Alfie felt his skin prickling. He leaned in as well.

"President Talin?"

"My parents left me something," Reggie said softly. "I think I know what's coming."

Alfie leaned in closer. Suddenly the doors of the gym burst open with a familiar gust of icy wind, and Reggie and Alfie fell back, toppling the bench and sprawling onto their backs. Alfie lay there, dazed, and then started to laugh despite himself. Reggie joined in, and they both clambered up and pushed the bench back upright.

"You guys all right?" Peño asked, raising an eyebrow.

"Yeah," Alfie said. "We're fine."

He glanced at Reggie, but he just mouthed, "Another time." Alfie nodded, and they grabbed their balls and went to warm up. He took threes. He practiced cutting in from the wings. He worked on low-post moves and bank shots. Alfie guarded Reggie on the perimeter, and they hit each other on passes, working in rotation, sweating, laughing, and urging each other on.

Rolabi appeared right at nine, summoning them to half-court. He looked the same as always—the same suit, the same bow tie, the same pocket watch. His eyes flashed emerald green.

"All but one of you have caught the orb," he said. "Why?"

"Because . . . you told us to?" Vin said uncertainly.

"But why? What did you find?"

"Our fears," Reggie said from beside Alfie.

Alfie nodded. He would never have thought to search for his fears. He had assumed they were obvious, right there surrounding him, every day—an inevitable reaction to external problems that he couldn't control. But they ran deeper. Doors he kept closed. Places he avoided.

And without even realizing it, they had been shaping his entire life.

"If one thing will stop you in life, it is that," Rolabi said. "To win, we must defeat our fears. For basketball . . . for everything."

"But . . . we did, right?" Big John said.

"Fear is not so easily beaten," Rolabi replied. "It will return. You must be ready."

He opened his bag and reached inside.

"For today, we will review what we have learned so far."

Alfie heard scratching and turned to the locker room door.

"Twig, you know the drill."

Alfie ran to the door and let Kallo out, who paused so he could give her an affectionate scratch on the neck. Rolabi began setting up an obstacle course, even more elaborate than the last. The lights flickered, half went out, and the shadow team emerged from the floorboards.

"Shadow Alfie," Alfie said, nodding.

The shadow gave him a pat on the shoulder and went to form up on defense.

With that, they started the drill. Or more accurately, *drills*. Alfie had to fight past his shadow again and again. He was tackled by Kallo. He climbed steep floors, slid down others, jumped divots, climbed endless stairs. He lost his hand and missed countless shots and passes.

And still he kept pushing until every single article of clothing was sopping wet.

On the fifth lap, he came to the vertical hoop for the pass. He had missed the target every time so far. His stronger right hand was gone again, and so he had to try and make it with his left.

He took a deep breath, steadying himself.

The hoop vanished, and a towering mirror formed instead. Twig found himself staring at his reflection, and as before, it began to change. His father appeared. Then the image warped again, and Twig was looking at the older version of himself: forlorn and lost and disappointed. It was the future he had feared. The secret in his dark room . . . that he would become his father. That he would never be happy with himself. The gym went still, and he was alone with the reflection.

He heard nothing else as he stared into the faded brown eyes. Then he threw the ball.

It shattered the mirror into a million pieces. The shards littered the floor and melted away, leaving only the ring, and his ball sitting behind it. Twig scooped it up and kept running.

There is only one person who can rebuild that mirror. Take your time.

When the drill finally ended, the shadows vanished with a flash of light, and Kallo strolled back into the locker room. Alfie grabbed a water bottle and chugged it as the team gathered around Rolabi.

"Are we done?" Jerome asked.

"One more thing."

A-Wall snorted. "The walls aren't going to try to crush us again, are they?"

"You think they would have?" Alfie said, glancing at him.

"Sure seemed like it," Vin replied.

"I don't think so. I think Fairwood is a little grateful for all our hard work, actually," Alfie said.

The rest of the team turned to him, frowning.

"Is he talking like the building is a person, or is it just me?" Jerome asked.

"No, he is," Vin said. "What are you talking about, Twig?"

Alfie glanced at Rolabi.

Go ahead.

"I'm sure you've noticed all the changes in here?" Alfie said, gesturing around the gym.

"So?" Jerome said.

"Well, we did this," Alfie replied.

"Twig has lost it," Big John muttered. "If he ever had *it* to begin with."

"What do you mean *we* did it?" A-Wall asked. "I didn't do anything."

"Yes, you did," Alfie said. "The sweat. Did anyone else notice anything weird about it?"

"Like . . . how it seeped into the floors?" Reggie said. "Yeah . . . I saw that."

"Exactly," Alfie said, nodding excitedly. "That was the first day it started. The floors just soaked it all up like a sponge. The next day, the banners were fixed. And every day it continued."

He had finally put the pieces together last night. Rolabi said that sweat could forge the greatest change. It turned out he was being literal, for once. Fairwood was absorbing their sweat, using it to pump the great heart and bring the old building alive again. All along, it had just needed *work*.

"So the building is alive . . ." Reggie said.

Alfie grinned. "I don't know. It did try to eat us."

Everyone looked at him. He wondered if they would make fun of him, or tell him he was crazy, or just go back to ignoring him. And then Vin burst into laughter. Reggie and Jerome joined in, and soon they all did. He noticed to his shock that Big John was smiling too.

"Twig telling jokes," Peño said, shaking his head. "What's next?"

He started beatboxing:

"Camp is almost done
We probably still got to run
Putting champs on a banner
The quiet over clamor
Peño waits to watch
Cheers and stops
He wanted rhymes with 'Badger'
But the words didn't matter
Ball is roads and ramps

No more time for losses
Only time for champs."

Everyone started to laugh, and Peño was swarmed with hands. Alfie joined as they jumped around him and cheered. Big John leapt in as well, colliding with Alfie and sending him stumbling back. But just as Twig was about to fall, Big John grabbed his shirt and held him up.

They stared at each other for a moment, and then Big John let go of his shirt and grinned.

"I'm still coming for that starting spot, Alfie," he said.

Alfie smiled. "I would expect no less. And you can call me Twig. Every West Bottom Badger needs a nickname."

Big John smiled. "Fair enough, Twig."

Rolabi just picked up his medicine bag and headed for the doors.

"I thought you said we still have a puzzle to solve?" Rain called after him.

"You do," Rolabi said. "One for each of you. And by the way, welcome to the Badgers."

Another cheer went up as he disappeared into the sunlight, and the doors gently eased shut behind him. Everyone broke into different conversations. Twig fell into step with Reggie, heading for the bench.

"You really think we're gonna put *Champions* up there?" he asked.

Twig shrugged. "It seems anything is possible."

They sat down together, staring out at the court, listening to the laughter.

"It's going to be some season," Twig said.

"Yeah, man. Who knows what's coming next," Reggie agreed.

"Well, we'll just have to be ready."

Reggie glanced at him. "You ain't the same Twig who started this camp, are you?"

"I just set some roots, is all," Twig said, smiling.

Reggie laughed and shook his head. "You know what your puzzle is?"

Twig frowned. "No, actually."

He thought about that as he pulled off his shoes. He shoved them in his bag, frowned, and pulled out a small piece of paper, about the size of a card. There were words written in silver ink.

How does one master the mirror?

Twig held the card for a moment, considering. He realized how much of his issues had come from a mirror—not the physical mirror, but what it represented. His image of himself.

He smiled and tucked the note back into his bag.

"He learns to like himself," Twig murmured.

He realized that was part of his name too. *Twig* had always been something he hated, because he took it to mean skinny and weak and unwanted. But he had made those connections.

Now he decided it meant that he could always grow.

They finished changing and waited for the others. It seemed everyone was waiting today. When the last player, Lab, stood up, they all got up with him and started for the doors as a group.

As Twig walked, he saw the silver beneath him and the great beating heart of Fairwood.

"You all going to be here Monday night for practice?" Reggie asked.

"You know it," Lab said. "You?"

"Wouldn't miss it," he said.

Rain walked out first, then turned and held the door for them. Sunlight poured inside.

And for the very first time, the West Bottom Badgers walked out of the gym together.

BOOK THREE

CASH

THE NEW FACE

When we dwell on regret,
we make the past our future.

◆ WIZENARD ◇39◇ PROVERB ◆

FOR A CRAZY moment, Devon thought about running. The door to the gym was open, but he didn't have to go in. He could still make it home. He could sprint down sun-blasted, cracking concrete. He could hop over collapsed fencing, cut overgrown driveways, dash past row houses with flaking black shingles like snakeskin and bricks crumbling to dust—his own just another in the endless maze.

He would be safe there. He wouldn't have to face the world again.

But that was the whole point, wasn't it? he thought. *To start over.*

Freddy turned, gesturing for Devon to follow him. Devon paused, took a last look at the road beyond the parking lot, and went inside.

Humid air fell over him, thick with dust. He tried to breathe and felt the particles stick in his throat. His stomach was hard and heavy and sitting somewhere near his white sneakers.

What was I thinking? he asked himself for the hundredth time that morning.

He had been thinking he needed to change. It made a lot of sense when he was sitting in his bedroom with his books and his posters of

Dren Basketball League pros, thinking: *I could do that*. But that was at home. At night. Alone. It was different when the morning came and he had to get into the car.

"Here we are, my man," Freddy said happily. "Fairwood Community Center."

Devon ignored the gym and focused on the players warming up and laughing and playing together. He tried to calm down, but it was hard when all he could hear was his pounding heart. His nana had said meeting the team would probably be an "anxious experience." She didn't say that meant it would be hard to breathe, and his chest would feel like it was in a vise, and he would be able to taste breakfast again.

"My boys!" Freddy said. "All here? Come on over. Let me introduce Devon."

Devon watched the group as they approached. Freddy had given him a team photo a few weeks ago and listed off their names and nicknames, and Devon had studied it carefully since. He began to match the photo to the faces in front of him. The star player, Rain, looked him up and down with an appraising eye like he was a horse at auction. Devon felt his throat seize up.

"What up, big man?" Rain asked.

Devon knew he should say something polite. He had practiced this moment for hours, but all that was forgotten now. It had been so long since he had faced so many strangers. Years.

"Nothing," Devon said. Even to him, his voice sounded like a whimper.

"Speak up, bro!" Big John said.

Devon felt his cheeks burning. He didn't have to do this.

"He's quiet," Freddy said. "But a big boy."

Peño snorted. "We can see that. He looks like a Clydesdale."

Devon flinched and hoped no one noticed. He heard old, angry words: *animal* and *thug* and *dangerous*, and he wanted to block his ears. His heartbeat was so *loud*. Couldn't they hear it?

"Where you from?" Lab asked. "I never seen you at school before. Hard to miss."

Devon took a breath, forcing his lips to move. "Homeschooled."

"Homeschooled!" Peño said. "Crazy. My pops barely wants me there *after* school."

Big John laughed. "Who can blame him? Still . . . kid got muscles I didn't know existed."

Devon rubbed his arms self-consciously. He had always been big, but the muscles had grown in the last few years. He worked out in the basement at home with his dad. It was his only real release of energy, other than the old hoop in his driveway.

Freddy grinned. "He ain't here to read poetry, boys. Devon is a power forward and a great defender. Well, he will be when we're done with him. He's going to play well with Twig."

Devon kept his eyes down, hoping they would stop talking about him. He just had to make it through today. Then he could tell his parents and his nana that it wasn't working. They would be disappointed, but he knew they expected him to quit. So did he. A part of him knew this plan would fail.

What have you come to find?

The voice was low and deep. Devon's eyes flicked around the room. Nobody seemed to have spoken, and it didn't sound like any normal voice, anyway. It just appeared inside his brain, but he knew the thought wasn't his own.

The lights suddenly blinked off, plunging the gym into darkness. Devon flinched as the front doors burst inward, flooding the room with cold wind. He turned to the open doorway, shielding his face with his arm. Something appeared—a huge silhouette, blotting out the light like an eclipse. The wind died as the figure stepped into the gym.

It was a giant of a man. He wore a suit, polished dress shoes, and a red bow tie. But neither his suit nor his size was as bizarre as his eyes: a striking fluorescent green. They moved around like twin searchlights and fell on every person in the room, freezing them in place.

When his gaze landed on Devon, the greens of his eyes flashed, becoming impossibly bright. The deep voice returned.

Who built the cage? the voice thundered through his mind.

Devon stepped back without thinking, nearly tripping over Freddy. He knew without question that the voice belonged to this towering man, and that scared him even more.

"You're early—" Freddy said.

"Being late or early is simply a matter of perspective."

Spoken aloud, the man's voice was remarkably controlled—each word seemed to have a tangible weight, like it was the most important thing ever spoken. It was almost hypnotizing.

Devon watched as the stranger approached. He dwarfed Devon easily. His feet seemed to float over the ground, and even from where the team was huddled at center court, Devon caught a scent of . . . salt? He breathed it in, bewildered. His nana cooked mussels whenever the local market had a batch—they were old and withered generally, as the ocean was far off, but she cooked them in a pot of salty brine.

It reminded him of that, but fresher somehow. Like it was carried on a cool breeze.

Devon blinked. He'd always had a habit of daydreaming, and he realized his thoughts had wandered off again. The man introduced himself as Rolabi Wizenard and promptly dismissed Freddy. Freddy paused for a moment, then fled the gym.

Devon was confused. The flamboyant team owner had told Devon he was in charge of the Badgers—apparently, he had forgotten to mention that to the coach. The gym suddenly fell silent. Devon wasn't used to such quiet; someone was always up and about in his house. His nana cooked and served as his teacher, his parents were in and out of work, and his little sister, Keya, was usually firing pretend blasters at aliens. But this moment was empty. Not even a breath disturbed the stillness.

Then, without a word, Rolabi pulled a sheet of paper from an inner pocket of his suit jacket.

"I will need everyone to sign this before we can proceed," Rolabi said.

When the paper came to him, Devon read it over:

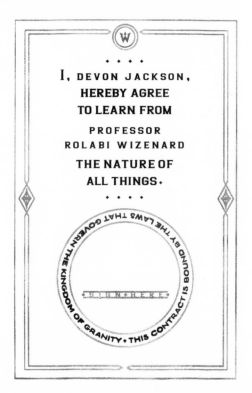

The Kingdom of Granity. The name stirred a memory, but it was vague and half-complete . . . a conversation he'd had as a child, perhaps, or something in a book. He read a lot of fantasy stories—the ones with knights and castles were his favorite—so it seemed entirely possible.

He realized the others were watching him, including Rolabi himself, so Devon quickly signed on the line and stepped into the group.

Twig was the last to sign, and when he handed the paper back to Rolabi, it vanished.

"What . . . Where did . . . How . . . ?" Twig murmured.

Devon stared at Rolabi's empty hand, flabbergasted, but the professor gave no indication that something strange had happened. Instead, the coach opened his bag and began to search for something, reaching deeper and deeper until most of his enormous right arm was buried inside.

"Here we are," Rolabi said.

Then he threw a basketball to Big John, and it smacked him in the cheek with a clap.

He had thrown out four more basketballs—each little more than a blur of orange—before one came whizzing toward Devon's forehead. He snagged it just inches before the impact and lowered the ball, eyes wide. The gym was full of people—hundreds of them. They packed the bleachers and the court, standing shoulder to shoulder, pressing ever closer. Young and old. Poor and poorer. The whole Bottom seemed to be here. They closed in, eyes hard.

"He's dangerous!" one man yelled.

"Send him home!"

"I don't want him near my boys!"

"Get out of here, kid!"

Devon spun around, his face burning with humiliation. He knew this would happen.

He knew they didn't want him here.

"Leave, you big freak!" said a little girl, no older than six.

Devon whirled around in panic, watching as the bodies closed in. Their cruel voices grew louder and louder. The crowd looked like it might turn violent, and he raised his fists, ready to protect himself, though he knew there were too many of them. The mob would surely kill him.

He put his fists down. He wouldn't fight. Not again. He just waited for them to come.

Then Devon saw one person standing apart from the crowd, quietly watching: Rolabi Wizenard.

The crowd fell silent all at once.

"Hmm," the coach said. "Interesting. That will be all today. I will see you here tomorrow."

The crowd was gone, leaving just the team. He felt his knees buckling. Where had the people gone? His heart was pounding again, and he whirled around, searching for them. But it was only the team, and Rolabi heading for the doors.

"What time?" Peño called after him.

Rolabi kept walking. When he reached the doors, they blew open with another blast of frigid wind, and as soon as he was through, they slammed behind him like castle gates.

"Do we keep the balls?" Peño shouted.

He ran after Rolabi and pushed the doors open.

"What . . . Professor?"

Rolabi was already gone.

A PROMISE

We fear what is different
only because we think it makes us less.

YOU SURE YOU don't want me to come inside with you?" Devon's nana called after him, leaning out of the open driver-side window and eyeing the gym. She was a big, broad woman, like everyone else in Devon's family, and even at seventy years old, she had just the first hints of wrinkles forming in the corners of her eyes. "I would like to meet this Rollybolly fellow!"

Devon turned back, trying not to sigh. "No, Nana. Thank you. And it's *Role-ah-bee*."

"Same thing! Now go make some friends," she said, wagging a finger at him. "Talk!"

"I will."

"Liar," she said wryly. "You think I was born yesterday?"

"Of course not—"

"Oh, so now I'm old?" she said. She pointed at the gym. "Go hoop some balls already."

"That's not a thing—"

"Then ball some hoops!"

She took off, her slender hands holding the wheel in a death grip. Devon's little sister, Keya, was sitting in the back with a dinged-up Space Voyagers toy helmet on—she refused to leave the house without it, claiming that "you never know when aliens might show up." She pretended to shoot a laser blaster at Devon as they pulled out of the parking lot. Devon put on a brave smile. He was the older brother, after all. But as soon as the car rumbled away, spewing smoke and sounding like the axle might fall off at any given moment, his courage evaporated.

When he had walked out of the gym yesterday, he'd told himself he wasn't coming back. At home, his parents had even said that quitting was his choice to make, disappointed as they obviously were. And yet here he was. He had decided to stick to his promise: ten days. Ten days to try to be a happy, normal kid again.

Because promising yourself to be normal is perfectly normal, he thought glumly.

It was Freddy who had started this. He had seen Devon playing with his dad on an old hoop on the street, stopped the car, and immediately asked if he wanted to join the Badgers. Devon hadn't played organized sports in four years. He hadn't hung around with other kids in four years. But he'd said yes. He knew his family wanted him out of the house. For ages they had been trying to get him to go back to school or join a team or even make a single friend. His dad had built the hoop so he could invite people over. His mom tried to get him to join her for walks—always by a ball court or a schoolyard or a neighbor's house. His nana had ably taken over his homeschooling, but she told him ten times a day that she couldn't teach him to be a kid again.

So for them, he decided to give it a chance. He made his promise.

You don't have to talk, he told himself. *Just play the game and you'll be fine.*

Pulling open the groaning double doors, Devon stepped into Fairwood Community Center. The morning was a little cooler than yesterday, the sun covered behind a veil of wispy clouds, but the drop in temperature didn't seem to have any effect on Fairwood. The community center was its own little self-sustaining ecosystem, the air humid and stifling. Devon let the doors swing shut behind him, and they clattered so loudly that he thought the door frame might detach from the wall. The old building grunted and settled cantankerously back into place.

Oddly, Devon thought he heard a grumpy voice: "Back again? Lost me ten bucks, you rapscallion. Now how about you find me a mop!"

Devon looked around, frowning. It was different from the voice yesterday . . . old and raspy.

"No, why would you?" the voice continued. "Kids these days. Play but no pay."

Most of his new teammates were already shooting around. He had gone over their nicknames again last night—it seemed that everyone went by something other than a regular name. Devon wondered what his would be: freak, giant, ox. He'd already heard them all.

No one said anything to Devon as he made his way to the bench, and he in turn kept his eyes fixed on his size fourteen shoes. He plunked onto the bench and found himself staring at the bleachers across the room, stretching out from the wall like an ancient metal accordion. They were ten rows deep and accessed by three narrow aisles. Railings bordered either end, although they were broken off in a few places and hanging pitiably. Devon tried to imagine what they would look like filled with spectators. The people would all be looking at him. Talking. Pointing. Laughing.

Or maybe just afraid.

Devon took his new shoes out of his father's old duffel bag—it had been his grandfather's before that—and slipped them on. He tied them slowly . . . almost lovingly. His parents had bought them for the training camp—crisp and white and fresh. He had told them a hundred times it was unnecessary, but they were so excited he was joining a new team that they insisted. Even his nana had approved—and she was notoriously frugal.

Devon tried not to think about the fact that the shoes had cost almost as much as a month's rent, and that his parents had worked extra hours to pay for them. His mom was a nurse at the Bottom's lone hospital, and his dad a payroll administrator for one of the gravel pits. They were considered good jobs in the Bottom, and they still struggled. Their work would be wasted if he quit the team now. As difficult as it was to come back, he wasn't going to let that happen.

Rain sat down and glanced over at Devon. "Hey, how's it going, man?"

Devon paused. He hadn't done very well the last time Rain had asked him something.

"Good," he said, deciding to just keep it simple.

Rain sighed and started to tie his shoes. "Good."

Devon hurried away from the benches before he was forced to talk to anyone else. The ball Rolabi had provided yesterday was still sitting in his bag, but he ignored it. For one, he didn't really want to risk having any more visions. More important, he didn't want to shoot around in the open yet.

So far no one knew he was absolutely terrible on offense, and he wanted to keep it that way for as long as possible. He'd been working on it, but he seemed unable to improve his shot.

Devon began to run along the sideline, swinging his arms to loosen up. He watched the others warming up and saw Rain draining one jump shot after another. Devon tried to note how his body moved in one smooth motion, every joint and muscle flowing in unison. He could almost see a clean, arching line from Rain's springing ankles to the hoop.

Devon's jump shot always felt clumsy and out-of-control, his body cumbersome.

The body reflects the mind.

Devon flinched and looked around. "Professor Rolabi?" he whispered.

"Maybe he's already here."

Devon jumped as the deep voice boomed across Fairwood. He whirled to the bleachers, where Rolabi was eating an apple. He looked just like he had the day before. Not similar, but the *exact* same. He wore the same pin-striped suit, the same scarlet bow tie, the same polished shoes.

He seemed to glide across the floor to the center circle. "Put the balls away."

Devon had no ball, so he tentatively made his way to Rolabi while the rest of the team sprinted to their bags.

"You're back," Rolabi said, his eyes falling on him.

Devon stiffened. "I . . . I am."

"And I won my bet. Do you know what one of my favorite traits is in a person?"

"Umm . . . no," he said.

"Someone who keeps their promises."

Devon stared at him, his mouth opening and closing without sound. How could he possibly know about his promise? He had made it to himself in the mirror three nights ago, gripping the bathroom counter and whispering each word. *Ten days to try.* His parents didn't even know.

Was it a coincidence?

"It's good to have you back," Rolabi said, smiling. "Nine more days to go."

Devon blanched, opened his mouth, closed it, and managed a weak nod.

In a moment, the Badgers were gathered before the coach.

"Umm . . . Professor Rolabi?" Twig said.

Devon glanced at him. He was tall—maybe six five—but skinnier than Devon's wrist, with almost skeletal features and cheeks rippled with small divots and scars. He had his hand up as if he were in a classroom.

"Yes?" Rolabi said.

"My dad was wondering when the parents can come meet you?"

Rolabi nodded. "Following the tryout, I will meet with parents."

Devon glanced at Rolabi, confused. Tryout? Freddy had told him that he was automatically on the team if he showed up. He had been so worried about getting through the training, he hadn't even thought about having to try out. What if his offense got him cut?

Of course he would be cut. It would be better for everyone, himself included. This had all been a mistake. But he couldn't shake a little feeling of dismay, even fear, at the prospect of being kicked off the team. It surprised him.

If you really want your cage, it will be waiting.

Devon glanced at the big man. *That* voice had been his. There was no doubt.

What cage? he thought.

The one you built for yourself. Why did you build it?

Devon turned away, his eyes screwing shut, his cheeks hot. Images and voices snuck into his consciousness—wisps of smoke from an unseen fire—but he drove them away. Pushed them down and down into some lockbox he had created. That was where they belonged. Hidden away.

And then you joined them.

"We are going to start with a scrimmage," Rolabi said.

Devon tried to hide his disappointment. He had hoped they would start with some physical drills so he could showcase his athleticism. Now he might have to shoot the ball and be immediately humiliated. What if he got cut on the second day? What if they all laughed at him?

He looked at the others, feeling his throat tighten. He tried to clear his throat and coughed, then saw someone looking at him, and flushed.

Last night, he had admitted to his nana how nervous he'd been at practice . . . almost sick from it.

She'd said, "Anxiety has a feeling to it, Devon. It sits in your bones like a cold weight, and the more you ask it to leave, the more comfortable it gets. You get nervous about the anxiety itself, and that makes a nasty little circle. I saw it with your grandpa, rest his soul. So don't bother asking it to leave. Let it sit. If you don't ask for its opinion, it will stop giving you one."

He tried to remember that. Just let it sit. Play the game. One possession at a time.

"You think you're nervous?" a grumpy voice said. "I get to be a giant drum set."

Devon glanced around, then scowled. *Buildings don't speak*, he reminded himself.

"Or humans don't listen," the voice retorted.

"We are going to use a different ball today," Rolabi said, drawing one out from deep inside his bag. "Last year's starters versus the bench players. Devon will play for the latter."

Devon tried to remember who the bench players were. He saw a few boys look at him appraisingly and assumed they must be from the bench team: Reggie, Vin, Jerome, and Big John.

Twig and Big John stepped up for the toss, so Devon matched up with A-Wall.

Just play the game, Devon thought again, trying to control his already-pounding heart.

He played with his father in the street most nights, but it was different to be back on a real court. There was pressure here. Less time to think. Moving bodies and shouting and run-ins. He decided to be very careful— he was *not* going to start the training camp by hurting somebody.

Devon gingerly sidled up to A-Wall. He was a slightly stooped kid with an Afro and a smattering of freckles beneath his eyes. He was chewing on a mangled toothpick.

"So you're the new power forward," A-Wall said, eyeing him over. "You're big."

"Uh . . . yeah," Devon said.

"A-Wall," he said, extending a hand. "They call me that because I lose my temper. Just in games, though. Never at my own team. I mean, besides a few times. But rarely. Don't sweat it."

Devon frowned and shook his hand. "Oh. Devon. That's . . . just my name."

"Cool. I think I met a dog named Devon once. He was a stray. Had fleas, I think."

Devon stared at him, wondering if it was a joke, but A-Wall seemed quite sincere.

"Cool," Devon murmured.

"I think your team has the ball, bro," A-Wall said.

Devon realized that Vin was dribbling up the floor, so he sprinted to the post to get open. A-Wall stomped after him. Devon spread his legs, bracing himself, and A-Wall hurried to get in position and tried to push him off the low post. Devon didn't move an inch.

"It's like pushing against a wall," A-Wall muttered. "And I would know."

Devon glanced back. A-Wall was certainly . . . unique. But when he saw the sweat beading on A-Wall's forehead, and the strain on his face, he let himself be pushed out. He didn't want to make anyone nervous. Or *afraid*.

"New kid . . . switch!"

Devon turned to see Big John running toward him, gesturing for Devon to move. He quickly ran to the other block, keeping clear so he didn't run into Twig, who looked very fragile. A-Wall hurried after Devon, grabbing on to his arms and holding on like the reins of a dogsled.

"I foul a lot," A-Wall said conversationally. "Devon, huh? You could be D-Wall."

"I . . . uh . . . Why?"

A-Wall snorted. "Devon . . . strong like a wall. What's to get? Uh-oh."

Rain had stolen the ball, but he heaved a three and missed badly.

Devon got into position down low again. His guards—Vin, Jerome, and Reggie—moved the ball around the three-point line, and then Reggie threw the ball to him. Devon caught the pass and glanced back. A-Wall had stepped away, maybe wary of Devon's looming elbows, so Devon was wide-open for a shot. He turned to the hoop, bringing the ball up for a quick bank shot.

"Just take your time," his dad always said—usually right before Devon missed.

He looked toward the basket, trying to remember to tuck his elbow. His eyes widened.

The hoop was the size of a coin. The backboard was the same, the ball was the same . . . the hoop was just *minuscule*. He couldn't have fit his index finger through it. Devon stared at the miniature net, bewildered. There was no conceivable way he could get the ball through that rim.

Short of options, he turned and passed the ball back to Vin at the point.

"Take that shot, big man!" Vin shouted angrily.

Devon was about to gesture to the hoop to show him how small it was when he saw that it had gone back to normal again. Had he imagined the tiny rim? He scratched his head.

"Yeah," the surly voice said, "you're bonkers. Might as well do some cleaning instead."

"Who are you?" Devon whispered, looking around.

"Your conscience," the voice said sarcastically. "Now stop stepping on me, you clod."

The rest of the game wasn't much better. Devon soon realized that everyone was acting strangely . . . that, or they were all really bad at basketball. A-Wall kept trying to touch something invisible, and he was pretty sure Reggie started crying at one point. Devon constantly found himself facing a mini rim with an oversize beach ball. Combined with his reluctance to bump into anybody or fight for rebounds, he was pretty much useless. His unwillingness to shoot clearly irked his point guard, Vin, who kept shouting, "Take the shot, dude!" or "What are you doing, big man?" or "You were so open, bro!"

At one point, Vin ran past him with a pronounced scowl.

"You join the team to never score a point?" he snarled. "Step it up, man!"

Devon didn't know what to say. To him, the message was clear: *We don't want you here.* He remembered it well. Devon wanted to storm out of the gym. Instead, he kept running and moving and refusing to take a shot.

After a strange sequence where Rain seemed to be trying out some sort of slow-motion strategy, Rolabi walked onto the court. He hadn't said a word throughout the awful scrimmage.

"That will be all for today."

"We aren't going to do any drills?" Peño asked, frowning.

Rolabi didn't seem to hear him. The coach just put the game ball in his bag, sat on the bleachers, and checked his watch. The instant he did, Devon heard a deafening crash. He turned to the far wall. A gust of freezing wind came roaring in from the now wide-open locker room door. Then, just as suddenly, the wind stopped, and the door slammed shut.

"Where . . . How did . . . ?" Big John said, sounding almost faint.

Devon turned back to the bleachers.

Once again, Rolabi Wizenard had suddenly and inexplicably vanished.

"He never says goodbye," the grumpy voice said. "Rude, really."

Devon rubbed his temples and went back to his duffel bag, trying to remember if the world had always been this nonsensical. Clearly, he'd spent a little too much time alone. He wondered if everything he was seeing and hearing was because of the anxiety too. Maybe his nana would know.

He sat down on the bench and pulled his ratty old bag out from underneath. After the new shoes, they hadn't had the money for a bag, but he didn't mind—it reminded him of his grandpa. Devon frowned. There was a card resting on the bag—blue and white with a big *W* and a number. So Rolabi *had* left a way to contact him. Devon tucked it in the bag. Nana would be happy, at least.

"So," Peño said, sliding up beside him on the bench. "New guy. Home-schooler. Big baller."

"You're not going to rhyme, are you?" Lab asked from Peño's other side.

"Maybe later," Peño said. "Just want to get to know the new kid. For instance, I noticed you don't like to shoot. Or rebound. Or push people. And yet you're huge. I'm a little confused."

Devon forced a smile. "I . . . I was just getting used to the team."

"Understandable," Peño said. "Usually I can dribble. I just . . . well . . . It was a weird day. But, man, be big. Or at least show me some workouts. You're like an ox. A box. A lock stock and—"

"Please stop," Lab moaned.

"My brother doesn't get my genius," Peño said, sighing dramatically. "Well?"

Vin hung up his cell phone. He seemed to be the only player who had one.

"A recording. It said the line was for parents. And it said 'Good night, Vin,' which was creepy."

"He's a witch," Big John said.

They proceeded to launch into an argument, and Peño patted Devon's knee.

"See you tomorrow, bro. Step on somebody, will you? Just not me. I'm too beautiful."

Devon laughed without thinking, and Peño shot him a grin and joined the debate.

"You see any warts?" he said. "And witches don't wear suits, dummy."

"How many witches you know?" Big John rebuked.

"Well . . . we got your mama—"

Big John chased after him, and Peño scampered away, laughing uproariously. Devon watched them run around the gym and laughed again. Maybe he could give it *one* more day.

THE
DAISY

Victory happens in the mind first.

❖ WIZENARD ◇ PROVERB ❖

YOU LISTEN TO that Rolabi," Nana said, wagging her finger again. "Don't talk back to him."

Devon sighed as he swung one leg out of the car. Last night, Nana had dialed the phone number Rolabi had given out and proceeded to stay on the phone for nearly thirty minutes, talking like she'd reconnected with a childhood best friend. And after, she had told anyone who would listen that Rolabi Wizenard was a "blessing." She wouldn't tell them anything else, though.

"When do I ever talk back?" Devon said. He closed the car door.

"Don't make me point out the irony here," Nana said.

From the back seat, Keya leaned out an open window and pointed a finger-gun at him. "Pew . . . pew . . . pew—"

"Enough with shooting people!" Nana shouted. "I'm going to ship you off to space soon, girl."

"Good," Keya said.

Nana massaged the bridge of her nose. "I'm supposed to be retired. Taking it easy. Ha!"

She drove off, leaving Devon to wave from the parking lot. The car pulled out into the road, squeaking and bumping and barely getting along. They had only the one—both his mom and dad took a bus to work so his nana would have a car for emergencies. It meant they both had to leave before sunrise, but they never complained, even when they returned after dark.

He kicked a rolling paper bag. Devon had lived in the Bottom his whole life, but he had confined himself to his house for so long, he had almost forgotten how destitute the streets were.

He pulled open the creaky old doors and walked into the gym. Rolabi was nowhere to be seen, but a few guys were already getting ready on the benches: Reggie, Peño, Lab, and Vin.

"What up, big brute?" Peño said.

Devon just nodded and sat down.

"Not much of a talker," Peño said, as if explaining to the others.

"We noticed," Vin muttered.

Devon busied himself in his bag, pretending he didn't hear them. He slid his shoes on and started walking around the gym, tuning out their conversations. Nana was forever snapping him out of his daydreams. She was a strict teacher. He didn't get summer break, and she had given him these ten days off only because she wanted him to make friends. Everyone in his family wanted him to be the kid he had been before that day. They wanted him to forget what had happened.

But Devon couldn't just talk to these boys like he was a normal kid. He wasn't.

Normal—a common and impossible goal.

Devon sighed inwardly. When he had loosened up, Devon went back to the bench and sat down. He had a ball now, of course, but it seemed everyone else was talking. He wasn't going to go shoot alone where they could all watch him. So instead he just sat there, hands in his lap, listening to the others talk about Rolabi.

"It was magic, man," Big John was saying.

"There's no such thing as magic," Lab replied, rolling his eyes.

"Is that so?" a deep voice asked from behind them.

It was like someone had flipped the benches. The entire team—Devon included—spilled forward, twisting to look and shouting as they toppled awkwardly to the ground. Devon smacked his chin hard enough to rattle teeth.

"If you don't believe in magic," Rolabi said solemnly, "you need to get out more."

Devon massaged his sore chin. Everyone else was still groaning.

"We will start with laps," Rolabi announced.

The team climbed back to their feet and took off. They were moving at a slow pace, but Devon noticed that some players looked exhausted after only a few laps. Big John was already teetering. Devon wondered if they had done any cardio in previous seasons. It didn't look like they had.

"How many laps we got to do, you think?" Vin asked.

"I don't know," Jerome muttered. "Could be all day."

"Don't say that," Big John said, wheezing.

When they had circled the court five times, Rolabi spoke again.

"We will take free throws, one at a time. As soon as someone scores, you will stop running for the day. If you miss, the team runs five more laps."

Devon felt a lump form in his throat. Would *he* have to shoot? He was terrible at free throws. His dad had estimated him at about a 9 percent shooter on their old hoop, which even he said had to be some sort of record.

"I got this," Peño said, heading right for the free-throw line.

Most of the team had already doubled over, so there were no complaints. Devon looked around, amazed. Why were they in such bad shape? How could they actually play a full game?

Peño accepted a pass from Rolabi and proceeded to the free-throw line, moving with exaggerated slowness. He dribbled a few times, took a deep breath, looked up, and then froze.

He seemed uncertain. He kept glancing from Rolabi to the hoop, mumbling something.

Finally, Peño crouched down and heaved the ball over the net and out of bounds.

Devon stared, bewildered. That shot was even worse than his. Maybe he would fit in here after all.

"Five more laps," Rolabi said.

Devon felt it before he saw it—a shift in balance, a sudden pull. He crouched down in alarm as the entire gym suddenly tilted up on one end. They were now at the base of a steep hardwood hill, and the far wall was *up*. He blinked, disbelieving, but the steep incline remained.

"I think I pulled something." The cantankerous voice was back. "A left support strut, maybe."

"Does anyone else see this?" Jerome whispered.

"Begin," Rolabi said.

There was a pause, and then Twig started up the hill. The team, short of options, trudged after him. Devon threw himself forward with every step, fingers gripping the floor and feet driving him upward with splayed steps to avoid slipping. When they reached the top, Devon turned to the baseline, ready to climb. The team bunched up again. The floor was tilted down now, steep and smooth.

"Told you he was a witch," Big John said.

"I stand corrected," Peño admitted.

Devon shuffled down and then found himself facing a steep staircase— the floor had morphed into huge steps that built up toward the far wall. Rolabi was perched on one in the middle, seemingly unaware of the changes to the gym. The team broke into another argument, but Devon was beginning to enjoy himself. He leapt up the steps, passing one teammate after another.

Sweat beaded and fell, covered him in a sheen. He felt his worries leaking away.

"A little help, big man?" Peño said.

He was gripping the end of a step, clearly about to slip, and Devon hoisted him up.

"If I wasn't about to pee myself, I'd give you props," Peño muttered.

Devon laughed and kept climbing. Around the next turn was a valley, and he sidled down one end and then exploded up the other, pulling just behind a struggling Twig. He stayed in second place, not wanting to take the lead. He leapt over holes and hurdled obstacles and relished the exhaustion.

He was almost disappointed when they stopped for another shot. But he didn't need to wait long—Rain missed his attempt, screamed at Rolabi, and then stormed off to the bathroom. Apparently, Rain didn't like to miss. But so far, he seemed to do a lot of that.

"Everyone, grab a drink," Rolabi said. "The laps will continue shortly."

As Devon downed the majority of his bottle in one thirsty gulp, he knelt and put one hand to the floor. It seemed like regular hardwood, but it couldn't be. What was this place? How was this all happening?

Did he dare ask someone? He looked at Twig. The words caught in his throat, and he coughed a little, summoning his courage. This was good practice. Just a question. That was it.

"The floors . . . They were moving, right?" Devon asked.

"Yeah," Twig said.

Devon looked away, not wanting to stare at the pockmarks on Twig's cheeks.

"Just checking."

Devon left it there, but he was secretly pleased. He had asked someone a question, and even had a conversation. Sort of. Still, Twig was the first kid he'd talked to other than his sister in years. Nana would be proud.

He finished his bottle with a shake of his head. He had a magic coach and a gym that could shape-shift, and he was busy thinking about a tiny conversation. His priorities were a mess.

Rain returned from the locker room, still looking a little distant, and the drill resumed. Devon continued to excel—always staying just behind the leader. Finally, after what must have been another thirty laps, Reggie hit his free throw. Most of the team looked ready to collapse.

"So you got the cardio too, huh?" Peño said to Devon, wiping his face. "Figures. You can bench-press me and my bro and then run laps around us. I can bench-press a sandwich to my face."

He patted his belly mournfully. "Think I can borrow some abs?"

Devon laughed. He didn't know why, but Peño made him feel at ease. He was the shortest on the team by far—his head was in line with Devon's chest. He was squat and perhaps a *little* flabby, and he had about seven mustache hairs that moved with his quick smile.

"Water break," Rolabi said. "Bring your bottles over here."

They gathered in a seated circle around Rolabi, who dug into his bag and pulled out a potted flower. Devon's mouth fell open. His nana loved flowers and constantly showed him pictures of her old garden. Things like that didn't grow in the Bottom anymore. No one knew why, though his nana said acid rain was to blame—apparently it used to fall all the time when the industries were booming. He had never seen a daisy in person, and he couldn't wait to tell his nana later.

Rolabi gave no instructions. He just stood there and stared at it intently. Devon looked between the coach and the daisy. Maybe they were just supposed to admire it. He certainly liked it.

Peño was sitting beside him, legs flopped out in front of him. He seemed confused.

"What are we supposed to do with the flower?" he asked.

"Isn't it obvious?" Rolabi replied.

Peño looked at the daisy for a moment as if trying to figure out the answer. "No."

"We are going to watch it grow."

"Why?" Lab asked incredulously.

"Small, nearly imperceptible things make the difference between victory and defeat."

Devon thought about that. He was used to staring at nothing, so he figured he might be an expert at this. He shifted and felt himself relax. The flower didn't seem to be moving, but he focused on the petals anyway and rested his hands on his knees, trying to take deep breaths like his nana had taught him when he was feeling anxious. She said breathing was the enemy of panic. He closed his eyes for a moment, relaxing.

Then he felt someone watching him. He opened his eyes and found Rolabi sitting on the other side of the potted flower, cross-legged, hands on his knees. Everyone else was gone.

"Why did you come to this training camp?" Rolabi asked.

Devon looked around, alarmed. He wondered if he had fallen asleep. He hesitated. "I . . . I don't know."

"Yes, you do."

Devon fidgeted, sensing there was no point in lying.

"I knew my parents wanted me to try. To . . . you know . . . make friends."

"I'm not concerned with what they wanted. What do you want?"

Devon was silent for a long time. He wasn't exactly sure. He wanted lots of things, of course, but there seemed to be one connector. One problem that tied everything else together.

"I want to stop being so afraid," he whispered.

"Of?"

Devon looked away. "I don't even know anymore."

To his surprise, Rolabi smiled. "People think fear is a specific thing. Spiders or heights or speaking in public. Not always. Sometimes fear is just darkness itself. In those times, we need only find who turned out the light, and why, and where the switch has gone."

"How do you do that?" Devon whispered.

"Simple. You learn to see in the dark."

The others reappeared, and Rolabi was tucking the daisy into his bag.

"Water bottles away," he said. "We have one more lesson today."

Devon hurried to the bench, glancing at the professor. That conversation hadn't *felt* like a dream. There was no blurring at the edges, no tiredness when he snapped back into reality. It had felt more like the vision from the first day. He shivered at the memory of it. The frightened faces.

Rolabi was now setting up a sort of obstacle course, pulling objects from his bag and tossing them around haphazardly, yet there was nothing random about where they fell. In moments, a full circuit had been assembled, and when he was done, Rolabi took out three basketballs and placed them at half-court.

The team warily gathered in front of them.

"You will complete the circuit," Rolabi said. "A layup on the first hoop and a shot from the elbow on the other. When you return, pass the ball to the player who is first in line. Three may go at a time. You may begin."

It seemed simple enough. Devon wasn't thrilled about having to take the shots, but at least everyone would be busy and there wouldn't be much time to watch one another. He hoped he could make the initial layup, at least. But before they could begin, Rain started screaming.

A chorus of shouts and cries followed. Devon whirled around, bewildered, and then looked down. His stronger left hand was gone. His wrist now ended in a fleshy wall, perfectly flat, as though there had never been a hand there at all. He ran his right fingers through the empty space and felt nothing. The hand had simply vanished.

"What is this?" Big John shrieked, his cheeks quivering.

"An exercise in balance," Rolabi said. "Proceed."

"No!" Lab said, storming out of the line. "This is too much!"

He started for the bench, seemed to remember something, and whirled back to Rolabi. "And give me back my hand, you wack job!"

Devon felt the smooth stump again, too stunned to think. He vaguely wondered how he would he tell his parents. And Keya. They would be devastated. He pictured his nana's reaction: "You're still doing your homework!" He frowned. Well . . . the other three would be sad.

"Shall we begin?" Rolabi said.

There was a long pause, and then Rain picked up the ball with his left hand and started the circuit. Devon looked uncertainly at his missing hand as he moved up in the line. He could barely play offense with his left hand . . . he had no chance with his right.

When he received a pass, he awkwardly dribbled with one hand toward the hoop. It felt like he was dribbling with a wooden club, not part of his own body. It got worse from there. He hit the bottom of the backboard on the layup. He lost the ball four times through the cones. When he emerged, thoroughly humiliated, he tried to pass the ball through the vertical hoop and missed by ten feet. His right hand wasn't just weaker— it was *useless*.

He finally made it back to the line and threw the ball to Reggie, his cheeks burning. His performance was even more awful than he could have imagined. He didn't make a single layup or jump shot. He wasn't even close on the passing drill. As an hour or maybe even hours rolled by, frustration set in and made his efforts even worse. He rushed, fuming, and chucked wild shots. At one point, Devon retrieved his rebound— exasperated after yet another air ball—and passed to the front of the line. At least, he tried. The ball sailed wide and smacked Vin in the head so hard that he toppled over.

Devon froze.

He saw it again and felt his stomach turn. A boy on the ground. People shouting. Crying. Devon always hurt people. That's what he did. He was a big stupid brute, and he always would be. He felt the weight of that fact settle in. He shouldn't have come here. He could never be a Badger.

Regret is another word for self-pity.

Devon felt a little stirring of anger at the voice. What did Rolabi know about his past?

It's the truth, he fumed. *If you knew me, you would understand.*

If you knew yourself, so would you.

Devon glared at the professor, his body shaking. He could still leave. He could forget about this whole stupid idea. He didn't want to face the past. He didn't want to remember what he was. Maybe he did have a cage. But it was safer there. He could hide and be done with this.

Rolabi's green eyes turned to Devon, shimmered, and held him in place. The gym was gone.

Iron bars sprang up in front of him, leaping out of the floor and racing for the ceiling. They bent and converged over his head. The lights dimmed. Soon there was only the cage, and darkness beyond, interrupted by some ominous orange glow, like firelight. Devon gripped the bars with his remaining hand, panicked.

"Hey!" he shouted. "Rolabi! Anyone!"

He spotted a door on the side of the cage. He ran to it and heaved, but it was locked. He found the lockbox and the keyhole and tried to shake the door loose but couldn't. He was trapped.

"Let me out!" he said.

The darkness seemed to close in. Even the meager firelight was fading. He shook the bars again, frantic, trying to break the door down. He lowered his shoulder and charged into it, bouncing clean off and clattering to the floor. He lay there, shoulder bruised, watching the dark.

"Why don't you just ask the jailor?" Rolabi said.

He was standing outside the door, in a spot that Devon knew had been empty a moment ago.

Devon climbed to his feet. "Rolabi! Yes, please. Let me out."

"Who said the jailor was me?" he asked.

Devon heard something jingle. He looked down to see a key ring dangling from his shorts. He unclipped it and held the keys up in his trembling hand. *Just ask the jailor.*

"When will the sentence end?" Rolabi asked.

Then he was gone, and so was the cage, and Devon was back in Fairwood. He whirled around. The team was arguing. The practice seemed to have ended. He stood there, shivering, looking down at his remaining right hand. It had seemed so real. He'd felt the bars. The cold.

Devon rubbed his forehead. There was no such thing as magic. It was impossible.

"Tell that to him," the grumpy voice said.

"I am not talking to a gym," Devon muttered, heading for the bench.

"So talk to yourself," the voice said. "That's *much* less crazy."

Devon scowled and plopped onto the bench. He ran through the day in his mind. He had made his way through a shape-shifting gym, stared at a daisy, lost a hand, ended up in a cage, and was now talking to a gym. He had come to this training camp for normalcy. That was proving to be tough.

Devon changed his shoes and shirt and started for the doors, ignoring the others. He kept picturing the cage, even here. He felt as though he could almost touch the cold metal of the bars. As he reached for the doors, he heard the grumpy voice:

"What did you do that was so bad, anyway?"

Devon paused, his fingers on the handle. "I left my cage," he whispered. He hurried out just as the first tears clouded his eyes.

THE BEAST

*If you worry about what others think of you,
you don't think enough of yourself.*

✧ WIZENARD ③② PROVERB ✧

DEVON RAISED HIS left hand to wave goodbye, hesitated when he saw the stump, and then awkwardly waved with his right hand instead. His nana waved back and drove away with no mention of his missing hand.

An old paper bag rolled past his feet, heading toward a rapidly growing pile that was forming in the corner of the parking lot. Piles formed at odd places throughout the Bottom, like coral reefs slowly spreading out across the concrete. Over time the garbage grew sodden and began to decay into a multicolored mush, which only made the smell worse. He knew the trash was a Bottom problem only—his nana had taught him all about the rest of Dren. She had actually been outside of the Bottom—when she was a little girl, before the ban on its residents. She had even been to Argen.

Argen was the nicest region—pristine white streets, wide boulevards lined with trees. It was the seat of President Talin's loyalist government and about as different from the Bottom as possible. His nana said President Talin had always hated the Bottom, but she never said why.

It seemed obvious to Devon. It was a dump.

As he stepped into the gym, Devon felt his stomach give a familiar anxious flop. Every night since training started, he'd told himself that the next day's practice would be different. That he would talk and be funny. His new teammates didn't know him. So why couldn't he be the joker? The smart one? The cool, composed one?

He could be *anyone* he wanted. And yet, he had chosen brooding, troubled Devon. And every morning he made the same choice again. He was silent. Afraid. The same broken, timid brute he'd been since what seemed like forever.

Devon sat down at the end of the bench and pulled on his shoes, listening to the others.

Their conversations only made him lonelier.

"She definitely likes me, man."

"My brother doesn't have to do nothing . . . you know? I got every chore going."

"You see the Aces last night? Porter was on fire, man. Just draining threes like crazy."

Devon had seen the game—they had a lone television, and his dad always caught games with him when he got home. Devon wanted to talk about it. But the words died on his lips, and the front doors of Fairwood swung open at the same time. Rain and Freddy walked in, and Devon could immediately sense their uneasiness. Freddy looked like he might turn and run. His eyes were darting around, looking for something. No . . . *someone*. Devon frowned. What did he want?

They said their hellos, and then Freddy got to the point.

"Rain tells me there are some problems with Rolabi."

Devon looked from Rain to the rest of the team. Realization dawned on him. Were they going to *fire* Rolabi? Some of the reactions to Freddy's announcement seemed relieved or at least unfazed, but Twig and Reggie looked as concerned as Devon felt. Had there been a vote? When had that happened? Why had no one asked him?

Because they don't want you here, he thought glumly.

"Were you on any of these teams, Frederick?"

Devon jumped and turned to the north wall, where Rolabi Wizenard was staring up at the banners. Devon heard sharp intakes of breath and muttered curses from the others as they realized he must have been listening. Freddy looked like he might faint and took a big step back.

"What . . . Where did . . . ?" Freddy said.

"I suppose you were too young," Rolabi said. "It's been so long. Can I help you?"

"Yes," Freddy said. "Can I speak to you privately?"

Rolabi walked toward them, stopping just a few feet from a petrified Freddy.

"No need," Rolabi said, his eyes flicking around the group. "Go ahead."

Devon turned to Freddy, but he was gone. Everyone was. Devon was sitting alone.

"I was quite a large child growing up."

Devon flinched and turned to find Rolabi sitting on the bench beside him.

"I . . . can imagine," he said.

"Tall, of course, but also broad. Strong. My mother said I was born of the mountain."

Rolabi smiled—the first time Devon had seen him do so. It made his face soften—the long scars on his cheeks crinkled and faded into his warm brown skin, and laugh lines formed at the corners of his eyes.

"I could dunk at seven," Rolabi continued. "I broke the net at eight."

"That's kind of awesome," Devon said.

"But I stood out, I suppose. And I always asked myself: What is the purpose of strength?"

Devon frowned. "What do you mean?"

"If we are stronger than others, or wealthier, or wiser . . . *why*? What do we do with our difference?"

"I . . . I don't know. I don't think we have to do anything with it."

"Ah," Rolabi said, glancing at him, "that is where we disagree. I think we *must*."

The team suddenly returned, and Freddy and Rolabi were facing each other.

"Rolabi will remain the coach," Freddy whispered. "I . . . I look forward to the season."

With that, he walked out of the gym. The doors closed, and a hush fell over the team. Devon glanced around, looking at the team's reactions. He for one was glad Rolabi was staying. The magic could be unnerving, but Devon knew he needed some help. Rolabi was offering it.

"Today we will be working on defense," Rolabi said. "Before I can teach you proper zones and strategies, I must teach each of you how to be a defender. They are not the same lessons."

Devon's mind was spinning with questions, but a noise interrupted with a more pressing one. Something was *scratching*. It raked over and over, a few seconds apart, as regular as a chime. The sound made the hairs on his arms stand on end. Devon looked around warily.

"What must a defender always be?" Rolabi asked.

The scratching was growing louder. Devon noticed that Twig was staring at the locker room door, and he followed his gaze. The door was trembling on its hinges. There was something in there. Something *big*. And it was trying to get out. An animal, maybe.

Everyone was talking, but Devon just watched the door, transfixed, curious.

"*Ready*. They must always be ready. A defender must be a step ahead of their opponents. They must outthink and outwork and out-strategize. They must always be ready to move."

"What is that?" Rain asked finally.

"Can someone open the locker room door?" Rolabi said.

Everyone who hadn't already figured out the source of the sound whirled to face the door. It was still pulsating with every long, gouging pass of claws on steel. Devon could feel the noise in his teeth.

"What's in there?" Peño said.

"A friend," Rolabi replied.

No one moved for the door. Devon felt frozen, despite his curiosity, and no one else seemed to be able to summon the courage either. Rolabi waited, saying nothing.

Finally, Twig started for the locker room. Devon was surprised. He seemed to be the outsider on the team—though Devon was vying for the title—and always acted so nervous. Yet here he was, laying his trembling fingers on the door handle.

Twig pulled the door open, and a tiger strolled out. Devon stared, awestruck. He had never seen anything so big—apart from Rolabi. The creature was muscular and lithe but moved with easy grace.

"Meet Kallo," Rolabi said. "She has graciously volunteered to help us today."

Kallo sat down beside Rolabi, accepting a scratch behind the ears with a purr.

"Rain," Rolabi said, his eyes flicking to him. "Step forward."

Rain took a moment, and then stepped forward, his skin ashen. "Yes?"

Rolabi rolled a ball to center court, where it stopped perfectly on the dot.

"The drill is simple," Rolabi explained. "Get the ball. Kallo will play defense."

Devon frowned and looked at Rolabi. Did he just say they had to get by the *tiger*? The animal was magnificent, but Devon had heard those claws raking through metal like it was nothing—he could see the tips poking from their sheaths even now. Kallo paced, her fangs bared in something like a smile.

Rain certainly wasn't smiling. His knees were wobbling, his left hand clenched at his side. Devon could sympathize. He wasn't sure he would have the courage to face Kallo either.

To Devon's surprise, Rain went for it. He faked left with a drop of his shoulder and then drove hard to the right with a burst of speed. It was futile. Kallo pounced on him, licked his face, and then slipped off. Rain lay there like a corpse.

"She killed him!" Peño shouted.

"I'm fine," Rain said, climbing to his feet. "She didn't hurt me."

"Devon," Rolabi said.

Devon turned to the professor, wondering why he had been chosen next. Had he done something wrong? Could Rolabi see his shaking knees? Devon turned to the tiger, trying to steel himself. Rain had survived, so he couldn't back out now without looking like a complete coward in front of his teammates. He took a deep breath and charged.

Devon tried Rain's move in reverse—right and then left—and a blur of orange-and-black fur hit him before he could even blink. He found himself flat on his back, staring up at intelligent purple eyes. Kallo licked him right across his face with a tongue like Velcro hooks.

"Thanks," Devon muttered.

He climbed back to his feet, embarrassed that he had been tackled so quickly. But that embarrassment didn't last for long. No one got close to the ball. Big John flat-out refused to go, which resulted in a heated exchange with Twig and an intervention from Rolabi. Big John stormed into the locker room and slammed the door so hard that the paint came off. Devon was surprised at how many hissy fits the team threw.

"I've been clinging to that paint," the surly voice said.

Stop talking to me, Fairwood, thought Devon. *Gym. Or whatever your name is.*

"Of course. Why would anyone want to talk to me?"

Devon frowned and stared at the closest wall. *Does everyone else hear you?*

"You are the one using grana, kid. You tell me how it works."

The . . . grana?

"Oh, boy. Rolabi has got his work cut out for him."

"None of you got the ball," Rolabi said, scratching Kallo behind her ear. "But you all showed real courage. That is a good start."

Devon felt his left hand before he saw it. He held it up for a relieved inspection, flexing his fingers. The hand didn't feel sore or tight at all from its daylong absence. The other players celebrated with high fives and props, but Devon stood alone and clasped his hands together.

It hadn't always been so hard. When he was in school, he had been shy, but he had a few friends. He played basketball and dominated in gym class, and he always joined the pickup games during recess. It had been one of those games that had ended his time in school. A split-second decision that he had replayed every single day since.

Step away. Breathe. How many times had he said those words to himself? Whispered them in the dark?

A flash of movement caught Devon's eye. He turned and saw a floating ball, black as outer space and fluctuating like a droplet of water. Its shape changed constantly, stretching and pulsating before returning to a sphere. Devon was transfixed, but he felt strangely cold, and his skin was prickling like mad. Something about that orb made him nervous. Even afraid.

Devon stepped back, nearly falling. He saw something in the blackness.

"Ah," Rolabi said, turning to the orb. "Just in time."

"What . . . what is it?" Peño asked. Judging from the hush in his voice, he was disconcerted too.

"That is something you all will want to catch," Rolabi said. "No, it is something you all *must* catch. We can call it the orb for reference. Whoever catches it will become a far better player. But it won't last forever. If no one catches it, we run laps." He nodded to the orb. "Go!"

The others took off after the orb like a pack of wolves. Devon held back for a moment, but soon the shouts and enthusiasm of the others took over. He joined the pursuit—a chaotic mass of players stumbling and tripping and diving atop one another. The orb was incredibly fast. It dodged between them like a bullet, always seemingly just within reach until the very moment it wasn't, tempting them into disaster. Peño went flying. Jerome smacked his chin off the floor. Devon lunged and landed on his stomach, knocking the wind out of him.

"There it goes!" Vin shouted.

"I got you now!" Lab cried, before missing and diving face-first onto the hardwood.

"Look out!" someone else called.

"Get it!"

"What the heck is this thing?"

In the end, none of them caught it. The orb flew too close to Kallo, and she jumped up and swallowed it whole. She settled beside Rolabi, flashing the team another toothy grin.

"A true defender," Rolabi said admiringly. "Get some water. Laps and free throws."

There was a chorus of sighs, and the players marched to the benches, defeated. Devon gulped back some water. Whatever else this training was accomplishing, he figured the team was certainly getting into better shape. Big John re-emerged from the locker room, and the laps started again.

As before, the gym changed with every turn: inclines, declines, stairs, valleys, and at one point, a seemingly never-ending spiral staircase, which caused at least one player to get nauseous.

As before, no one seemed to be able to hit a free throw.

Rain missed, then Peño and Lab and Reggie. As the team cycled through, Devon kept shrinking back, hoping desperately that he wouldn't have to take a shot. Finally, just before he would have had to step up as the last man to shoot, Twig hit his free throw. Everyone doubled over, gasping in relief, and Devon most of all. How long could he hide his game? What would he do when the time came for him to shoot? The thought made him more nauseous than the stairs. "Tomorrow we will work on team defense," Rolabi said. "Get some rest tonight."

He headed for the front doors with Kallo at his side.

"Are . . . are you taking the tiger?" Peño asked uncertainly.

The doors burst open, slamming into the cinder-block wall on either side, and Rolabi and Kallo strode into the daylight like two friends going out for a coffee.

"He should really learn how to say goodbye," Peño muttered.

Everyone shuffled to the bench. Devon struggled to pry off his sopping shoes—it was like they were sealed to his feet with glue. He finally wrenched them off and grimaced at the smell. He would have to leave them on the porch tonight or Nana would have his head. She always said, "Body odor is perfectly natural and perfectly un-allowed near me."

A-Wall sat down beside him, wiping the sweat from his eyes.

"My ma ain't gonna believe there was a tiger here," he said mournfully. "Last night she was like: 'Boy, your gym ain't changing. Your puny brain is.' And never mind that elevator, man!"

"What elevator?" Devon murmured.

A-Wall glanced at him. "You wasn't on that? Lucky you. I almost puked up my muffin."

Devon frowned and started zipping up his bag. So they were all having visions . . . but why? If this magic, or grana, was real, why was it happening now? Here in the Bottom, of all places?

If you were to plant a seed, where would you put it?

Devon recognized Rolabi's deep voice. *A seed for what?*

The beginning.

"Drop some lines, Peño," Jerome said, cutting into his thoughts.

Devon had no idea what Jerome was talking about, but he didn't have to wait long. Peño began to bob back and forth, waving his hand in front of him with his index finger pointed out, and freestyled another verse. They laughed as Peño struck a dramatic pose for the banners.

The laughter slowly died off, and the team began to file out of the gym. Devon held back, waiting for the others to leave. He wanted to enjoy a little silence before going home, and it wasn't long before he was sitting in an empty gym. He walked out onto the court, his socks leaving sweaty trails in his wake like imprints in the sand. Devon stopped at center court, listening to the silence. He breathed in the must and the dry rot and relished the feel of the wood. "The kid is a danger," an unfamiliar, faraway voice said.

Devon stiffened and looked around, but the gym was still empty.

"It was an accident," someone said.

Not someone . . . his mom.

"It was no accident," an angry voice replied. "He just snapped."

"They were calling him names—"

"My son is in the hospital!"

Devon spun around, cringing at the voice. It seemed to echo around the gym.

"Devon doesn't know his own strength—" his mom said.

"He's a brute. He can't be trusted around other kids."

"What do you want?"

"I want him out of this school."

Devon closed his eyes, feeling the pressure welling up behind them. It had been his choice, ultimately. The principal suspended him but didn't actually expel him. She had wanted to give him a second chance. But

Devon was tired of the comments and hushed voices and the parents looking at him warily as they dropped their children off. Devon, the big, ugly beast. Devon the loose cannon.

Devon the animal.

Tears slipped down his face. After the suspension was over, he didn't go back. As the weeks went by, he drifted. He didn't want to see the kids at school. After a few months, he didn't want to leave the house.

Devon opened his eyes and stepped back, alarmed.

Kallo was sitting across from him.

"Oh," he murmured. "Hey, Kallo . . ."

She growled, baring her teeth, and he took a cautious step back.

"Umm . . . are you okay?" he whispered.

She lunged at him. Without thinking, he grabbed on to her neck as they both fell backward in a rolling tangle of limbs. She pinned him, gnashing her teeth, getting closer and closer. She wasn't playing this time. Panicked, he used every ounce of strength he had to hold her back, crying out, straining. He cocked his legs, placed his socked feet on her chest, and launched her backward. He scrambled up again and faced her, fists raised, panting.

She sat down and gave him another toothy grin.

"People have many names for those whose strength they cannot match," a deep voice mused.

Devon spun around, but Rolabi was nowhere to be seen.

"But their names do not define us. We should never be ashamed of our strength."

Devon turned back to Kallo, but she was gone. He stood there, breathing shallowly, adrenaline coursing through him. Raw energy, ready to be unleashed. He stared at his hands.

Be the beast.

⑤
THE TIGER INSIDE

*Courage is understanding that it is okay to be afraid,
and then to walk on regardless.*
◆ WIZENARD ㉒ PROVERB ◆

THE NEXT MORNING, Devon pulled open the doors to the gym and froze, an unbidden smile forming on his lips. There was a castle on the court. Not a jumping one. An actual castle.

"Cool," he whispered.

It took up about a third of the gym, rising up from the hardwood like a great stone tree that had sprung up overnight. A smell of rubber hung in the air, and salt beneath it. Devon's eyes fell on the trophy that sat atop the castle: the Elite Youth League national trophy. He had never dreamed of playing for it—not for four years, anyway. But now it drew him in. He wanted it.

It was an impossible dream: no team from the Bottom had ever come close to winning it. But playing for the Badgers, or any team for that matter, had been an impossible dream a few weeks ago as well. What was one more?

Devon realized he didn't hear any voices. He looked around. The gym was empty.

"Why do you play this game?"

Devon turned to find Rolabi leaning against the wall, staring at the castle. Devon's eyes fell on the scars that ran from cheek to chin—thin and long, as though they were made by the point of a sword, or sharp claws.

"I . . . I always played it growing up," Devon said. "And then with my dad."

"And you love it enough to leave the house after all this time. To try again. Why?"

Devon hesitated. It was true. A part of him had thought he would never leave the house, but the prospect of playing ball again had lured him out. He had dreamed of it. Yearned for the court.

"Because it's simple. It's the only place where I know what I am supposed to do."

Rolabi was silent for a moment. "Yes, simple things are often the most beautiful." He laid a hand on Devon's shoulder. "You should be proud that you came here. Now take it further."

"How?" Devon murmured.

"Kallo showed you last night."

Devon suddenly heard voices and saw the team gathered on the benches, laughing and talking. He glanced at Rolabi and then went to change his shoes. So Rolabi wanted him to unleash his strength. But what if that meant someone got hurt? How could he take that chance?

The last few players filtered in, each stopping to speak with Rolabi. When everyone was ready, Rolabi called them to the castle that dominated the center of the gym. Devon gazed up at it, running his fingers along the walls. They were smooth, explaining at least part of the smell. It was made of rubber. He supposed the salt in the air was just Rolabi. It seemed to hang on him.

"Today we are working on team defense," Rolabi said.

"Like . . . zone defense?" Peño asked.

"In time," Rolabi said. "First you have to learn the fundamentals."

Devon stared up at the fortress, thinking of the castles in the old stories his nana told him. He used to love them. He still had the books. When he was younger, he used to picture himself as a knight. Tall and strong but also noble and composed. Sir Devon the Strong. A true hero.

He heard a thud and turned to see a pile of red and blue items scattered about the floor.

"Take one of each, please," Rolabi said.

Devon pulled on a red helmet, clipping it beneath his chin, and grabbed a matching red pad. It was tough and sturdy, with two handholds on the back. He glanced at the others as they picked up their own helmets and pads and divided into their colors. His teammates were Reggie, Lab, A-Wall, and Vin. They glanced at him, probably wondering if he would actually use his size or stay invisible like he had during the scrimmages. Devon was wondering the same thing.

"The game is simple. One team will attack, and the other will defend. The team to get the trophy in the least amount of time wins. The losing team will run laps while the winners shoot around."

"How did you get the national championship trophy?" Peño asked, staring up at it.

Devon could see his hand opening and closing at his side as if itching to touch it.

"I borrowed it," Rolabi said. "Blue team will defend first."

Devon chewed his lip. Was he going to have to . . . *hit* people? What if he hurt them? Was this what Rolabi was preparing him for? Was this all designed for him?

"Come on," Vin said, heading for the benches. "You too, gentle giant."

Devon forced a smile and followed, still trying to decide what to do.

Devon had always been strong. His nana said that when Devon was born, she thought the hospital had mixed him up with a toddler. His mom said the nurses felt sorry for her. As a baby and a little kid, Devon had kept growing and growing. His dad was a weight lifter, and Devon had joined him as soon as he could. When he was five years old, he looked ten. Now that he was twelve, he looked eighteen. It should have been a good thing. But it didn't work out that way.

As soon as they figured out Devon wouldn't thump them, the other kids started calling him names. One time a frustrated basketball coach had called him a dumb ox when he was only seven and trying to learn a zone defense. His teammates called him Dumb Ox after that. He always hated it. He wasn't dumb. He had issues in school, and reading was difficult for him—the words seemed to jumble together. The problems had grown and grown and gone so wrong . . .

Devon shook his head. He needed to focus. He needed to decide if he could take the risk and use his strength.

The red team formed a small huddle.

"What's the plan?" Vin asked.

"Everyone should just take one ramp and go," A-Wall said.

"There are five of us and four ramps," Vin pointed out.

A-Wall sighed. "Does this mean I have to sit out?"

"No, you dolt," Vin said. "We can double-team one of the ramps."

Reggie was staring at the castle. "They'll probably keep one guy to double on defense too."

"Rain, probably," Vin agreed. "Let's just get Devon to run over somebody. *If* he will."

Vin glanced at him with a raised eyebrow, and Devon looked away, cheeks hot.

"Never mind," Vin said. "I forgot he's about as vicious as a fruit fly."

"Listen," Reggie cut in, "we have the advantage. We can choose where we target. I say we start just like you said, A-Wall. Pick your target and go. But if we don't get through after a couple tries of double-teaming, then three or four of us will attack *one* ramp. They won't be able to respond in time.

We'll push through and get to the trophy, with Devon at the lead. Cool?"

He looked right at Devon, challenging him. Devon managed a nod.

"Begin!" Rolabi said, his voice echoing around the gym.

Devon turned to the castle and froze. The old stories had come to life.

They were now facing a castle surrounded by a brackish moat. Wooden bridges stretched to each stone ramp, and blue silk flags billowed from the parapets. Devon realized with a start that even his outfit had changed—he was wearing shimmering silver armor accented with red trim, and his shoes had turned to armored boots. He ran his fingers over the fresh steel, smiling.

Sir Devon the Brave, he thought. *The hero of Fairwood Kingdom.*

For the first time in years, he wanted to show his strength.

"Charge!" Lab shouted.

Devon took off. He spotted Jerome guarding one of the four ramps and headed for him, pad lifted. Devon saw Jerome's eyes widen. They slammed together with a thud of hard leather.

Devon drove his legs forward—short, powerful steps—and Jerome slid back rapidly.

"You're . . . a . . . monster," Jerome said, still sliding up the ramp. "What they feeding you?"

Devon planted one foot after the other, ignoring him. Jerome continued to lose ground.

"A little help!" Jerome cried.

Devon looked up and saw that he was almost to the first level. It was wider there, so he could simply fling Jerome aside and head for the trophy. But before he could push past him, Rain joined the fray. Devon pushed against both of them, and Jerome's steady slide stopped. Rain and Jerome pressed forward, taking ground, but Devon found his footing again about halfway down, matching them. His arms bulged inside their steel casings, the muscles straining.

"Help!" Peño called from elsewhere in the castle. "I got two!"

Jerome looked up. "Rain—"

"You'll be fine," Rain said, disappearing around the corner again.

Devon knew his opponents were in trouble now. He drove forward, pushing Jerome up the ramp.

"A-Wall just took off!" Big John shouted from somewhere else in the fortress.

"So did Lab!" Twig called.

Devon heard feet lumbering across the bridge behind him. He glanced back and saw that both A-Wall *and* Lab had come to join his attack. Jerome saw them too and blanched.

"Oh no," he whispered.

Devon felt the others collide with his back and pushed at the same time. The combined assault sent Jerome flying into the far wall, and Devon, Lab, and A-Wall streamed into the castle and turned for the final ramp, where Rain was facing them alone. Rain lifted his pad, stunned.

"Help!" he shouted.

Devon paused, seeing the dread on his face. But this was the point of the drill. To use his strength. That was what Kallo had shown him. Devon lowered his pad and charged, sending Rain airborne as well, then led the red team up the final ramp to the trophy. He hoisted it with one hand, its rim catching the light.

Sir Devon the Brave saves the day! he thought.

"Way to go, big man!" Reggie said, clapping him on the back.

"The beast!" Vin shouted. "I knew you had it in you!"

Devon felt a flush of pride.

"One minute and forty-seven seconds," Rolabi said. His voice carried over the celebrations, muting them. "Blue team, you will now attack. You have two minutes to prepare."

The blue team dejectedly headed down the nearest ramp to huddle.

Devon put the trophy back and wondered how they would stop the blue team from doing the same thing to them—overwhelming one of the ramps.

"We need a plan," Lab said.

Vin nodded. "It's tough. Devon and I can each take a ramp. Lab, you and Reggie—"

"No," Reggie said.

Everyone turned to him. He looked around the castle and laughed.

"What's funny?" Vin asked.

"It's actually pretty simple," Reggie said. "The other ramps are just distractions."

"What are you talking about?" Lab asked.

Reggie gestured to the trophy. "All we have to do is protect the trophy."

Vin frowned. "Right . . ."

"So we only need to block the last ramp," Reggie said. "That's it."

"Of course," Lab said, whistling.

"We defend it *together*," Reggie said. "Big man, you take the front spot."

He patted Devon on the shoulder, then took the spot closest to the trophy. One by one they stepped in front of Reggie, placing their pads one behind another as if laying bricks. Finally, Devon stepped in front, hoisting his own pad into position like a great iron gate. He set his feet apart and waited, fighting back a smile. Sir Devon the Strong was now literally holding the fort.

"Begin!" Rolabi said.

Devon soon heard the pounding of armored footsteps on the ramps. The blue team charged onto the second level with a triumphant-looking Rain at the lead. But his grin didn't last long: he saw Devon and slid to an abrupt stop, frowning. The rest of the blue team slammed into his back.

Rain narrowed his eyes. "Push!"

The blue team charged into Devon, but he held them easily. The plan was flawless. The attackers strained and pushed again and again, but they couldn't get past the combined resistance of the defense. Finally, when he sensed them weakening, Devon pushed forward with all his strength. The entire blue team crumpled and fell back into a tangled pile against the wall.

"The time is beat," Rolabi said. "The red team wins."

"The beast strikes again!" Lab shouted, shaking Devon's arm and laughing.

This time, Devon didn't bother to hold back the smile. The armor returned to their normal clothing, the moat dried, and the stones turned back to rubber.

"The red team may grab some balls and shoot around," Rolabi said. "Blue team, laps."

As the blue team took off around the gym, Devon and the other reds grabbed their balls and worked on their shots—though Devon was reluctant to attempt anything but layups. He didn't want to ruin his good day. As they shot around, the blue team circled them.

It took the blue team nearly an hour to hit a free throw. When they finally collapsed onto the bench, downing their water bottles, Rolabi called the red team over as well.

So the beast poked its head out.

Devon glanced at the big man. *I . . . got carried away maybe*, he thought.

And you carried them with you.

An old image flashed in front of him, turning his stomach.

There aren't always helmets to protect people, he thought.

In a single breath, all the pride and competitive fire faded away into dread and guilt. Devon had been reckless today. He could have lost control so easily. He could have hurt Rain and Jerome. He stared down at his hands. He really was dangerous.

And so the cage returns.

"What must a defender always be?" Rolabi asked.

Devon blinked. The castle was gone. Not even a scuff or scratch had been left behind on the hardwood.

"Ready," Reggie said.

"The same goes for the entire team. If you are not ready, we are wasting our time." Rolabi turned and headed for the doors.

"Are we done for today?" Peño asked.

"That is up to you."

The doors burst open, and Rolabi walked out. After they closed and the wind died, a chill remained, like a fine mist of icy rain. Devon turned and found the orb waiting at half-court, and it almost seemed to be calling to him. He heard a voice as if from somewhere far away.

Animal. Dangerous. Beast.

Devon shivered and turned away. It fell deathly quiet in the gym.

Twig was the first to go. He charged, missing wildly, and spurred the team to join him. Devon joined in as well, caught up in the chase, and once again the race quickly descended into chaos. Devon managed to hyperextend an elbow and barely avoided a collision with Big John, who tripped regardless. The orb was devious: always just within reach but then too fast to grab. It was maddening. Finally, after ten minutes of chasing, the orb zoomed into a wall and was gone.

Devon rubbed his now-sore elbow, annoyed.

"Still up for that scrimmage?" Peño asked.

"Nah," Rain muttered. "Let's just get out of here."

There were no arguments. The team kept discussing the orb, but Devon plunked himself on the away bench, loosely bending his elbow to work out the kink. He hoped it wasn't going to be sore tomorrow . . . Clearly his right arm was not a viable alternative. He wondered if he would ever catch the orb, and if he ever wanted to. There was something *in* there. Something that wanted him to feel cold and small.

"Who cares!" Rain snapped. "What did that game have to do with basketball?"

"Everything," Reggie replied. "It was about playing defense the right way. As a team."

Rain was on his feet now. His whole body was shaking.

Here we go again, Devon thought. *Another hissy fit.*

"This is a big year for me," Rain continued, ranting.

"You mean for *us*," Lab said.

"Yeah," Rain said. "Rain Adams and the West Bottom Badgers."

With that, Rain stalked out of the gym. Devon glanced at the others, wondering if that was usual behavior for him. He'd seen at least two of Rain's angry tirades already. The kid seemed very selfish. Devon wasn't sure he liked him—of course, he doubted Rain cared what he thought.

Devon changed his shoes and shirt and went to the bathroom. As he was washing his hands, he looked up at his reflection. He ran his fingers over his shaved head, his broad nose.

"Maybe we should just let him stay home for the rest of the year. To be safe."

That was his father's voice now. He didn't bother looking for him. It was a memory.

"I guess," his mom said. "Just the rest of the year, though. Then he should go back."

"Agreed. He just needs time."

Time.

Four years later, he'd had plenty of that. Devon frowned as in the mirror he saw slowly looping words appearing on the wall behind him, written in silvery ink. When he glanced over his shoulder, the wall was blank, yet the writing continued to form in the reflection. He leaned toward the mirror, struggling to read the backward words. His mind untangled the message.

"We only . . . see . . . what . . . we . . . believe," he said slowly.

He thought about that for a moment. He usually saw a freak and an animal. But that wasn't what he had seen today. He straightened and puffed out his chest. Now he was wearing shiny armor again, and a determined expression. A castle sat behind him on a distant hill.

"Sir Devon the Brave at your service," he whispered. "But my friends call me the Beast."

He heard someone else walk past the stall, and Devon hurried out.

"Were you talking to yourself?" Vin asked on the way to another stall.

"Umm . . . yeah."

Vin laughed. "I do the same. Nice work today, big man. Let's bring that to the court."

Devon went to grab his bag, thinking about what he'd just said to his reflection.

"My *friends* . . ." Devon repeated.

He left the gym with a smile.

6

THE DARK ROOM

*You know nothing of your strength
until you have felt truly weak.*
❖ WIZENARD ⑰ PROVERB ❖

DEVON CLUTCHED THE ball to his chest, his fingers splayed across the pebbling. He could feel the shift of rubber beneath them as he prepared himself. Then he spun around, lowering his shoulder and driving toward the rim for a layup. An imaginary defender missed. An imaginary crowd cheered. He grabbed the rebound and hurried to the other side of the key, ready to go again.

Devon had been working on his shot for nearly half an hour now. He had arrived especially early and *still* not been the first one in the gym. Devon wondered if Reggie ever left. He gripped the ball, preparing to attack again, but a voice split the air.

"Gather around. Put the balls away."

He glanced back and saw that the whole team had arrived, and Rolabi was standing at half-court. Devon quickly put his ball away and hurried over with the others, noticing obvious tension around Rain—angry looks and mutters.

"Today we are going to work on offense," Rolabi said. "We'll start with passing: the foundation of all offense. What do all the great passers have?"

Devon tried to think. The only passing he did was to his dad when they shot around in the street, and that probably didn't count.

"Vision," Peño said.

"Very good. A great passer must be quick and agile and bold. But mostly, they must have vision. Both of what is and what will soon come. They must see *everything* on the floor."

"So, we just have to practice seeing more—" Lab said.

"Yes," Rolabi said. "And the best way to start is by seeing nothing at all."

The gym was enveloped in darkness. Not even sunlight crept in around the doors. Devon closed his eyes, and it made no difference. He realized he was trembling. He didn't like the dark. He'd spent too many nights lying awake in it, watching bad memories play across the shadowy ceiling.

"Hey, watch it," Peño said. "That's my toe!"

"Well, how do you want me to avoid it when I can't see anything?" Big John said.

Devon felt himself relax. He wasn't alone here. This was different.

"What do you hide down in the dark?"

Devon flinched. "Professor Rolabi?"

He no longer heard the others—no shifting or breathing or quiet conversations. He suddenly felt alone again, though he could sense Rolabi and smell the faint tinge of salt water.

"What did you hide there?" the deep voice repeated.

"I don't know what you mean—"

"Are you ready to face it?"

His voice was terribly loud in the darkness. It made the floors vibrate beneath Devon's feet.

"Face what?" Devon asked.

"The heart of the cage."

"I . . . want it to go away."

"Then you are ready," Rolabi said. "Start by finding your own center."

Devon took a deep breath. He closed his eyes and kept them shut. He imagined he could open them at any time and find light. When it felt like *his* choice, darkness lost some of its threat.

Now he could hear the noises around him again. Feet shifting. Breath. Whispers.

The team was back.

"Starters versus last year's bench," Rolabi said. "Starters will go first. Find the ball."

While the starters set off in search of the ball, shouting, cursing, and bumping into things, Devon followed the voices of the bench players to what was hopefully the center line. Devon kept his eyes shut, waving his hands in front of him. He smacked something warm and fleshy.

"Ow!" Jerome said.

"Sorry," Devon replied quickly.

"It's like being hit with a slab of ham," Jerome grumbled.

"How do we find the center line in the dark?" Big John asked.

"Look for the bleachers," Vin said. "We can find the middle of those."

"This is ridiculous," Big John said. "I hate these stupid— Hey! Who just kicked me?"

"My bad," Reggie said.

"Didn't feel like an accident," Big John muttered.

It took at least five minutes to establish what they thought was the center line, and a few minutes more for the starters to get ready beneath the net. Devon wasn't even sure he was facing in the right direction, but he spread his hands out and tried to keep track of the voices.

"Remember when we used to just do layup drills and scrimmage?" Vin said wistfully.

"Remember when we went three and twelve last year?" Reggie said. "We sucked."

"And you think this is going to help?" Big John said.

"Couldn't hurt."

"Tell that to my shin," Big John said.

The starters finally set off—or at least it sounded like they did. Their shouting voices and shuffling steps slowly closed in. Finally, when the voices were nearly on top of the defenders, everyone started to shout, and Devon lost track of the attackers. Somebody ran into his chest. Teammates cried out for the ball. Someone missed a pass, and it went bouncing off the court.

"Switch," Rolabi said.

It took another five minutes to get the bench team organized beneath the net. Devon bonked his nose on the wall, and then Vin missed the very first pass and lost the ball again.

"This is going well," Jerome said.

"Hmm," Rolabi said. "Perhaps we will work up to complete darkness."

Devon eased open his eyes. A crimson ball of light moved in the darkness. He could make out thin black lines curving around the sphere and the soft glow between them, though the ball cast no extra light. Armed with the illuminated ball, the starters moved a little faster, but Jerome still picked off a pass.

"Switch sides," Rolabi said.

The play went back and forth for what felt like hours. Devon started to get used to the sensation of darkness. He had never noticed how helpful his other senses could be on the court. He knew the pros called out plays, but he had never thought to listen to the flow of bodies running and breathing. He used his hands to grab the ball, but he had never enlisted them to track the other team like probing tentacles. He supposed he could always smell, but he had never been aware of the pungent body odor moving around him with the cutting players. He even got an unfortunate taste of a sweaty arm.

Finally, the starters managed to get across the gym, and the lights flicked back on.

"The starting team wins," Rolabi said. "Water break."

Devon shuffled over to the bench, blinking against the sudden fluorescent glare. He wondered what Rolabi had meant about him being ready to find his center. To face his cage. He had already been there, and yes, he had possessed the keys. But that didn't mean he could use them. He gulped back some water, watching as the others did the same. Why couldn't he just be normal like them? Rain and Twig and Lab—they were fine. They didn't have to be afraid.

"Twig, come up here, please," Rolabi said.

Twig shuffled over to the big professor, who made even the gangly center look short.

"I want you to tell the team one thing you would like to say to them. One *honest* thing."

Devon frowned. He didn't like where this was going. Was it just Twig who was going to be put on the spot? Rolabi had to cajole an answer out of him. Devon could sympathize with his reluctance to talk.

But then Twig spoke. "Okay, well, I have been working really hard," he murmured. "You know, in the off-season. And I am trying really hard to be better. I know maybe you guys didn't want me back this season, but I really am trying to help the team. I want you guys to know that."

Devon focused again on the scars and pockmarks on Twig's cheeks. A small part of him wondered if Twig had secrets too.

We all have secrets and scars. Only the fool chooses not to see them.

"Jerome," Rolabi said.

They began to cycle through, and Devon grew increasingly nervous. What would he say? Could he bring himself to talk in front of the team? His throat felt dry, and he downed more water. He felt his chest growing tighter as each person took their turn:

"I want to kill it this season."

"I've been working on my jumper, and I know I'm going to hit some shots this year."

"I'm going to be a starter this year."

The statements were mostly generic. Devon tried to think of something. He would . . . play hard? That sounded stupid even to him. He was still rehearsing answers when Rolabi called on him. He walked to the front, racking his brain, and then just mumbled the first thing that came to mind.

"I . . . I want another shot."

That seemed to confuse everyone, so he just hurried back to the bench. Why did he say that? He meant take shots. Or score. Not *another* shot. He stared at his feet, his cheeks blazing.

You have come to the right place. But you have to earn it.

How? he thought meekly.

Tell me what we must do with our strength.

Devon frowned. *What?* He didn't know.

Then pay attention.

"Let's scrimmage for an hour," Rolabi said.

"No tricks?" Peño asked.

"Just working on our vision. Rain, Vin, Lab, A-Wall, and Devon versus the rest."

Devon looked around in surprise. He was playing with Rain now? Was he a starter? Both the centers from last year—Twig and Big John— were on the same team, so he figured he was now the opposing center by default. He stepped up across from Twig, and Twig nodded at him.

"We can see so much, and yet we choose not to," Rolabi said. "It is an odd decision."

It didn't go fully dark this time. Instead, it was like a strange blockage had been placed in front of Devon's face, leaving only two narrow slivers of visibility on either side. Devon turned this way and that, but the blockage remained. He rubbed his eyes, but that had no effect either. Devon sighed. It was another test. He just had to stay calm and play.

Now you are getting it.

The others didn't seem to be taking it as well.

"Not cool!" Lab shrieked.

"I'm half-blind!" A-Wall said. "Maybe even three-quarters!"

Rolabi tossed the ball up, and Devon jumped blindly. He caught a flash of orange and a confused Twig on the way back *down*. Then he felt someone smack him in the shin and spotted Twig hunched over below him, clearly having chased after the ball.

"Sorry!" Twig said sheepishly.

Vin scooped up the ball, and the scrimmage began. It didn't take long for Devon to see the point of the exercise. It made passing and running in straight, direct lines nearly impossible. The ball had to be spread *outward*. Everything had to slow down to facilitate that. Devon moved constantly, shifting and turning to keep his teammates in view. Because his field of vision was so limited, he relied on his teammates to call out cuts and rotations and to let him know when shots were taken.

He began to recite actions in his head on offense: Move to the ball. Catch it. Weigh your options. Choose the best one. Repeat. It was almost mathematical. He calculated the best odds every time he touched the ball. If he was going to shoot, he made sure he had a path. There was no guesswork—if you guessed, you were liable to run into something. It was a new style of play.

All this time he had thought basketball was a mindless release—a battle of talent and strength. But there was much more going on if you slowed the action down. A game within a game within a game.

"That will do," Rolabi said finally. "Grab your bottles and join me in the center."

The blockage in his vision vanished, and Devon downed the rest of his water and started back for Rolabi. A-Wall fell in beside him, wiping his sodden face. His Afro was matted to his forehead as if it had been left out in the sun and wilted.

"So you liking the Badgers so far?" A-Wall asked.

Devon glanced at him. "Uh, yeah."

"We used to have less wizards," he said conversationally. "That's new."

"Yeah, I kind of figured."

He noticed that A-Wall was staring at his chest. A-Wall stopped and looked him over.

"So do you, like . . . do a lot of push-ups? I'm trying to work on my pecs." He flexed and looked down at two pointy protrusions the size of bottle caps. "They're small, right?"

Devon frowned. "I—I don't know. I guess you could do some push-ups."

"I knew it." He rolled up his sleeve. "What do you think about my bi—"

"Now, I am owed some laps," Rolabi announced.

Devon was actually grateful when they took off running. It wasn't much of a run—they did a quick five laps, and then Reggie proceeded to hit his very first free throw attempt. They were back in the center circle in a couple of minutes.

Rolabi opened his bag. "You all have your full eyesight again. But are you really looking? We must relearn to see." Devon hurried to join the group just as Rolabi set down the potted daisy.

"Not again," Peño muttered.

"Many times more," Rolabi said. "If you wish to win, you *must* slow down time. Begin."

He turned on one heel and headed for the doors, his bag swinging beside him.

"Where are you going?" Peño asked.

"You will take the daisy home tonight, Peño," Rolabi said. "Be careful with it, please."

Peño gulped.

"How long do you want us to stare at it?" Rain called after him.

"Until you see something new," said the professor.

The doors slammed shut behind him.

Devon hesitated, then sat down and folded his legs beneath him. The others were talking, but he let their voices fade away. He focused on the petals and tried to see them move. That wasn't likely to happen, of course—he had figured that out the first time. To watch the flower grow simply meant to appreciate time. To slow things down in his head to the point that even something as imperceptible as the growth of a flower *might* be seen. It didn't really matter if it ever was.

Most of the team didn't join him. Big John left altogether, while several others shot around. Only Reggie and Twig remained seated. Devon ignored them all.

It was some time before he felt the mood change. The entire gym fell quiet. Still. *Cold.*

A deep sense of dread swept over Devon. He heard whispers and faraway voices. Twig and Reggie were rigid, their eyes focused just above his head. Devon guessed that the orb was floating right over him.

He kept his eyes on the flower. He knew this might be his best shot. The orb had come for him. He stared at the flower for a minute, hopefully lulling the orb into false complacency.

Devon took a last steadying breath. Then he made his move.

He jerked his hand up without looking and felt it close on something viscous and icy cold. Devon looked up at the captured orb, watching it seep through his fingers. And then the gym disappeared.

He was sitting on a concrete floor, surrounded by darkness. He slowly stood up.

Where am I? he wondered numbly.

The air was cold and damp, like a late-winter morning. It seeped into his bones, made them ache, made his skin prickle. Devon turned, peering into the darkness. There was no cage this time. No keys. But something appeared at the edge of shadows. He paused, gripped with fear.

But his curiosity was stronger. He walked toward the hulking shape, his breathing shallow.

As he closed in, Devon's eyes widened. It was a door. He *knew* the door—it was the one from his old public school—a creaky metal one like Fairwood's. Unexpectedly, Devon felt his eyes watering at the sight. He missed that place. Or maybe . . . he missed who he had been when he was there. Before everything went so wrong. Without thinking, he opened the door and stepped through.

A scene appeared in front of him. A younger version of himself— already tall and broad—dribbled down a court for a layup, shouldering aside a smaller boy on the way. The younger Devon smiled as he hit the layup. The other boy didn't. Greg Nennitz. It was *him*.

"I didn't know stupid meat loafs could get the ball through the hoop," Greg said. "Hey, everyone, did you see the loaf of meat get a basket? It's a miracle!"

"Don't call me that," the younger Devon growled.

Step away, Devon thought. *Breathe.*

But his younger self didn't listen. It had been going on for a year already. Little comments. Laughs and jokes. Greg always seemed at the center of it. He told the girls that Devon was dangerous, and they all stayed far away. He told the guys that Devon was stupid.

They joined in with the name-calling.

"Or what?" Greg said. "You're too stupid to do anything about it. You're a freak."

Breathe. Walk away. Play the game. Don't do it. Don't do it.

"Shut up," the younger Devon said.

Greg took the ball and smirked at him. "Your mom must be an ogre. Ugh. Nasty."

Devon closed his eyes. He had tried so hard to forget. He spent countless hours burying it, shunting it aside, trying anything to lock it all away. Why was he seeing this again? *Why?*

Breathe, he pleaded with his younger self. *Walk away. This time, walk away.*

"Don't talk about my family," the younger Devon said, stepping closer now.

Greg laughed. "What, how ugly your mama is? Or that your grandma is a cow—"

Devon couldn't really remember doing it. It was a stupid comment—nothing really. Maybe it was the accumulation of a year's worth of taunts. Maybe it was his own issues with his size. Whatever it was, he snapped.

And as he watched in horror, his younger self shoved Greg with every bit of strength he had—a considerable amount. The boy's head smacked the ground with a sickening thud. His body went limp, his eyes closed, and blood trickled from the corner of his mouth. Other kids started screaming. So did the younger Devon. He called for help, wiping the blood with his own T-shirt, crying and shouting for teachers or an ambulance or his parents. Greg had suffered a severe concussion. He was in a coma for a few days. Away from school for months.

Devon had overheard that it could have easily been fatal.

Devon fell onto his knees as he watched the scene continue. Greg stayed on the ground for an excruciatingly long time, just like Devon remembered. The attack was just as bad. He really was as dangerous as they said. He could have killed him . . . just like that. In one moment of anger. The scene blew away in a wisp of smoke, and Devon knelt in the midst of it, ashamed.

"It was a terrible thing to do. You were prodded, yes. But it was a mistake to push him."

Devon turned and saw Rolabi standing behind him, emerging from the tendrils of smoke.

"But if we cannot grow, what are we?" he asked.

"What is this place?" Devon whispered. His eyes were watering, his vision blurred. "Why did you bring me here?"

"Actually, you brought me here," Rolabi said. "This place is yours."

"What is it?"

"Your fears," Rolabi said. "Your scars. We are *in* them. The orb contains fears, which are different for everyone, of course. Not your everyday fears. Those are easy to see. This is far deeper. It is a place where few people go—the heart of their own fears."

Devon stared into the darkness. The smoke had faded now, leaving nothing.

"Why did I see that?"

"You tell me."

Devon tried to process . . . tried to quiet the terrible guilt inside of him. He knew it well.

"I . . . think about it a lot," he murmured.

"This was the day things changed for you. It was the day you gave up."

"You saw what I did," Devon said.

"I saw a boy pushed too far, a boy who let himself down. Nothing more."

Devon whirled on him. "They said I was dangerous. They didn't want me back."

"We should never listen to those who speak from fear. Why did you lock yourself away?"

Devon was silent for a long time. "Because I believed them."

"And you have punished yourself since. Self-doubt is an invasive seed. It grows and grows until it takes over everything. It becomes anxiety. It chokes you. In time, you fear yourself most of all."

Devon looked down at his hands. They were trembling, and he knew that what Rolabi was saying was true.

"What are you afraid of?" Rolabi asked.

Devon hesitated and looked away. "That they were right," he whispered. "That I am a bad person. That I am dangerous and an animal and all those awful things they said I was."

The whole room seemed to tremble.

"You know," Rolabi said thoughtfully, "only good people are ever afraid of being bad ones. But if you never beat that fear, then you can never reach your true potential." He laid a hand on Devon's shoulder. "Greg made a bad choice that day. So did you. You can make yourself a monster for the rest of your life, or you can become something more."

"But the other kids—"

"They have moved on. Even Greg. The only forgiveness left to find is your own."

Devon wiped his nose. "How will I know if . . . if I'm a good person?"

"The people you love will tell you. Stop isolating yourself, Devon. Learn from the past. Build yourself a future. Create new friendships here. Build them strong. You will need them."

Rolabi withdrew his hand.

"The good news is that you have the strength to do it. And I don't mean your biceps."

Light flooded into the dark room, and once again, Devon was standing in Fairwood. There were shouts and pointing fingers and stunned faces all around, but he didn't pay any attention. He didn't feel like talking. He just grabbed his duffel bag and headed for the doors.

It was true. He had locked himself in that moment. Inside that old school. His memories were a cage. Maybe he had been waiting for someone to invite him out, to break the bars for him, to tell him he was *good*. But the cage opened from the inside. No one else could unlock it for him.

The fear was still there—the guilt and the shame and the self-doubt. At least Devon knew what was at the heart of it now.

It wasn't a victory. But it was a start.

The monster had a face. Now Devon had to figure out if he was strong enough to defeat it.

7

THE BIG SHOT

If you assume someone is perfect,
you miss the opportunity to help them.
❖ WIZENARD ❀ PROVERB ❖

THE NEXT MORNING, Devon took a deep breath, staring at the doors. He had been planning his new approach all night. It was always easier before the fact, and now he had to follow through.

"Just ask someone how they're doing," he whispered. "One person. Just try it."

"You grab them and pull," someone commented.

He jumped. Nana was still parked behind him—he had completely spaced out and forgotten they were there. Keya was playing with an action figure in the back seat, her helmet reflecting the smog-infused sunlight, while his nana was leaning out the window, grinning.

"You're still here," Devon said, embarrassed.

"Amazingly, yes," Nana replied. "Though at a ripe old age. Come here."

Devon walked over to the car. Nana licked a wrinkled thumb and wiped his chin with it.

"You eat like a barbarian." She cupped his chin. "I'm proud of you."

"What?"

She sighed, gave his chin a little shake, and smiled sadly.

"And you still have such a hard road ahead. See you tonight."

With that, she drove off. He watched as the car rounded the corner, bumping and rattling along, and wondered what she meant by *a hard road ahead*. Did she know something about what his future held?

Devon put the question aside for later and walked into Fairwood. Twig and Reggie were stretching by the benches, and Devon glanced at them as he sat down. He had promised himself to ask someone a question. Start a conversation. It scared the heck out of him, but he was going to try.

Just not quite yet, he thought.

He pulled on his sneakers and went to shoot around. For the last six days, he had been taking layups or avoiding shooting altogether. But he knew he couldn't hide his inept form forever. Eventually, he would have to play a real game . . . *if* he made it through the camp. So, he just started to shoot.

He shot jumpers from the elbow and threes and free throws. They clanged off the rim. They hit the backboard or nothing at all. But he didn't stop. He shot until the ball was slick in his hands. He shot from each new location until he hit one—sometimes it took ten or twenty attempts. But every time he made a shot, he grinned and remembered exactly what he had done—the feel on his fingertips, the bounce in his toes, the direction of his elbow. Then he worked to replicate it again and again. Sweat began to stream down his face.

Peño came up behind him, grinning:

"my boy taking shots
From every side we gots
They not falling yet
But it'll follow and sweat"

"Less terrible than usual," Lab muttered.

Peño threw his hands up. "I have impressed my brother!"

"You rhymed *shots* with *gots*," Lab said. "Don't get too excited."

Devon snorted and kept working.

"Today we work on your shots," Rolabi's deep voice announced. "Balls away."

That's a coincidence, Devon thought.

He wondered if Rolabi believed in such things.

Devon looked around and realized the entire team had arrived. He quickly put his ball away and joined the group around Rolabi, lingering on the edge of the circle. The professor looked over their faces as if searching for something. His gaze fell on Devon, and he smiled.

"Your grana grows stronger," Rolabi said. "It is time to share it."

Rolabi tossed Devon a ball. As soon as he caught it, the gym fell away beneath him like melting wax. It was replaced with black skies tinged blue, dark enough to see a smattering of stars. Devon whirled around, his lungs flooding with cold, thin air. Thin, because the team was standing on a spiraling summit. The peak was small, chopped away at the edges into sharp lines and teeth. Devon's breath caught at the sight of the clouds far below them. He spotted a second mountain facing theirs. Atop it was a pristine basketball hoop, and between the two mountains was ten feet of open space and a very long fall.

Devon looked down at the ball. What had Rolabi meant? Had *he* brought the team here? And *grana*...That was the same word the grumpy voice had used. Why did it seem so familiar?

You have always known it.

What is it? he thought.

It is shaping your world.

The silent conversation was cut off by a crack like thunder. The team cried out as an enormous chunk of the mountain detached and fell toward the waiting clouds. New fissures rapidly spread out around the shorn cliffside, threatening to pull the rest down, and Devon immediately understood what was happening. The mountain was a giant hourglass. This test would be timed.

"We're supposed to be practicing shooting," Twig said. "Maybe we need to shoot the ball."

The mountain splintered, sending another boulder plummeting toward the clouds, and the team turned to Devon. He looked down at the ball and felt his throat catch. *He* had to shoot it?

"Take the shot, Rain," Reggie said.

Devon was relieved. Giving Rain the ball was definitely the smarter choice—hopefully only one of them needed to score. Devon tossed Rain the ball, though he noticed that Rain was trembling even more than he was. Rain barely caught the ball, and another boulder fell away. The mountain was collapsing faster now.

Rain brought the ball up, his hands shaking madly, and missed. The ball fell into the abyss between the mountains, and Devon watched it numbly, wondering what they would do now. He needn't have asked. The ball rocketed right back up again directly into Vin's hands.

"Keep shooting!" Twig said.

They began to shoot, and each time, make or miss, some invisible force rebounded the ball back up over the mountain and into someone's reluctant hands. When it came to Devon, he tried to stay calm, knowing he would never hit the shot otherwise. But he could feel the team's eyes on his back. He could hear the cracking of stone. The short, shallow breaths of the nervous players.

He took the shot and missed everything, eliciting a chorus of groans. Devon backed away from the cliffside. Only Twig made a shot the first round. The second round of attempts started with a miss by Rain.

"I don't like heights," A-Wall said. "At least not when I'm on them."

Devon missed again as well—hard off the rim. Only a few of them had made their shots on the second round, and it started again. Rain missed. Vin made. Lab missed. Peño missed. Reggie made. A boulder fell. Devon missed again, this time off the back of the rim.

"We're dead," A-Wall said.

Devon ran his hand down his face, angry and afraid.

Where is this grana now? he thought furiously.

In every miss.

Another chunk of mountain sheered away. The ball arched back up again, and Rain missed to the left.

"Come on, Rain!" Vin shouted.

Rain looked stunned. Lab missed. Peño made. Devon missed off the front rim and nearly screamed in frustration. He couldn't do this. He wasn't a baller. He was a coward and a failure, and there were too many eyes on him. He belonged at home, alone. Rain missed again.

"Come on!" Rain screamed at the mountain.

Lab made his shot. Just like that, there were only two players left: Devon and Rain. Rain missed. Devon missed again. Of course he did. This was a mistake. A failed effort. It was all a missed attempt. He had wanted friends, and now he was letting them down.

Devon could hear them whispering:

"He'll never hit it."

"What do we do?"

"He's not even close. We're gonna die, man."

The guilt was like a red-hot weight sitting in his stomach. His eyes welled.

This isn't worth it, he thought. *I was better off alone. I was the only person I could let down.*

The bars spring up again.

Good! he thought, raging now. *Leave me alone!*

There was no response.

Rain missed again. Another boulder fell. The mountain was shrinking fast; they were almost out of time. The ball came back to Devon. His temper flared, replacing the humiliation. He couldn't do this, and he shouldn't be forced to. He never should have joined the stupid West Bottom Badgers. He lifted the ball quickly, not thinking, not focusing, just wanting it to be over.

"Wait!" Twig said suddenly. He hurried over, gesturing for Devon to hold off. Devon looked at him, confused.

"Just *breathe*," Twig said quietly.

Devon paused and then took Twig's advice. His lungs flooded with cold, thin air. He took another gulp, and then another. The trembling in his hands calmed. The fire subsided.

"Tuck your arm in. Yeah . . . perfect," Twig continued, coaching him. "And follow through toward the net. Your wrist will flick at the end. Flick it like you're dropping it in there."

Devon followed his instructions carefully. Twig wasn't calling him a failure. He was trying to help. Devon turned to the basket and breathed deeply again. Then he took the shot.

It hit the front of the rim, then the backboard, and dropped in. Elation surged through Devon, and he clapped Twig on the shoulder so hard that he nearly knocked the slender boy right off the mountain. Devon quickly grabbed his shirt and pulled him onto solid ground again.

"Sorry," Devon murmured.

Twig managed a smile. "No problem."

The ball flew back to Rain. He stood at the edge of their shrinking huddle facing the basket. The rock cracked again, and Devon realized the sound was coming from right beneath them. His jubilation at hitting his own shot faded. The mountain was about to fall.

"Make it, Rain!" Peño shouted.

The splintering intensified.

"Hurry!" Vin said.

The ground shook and rolled beneath Devon's feet. His breath caught in his throat.

"Shoot it!" A-Wall cried.

The mountain gave way just as Rain released the ball. The mountain fell backward, and Devon felt gravity tug at his limbs. He tried to scream, but no sound came out. He watched as the ball floated toward the hoop, spinning beneath the stars. It seemed to take hours to arrive. Then it flew through the rim with a gentle ripple of mesh.

Instantly the team was back in Fairwood, and Devon slumped over, gasping. The team cheered and pumped their fists or dropped to kiss the ground. Rolabi stood in front of them, watching with calm bemusement. Devon looked at him, meeting those curious emerald eyes.

"Welcome back," Rolabi said. "What makes a great shooter?"

What did you find?

Devon paused, still trying to stop the shaking. *I don't know . . .*

What did you lose?

"Think about the *heart* of a great shooter," Rolabi said. "What does he lack?"

Devon thought back to the mountain. To the moment when he finally made his shot. What did he lose in that moment? What was different from the shots before? What did he lack?

"Fear," Devon said, forgetting his shyness for a second. "He lacks fear."

"All great shooters are fearless. If they fear missing, or being blocked, or losing, then they will not shoot. Even if they do, they will rush it. They will allow fear to move their elbows or turn their fingers to stone. They will never be great. And how do we get rid of our fears?"

Devon realized it was never the mountain he feared. It was the *shot*. It was letting down his new teammates. Stepping into the spotlight. The drill made him face everything he had been hiding from. He could see it clearly now. His fear had grown into a mountain, invisible only because he had chosen not to look.

"We face them," Devon whispered.

"Yes, and one thing we all fear is letting down our friends," Rolabi said. "Basketball is about confronting fear. If you won't face it, you will lose. We will practice a thousand shots. Ten thousand. Twenty. If you take them all from a crumbling mountain, you will become great shooters."

Devon looked at the closest basket and smiled. He could see faint stars behind it.

"That will do for today," Rolabi said.

Rolabi walked toward the nearest wall, and with a brilliant flash of fluorescent white, he was gone. Rain headed for his bag, grabbed a ball, and then proceeded to the top of the key.

"What are you doing, Rain?" Peño asked.

"Shooting," Rain said.

Devon could see the grim determination on Rain's face—he was promising himself not to be last again. Devon smiled. Maybe the star player had a little more grit than he had realized. The others got their balls as well and formed a free-throw line. Devon hesitated, then went to join them. They shot one after another, and Devon stepped up last of all.

He breathed deeply and took the shot, for once not thinking about how he might miss.

8

THE SPOTLIGHT

Wake up with a purpose
or risk going to sleep without one.
✦ WIZENARD ◈ PROVERB ✦

DEVON STARED AROUND the locker room, confused. He had been in here to use the bathroom only a few times, and it had been thoroughly smelly and dilapidated to the point that he had been almost afraid to touch anything. Now the locker room sparkled. The mirror, once cracked and spotted, was freshly polished. The white sink was spotless, and the floor tiles gleamed a calming sky blue. Someone had renovated the bathroom in a single night.

That was enough to puzzle over, but for the moment, Devon was focused on himself. Not his appearance. Nobody here cared what he looked like—they just cared if he could play ball. He liked that about coming to Fairwood. Instead, he was asking the boy in the mirror if he was going to be strong. If he could remember the mountain and the dark room and try something different: a day without fear. He realized that meant the likelihood of failure. Of a bunch of missed shots, of saying things that might not be very funny or smart or cool. That was what he had to accept.

If he wasn't afraid of the results, he could take the risk.

"You are going to go out there and shoot from everywhere," he said. "You're going to talk too. Just say hi or shout out some plays. You are going to try. You are going to be a beast."

The boy in the mirror said it back, and Devon thought he looked a bit braver today.

It occurred to him again that normal kids probably didn't have to talk to themselves in the mirror. They probably didn't have to give themselves pep talks. Normal kids didn't have to try to be normal. Normal kids didn't have to promise themselves to speak. Devon sighed.

"I know, I wish this was easier," he whispered to his reflection.

It doesn't matter what you wish for, a deep voice said. *It only matters what you work for.*

Devon wondered what he meant. Weren't wishes and dreams necessary?

The reflection suddenly changed. It went pitch-black and then pulled Devon in headfirst. He screamed as he tumbled end over end and then found himself standing in the darkness, looking around wildly. Light broke the blackness, illuminating piles of bricks in a ring around Devon. Mounds of them. Bricks and mortar and assorted tools, and it was all a chaotic mess.

Devon picked up one of the bricks, confused.

"A great many people have stood among these bricks."

Devon turned toward the familiar voice. Rolabi was standing behind him, hands clasped at his back.

"Practically everyone in the world, in fact."

Devon frowned and put the brick down. "What for?"

Rolabi walked past him and gestured to a great, open space beyond the piles. Grass sprouted up, green and fresh, and without thinking, Devon hurried over and knelt in it.

"They stand here and wish for a house," Rolabi said.

Devon was unable to hide his excitement. "Do they get one?"

"No," Rolabi said with a sad smile. "They stand still and they wish.

They wish for the biggest mansion, normally. Or for nicer cars. For better friends. Closer family. More money."

"Out of bricks?" Devon asked, frowning.

"Or something similar," Rolabi replied. He picked up one of the bricks. It was small in his hand. "They stand amid all they need, and they wish. But, of course, nothing happens."

Devon ran his fingers through the blades of grass. They brushed his palm, soft and warm. He had never seen this sort of healthy grass in person before—all that was left in the Bottom was starchy, yellow, poisoned.

"They don't realize that each brick must be laid. That they must begin now what they seek in a year, or two, or ten. That they must set a foundation, and labor, and build it strong."

Devon stood up and faced him. "But how do I know what to build?"

"You are the architect," Rolabi said. "Envision what you want. But don't just focus on the exterior, the facade. Remember that it needs beams and posts and strong walls. If you build your dreams on straw, the whole structure will fall as soon as the wind picks up."

Devon grabbed a brick and stared at it. "These aren't literally bricks, are they?"

Rolabi chuckled. "No. They are kind deeds. They are early mornings. Long nights. They are moments of reflection. Hard choices. They are every action you make. Use them all to build."

Rolabi put his brick down and met Devon's eyes.

"The time to build is now. We will need strong shoulders to bear the weight."

The room suddenly vanished, and Devon was back in the locker room again. He blinked, dizzy for a moment, and gripped the sink to steady himself. He wondered about Rolabi's last words—they seemed almost like a warning. His mind flicked back to the bricks. To the house waiting to be built. Devon hadn't seen his future, but Rolabi was helping him find it.

The hard way. Little steps and struggles and setbacks, all inching toward a change that would take far longer than a day to achieve.

Somehow, that seemed calming. Devon had time to do it right.

He walked out to the gym and saw that a few of the other guys had arrived. Devon cleared his throat, grabbed his ball, and nodded at Peño, Lab, and A-Wall.

A good start, he thought.

He walked over to the three-point line, hesitated, and took the shot. He airballed it by at least three feet. Sighing, he hurried to grab the rebound and went back again. Another bad miss.

Just keep shooting, he told himself, grabbing the ball again.

"You . . . uh . . . planning to shoot a lot of threes?" Jerome asked.

Devon forced a smile. "I doubt it."

"Cool," Jerome said. "It kind of looks like you are doing shot put or something."

Devon flushed and went to try some elbow jumpers. He was halfway through a shot when the front doors crashed open. Snow came billowing inside. It swept through the gym, twisting into shapes and faces and a thousand doors opening into pure white. He watched in wonder as they swirled together in the middle of the gym and then blasted like fireworks, evaporating away.

He smelled salt again, carried on the cold breeze.

A mountain on an island, he recalled suddenly. A place of grana.

Where had he heard that before?

Rolabi walked inside, the doors slamming shut behind him.

"Am I still dreaming?" Lab murmured.

"Dreams are fleeting," Rolabi said, heading right for center court. "A wisp of smoke and they're gone. The question is whether you can find their heart."

"I got dreams," Peño said. "You need dreams. They keep you going sometimes."

Rolabi glanced at him. "A dream is nothing without vision. Don't dream. Aspire. Find the rungs of the ladder and climb. And choose correctly. If a dream can be achieved without work, without sacrifice, then it is meaningless. It will bring you no joy. You didn't earn it, and so you do not own it. Don't wish for fleeting dreams. The road to your dreams is paved with hardship."

You must show them the bricks.

Devon frowned. *I don't even talk to—*

Who said you had to talk?

Rolabi set his bag on the floor and turned to the team. "Line up facing me."

They rushed to comply, and he looked them over. His eyes darted from face to face.

"Three of you have caught the orb so far."

Devon glanced at the others, surprised. He had thought it was only him. Nobody said anything, though he thought that Twig was standing a bit straighter than usual. His shoulders—forever reaching for his knees—were set back, and he was right in the middle of the group today.

"I can see some changes," Rolabi continued. "The rest must stay vigilant. They must be ready when the moment comes. Today we will be focusing on team offense. You have worked on your passing and vision. You have worked on your shot. But this is not a game of one."

Devon noticed a lot of glances flick toward Rain, and he wondered about him. This morning he seemed sullen . . . almost sad. Maybe even Rain was hiding secrets and scars.

"It is good to recognize who is defending us at all times," Rolabi said. "To use size and speed advantages. But before that, we must understand what it means to attack as a team. And so we remove those advantages and create fully equal defenders."

Half the lights suddenly switched off. All the lights in *front* of the team remained on, fizzling with a strange new intensity. The light was almost blinding, and Devon lifted a hand to shield his eyes.

"We will learn to attack as one," Rolabi said. "But first, we need defenders."

Devon felt it before he saw it. Something was watching him. He turned around slowly, warily, and then gasped. The brilliant remaining lights had cast his own vivid shadow behind him, and it was *getting up*. Devon stepped back as the shadow placed its hands on the hardwood and heaved itself up like it was popping out of a cake pan. It straightened into an exact replica of Devon—no features, but the same squared head, broad shoulders, and thick arms. It began to limber and stretch.

"Mommy," A-Wall murmured.

"Meet today's defenders," Rolabi said. "You should know them well."

Devon's shadow stuck out its hand. Devon reluctantly met it, and his shadow squeezed tightly enough to crack Devon's knuckles. Devon scowled and squeezed back. For a moment, they were locked in a perfectly even match of strength. Devon's whole arm strained, his fingers creaking. Finally, his shadow nodded and stepped back.

"Into position, defenders," Rolabi said.

Half the shadows moved in front of the basket to form a defensive zone, while the other half hurried to the sideline to wait. Devon's shadow didn't look happy to be on the "bench," pacing and jumping on its heels and boxing the air. His shadow was . . . intense.

Devon moved to the sideline, happy to watch the starters try first.

Peño shot a resentful look at Rolabi and began to dribble. "Line it up," he said weakly.

Devon glanced at his shadow. It was watching the drill impatiently on the sideline, still bouncing around. Devon rubbed his nose—this was a whole new level of weird. Within thirty seconds, the starters were stymied by their shadows, who played hard and close. Their attempt ended with Twig's jumper being swatted away.

"Switch it up," Rolabi said.

"Okay, let's do this," Vin muttered, retrieving the ball.

Devon hurried to the post, where he met his shadow. They jostled for position. The shadow kept pushing and jockeying him, reaching out simultaneously to deny the entry pass. It played defense like his dad had taught *him*—aggressive and physical. At first, Devon let himself be pushed around, but then he took an elbow in the rib cage and felt his temper flare. He pushed back, setting his legs, and they fought for the block, matched evenly, neither giving up an inch.

When Devon did get the ball, he tried to turn to the hoop, but his shadow was right on him. He couldn't get an open look and was forced to pass it back out again. Twice more the same thing happened. Finally, after everyone was frustrated, Reggie drove to the hoop, and the ball was stolen.

"Switch," Rolabi said.

The starters were stopped again. So was the bench. They went back and forth repeatedly, and soon Devon was annoyed and exhausted. He was shoved around on the block, or had the ball stripped, or was stuffed. He was being outmuscled.

"Grab some water," Rolabi said.

Devon drained his bottle in one gulp. All the jockeying and pushing was exhausting. He felt like he'd been wrestling for the last hour. Of course, it was a good strategy. His shadow was making him work so hard for position that by the time he got the ball he was tired. Each shove and counter-shove and shift of weight took his attention from the game and sapped his energy.

It is playing the same defense you are capable of.

Devon glanced at Rolabi. He was talking out loud to the team, but his eyes fell on Devon.

I need you to be the pillar at the middle of our defense. The inexorable force.

What do I need to do? Devon thought warily.

Exactly what your shadow is doing to you. Exert yourself. Wear the offense down.

But—

You will show the others what it means to be a tiger. On defense and offense.

"We attack as one," Rolabi said aloud. "And that starts with a simple spotlight. Into your positions, please."

Devon looked around, realizing the internal voice was gone. The starters were heading back onto the floor, none looking too pleased about it. He considered Rolabi's words: that he could become the pillar at the center of the defense. The tiger. That would mean jostling, and closedowns, and blocks, and controlling the paint. Once again, it meant being the beast.

It is time.

The drill began again, but with a new element—the lights grew dim, and the shadows grew larger. That continued until someone moved and got open, at which point a spotlight fell on the open player. If they stayed still, or held the ball without action, the spotlight faded. It took the starters a minute, but they started to cut and move the ball more rapidly, and more and more spotlights fell.

"Of course," Reggie said from behind him. "Lighting up the court."

"I don't get it," A-Wall said.

"You got to get open," Reggie said, drawing out the movements like he was finger-painting. "Watch Peño—he should pop out."

Peño popped out to the wing for the ball, and the spotlight fell on him.

"Now, Rain," Reggie said, almost at a whisper. "Cut across the zone."

Rain did just that, lighting up, and he got the pass as well.

Devon glanced at Reggie. His small eyes narrowed as he mouthed each movement and play to himself. He urged each player to get open, or guessed at the cut, or described the setup of the defenders. And for just a moment, it seemed like there was a spotlight on him as well.

When the bench team went in, Devon worked harder than he ever had. It wasn't enough to sit and wait for rebounds. He needed to cut and post and set screens for the guards, even if his movements took him to the top of the key or out to the three-point line. He had to move and throw his weight around to help the others get open.

With shadows as defenders, there were no faces or voices to trigger Devon's memories or guilt. So he threw hard screens and knocked one shadow player after another onto their butts. Shadows bounced off his chest. He shouldered others out of the lane. And as he did, his team began to work around him, using the space. He didn't even need to touch the ball to help them—if he knocked the defenders around, his teammates got open, and the spotlight fell on them.

And now you begin to see.

Before long, everyone was sweating. But as the team rotated and talked and worked to get open, they began to score. As the screens and cuts continued, Devon's shadow grew frustrated.

Devon had thought playing on a team would be like playing on the street. It wasn't. Being big got him *on* the court. It didn't make him effective. He had to use his size intelligently. He had to think of where to move next. Of where he could apply pressure. Where he could open up space.

As another hour went by, the Badgers started to score more than they were stopped. Even Devon hit a few layups. He took rebounds from his shadow with hard box outs and better positioning. He started to beat *himself*—but only with the help and spacing of his teammates.

Rolabi finally ended the drill and placed the potted daisy in the center circle.

"Sit and watch," he said, and then nodded at the shadows. "Thank you, gentlemen."

The lights flicked back on, and the shadows disappeared. Devon sat down in front of the daisy, plopping his legs out in front of him. He was beyond exhausted. But he was also strangely satisfied. He hadn't been mean or aggressive. He had just applied calm strength. An inexorable force.

That, he could do.

"We are a team on both ends of the court," Rolabi said. "If you use the Spotlight Offense, you will be more effective. Follow the light, invite it to yourself, and you will conquer any darkness."

"Pretty heavy for basketball," Big John muttered.

"And perfect for life," Rolabi said. "Why not live every part with the same values?"

He fell silent, staring at the daisy, and Devon followed suit. But he soon noticed a change in the gym. The orb was floating near center court. He didn't hear the whispers this time or feel the same chill. He knew it wasn't here for him. He had found his dark room.

"Here we go again," Lab said.

Seven players jumped to their feet and charged. Twig and Jerome remained seated with Devon. They met eyes and nodded. Nobody asked about the orb or what had happened when the others had caught it. Devon suspected they felt like he did: that the dark room was for them alone.

"Split up!" Lab shouted.

He was still chasing the orb along with the others, jumping, weaving, and running into one another. Players collided and ended up on the floor.

Big John doubled over, exhausted. "I hate this thing," he said, gasping.

At last, the orb seemed to settle, facing Rain in a one-on-one challenge. Rain made a slick pivot move and caught it, vanishing instantly.

Devon looked around and noticed Rolabi had left during the chaos. So had the flower. He climbed to his feet, stretching, and started for the bench. Peño fell in beside him.

"Lab and I have a bet," he said. "Why do you do homeschool?"

Devon looked around. Everyone else seemed preoccupied.

Just stay calm and talk normally, he thought.

"I . . . I like it better," Devon said.

"Oh," Peño said, sounding disappointed. "I was betting your parents made you. How long you been doing that? Don't know anyone who is homeschooled, you know? Seems kinda cool."

"This is the fourth year."

"So you used to go to regular school?" Peño asked.

"Yeah."

"Why'd you leave?" Peño asked, leaning in conspiratorially.

Devon hesitated. He didn't want to get into the details, but he didn't want to lie either.

"I . . . didn't fit in."

"Oh," Peño said, disappointed again. "I bet that you were expelled. No offense."

Devon pulled his bag out from under the bench and noticed that Peño was watching him.

"Man, I wish I looked like you," Peño said. "Your arms are thicker than my waist."

Devon shifted uncomfortably. "Sometimes I feel a bit . . . too big."

"Too big?" Peño said, scoffing. "Own it, big man. You know what people call me?"

"Umm . . . no."

"Shrimp, lil'boy, baby mustache . . ."

Devon snorted.

"Yeah, I guess that last one isn't about my height," he said, stroking the wispy hairs on his lip. "The point is, I don't let that get me down. So what? I'm short, and I'll still outplay them all. You're a beast, bro. Throw it down. Use it. And if people call you names, smile and ball 'em."

Devon rubbed his arm, smiling nervously. "Yeah . . . you're right."

"Of course I'm right! You'll figure that out soon." Peño suddenly gaped and slapped his forehead. "Hey, you don't have a nickname!"

"I . . . well, no. Not yet."

Peño's brow furrowed. "It's kind of my job. I've been neglecting my duties."

"Don't worry about it—"

"Nope, you can't be the only one. See: Lab is lazy, like a lazy Labrador, you know. Rain scores a lot. 'Make it rain' kind of deal. A-Wall goes, well, A-Wall. Wait for games. The guy is a nut. Jerome, Reggie, Vin—they made their own before I could get to them. That's why they're boring and terrible. Big John, well, that's easy to figure out. Rain gave me Peño because I get a little heated sometimes. Like a jalapeño. It's not bad, I guess. Twig is skinny like . . . a twig. And you . . . well, you're just huge. A brute. Beast. The Bull?"

Devon tried not to let his disappointment show, but Peño seemed to catch it anyway.

"Ah, skip that. Too obvious." He paused. "Big D?"

Devon shook his head, and Peño nodded, still playing with his mustache.

"Yeah, not great. Tell you what . . . let's give you one you're going to have to *earn*."

"Like what?"

"Cash Money," he said proudly. "Cash for short. Like every time you get the ball down low, you can just cash it in 'cause nobody can stop the big man."

Devon laughed without thinking, and Peño clapped his hands together.

"Cash it is!" he said. "Let's get it, boy! Cash coming for the title!"

Devon sat down and changed his shoes, mouthing his nickname and trying to hold back a smile. He wasn't alone anymore. His teammates *wanted* him here. He was officially a Badger.

"*Cash*," he whispered. "Yeah . . . that works for me."

THE BIG MAN AT
THE BOTTOM

Never let your desire for more
supersede your gratitude for any.
◆ WIZENARD ㉟ PROVERB ◆

CASH!" PEÑO SHOUTED.

Cash pivoted, and Peño lobbed a ball down to him. He caught it high—keeping it up over his head as Peño had instructed him—turned sharply, and laid it in with a power move to the basket, neatly placing it on the backboard and in.

"That's it, my brother," Peño said, pretending to open a register. "Cash it in."

Cash smiled and threw the ball back to him. The little point guard had insisted he work on his low-post game today. Peño seemed to have warmed to him for some reason. Cash wasn't complaining. Rain was the best player, but Peño was clearly the leader on the team. The engine.

Peño started to bob his shoulders, dancing.

"Cash is a beast
down low he will feast
he may be schooled at home
but on the court, he's the..."

Peño paused, thinking.

"The mome... lume... hold on
He's schooled at home,
but on the court he will roam
he's the kid with the muscles
he must eat his brussels...
Sprouts?"

Peño sighed deeply. "Definitely not my best work."

"That's an understatement," Lab said. "But wait . . . do you have any best work?"

"Shut up."

Devon grabbed his ball and prepared to work on some turnaround jumpers.

"How come you don't talk, anyway?" Lab asked, going in for a layup.

Devon shrugged—he had never really spoken to Lab and wasn't as comfortable with him as he was with Peño. Lab seemed moodier than his older brother, and he was definitely quieter.

"Yeah," Lab said, "I kind of feel the same way sometimes. And by the way, Peño has to clean our room by himself for a week thanks to that bet he lost." He grinned. "Thanks for not getting expelled or locked at home by your parents. I knew you were way too cool for that."

Devon smiled at the word *cool* . . . though Peño's bet wasn't that far off. "You're welcome," he said.

Lab opened his mouth to continue, but another voice cut across the gym.

"Vision can be a dangerous thing."

Devon saw Rolabi walking onto the court. He noticed Rolabi wasn't carrying his usual black bag—for the first time in nine days. He stopped at center court, hands at his back.

"The question is, do we turn away, or do we stand and meet it?"

The team quickly gathered around him, and Devon wondered what Rolabi was talking about. It sounded ominous, whatever it was. He caught a glimpse of Reggie in the corner of his eye, nodding along. Did Reggie know something the rest of the team didn't? Devon thought back to the spotlight that had surrounded Reggie yesterday when he was anticipating the plays. Devon was starting to think there was more to Reggie than met the eye.

"We have two days left of our training camp," Rolabi continued. "And two left to catch the orb. We will return to three evening practices a week until the start of the season. We will practice everything we have discussed here until it becomes second nature. In your free time, you will focus on your mind. Read. Study. Learn to see. The mind and body are intertwined . . . if you neglect one, the other will fail. Never stop."

"It's summer break," A-Wall said. "We're not supposed to be studying."

"No break is needed or wanted for the tenacious mind. I will see you tomorrow."

"There's no practice today?" Peño asked suspiciously.

"Oh yes," the professor said, though he was headed for the doors. "You just don't need me."

"What should we do?" Rain said.

Rolabi glanced back. "I leave that to you."

Rolabi stalked through the open doors, the wind howling as ever. But this time, when the doors slammed shut, they vanished. There was only one doorway into and out of Fairwood, and it was now gone. Thick yellowed cinder blocks stared back at Devon in its place, impassable and unmoving.

"Now I'm stuck with you guys?" the grumpy voice said. "Oh . . . this will be fun."

Devon flinched. He had almost forgotten about the other disembodied voice in Fairwood.

The gym rattled as the two longer walls that ran down the court began to slide forward like an enormous trash compactor. Devon whirled around, watching as they slid toward them.

What are you doing? he thought.

"Not my doing," the voice said. "But it's nice to stretch. Not so nice for you, of course."

Can you stop it?

"No. I think this is a one-way trip. Going to be messy. Ugh. Just what I needed."

Devon tried to think. Was there a trick to this test? There were no windows or ducts or obvious weak spots in the brick. Escape seemed impossible . . . so there had to be something else. A clue they were missing.

"Maybe we need to score the ball again?" Vin suggested.

That didn't sound right to Devon, but he followed Vin anyway. Every player hit a shot—Devon choosing a layup to expedite things—but the walls drove on. The noise was terrible: the rumbling of an unseen engine, the screech of the bleachers as they dug grooves into the hardwood, the panicked shouts of the team. The disgruntled voice complaining continually in the background.

Devon realized he was chewing his nails to nubs and lowered his hand. *What now?*

"This is useless," Lab said. "We did shooting two days ago. He wouldn't repeat it."

Devon tried to take stock of what they had around them. Team benches, bags, bleachers . . . He turned to the bleachers. Maybe there was no trick this time. Maybe they just had to *survive.*

"We need to stop the walls," he said.

He ran to the bleachers and grabbed on to one end, setting his legs like two anchors and pulling. But he hadn't realized it was one giant steel structure. It was outrageously heavy. He pulled with everything he had, but they moved a few inches at most. He couldn't do it alone.

"Help!" he called, turning back to the others.

The team rushed over, some pulling on corners and benches, and some pushing. Together they managed to turn the clunky bleachers sideways before the walls had closed too far . . . though just barely. Everyone stepped back just as the lumbering walls closed in, and Devon waited anxiously. He knew that if the bleachers didn't work, nothing else in here would.

The walls pressed in, there was an awful screeching, and then the bleachers began to fold.

Devon slumped as the walls rolled on, swallowing the gym. The old banners were torn from the walls and shredded. The benches caught between the sliding walls and tore as well. As the walls came closer and closer, Devon realized with horror that the team would be flattened into nothing along with the rest of Fairwood.

Devon watched as the bleachers folded into an abstract metal sculpture. He started to tremble when he thought of bones and sinew doing the same. He thought of his parents and his sister and his nana. What would they say when they found out? He had come so far, and made friends, and he had *tried*. It seemed unfair. Pointless.

"Rolabi!" Peño shouted, pounding on the wall. "Help us! Someone!"

Then something caught Devon's eye. A black ball floating high above them. The walls were well past the sidelines now . . . sliding forward with the same steady, inexorable progress. The team had perhaps a few minutes to live.

"Someone can get out of here!" Twig shouted. "You vanish, remember?"

"Get up on the bleachers!" Lab cried.

Devon went first. He climbed up onto the folding metal, grabbing on to the rails and benches and heaving himself up toward the arch that was now the highest point. His shoes slipped on the metal, but he kept going, pulling others up behind him until they were all perched precariously atop the rising steel structure like a flock of pigeons.

"It's too far!" Lab said, panicked.

The walls were only about ten feet from each other now. The gym floor was carpeted with splintered wood and shards of glass. Someone's lunch had been ground into a gray paste. Everything had been destroyed. Devon thought of the dark room and Rolabi's advice there:

Create new friendships. Build them strong, he had said. *You will need them.*

Devon thought of the bricks. Mounds of them. He knew what he wanted his house to look like: the outside was solid and unassuming, but inside, it was packed full of friends, teammates, and family. If he was going to build it, then he could place the first brick right here. He knew what to do. Devon dropped to all fours, bracing himself against the benches.

"Come on!" he shouted at the others. "Make a pyramid!"

They saw his intention quickly. Twig, A-Wall, Big John, and Reggie dropped to their hands and knees beside him. They pressed their shoulders together even as the bleachers continued to warp beneath them. Devon noticed with a sideways glance that A-Wall had tears rolling down his face, but he still stoically held his position as the others clambered on top of him. Jerome, Rain, and Vin formed a second level, and finally Lab and Peño climbed to the third.

Devon felt their combined weight on his back and grimaced. The bench was so distorted now that his arms and legs were sloping downward on either side, and he had to grip the steel to keep the pyramid steady, holding with every ounce of strength he had. There was pressure on all sides of him, leaning into him. He knew that if he slipped, the whole pyramid would topple, and time would be up. Every muscle in his back and arms seemed to tremble. He gritted his teeth. Still he held.

"Hurry!" Rain shouted. "Get it!"

Devon couldn't hear what Lab and Peño were saying. The walls were only a few feet away, and the sound was like an oncoming train. But he had his job. Holding steady required all his concentration. He vaguely thought he should be crying, but tears didn't come. He simply remained in the center of the pyramid, keeping his teammates up. That felt good to say, even in his mind. His teammates. His *friends*. The pressure increased as others began to weaken, and he flexed every muscle he had, his whole body rigid. He became the pillar in the middle. The walls were close enough to reach out and touch. He closed his eyes.

Devon felt a sharp pressure on his back and heard his teammates crying out—though he didn't know whether it was from joy or fear or pain. He guessed that someone had jumped for the orb. Seconds ticked by as he waited for the end.

And then the walls stopped. One voice rose up over the noise:

"Badgers!" Peño cried.

Everyone started to cheer. Devon shouted, "Badgers!" even as the others crawled off his back. The walls retreated, and the bleachers went with them. The human pyramid broke apart, and Devon rode the bleachers back to the ground, looking around in wonder as Fairwood was remade from the devastation. The splintered benches reformed. The banners were resewn and flew back into place. Doors appeared in the walls. But nothing was the same as it had been. Everything was gleaming now, fresh and new. He smiled. All of the broken things had been remade better than before.

As the team started for the benches, Twig fell in line beside Devon.

"You saved us," Twig said.

Devon shook his head. "I was just doing what I thought was best."

"No," Twig said. "You kept your head. You knew you wouldn't be saved, and you did it anyway. That took heart, man. Even if you're quiet, you have a whole lot of heart."

Devon stared at his shoes, his eyes welling up unexpectedly. He had spent so long thinking he was dangerous. A bad person. An animal to be caged. And to hear that—that he had *heart*—felt like another blow to that idea. Maybe he had done something bad. But he could still do good.

He could be a pillar, and he realized he wanted nothing else. He nodded, turning away.

"Thanks," he managed.

Out of the corner of a blurry eye, he saw Twig smile and start for the bench. Devon hurried to the locker room to dry his eyes, but as he ripped off a piece of toilet paper and turned to the mirror, he paused. Who cared if he was crying? He was a person. A good one. A teammate and a friend.

And he realized he could be all those things *and* a beast. That was what basketball gave him.

The chance to be a tiger.

He smiled at his reflection, and for a second, he saw stripes and fangs, and he laughed.

He couldn't wait for the season to start.

THE
WEST BOTTOM
BADGERS

If you want to be stronger,
lift the ones who need to be carried.

WIZENARD ❰43❱ PROVERB

THE NEXT MORNING, Cash stood in front of the gym doors. This time he waited to open them until his nana drove away. The sky was overcast, the air a bit cooler than the previous days. A breeze whispered across the parking lot, carrying a hint that autumn was on the way.

Devon was completing the ten-day camp. He was living up to his promise. Ten days to try to face the world again. It felt like a long time ago that he'd made the vow. He had wanted to return to the old Devon, but instead he felt brand-new.

He opened the door and froze. The gym was gone. Instead there was an open space. He remembered it: no walls or ceiling, just mounds of bricks on a white floor, and an area in the middle blanketed with fresh grass. Cash walked inside and let the doors close.

He noticed a few bricks placed in a line on the grass, as if beginning a foundation. It was barely even a wall—twenty bricks or so, ten wide and two high. Cash couldn't help but feel disappointed. He had changed so much in the last ten days, and that was all he had managed to build?

"Beginning is the hardest part of building something," Rolabi said, appearing on the other side of the grass. His eyes seemed to reflect its dark green. "The better you do it, the slower it goes."

Devon frowned. "I guess, well . . . I thought I built a whole foundation yesterday."

"If we think we can change ourselves that fast, we open ourselves to collapse. To build a strong house, there must be many careful placements. Backups and safeguards. A million small but meaningful choices. If your house cannot sustain the first storm, it means nothing. And the storm is coming."

Rolabi gestured to something behind Cash, and Cash turned. Dark clouds were creeping across the pale gray sky, sweeping up out of the abyss beyond. A tumultuous wall of them approached, flashing at its heart, and Devon felt the cool wind pushed before the storm. Voices sounded, low and deep.

They must be stopped.

The boy is dangerous.

"What sort of storm is that?" Cash murmured.

"One that demands strength," Rolabi said. "And I don't mean muscles."

Cash watched as a face appeared in the clouds. It looked oddly familiar.

"I think I know that face—"

"The storm will fall on everyone. Friends. Family."

Cash stiffened and turned back to Rolabi. Behind the professor, the sky had brightened, and more light shone on the horizon, like a distant sunrise. Devon sensed a collision coming. Soon.

"Is my family in danger?" Cash asked.

"Everyone will be in danger when it comes. Will your house be ready or not?"

Cash turned back to the clouds. He would do anything to protect his family. If that meant making the right choices and building something strong, then he could do that. At least he had something to build on. He picked up a brick and placed it on the little wall.

"It will be ready," Cash said.

Rolabi smiled. "Then welcome to the team."

Devon was back in Fairwood, standing on the threshold, just inside the doors. He blinked against the fluorescent lighting and looked around. The team was mostly there, getting ready and warming up. A few of them glanced over at him, some waving or nodding, and Cash joined them on the home bench.

Peño jogged over to give him props.

"What up, big man?" he said. "You daydreaming at the door or what?"

"Something like that," Cash replied.

"Yeah, I hear you. That was crazy yesterday, right? Check this—"

"No," Lab groaned from farther down the bench.

Peño ignored him:

"Cash Money is comin'
flex on him you runnin'
Big as a house
quiet as a mouse
He holds the whole team up
Cash gon carry us to the cup"

Devon laughed. "I like it."

"What cup?" Vin said.

Peño glanced at him, then frowned. "I don't know. Just rhymed, I guess."

"Gather round," a deep voice announced.

Rolabi was standing at center court, his bag once again at his side. The team circled around him. There was an easy feel to their movements today. No drama. No fear.

Cash wondered if they had seen the storm on the horizon too.

"All but one of you have caught the orb," Rolabi said. "Why?"

"Because . . . you told us to?" Vin said.

"But why?" Rolabi asked. "What did you find?"

"Our fears," Reggie said.

Devon nodded. So it had been the same for everyone.

"If one thing will stop you in life, it is that," Rolabi said. "To win, we must defeat our fears. For basketball . . . for everything."

"But . . . we did, right?" Big John asked.

"Fear is not so easily beaten," Rolabi replied. "It will return. You must be ready." He opened his bag and reached inside. "For today, we will review what we have learned so far."

There was a sudden scratching.

"Twig, you know the drill," Rolabi said.

As Twig hurried to the locker room to let Kallo out, Rolabi dug into his bag and began setting up another obstacle course. Objects came flying out, seemingly at random, and fell into perfect patterns. As Rolabi worked, the lights flickered, and the team's shadows stood up behind them.

"Oh, great," Big John muttered.

In minutes, an elaborate obstacle course had been set up around the gym.

"In a line, please," Rolabi said.

They assembled behind Rain, and Cash waved his arms to loosen up. After the last few days, the visions and the collapsing gym and everything else, he was ready to work. To sweat.

"We'll start with the free-throw circuit: laps until someone hits. Once through we watch the daisy. We'll work on getting past Kallo and then strap up the pads for a defensive drill. After that we run the Spotlight Offense in the dark with a glowing ball, then with our shadow defenders. Following that, we run a circuit with our weaker hands. Finally, we shoot to end the day and solve another puzzle."

"Is there going to be weird stuff happening?" Vin asked.

"Weird stuff?" Rolabi asked with genuine curiosity.

Vin sighed. "Never mind."

The drill began. It was ten days in one—harder than anything they had done. It was falling and climbing and challenging shadows and a prowling Kallo who sprang on him again and again. It was Greg calling Devon a freak at every turn. It was the disappointment and pain in his parents' eyes when he failed to leave his room. He passed through one image after another as though he were running through a heavy fog.

At one point, Devon came to the basket for a shot. With a jolt, the floor warped upward and formed a wall in front of him, and then split again, turning into a cage. He cried out as it closed in, blotting out the lights. But no one called back to him. No one came over to help.

You built this.

He looked around at the bars. They had been in his way for years. But his team was out there. He was not going to give up again. Suddenly he felt angry, and he didn't even look for the keys. He clenched his teeth, lowered his shoulder, and charged.

He smashed through the bars like a battering ram, and they broke and melted back into hardwood slats, leaving Devon alone with the hoop. He was ten feet away. He breathed and took the shot, flicking his wrist like Twig had taught him. The ball hit the rim, rolled, and dropped in.

"Cash Money," Rain said, coming up from behind him for a shot. "I like that stroke."

Devon smiled and went to get his ball.

When the drill ended, the shadows vanished, and Kallo strolled back into the locker room.

Devon went to grab his water bottle and finished it, vaguely hearing the others talking behind him. Water dribbled down his chin, and he thought about the shattered bars and the years he had spent building them up. It had felt much better to bring them down.

"So you're sticking around?" the cranky voice said. "I lost another bet."

"You should stop betting against me," Cash said.

He heard something like a wheezy laugh, and it seemed like the whole gym vibrated.

"Fair enough," the voice said.

Devon tucked his bottle away and went to join the others just as Rolabi headed for the doors.

"I thought you said we still have a puzzle to solve?" Rain called after him.

"You do," Rolabi said. "One for each of you. And by the way, welcome to the Badgers."

The team cheered and the doors blew open as the professor walked outside, a fading silhouette in the sunlight. They started for the benches, but Cash just stood there for a moment. A puzzle. Or a riddle, maybe.

"What must we do with our strength?" he murmured, recalling Rolabi's question.

It occurred to him that the question didn't necessarily refer to physical strength. It could be anything. So what did people have to do with their strengths? He thought back to the last ten days. To the tiger. The castle. The closing walls. The answer was obvious.

He almost laughed.

"We must use it," he said.

Then let's get to work.

Cash changed his shoes and put on a clean shirt. When the team was ready, they stood up as one and started for the doors. Rain pushed one open and held it, letting sunlight pour inside. Devon remembered the storm clouds blotting out the sky. He remembered his nana's warning that the road would be hard. He wondered what was coming for him. What waited beyond the sunshine. But he supposed it didn't really matter. He was a part of a team now. Whatever happened, he would face it with them.

The group walked out together. Devon smiled, right in the middle, ready to hold them up.

BOOK FOUR

PEÑO

ALL BUT ONE

A true leader stands at the bottom,
pushing his team up.

✧ WIZENARD ◈ PROVERB ✧

PEÑO PULLED OPEN the doors and paused, arms spread, eyes closed, a smile slipping across his face. He breathed deeply, drawing in the partnered scents of cedar and sweat, crisp and sharp.

He was home.

Fairwood was old, to be sure. Decrepit, even. But it was also Peño's favorite place in the world. Old was fine. The important thing was that it was the *same*. The same tattered nets. The same dull paint on the cinderblock walls. The same creaking floorboards. Outside, there were only levels of decay. Things got *worse*. Buildings crumbled. Cars were abandoned, like rusted tombstones. Even the people faded.

Rain's dad was gone. Big John had lost his dad and an older brother. Peño's mom . . . that had been three years ago. Three years. Surely it was last week. Maybe a month. How could it have been so long? How could he not have heard her voice for three years?

"It's so early," Lab moaned, shuffling in behind Peño, rubbing his eyes.

Lab was a year younger than Peño but already three inches taller, a fact Lab conveniently slipped into 95 percent of their conversations. He was lanky where Peño was stout, his hair messy where Peño maintained a meticulous fade—which was no small feat with a pair of ancient clippers he'd reclaimed from a dumpster. The only similarity was their eyes—round and rich brown, like toasted almonds, someone had once said—but no one mentioned them now. They were their mom's eyes, and they brought memories.

"It's ball time," Peño said. "It's never too early."

He started for the bench, adjusting the strap of his bag on his shoulder and flashing Reggie a grin. He didn't need to dwell on things here. That was the point. That was the beauty of this place.

"Debatable," Lab replied.

"It's going to be a big year, Lab. Things are going to change."

"You mean you're going to grow?"

"Shut up."

Peño gave Reggie props and then turned to the away bench, where Twig sat alone.

"Twig," Peño said. "Yo, dawg."

"Hey, Peño," Twig mumbled, waving awkwardly. "I mean . . . yo . . . dog."

Peño snorted. He liked Twig, but the gangly starting center frustrated Peño to no end. If he had his height, he would be a superstar. Peño had to make do with being the shortest player on the team: five foot one with shoes on. He *hated* being short. There were other things that bothered him, like his big nose, the freckles under his eyes, and his always-rounded belly, but he would accept all of that if he could have a few more inches. Lab had caught him many times holding on to an exposed beam in their kitchen with a heavy bag tied to his feet. It gave him sore fingers, but little else.

Peño sat down and pulled out his beloved kicks. Freddy had pushed for them all to get matching shoes two years ago, the first official year of the West Bottom Badgers. That was no small task for families in the

Bottom, especially in the desolate west end. Most families had scrounged shoes from flea markets or secondhand stores, but Peño's dad had saved up and surprised his boys with two brand-new pairs. Peño had almost fainted when he opened the box. He had slept with it next to his pillow for the first few months, and he still kept the shoes beside his bed and cleaned them every single night with an old toothbrush, even in the off-season. They were his most prized possession. The only new thing he had ever had in his life. He laced them slowly . . . delicately.

As the other players filed in, Peño stretched and loosened up. They had been off for about a month now—the season had ended with their second straight last-place finish. It had been seven losses to close the year out, the last of those being an absolute thrashing by their crosstown rivals, the East Bottom Bandits. Their starting point guard was Peño's arch-nemesis: Lio Nester. They had a personal war every time the teams met—smack talk, hard fouls, and occasional fights. Peño didn't like to admit it, but Lio usually put up the better numbers. He also called Peño the "Little Peanut," which didn't help matters. He felt his cheeks warm at the memory.

"Peño, you aren't blinking again," Lab said.

"I'm fine."

"Okay . . . Peanut."

Peño glared at his brother and grabbed his ball. The Badgers had only a single team ball, but Peño had managed to scrounge one at a yard sale and clean it up. It was worn and warped like an old tire, but it did the job. It made echoing beats as he dribbled, the sound traveling through the hardwood.

This is my year, he thought. *This is when I become the best point guard in the Bottom.*

"You got a rhyme for the season yet?" Jerome called after him.

Peño grinned. He'd been working on one for a week. "You ain't ready for it."

"No, we aren't," Lab confirmed.

"Beats, please," Peño said, passing Jerome the ball and waiting for Big John's rhythm.

Peño took a breath, trying to remember the lines, then:

"The badgers are back
And yes, our gym is wack
But the boys are better
Down to the letter
We comin' for the win
Uppercut to the chin
Dren best watch for the badgers
Because we are... well..."

Peño hesitated, cursing inwardly. He had lost track and started free-styling . . . but why did he always have to use the word *Badgers*?

"Mad . . . gers?" he said.

Everyone burst into laughter, and Peño sighed. He really had to figure out something that rhymed with their team name. Peño loved ancient animals, but why did Freddy have to choose *badgers*? He had read about them in one of his mom's books when he was picked for the team, and he liked the animal well enough. Badgers used to live in the grasslands of Dren a long time ago—back when there were grasslands. They had short, wide bodies and were small but vicious if cornered. It would actually be a perfect animal for Peño . . . if the name were better for rhyming. They could have been the Bears. The Bats. The Butterflies.

Well, maybe not that last one.

"Cladgers . . ." Peño said, still thinking. "Radgers . . . the Bad Curs— Ugh!"

He went for the layup and hit the bottom of the rim. Peño looked around, relieved that no one had noticed the miss. It was his offense that was killing his prospects. The ball always seemed to leave his hands too quickly. No matter what, he couldn't seem to slow his shot down, especially during games. Lio said he played defense on Peño "just to be polite." Peño scowled.

The front doors opened again, and A-Wall and Vin walked in.

"My man," Peño called, giving a mock salute to Vin.

Vin was the backup point guard, but competing for the starting position never seemed to get in the way of their friendship. A-Wall was the starting power forward and the team's resident blockhead. He had failed out of the school system but had managed to get a job shoveling dirt at a gravel pit. In the Bottom, school was considered a privilege: if you failed three exams, you were kicked out and expected to work. There weren't many jobs, but the pits had some openings.

Peño's dad worked there too . . . The odds were that Peño would end up in a hole with him.

Peño grabbed his rebound and started dribbling, mouthing some words:

"The badgers are the baddest
West Bottom ballin'
Peño be the man
You hear him shot
Callin nnnnng!"

He took a three-pointer and airballed it.

"Yeah," Lab said, walking out to join him. "I heard it."

Peño passed his brother the ball, and Lab promptly missed a jumper of his own.

"You shoot like Grandma," Peño said.

"You look like Grandma," Lab retorted. "Except I think she's taller."

Peño scooped up the rebound and headed for the point, dodging imaginary defenders.

"Mom said I would be the tallest eventually," Peño said. "I'm just a slow starter."

He regretted it as soon as the words came out. He saw a bit of the color leach out of Lab's face. Lips pursed. Eyes tight. It was always the same. Lab didn't like to talk about her. Ever. Maybe even *couldn't.*

"Yeah," Lab said quietly.

Peño felt an ache for his little brother. He struggled with the memories too, of course, but not like Lab. Peño could talk about her. He wanted to talk about her. Lab just wanted to forget.

Three years, Peño thought, *and he still can't admit she's gone.*

"Of course," Peño said, trying to lighten the mood, "who needs height when you got mad ups?"

He leapt and grabbed the rebound over Lab, getting the laugh he had wanted. They started playing one-on-one, shoving and pushing down low. Lab was the better scorer, but Peño was a tenacious defender. It was usually a close battle, although Lab had started to pull ahead over the last year.

As they scrimmaged, Freddy arrived with the new player in tow. The ever-ambitious team owner had phoned Peño and Lab a few weeks ago to tell them about his prized recruit, Devon Jackson. Freddy had said he was going to be a big presence down low, and apparently he hadn't been kidding.

Devon was the most muscular kid Peño had ever seen. His muscles had muscles.

"I need to get this kid's gym plan," Peño muttered.

"My boys!" Freddy called. "All here? Come on over. Let me introduce Devon."

The team slowly gathered around Freddy and Devon, and Peño gaped at him. He had thought Twig was lucky. This kid had it made. If he could run without falling over, he could be a star. Peño looked down at himself: round belly beneath his T-shirt, stubby legs, small hands. He'd gotten nothing to work with. No genetic breaks. How was he supposed to keep up?

"He's quiet," Freddy said, patting one of Devon's broad shoulders. "But a big boy."

"We can see that," Peño said. "He looks like a Clydesdale."

"Who's Clyde Dale?" A-Wall asked. "He a baller too?"

Peño rubbed his forehead. "It's a horse . . . Never mind."

"Where you from?" Lab asked.

Devon shifted for a moment, looking distinctly uncomfortable. Peño couldn't believe it—*that* kid was shy? If Peño had muscles like him, he would have thrown out his shirts.

"Homeschooled," Devon said finally.

Peño laughed. "Homeschooled! Crazy. My pops barely wants me there *after* school."

"Who can blame him?" Big John said. "Still, kid got muscles I didn't know existed."

"Yours are buried under Bad Man Blubber," Peño said, poking his stomach. "Well, how we gonna play with him if he doesn't talk? Maybe I can warm him up. What do you call a cat—"

"Boo!" the entire team shouted at him.

Peño scowled. "I had a good punch line this time."

"No you didn't," Vin said.

Just then, the lights flickered. Peño looked up, wondering if Fairwood's wiring was finally giving up. It was amazing it held out so long. The place probably hadn't seen an electrician in decades. But as he watched, the bulbs pulsated, grew brighter, drew him in like a moth.

What does it mean to lead? a distant voice asked.

Peño flinched and looked around. It had seemed to come from nowhere.

What is hiding in the darkness?

Peño looked around again. Freddy was still talking. But this voice was different . . . deeper.

It's time.

The lights blinked out altogether, plunging the gym into darkness. The front doors burst inward, though Peño knew for an absolute fact that they could only swing outward, as he had run into them many times before and smacked his nose. Gale-force winds roared inside, scooping up dust and trash into a towering wave.

"Dust tsunami!" he shouted, scrambling behind Big John. "Run!"

"Thanks," Big John said.

When the wind abated, Peño saw a man in the doorway. He was huge, crisply dressed, and carrying a purse. But it was his eyes that caught Peño's attention. They were a shimmering, radiant green, like lightning seen through smog. They flashed to Peño, boring into him.

The boy who couldn't breathe, the voice said.

Peño took a step back. He was imagining things. The voice was his subconscious.

Impossible. You never let it speak.

The man introduced himself as Professor Rolabi Wizenard, and the team was soon left alone with the enormous professor. His eyes flicked back to Peño. The green of his eyes paled and changed. Images flashed through Peño's mind: a stark white bed, slender fingers, nights alone, cooking through the night because it reminded him of her . . . His knees wobbled and he almost fell.

"You good?" Lab asked.

Peño nodded, uneasy. "Yeah, man. Breakfast is sitting weird."

"We ate leftover spaghetti," Lab said. "That *you* cooked. Of course it is."

Peño glared at him and tried to steady himself. What was happening to him? Why had those images returned so suddenly? He felt a weight on his chest, and his throat constricted. He pushed the fear away. These were thoughts for the dead of night, when Lab wasn't around.

Rolabi pulled out a contract. "I will need everyone to sign this before we can proceed."

When it was Peño's turn, he accepted the document nervously. Two important details made his pulse quicken. First, the paper was as hard as a rock. Second, there were no other signatures written there, despite the fact the same sheet had been passed along before him, and everyone had signed. He read the contract carefully.

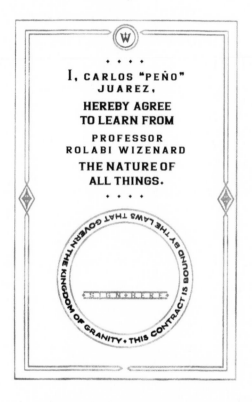

"I think I need my lawyer before I sign anything," Peño said.

"You can't even afford to look at a lawyer," Lab reminded him.

"Right," Peño said, signing on the line. "So . . . is the Kingdom of Granity a new association? It sounds a little overdramatic." He handed the paper to Reggie and took on a deep voice like a medieval herald. "The Kingdom of Granity will require all players to report in britches and poufy wigs."

He looked up at Rolabi, but the professor remained expressionless.

"Not a joke guy. I respect that," Peño murmured.

When everyone had signed, Rolabi opened his purse. Green light spilled out, and Peño could hear things moving. Big things. Something squawked.

"Was that a parrot?" he asked, trying to get a peek.

Without any warning, Rolabi passed a basketball to Big John. The next ball came whizzing toward Peño's nose, and he snatched it just before it would have collided. The room flickered and wobbled as if Peño were seeing through a crush of summer heat on concrete, and Fairwood was suddenly packed with spectators. Peño looked around, his eyes wide. He was standing in the middle of a game. Fans packed the bleachers. Reggie came sprinting up the court, and Peño yelped as he proceeded to run *through* his chest. He spotted his little brother and hurried toward him, relieved.

"Hey, Lab!" he called. "This is messed up, right?"

But his brother sprinted past him. So did Rain. Peño looked at the home bench and saw only four players sitting there: Vin, Big John, Jerome, and A-Wall. Devon, Twig, Rain, Lab, and Reggie were on the court—so the team was down to nine. He spotted his dad on the bleachers and hurried over, but his dad looked right through him, watching the other players.

"Dad! Hey!" Peño shouted, waving his arms. "Mrs. Roberts? Anyone? Hello!"

He tried to grab his dad's arm, but his hand went through flesh and bone like a wisp of smoke.

I'm not here, he realized. *Not really.* It was a vision, or maybe a dream. Peño spun around. The game was continuing without him. Everything was normal. He just . . . wasn't there. Peño crouched down, hugging himself, as the game raced around him. Cheers and laughter and shouts. His teammates didn't even notice he was gone. Didn't care. His stomach roiled.

Then he saw the professor standing on the sideline, staring at him.

"Hmm," Rolabi said. "Interesting. That will be all for today. I will see you here tomorrow."

The team was standing in an empty gym once again. Peño stood up and looked around, bewildered. His teammates seemed just as uneasy. Rolabi was walking out.

"What time?" Peño asked him out of reflex.

Rolabi didn't answer. When he neared the front doors, they burst open, propelled by another rush of ice-cold wind. The professor strode through, and the doors slammed shut.

"Do we get to keep the balls?" Peño shouted.

He followed, wanting an answer. Any answer. He hurried into the parking lot.

"What . . . Professor?" Peño whirled around, eyes wide.

Rolabi was already gone.

THE RIGHT WAY

2

Complacency guarantees failure.

WIZENARD ⟨27⟩ PROVERB

PEÑO STOPPED IN front of Fairwood, looking up at the pink building with real nervousness for the first time since he had tried out for the Badgers two years ago. That had been simpler. It was fear he would be cut, that Lab would make it, that he would be forced to watch the season from the sideline. He'd barely slept for weeks leading up to it and nearly vomited walking through the front doors. Thankfully, they had both made it. Seeing the team roster had been one of the best moments of his life.

This was a different fear. He was afraid of things he couldn't explain or understand. Voices. Memories. Peño looked down at his hands, saw they were trembling, and quickly stuffed them into his pockets before Lab could notice.

Peño didn't show fear. He was the big brother—he had to be strong. He didn't get to cry. He didn't get to be afraid. He cooked and cleaned and did everything around the house so that Lab and his father could push on. Still, he felt the tremors from his pockets. He hadn't trembled like this since three years ago, when he reached out for skeletal fingers, felt the warmth slip away, the grip go limp and cold . . . He shook the memory away. It wasn't the time to dwell on that. It was never the time.

"What are you doing?" Lab asked, peeking around him.

"Nothing," Peño replied quickly.

"Well, you're not going inside," Lab said. "Are you afraid?"

Peño sighed. They had both been dropping hints at each other that something had been amiss at training yesterday. But it seemed like neither wanted to be the first to admit it, and now they stared at each other appraisingly, both refusing to look away.

"Why would I be afraid?" Peño asked.

Lab shrugged, though he seemed uneasy. "Just calling it as I see it. Lead the way."

"Why don't you?"

"You always go in first," Lab said. "You basically skip through the door."

"Well, it's time you got your shot, little brother," Peño replied. He leaned in, lowering his voice to a conspiratorial whisper. "Unless there's something wrong . . ."

"Nope," Lab said. "You think I'm afraid of a weirdo in a suit? Like I said, Rolabi is clearly some two-bit magician who was trying to impress us on our first day so we behave."

He had said that about a hundred times now, but Peño wasn't convinced. There were street magicians in the Bottom—transients with tattered decks of cards or multicolored tissues stuffed up their sleeves—but they were sources of pity, if people paid them much notice at all. Magic was a scam, a last resort for a few Drennish pennies.

What Rolabi did was different. The images and visions, and the voice in Peño's head—they didn't feel fake. In fact, they felt strangely familiar, or personal, as if Peño was somehow complicit in the impossible things he was seeing and hearing, or maybe even responsible for them.

Are you ready for the road?

Peño looked at Lab, but he knew the question wasn't his brother's. It was the same voice as yesterday. *His* voice.

"Okay, then go ahead," Peño said, standing aside and gesturing at the doors.

Lab scowled. "Fine . . . *coward*."

Peño felt the heat rush into his face. He despised that word. They both did. Over the years he'd collected a broken collarbone and several ankle sprains because of it, while Lab had fractured three ribs jumping off the back of their roof on a dare.

Peño had been grounded for a long, long time after that one.

Peño grabbed the other door. "We'll do it at the same time, then, if it makes you feel better."

"Fine. But I'll walk in by myself. I don't need you."

"On three?"

Lab paused. "On three."

Peño turned to the doors. "One . . . two . . . three!"

They whipped their respective doors open, both taking small steps backward at the same time as if to ward off any blows. Reggie was alone in the gym, stretching by the bench, staring at them.

"Right," Peño said. "See? Nothing weird."

"I despise you," Lab mumbled.

The two brothers hurried inside, now racing and elbowing each other to be first.

"Anything you want to talk about, baby brother?" Peño whispered.

"Nope," Lab said. "You?"

"Feel great."

They plopped themselves onto the home bench and glared at each other.

"Fighting again?" Reggie said bemusedly.

"The usual," Peño replied.

He pulled out his shoes and eyed them for scuffs. There were none, of course. He had cleaned them yesterday when he got home, despite only having worn them for about an hour. He'd actually spent more time cleaning his shoes than wearing them, and he'd been bored by noon. Peño's family had no cell phones or computers—both far beyond their means—so Peño and Lab usually entertained themselves with a mixture of old books, a TV with four channels, and jump shots off the back wall of their house. Peño had drawn a small square with chalk that they had to hit. It wasn't exactly the same as a hoop, but they tried to work on their form, at least. Lab always said Peño would be an all-star if games could just be played on squares.

Trying hard not to flinch, Peño scooped the new basketball out of his duffel bag, took a hopefully inconspicuous look around for spectators, and, seeing none, hurried onto the floor. It was the one real bonus of yesterday's bizarre introduction—the new balls. The Badgers had never had their own balls before. And they were *brand-new.* Rubbery. Beautiful. Peño had spent half the night smelling his until Lab threatened to throw it out the window.

As Peño began to dribble, the fear ebbed. He listened to the beat in the floorboards and moved in a dizzying pattern: behind-the-back, through-the-legs, reverse. Step, dribble, crossover, step. It became a dance, hands flying about him in a blur, and he started a verse under his breath:

"Peño is the man,
The boy with the plan
His presence is a must
He's a basketball-O-pus."

Peño grimaced and decided not to share that one. He had been free-styling for years now . . . with mixed success. Lab despised it, but Peño thought he was getting better. Hopefully.

Lab soon joined him, and they fell into an easy routine—one shot the ball and grabbed the rebound, while the other cut for the layup. Even with a ball each, they still used only the one. Old habits, he supposed. Lab started draining threes, getting into a rhythm, and Peño hit him with one crisp pass after another.

"Oh, okay," Peño said. "Bro with the flow—"

"*No*," Lab cut in, glaring at him. "How about no freestyling today. Or, you know, ever."

"You're jealous, mad zealous, a BB gun with no pellets—"

Lab whipped a pass at him, and Peño caught it, laughing. He shimmied and moved around his brother, spinning off for a one-handed floater. He was planning to use that move a lot this year—he'd been working on it on their brick wall. He grabbed the rebound and ducked under a wild shot from A-Wall, who was not reliable shooting from anywhere but under the hoop.

"Getting closer," Peño said. "It stayed in the gym."

A-Wall scowled. "You just hit me with some open looks this year."

"Sure," Peño said. "If you are less than three inches from the net, I will pass it you."

"Thank you," A-Wall said solemnly.

Peño rubbed his forehead. It really was like talking to a wall.

He turned back to the hoop and froze. It was gone. Brick walls had risen up on all sides, soaring above to a distant sky, little more than a pin-prick of blue. He was trapped inside them.

"Lab?" he whispered.

Peño stepped to the nearest wall and tentatively brushed his fingers against the bricks. The wall was real, and it was impassable.

He walked around, confused, seeing no doors. "Rolabi!" he shouted. "Rolabi!"

Peño started to sweat. Walls had closed in on him before—they'd been imagined, maybe, but the threat had felt the same. His chest heaved as he tried to think. He couldn't panic. He ran his hands along the wall again, pushing, testing. To his surprise, one brick slid inward and fell to the floor.

The next wouldn't, but he gripped the side and pulled, and it too dropped toward him, revealing more light. He began to strip the wall, brick by brick, building an opening and letting sunlight pour into his walled cage. He could see Fairwood beyond the crumbling mortar—bleachers and faded walls.

"Do you know what it means to be a leader, Peño?"

Peño whirled around. Rolabi was standing behind him. "Where—"

"Do you?"

Peño paused, thinking. "I . . . To make people follow you, I guess."

"No," Rolabi said. "It's to suffer first. Sleep last. Work hardest. Enjoy least. It's to see walls as doorways. Every person has a way to unlock their potential. The builder leaves a key for others to use."

"What do you mean, 'key'?"

"It is usually hidden, yes. Most people don't bother to look. But a leader takes the time to bring down walls. They push and pull. They give and take. They bring out potential by helping others escape their own self-created confines. It is a difficult process. Arduous. Exhausting. Not everyone has the skill."

"That doesn't sound fun," Peño murmured.

"If we don't have a leader, we don't have a chance. We don't have a team."

Peño stiffened. "We need a team!"

"Why?"

"I love this team," Peño said. "I need it, man."

"But you're afraid of it too. Why? What are you so afraid of?"

Peño felt a chill seep through him and gulped. "I . . . I don't know."

"Then you are not ready to lead."

Peño was suddenly standing with the team at center court, gathered around Rolabi. He blinked, rubbing his eyes, but no one even seemed to notice that he had been gone. Lab stood in his usual slouch beside him.

He thought back to the walls. What did Rolabi mean? What was he supposed to do?

"My . . . uh . . . my dad was wondering when the parents can come meet you?" Twig asked.

Peño glanced at Lab. Their mom had always been the "involved one." Their dad worked long hours—and longer now—and could never meet with teachers or coaches. Peño missed coming home to her. He missed her singing in the kitchen, cooking meals she had learned from her mother . . . ones she never had time to teach to Peño. She sung every day—to wake them up, while she cooked, when they went to sleep. These days the house was quiet. No one sang.

"Following the tryout, I will meet with parents," Rolabi said.

Peño snapped back to the present. "Did you say tryout? This *is* the team."

"This *was* the team."

Peño's stomach turned. He could still be *cut*? He felt that old fear flare up again. What if Lab made it and he didn't? What if he was the only one cut? Would they all leave him behind?

"If there is pressing business," Rolabi continued, "they can call 76522494936273."

Peño started counting on his fingers. "That doesn't sound like a phone number . . ."

Twig was patting his shorts for a pen. "So . . . seven . . . eight . . . ? Can you repeat that?"

"We are going to start with a scrimmage," Rolabi said. "We are going to use a different ball today. Last year's starters versus the bench players."

Peño almost felt like he emphasized "last year's." Would Rolabi mix up the starters too? Even if Peño made the team, would he get relegated to the bench? That would be better than being cut, of course, but not by much. This was supposed to be his year. The chance to take a starring role and prove to everyone—including himself—that he had a shot at the next level. He eyed Vin nervously.

Was it his imagination, or did he look a little taller?

They quickly split into their respective teams. For the starters, it was Peño at point, Rain at shooting guard, Lab at small forward, A-Wall at power forward, and Twig at center. Each was matched by their respective backup, Vin, Reggie, Jerome, Devon, and Big John.

Twig and Big John stepped up for the jump ball.

"I'm coming for you," Vin said, giving Peño a playful elbow. "Taking that starting job."

Peño grinned, trying to hide his concern. "You got to catch me first, brotha."

The bench team won the tip, and Peño quickly backpedaled.

"Back into position!" Peño shouted.

Vin was a good player—broad and strong with a decent jump shot, but he wasn't as quick as Peño, and he didn't have the same handles. Peño stayed low, keeping one hand out to jockey him. He moved side to side with lateral shuffles, tracking Vin's stomach. His shot might be a work in progress, but Peño would put himself up against any point guard in the EYL on defense.

But within the first minute Jerome had already laid one in to take the lead.

"Pick it up!" Peño snarled.

He received the inbound pass and started dribbling up the court. Vin was playing a one-man press—a dangerous gamble, since Peño could shake anyone in the open floor. He faked left, dropping his shoulder to sell it, and then exploded right. Vin stumbled, waving at thin air, and Peño sprinted past him—straight into an invisible wall. He jolted back, his nose taking the impact. He tried again, and his head snapped back a second time, his eyes watering. He reached out and felt nothing.

"What is this?" he said, rubbing his nose.

"It's called tight D," Vin said with a grin.

"Not what I meant."

Peño faked left and tried to go right for a third time. Once again, he got a painful smack in the nose for his trouble. Peño had no choice. He dribbled onto his weaker left hand . . . and drove directly into Vin's chest. Within seconds, Vin stole the ball and went in for the layup. Peño just stood there. Was he losing his mind? He walked to the right, reaching tentatively with his hands, and felt nothing.

"What are you doing, Peño?" Lab asked, running past him to collect the ball.

I have no idea, he thought.

"Nothing," he said. "Just lost the ball. Get back and set a pick, why don't you?"

"I thought you had mad handles?" Lab said. "You look like Twig dribbling."

"Thanks," Twig muttered.

Peño caught the inbound pass and abruptly turned right, slamming yet again into a wall. He wanted to scream. But how could he explain this to the others? That an invisible wall was appearing and, oh yeah, only when he went right? The team would think he was crazy. So he kept quiet and grew more frustrated with every passing second. After an hour, the bench team was winning by four points, and Peño was deeply annoyed.

"This is ridiculous!" he said, shaking his head. "Come on! We're losing to the bench!"

He turned to catch an inbound pass and froze. He was alone again.

"Why me?" he murmured.

A knight suddenly appeared beside him . . . then three more. They all wore gleaming silver armor, their angular helmets were drawn shut, and ten-foot lances jutted from their gloved fists. Peño stood directly in the center of the group, feeling dwarfed. They were all at least a foot taller than him.

"Umm . . ." he said. "Hello?"

One of the knights looked at him, nodded, and then turned ahead. Peño followed his gaze and blanched when he saw another line of knights facing them across the gym—dressed identically, except that their armor was copper instead of silver. Ten of them stood at attention, their lances at the ready.

"Guys?" Peño said.

"March!" one of the silver knights shouted.

Peño tried to hang back, but the knights on either side of him pulled him along, marching headlong toward the opposing line. The beat of their steps quickened. The knights at the center of the line stepped forward, forming a V-shaped attack. The defenders mirrored their formation. Peño tried to get free.

"I think there's some mistake—" he said.

The knights at the centers of the lines crashed into one another with a jarring clang of metal on metal. Peño ducked down in the middle of the chaos, trying to make himself small. Meanwhile, the copper knights on either side of their defensive line marched forward unopposed, encircling Peño and the struggling silver knights in mere moments. Peño gulped as they all lowered their lances, pointing now at exposed sides and backs. One was leveled directly between Peño's wide eyes.

Everyone froze.

"And so the battle ends," a familiar voice said. "There were none to guard the flanks."

Peño wrestled out from behind the tangle of limbs, ducking under the frozen combatants, and saw Rolabi watching the scene.

"Why am I in a medieval war again?" he asked, waving his hand in front of a motionless copper knight.

"A team without a strong bench is half a team. That in turn means a swift and sudden defeat. The bench is all too often the tide that turns the battle. The team advances as one. The starters, the center of the formation, are no more critical than those who follow. You all must function as one unit, or you will never win."

Peño looked back at the encircled knights. "Are you trying to tell me I'm benched?"

"I am telling you that it doesn't matter," Rolabi replied.

"So what do I do?"

"Make sure everyone knows they have a job. Everyone must be ready. A weakness or crack in the line ends the battle," Rolabi said. He pointed a finger at Peño. "Seal the cracks."

With that, he walked to the bleachers, bag in hand. Peño realized the knights were gone, and the team was gathered around him instead. He wondered if they had disappeared, or if he had, or if any of them were seeing the same strange things. Lab had a dazed look in his eyes.

Rolabi sat down on the bleachers and was gone. The team stood around Peño, eyes wide.

"Where . . . How did . . . ?" Big John said.

Peño stared at the empty bench, mouth agape. "This ain't cool."

He thought of the strange vision, and the knights marching into battle, and Rolabi's instructions for him. What did he want from Peño? To keep the bench ready? More pep talks?

"So . . . we're pretty set on our coach being a witch, right?" Big John said.

Lab scowled. "What are you, six? There's no such thing as witches."

"I thought it was magicians that you didn't believe in," Peño said dryly.

He saw Devon plunking himself on the bench and thought about Rolabi's instructions again—to make sure everyone knew they had a job. To have them ready. He recalled that Devon hadn't said a single word in two days now, and Peño had noticed that he was playing soft. Timid, even. Maybe Rolabi wanted him to get the potential out of guys like Devon. He could do that.

Peño sat down beside him and noticed a card on each bag with a *W* and a number.

"So," Peño said, glancing at Devon. "New guy. Homeschooler. Big baller."

"You're not going to rhyme, are you?" Lab said, sitting down on Peño's other side to change.

"Maybe later," Peño said. "Just want to get to know the new kid. For instance, I noticed you don't like to shoot. Or rebound. Or push people. And yet you're huge. I'm a little confused."

Devon shifted, scratching the back of his neck. "I . . . I was just getting used to the team."

Peño could see his uneasiness. He was shy, to be sure. But they needed a beast down low.

"Understandable," Peño said, nodding. "Usually I can dribble. It was a weird day. But, man, be *big*. Or at least show me some workouts. You're like an ox. A box. A lock stock and—"

"Please stop," Lab said.

Peño sighed, shooting Devon a grin. "My brother doesn't get my genius."

He noticed that Vin was tapping numbers into his phone, glancing at the card in his other hand. Only Vin and Twig had cell phones. Twig lived in the suburbs, but Vin was from the run-down inner city like the rest of them. He never told anyone how he had managed to get the cell phone or who paid the bills for it.

"Well?" Peño asked as Vin hung up.

Vin frowned. "A recording. It said the line was for parents. And it said 'Good night, Vin,' which was creepy."

"He's a witch," Big John said.

"I think you mean a wizard," Vin replied.

"There's no such thing!" Lab snapped.

Peño gave Devon a quick pat on the knee. "See you tomorrow, bro. Step on somebody, will you? Just not me. I'm too beautiful."

That got a laugh out of him, and Peño slipped his shoes off, thinking. If he needed to get his teammates ready for battle, he could do that. But where would he be in all of that? How could he still become a star? That was his true focus this year. Peño felt a distinct flash of disapproval.

You are still not ready.

3

THE
COUNTING GAME

If your road is easy, use the time wisely.
Grow strong. There are hills over the horizon.

❖ WIZENARD ◈37◈ PROVERB ❖

THE NEXT DAY, Peño turned back to his brother and folded his arms, blocking the doorway.

"Last chance," Peño said. "Admit that you saw something."

Lab rolled his eyes. "I told you I did. But it was just a trick!"

"How can it be a trick? Have you ever seen a magician do those things?"

"It's called sleight of hand," Lab said.

Peño scowled. This had been going on all night. Lab refused to believe that Rolabi Wizenard was anything but a fraud magician. It was infuriating, and Peño felt his temper rising.

"But the visions—"

"Hypnotism," Lab said, walking around him to the doors.

"And the bag—"

"Prop bag."

Peño squeezed his hands into fists and hurried after him. "It was real. You know it was."

"If you're so sure he's magical, why didn't you tell Dad?"

Peño paused. "Well, because—"

"Because he wouldn't believe you," Lab responded. "Because magic doesn't exist."

"I didn't exactly say it was magic."

"Then what is it?" Lab snapped, turning to him. "Huh?"

Peño could see the red splotches on his brother's cheeks. Their mom used to call them "angry spots." They stretched from his narrowed eyes to his clenched jaw. *And they all call* me *the jalapeño*, Peño thought wryly.

"What is your problem?" Peño asked. "Why can't you admit that something is off?"

"Because that's not how the world works. It ain't magical, Peño. Sorry."

He turned to go inside, but Peño grabbed his arm. "Is this about Mom?"

Lab yanked his arm away. "It's not about anything."

"I miss her too—"

"And you saw her dying just like I did," Lab said, turning back. "Wasn't it *magical?*"

Lab yanked the doors open and stalked inside. Peño stood there for a moment, his throat dry and raw. He remembered. White beds. A beeping sound echoing in the hallways. Warm hands turning cold. A little voice inside agreed with Lab. There couldn't be magic in the Bottom.

Peño followed his brother into the gym. The musty air slipped over him like a glove, but it was no comfort today. Vin and Reggie were getting ready, and he nodded at them as he sat down. A strange silence had settled over Fairwood. It felt difficult to break . . . as if simply speaking or laughing wouldn't do it. It was a waiting, suspenseful quiet, and Peño fidgeted uncomfortably.

"Anyone's parents call Rolabi last night?" he asked, breaking the silence.

"Yeah," Vin muttered. "My mom liked him."

"My gran too," Reggie said. "You?"

Peño shook his head. He didn't like to tell the guys just how much his dad had to work.

"Pops got home late. So what did Rolabi say to them?"

"Wouldn't tell me," Vin replied. "My mom just looked like she was dazed."

The rest of the team started filing in, most confirming the same story. Their parents had called, listened, and then said nothing else. Peño kept thinking about what his brother had said—about the day she died. He wished his mom could have phoned Rolabi last night too. He wished for a lot of things.

"We're talking like this is normal," Big John said. "It ain't normal. It was magic, man."

"There's no such thing as magic," Lab snapped.

"Is that so?"

The booming voice caught Peño completely off guard. He toppled face-first onto the hardwood, and the whole team went over with him. Rolabi Wizenard was standing behind the bench.

"If you don't believe in magic," Rolabi said, "you need to get out more."

His eyes fell on Peño.

Did you find the cracks?

Stay out of my head! Peño thought.

"We will start with laps," Rolabi said, his voice as calm as ever.

They started around the gym, and despite the easy pace, many of the players were soon breathing hard, Peño included. At five laps, the sweat was running down Peño's face, and he vainly wiped it with an already-drenched sleeve, tasting salt.

"We will take free throws, one at a time," Rolabi said. He hadn't moved an inch since they started running—his eyes just followed them when they passed like the old oil portrait in Peño's grandpa's house. "As soon as someone scores, you will stop running for the day. If you miss, the team runs five more laps. You will continue walking while you wait for the shot."

Peño immediately stopped, grabbing his muffin-top sides. It was like someone was squeezing them with a pair of vise grips. He shuffled out onto the court, wiping his forehead.

"I got this," he said with as much bravado as he could manage through his wheezing.

Rolabi threw him a ball, and Peño dribbled it a few times on the way to the line. He needed to extend the break in case he missed, so he stopped at the free-throw line and dribbled again with either hand, taking a deep breath to steady himself. Then he lifted the ball to shoot.

Peño gasped. The rim was now fifty feet overhead, and the whole gym had stretched to accommodate it, so that he had to crane his head straight back to see the rafters. The banners were so far up he couldn't read the lettering, but his teammates were watching without comment.

"What . . . How am I supposed to . . . ?" he murmured.

Is this not what you always see? Too short to make the shot?

"Shoot it, please," Rolabi said.

"This is not possible, this is not possible," Peño said.

Grana makes it possible.

I am ignoring you today, magic voice that is probably Rolabi! he thought. *And . . . "grana"?*

You will see.

"Just shoot it normally," Peño whispered to himself.

It was impossible to judge the distance. He cocked the ball back with one arm and chucked it at the distant ring like a baseball pitcher. But as soon as the ball left his hand, the hoop returned to its usual height, and he watched in disbelief as the shot sailed well over, ricocheted off the wall, the backboard, the wall again, and then rolled into the far corner for a dejected time-out.

"What kind of a shot was that?" Lab said.

Peño turned back to the team. "I . . . I don't know."

"Five more laps," Rolabi said.

Peño shot the professor a look and then hurried to join the team. But when he fell into line, nobody moved. Peño suddenly started to slide backward, and he realized with horror that the gym floor was now sloping *upward* like a hillside. He crouched, trying to steady himself.

"Begin," Rolabi said.

"Professor," Vin said, "the floor . . ."

"When we are tired, the court can feel like a mountain," Rolabi said, nodding.

"It *is* a mountain," Peño said incredulously.

"Or is it a molehill?" Rolabi said. "Either way, the game continues."

"My brain hurts," Peño said, keeping his hands on the court for balance.

"Just run," Reggie said. "We can get up there."

The team hesitated, and then started up the hill. Peño was last in line now, and he was very conscious that if a player slipped, they would hit him on their way down. He kept a careful eye on Devon and Big John, ready to spring aside if they lost their footing. He didn't want to end up as a Peño-colored stain beneath one of those bruisers. When he finally reached the baseline, he realized the team had paused once again. They were now facing a steep *descent*. Peño felt his stomach turn. He hated heights.

It was just the beginning. Each turn presented a new challenge: Peño climbed up stairs, hopped over hurdles, sprinted along a treadmill-floor, and stumbled up and down slippery hardwood valleys. After five laps, he was so sweaty, he felt like he might wither into a block of salt. Thankfully, Rain stepped out for the next attempt. Rain was a cold-blooded free-throw shooter—the best one on the team. The laps were finally about to end.

Peño leaned against the wall, wiping his face. "Lab?"

"Yeah . . . I saw it," he muttered.

"Still a fake?" Peño asked dryly.

Lab didn't answer.

Peño snorted and glanced at Rolabi. He was still motionless in the center of the court, his hands clasped behind him, the purse on the floor. Peño frowned as something flickered into place behind the professor—a blurred image, as if wrapped in fog. There were people back there.

The road will not be easy.

Rolabi's lips weren't moving, but the voice was clear now.

"Who are those people?" Peño asked.

He felt a distinct chill—a threat. Whoever those people were, they weren't friendly.

The team must be ready. There is darkness on the horizon.

"Everyone, grab a drink," Rolabi said aloud.

Peño flinched and looked around. The team was already heading for the benches, and he followed, unnerved. One of the shadows had looked familiar—a sallow, skull-like face that was on the news almost every night. But it had to be a coincidence. He couldn't imagine why the president of Dren would be in Fairwood, of all places. He shivered as they took off again.

Lab, Vin, Big John, and Twig all missed. Peño figured he had lost ten pounds of sweat already. His limbs felt like cement blocks. Reggie finally hit a shot—though it rimmed around and almost reluctantly toppled in— and Peño doubled over, exhausted. Some guys managed a half-hearted cheer, but Peño could barely muster the strength to stay upright.

"Water break," Rolabi said, heading for center court. "Bring your bottles over here."

Peño straightened. "Maybe we should have jogged a few times in the off-season," he mumbled.

"No more jogging," Big John said. "Please, no more."

Peño joined the rest of the team in a seated circle around Rolabi Wizenard. He let his legs plop out in front of him like overcooked noodles and sighed in relief, propping himself up with one hand. Rolabi fished around in his purse for a moment and then pulled out a flower in a simple clay pot. He set it down, stepped out of the circle, then stared at it, enraptured.

Peño looked between him and the flower, confused.

"What are we supposed to do with the flower?" he asked.

"Isn't it obvious?" Rolabi replied.

Peño turned back to the flower, tried to think of something, and failed. "No."

"We are going to watch it grow."

Peño frowned. Watch a *flower* grow? Flowers didn't grow in the Bottom, period—not much did—but even *if* they grew out of the poisoned soil, he was pretty sure you couldn't see it happen. His mom used to keep a little herb garden in a box of soil on the back porch. She tended the green shoots meticulously, but the rain itself held poisons, and even the hardy mint withered after a season and never came back.

"Some things require a whole world to change," she'd said, emptying her dead plants into a trash bag.

Peño had never known what to make of that. It had always struck him as deeply sad . . . a sign that he was stuck with the world he was given. That they were all trapped in a broken one.

But can one person change the world?

Peño glanced at Rolabi, weighing that. Is that what his mom had meant?

Peño turned back to the flower, trying to focus. But sitting still, even for a few minutes, was not an easy task. At home he always had something to do: the laundry, cooking dinner, packing their bags for school, making lists of groceries, dusting. He *hated* doing nothing. He took a breath, stretched, grew bored again, and tried to come up with rhymes for later:

We chill watching a daisy
A coach who's mad crazy
Sitting with the Badgers
Going to . . . Ugh!

The minutes passed like hours. Peño started listening to the ticking of the clock and his own shallow breathing. They seemed to fall into a monotonous rhythm. He wanted to run around. Shout. Laugh. Isn't that why he was here? It was so quiet. So still. He couldn't bear it for another minute. His hands twitched at his sides. He was just about to give up when Rolabi broke the silence.

"What part of the body moves first?" Rolabi asked. "If you are defending someone, and they are approaching, what part of their body will move before the rest?"

"Their feet?" Peño said automatically. He was just relieved to say *something*.

"Feet are deceptive," Rolabi replied. "And never first."

Peño slouched. He knew that. He hadn't thought before speaking . . . kind of like he didn't think before shooting. Why was that? Why did it always feel like everything was so *unplanned*?

"The first thing to move is the mind. The opposing player must decide what he is going to do," Rolabi said.

Peño snorted. "So we're supposed to read his mind?"

"That would be helpful. But no. You are supposed to *understand* his mind."

"I don't get it," Peño said.

"When you know what your opponent is going to do, you will defeat him."

Peño felt his temper rising. Why did Rolabi always have to speak in riddles?

"And how do we figure that out?" he asked.

"That's simple. You need to see more. And for that, you need more time."

"And how are we supposed to get more time?" Rain asked.

Rolabi picked up the daisy and placed it back in his purse. "By watching the flower grow. Water bottles away. We have one more lesson today."

Peño rubbed his forehead in exasperation. It felt like his mind had just done as many laps as his body. People didn't talk like this. They didn't stare at flowers or try to slow down time.

Maybe that's the problem.

Can you just speak out loud like a normal person? Peño thought sourly.

Rolabi set up an obstacle course, and the team formed a line. It seemed simple enough.

Then Peño's hand vanished. He stared at the wrist, which now ended smooth as a tabletop.

"What . . . where did . . . but how can . . . ?" Peño whispered, prodding the fleshy stump.

There was no pain. No sensation. It was as if he had never had a right hand at all.

Did you ever have a left?

"What is this?" Big John said.

"An exercise in balance," Rolabi said. "Proceed."

Lab stormed out of the line. Peño recognized the expression: mottled cheeks, eyebrows squished into a V, hands shaking. He had lost his temper again. But why? Lab still had both his hands.

"No!" Lab shouted. "This is too much. The other stuff . . . fine . . . but this is messed up!" He stormed toward the bench, then turned back. "And give me back my hand, you wack job!"

Peño couldn't understand what he was talking about. Lab's two hands were right there, firmly attached.

"If anyone leaves the practice without cause, they are off the team permanently." Rolabi said it calmly but with an unmistakable note of finality.

Lab turned to Peño. He could see the fear on his little brother's face. Peño wanted to console him, to be the big brother. But Lab clearly still had his right hand . . . In fact, Peño wasn't sure why anyone was upset. *He* was the only one who had lost a hand.

"I can see your hand," Peño said, pointing at it with his left. "It's right there."

Lab lifted his right arm in disbelief. "No, it isn't. I'm the only one who lost it!"

It's just an illusion, Peño realized. *We can't see our own hands.*

He tried to calm down. It was magic again . . . or grana, or whatever Rolabi had called it. This was no different from the visions or the shifting floors. He tried to stop cradling his wrist.

Lab shook his head. "This isn't possible."

"Possibility is notoriously subjective," Rolabi replied. "Shall we begin?"

Lab turned to Peño again, clearly looking for support.

"Just come play," Peño said.

Lab scowled and joined the team, trembling. Rain was at the front of the line, and he picked up a ball with his left hand and dribbled it experimentally. With a last unhappy look at Rolabi, Rain started the course with a layup. It took about thirty seconds for the chaos to begin.

Peño knew his left hand wasn't as strong as his right, but he now realized it was completely *useless*. He missed his layup, lost the ball several times through the cones, ran right into a pole, missed the pass into the standing hoop by ten feet—hitting an annoyed A-Wall in the back—and then airballed his one-handed shot from the elbow. When he went to pass the ball to the front of the line, he misfired on that as well and sent Twig chasing after it into the bleachers.

He stared at his left hand, disgusted. How could he have ignored one of his hands?

The gym suddenly fell silent. Sensation flooded into his wrist, and he realized his right hand had returned. Relieved, he looked for Lab. But Fairwood was empty.

Peño sighed. "Not again."

A noise cut the silence: the low, ominous rumble of a distant thunderstorm. A second later, the front doors of the gym burst open, and water poured through the opening, frothing and thrashing like a river that had burst its dam. It spilled over Peño's feet and rapidly filled the gym. Peño whirled around in panic.

"Help!" he cried, but the water continued, rising past his ankles. "Rolabi?"

He tried to push against the current and escape to the front doors, but the water was already rising past his stomach. He felt a change in the current, looked back, and saw that a second door had opened at the back of the gym. The water was now pouring out the back. He frowned. There was something in there—flashing images, appearing like snapped photos in the darkness and then gone again. His house. His bed. His neighborhood. Familiar things. Comfortable things.

As he drifted toward the door, Peño looked over his shoulder at the front doors. He saw images there as well. Himself with a black granite trophy, a dark alleyway, shots going up, missing, scoring—they flicked by like a newsreel. The water rose. He saw the trophy again.

"It's easy to go with the current," a familiar voice said.

Peño felt the water churn, dragging him toward the back door. He fought to hold his ground and saw Rolabi standing nearby, the water flowing around his giant torso and rejoining behind his back.

"It's the easier choice," Rolabi said. "Water always follows the path of least resistance. We often do the same."

"What is happening?" Peño shouted, the water creeping up his neck.

"Can you see the uncertainty ahead?"

"Yes!" he shouted, keeping his mouth out of the water.

He had never swum before—he had no idea how. He just flapped and writhed and kicked.

"Glory and pain. Both. Or one. Do you want to take this path? It won't be easy."

Peño pushed his lips up, gasping for air. "I want it!"

"Then take it. Swim."

The current swept Peño's feet off the floor. The water was too high for him to stand. He thrashed forward, pumping his arms to fight the streaming river. He kicked and paddled madly. His arms were soon burning. His legs too. He couldn't do it. He wasn't strong enough. He let go.

Raging water took control of Peño's limbs. The back door swallowed him whole.

And then he was alone again, standing at center court. The river had disappeared. The floor wasn't even damp.

"I thought you said you wanted it?" Rolabi said.

Peño doubled over, hand on his knee. "It . . . it was too hard."

"And now you know why you neglect your left. It's easy to follow the path of least resistance. Even in little everyday decisions. People use their stronger hands because it's easier. They let the water take them—in all things. Show your teammates the harder road. Push them."

"How?" he managed.

Rolabi smiled. "Start with yourself."

The team reappeared, all hunched over and gasping. Peño looked around and saw that the obstacle course was gone. Rolabi was calmly walking toward a solid cinder-block wall nearby.

"He knows there isn't a door there, right?" Peño murmured.

Peño squinted as the lights flashed a brilliant, blazing white and then flicked off, leaving the team in darkness. A gust of wind roared into the gym, seemingly from nowhere. Before he could even move, the wind died, the ceiling lights blinked on again, and Rolabi was gone. Peño stared at the wall.

Lab was right. It was too much. Peño had almost drowned and lost a hand, and who knew what else was coming. Who was Rolabi to tell *him* that he took the easier road? What did he know about Peño's home life? Who was he to tell him he was a quitter? He didn't see Peño staying up late every night and waking up early every morning. He didn't see him packing snacks into his dad's lunch box while the old man slept on the couch. He didn't see him washing uniforms by hand. His temper flared. Peño didn't need to be tested. He didn't need to be doubted.

Maybe it was time to get rid of Rolabi. Freddy could still fire him.

And there was only one player who could make that call.

"Okay," he said, "I think maybe we should talk to Freddy. Rain?"

Rain was staring at the wall as well. He nodded. "It's time to fire Rolabi."

"Finally," Vin said.

"He just started—" Reggie said.

Peño stalked to the bench, ignoring the ensuing arguments. He was exhausted. The swim had felt so real—the throbbing limbs and the freezing cold water. A small part of him knew why he was upset. He had quit so *easily*. He had let the current take him.

He was supposed to be the strong one. The one who carried the family. The one who Lab could look up to. But was he really being strong? Or was he pretending that everything was fine because it was easier than admitting it wasn't? He stared down at his hands—the left, weak and uncoordinated, and the right, missing.

Start with yourself.

He realized his left hand was shaking.

There are different ways to lead.

Leave me alone! Peño thought.

Some begin by allowing ourselves to be vulnerable.

THE FIGHT

If you rise above the conflict,
you can see who needs your help.
✦ WIZENARD (20) PROVERB ✦

THE NEXT MORNING, Peño slowly eased his shoelace through its loop, moving at an almost-glacial pace. He had never realized that tying his shoe with one hand might be a bit of an issue. In fact, it was proving to be nearly impossible. He had managed to slip one lace through and was preparing to tighten the loop when Lab—who had spent the entire night complaining about his hand—decided to start up again.

"I don't like you right now," Lab said.

The loop slipped from Peño's fingers, and he sighed. "We'll get them back today."

He picked up the laces again. He was far from thrilled about his missing hand, but even after his initial dismay, he knew there was something to be learned here. Now that he was forced to use his left, he realized it wasn't just basketball where it was an issue. Eating, bathing, brushing his teeth—it was all awkward and difficult. How could he play with his left if he couldn't brush his teeth with it? This was a simple thing, yet he had never really considered it.

But his brother just whined. He spilled things—almost on purpose—and complained to their confused and very tired dad. It was annoying.

Peño was getting sick of Lab's attitude in general. Mopey, cynical, sullen. It seemed like it was getting worse with every passing week. They had both lost a mother. Why couldn't Lab toughen up?

The loop slipped out of Peño's left hand again. He sighed and leaned back, thinking about Rolabi. He had suggested having him fired. It had seemed right at the time. But now . . . he wasn't so sure. He realized it wasn't about the hand or the river or any of it. Those were pieces of the bigger lesson. Rolabi was showing them that they had spent a lifetime limiting themselves.

Something about that thought nagged at him. Something deeper he couldn't quite place.

"How are you so okay with this?" Lab said sharply.

Peño turned to him. "What do you want me to do, Lab? It's magic."

"Magic isn't supposed to exist. Remember?"

"Well, it does. And I think that's kind of cool, missing hands aside. Don't you?"

"You sound like a child."

Peño's own temper finally boiled over. He didn't get angry very often, despite his nickname—he considered himself the more levelheaded brother. Well . . . usually.

"And you sound like a whiny old man," he snapped. "All you do is complain. You complain about getting up. You mope around at home. You don't eat my cooking. You don't come play at Hyde anymore, and you barely seem to want to play ball. What is *wrong* with you?"

Lab recoiled like he'd been slapped, and for an awful moment, Peño thought his brother might cry. He started to prepare an apology. But Lab's temper rose to match Peño's.

"Nothing is wrong with me," Lab snarled, "except that my older brother is an idiot. A stupid, washed-up, know-it-all . . . idiot! Stay away from me!"

"No problem!" Peño said, sliding farther down the bench.

Only Reggie, Twig, and Devon were in the gym so far, and if they had heard the exchange, they were pretending they hadn't. Peño returned to his sneakers, his cheeks hot. He probably shouldn't have said anything. But it was true: Peño was sick of watching Lab shuffle around the house. He was sick of barely being able to drag him out of bed in the morning. Peño missed Lab—his real brother, the one he had grown up with. He left his laces alone for a second, puzzling over the thought. That was it. He *missed* his brother. But how was that even possible?

Now you are asking a leader's questions.

I'm not a leader, he thought angrily.

Not until you start swimming against the tide.

Stop bothering me! he thought.

Peño finished his laces—mostly just knotting them together haphazardly—and went to shoot around. Normally that cleared his mind, but not today. He couldn't hit a shot to save his life. Not a three or a free throw or even a simple layup. His left hand was like a cinder block.

He soon sat down again, stewing over both Lab's attitude and his own ineptitude with his left. He didn't fail to see the irony, of course, so whenever Lab looked at him, he tried to force a grin. Lab just glared at him.

Rain and Freddy arrived last of all. Peño could tell that Freddy was nervous: he had his hands stuffed into his pockets and was shuffling along like he was on the way to the principal's office. Peño had asked for this—and here it was.

But had he really thought it through?

He looked down at his missing hand. Was he letting the current take him again?

"Morning, team," Freddy said. "How are we?"

"*Bad*," Jerome said, pointing at his right hand—which was sitting in his lap.

Freddy followed Jerome's gaze, clearly confused. "Right . . ." he said.

Peño noticed that Lab's eyes had glazed over. He had stopped tying his shoes and was just staring at the far wall. Peño frowned and snapped his fingers at him. Nothing. He followed Lab's gaze to the far wall, and for a moment, he saw something: shifting light and shadow. The shapes moved fluidly, like reflections on water. He squinted, trying to make sense of what he was seeing. The motion had an almost kaleidoscopic effect on the far wall, and Peño phased out of the conversation, awestruck.

"Were you on any of these teams, Frederick?"

Peño jumped and turned. Rolabi was staring up at the banners.

"What . . . Where did . . . ?" Freddy said weakly.

"I suppose you were too young," Rolabi mused. "It's been so long."

Rolabi faced the team, then glided over to Freddy in three enormous strides. "Can I help you?" Rolabi asked him.

Then he clasped Freddy's hand and turned right to Peño. The gym was gone.

Peño was standing on the silt-covered shore of a lake, which was tucked into a valley and bordered on all sides by bluffs and snowcapped mountains. He reached down and dipped his fingers into the cool water—he had never seen anything so clean in his life. He thought of his mom's garden box. If only she'd had this water, maybe her plants would have grown.

Maybe she would still be here too.

"Do you see it? The boat?"

Peño looked up. There was a rowboat in the center of the lake. It was fashioned out of crude wood but had no oars. It looked like it was sinking.

"Slow leak," Rolabi said thoughtfully. "Almost imperceptible unless you are inside it."

Peño stood up, glancing at Rolabi. "Isn't Freddy—"

"Firing me? No. I'm afraid we have too much work to do."

"Oh. Sorry about that."

"Are you upset or relieved?" Rolabi asked.

"Both, I guess," Peño murmured.

An unexpected wave of embarrassment rolled over him. Not because he had wanted Rolabi gone, but because of *why* he had wanted him gone. Because he was afraid. He stared out at the sinking boat, ashamed.

"Honesty is the first step to conquering our fears," Rolabi said approvingly.

Peño caught a flicker of movement. "There's someone in that boat."

"Yes."

"Who?"

"That you must find for yourself," Rolabi said. "But hurry."

Fairwood took shape around Peño again, and he saw the front doors slam shut. Freddy was gone, and the team had gathered around Rolabi, looking uneasy. Lab seemed to have snapped out of his daze.

Peño frowned. What had he missed? Did Rolabi dismiss Freddy? Who was on the boat?

"Today we will be working on defense," Rolabi said. "Before I can teach you proper zones and strategies, I must teach each of you how to be a defender. They are not the same lessons."

Peño was still puzzling over what Rolabi meant when he heard something scratching. He'd heard scratching before: Fairwood was infested with mice. He had them at home too—they were one of the few animals that survived in the Bottom. Peño had a soft spot for them and slipped them crumbs almost every night. But this was no mouse. The scratching was grating and powerful, like a saw working on steel.

"What must a defender always be?" Rolabi asked, ignoring the scratching.

"Umm . . ." Peño said, still looking around. "They have . . . wait . . . what was the question?"

"What must a defender always be?"

"Well . . ." Peño said, speaking without thinking. "Umm . . . in position?"

The scratching grew louder still.

"Ideally," Rolabi said. "But before that."

Peño's every muscle was on alert. The scratching was so loud that it was difficult to focus on anything else.

"*Ready*," Rolabi said. "They must always be ready. A defender must be a step ahead of their opponents. They must outthink and outwork and out-strategize. They must always be ready to move."

The scratching reached an awful crescendo.

"What is that?" Rain asked.

"Can someone open the locker room door?" Rolabi said calmly.

Peño spun around. The scratching was coming from *inside* the locker room.

"What's in there?" he murmured.

"A friend," Rolabi said.

Twig suddenly started for the locker room door.

"What are you doing?" Peño hissed.

"I want to see what it is," Twig said. He hesitated, took a deep breath, and pulled the door open.

"Cool," Peño whispered.

An enormous tiger walked into the gym. Impressive as the tiger was, Peño knew enough about them to step behind A-Wall, using him as a human shield. Big John had Peño beat: he sprinted to the other side of the court, whimpering all the way. But the tiger didn't seem to care. It strolled right past the team and sat down next to Rolabi. Its big purple-and-gold eyes flicked between the players and the coach. Peño could have sworn the creature smiled at him.

"Meet Kallo," Rolabi said. He ran a hand through her thick fur, and she purred like an enormous house cat. "She has graciously volunteered to help us today."

"Is that . . . is that . . ." A-Wall was saying.

"A tiger," Peño interjected. "Long extinct. Well, supposedly. One of nature's most perfect predators. Ambush predators—they can sneak up and jump ten yards onto their prey."

"Perfect," A-Wall murmured.

"Rain," Rolabi said. "Step forward."

Peño turned to Rain, alarmed. Was Rolabi going to feed him to the tiger? Did he blame Rain for the firing attempt? Peño chewed his nails. It had technically been his idea. Should he say so?

Rain paused. "Yes?"

Rolabi opened his purse and fished out a ball with the now-familiar blue-and-white *W* on the side. He rolled it to center court, where it stopped perfectly on the black dot.

"I don't like where this is going," Peño said.

"Tiger food," Vin said numbly.

"The drill is simple," Rolabi said. "Get the ball. Kallo will play defense. We will take turns and go one at a time. I want everyone else to watch and take note of what happens."

Rain looked at him in disbelief. "What? I'm not going near that thing."

Kallo's eyes flashed reproachfully, and Peño took another involuntary step backward.

"Maybe don't call her a *thing*," he suggested.

Kallo began to walk back and forth, showing off her intimidating musculature. She moved with a silky grace, every step soundless on the hardwood.

Yep, the tiger is going to kill Rain, Peño thought.

Rain clearly had the same thought. "Okay, I get it," he gushed. "I'm sorry we asked Freddy to fire you."

"*We?*" Reggie said.

"This is not a punishment," Rolabi said. "It is a drill. Now get the ball."

"But—" Rain started.

"A true defender *must* be a tiger. The first one to get the ball gets their hand back."

Peño glanced at Rolabi. He had told Peño to earn his hand back. Peño took a deep breath and tried to summon his courage. Maybe this was his chance.

Rain stood facing the tiger, clearly caught between two minds: look like a coward and leave or face possible mauling and death. Peño figured it was an easy choice, but Rain was proud, and Rolabi had already made it clear that if anyone left the training camp, they were off the team. He didn't seem like the type to make empty threats. And that would be a problem.

There were no Badgers without Rain. If he left, the team would probably fold. Peño shuddered at the thought of life without basketball. Could he even make it onto another team? Would the East Bottom Bandits take him on? The thought of joining their archenemy made his skin crawl. Would he have to back up Lio?

Do it, Rain, Peño thought. *Get the ball.*

Almost as if on cue, Rain made his move. He was quick, but Kallo was faster. In a flash of orange, she was on top of him, her huge paws resting on either shoulder. Rain didn't move, and a surge of guilt and panic flooded through Peño.

"She killed him!" he shrieked in a much higher voice than he had intended.

"I'm fine," Rain muttered, climbing to his feet. "She didn't hurt me."

Peño slumped in relief.

"Nice squeak," A-Wall said.

"Shut up."

"Devon," Rolabi said.

Peño was the fourth to go. Rain, Devon, and Vin all seemed to have survived their attempts without any injuries, so he stepped forward, sweating profusely. Kallo watched him like he was a delicious gazelle drinking peacefully at the riverside. Peño felt like one at the moment.

"Please don't eat me," he whispered. "I would taste awful. I love spicy food."

Kallo only smiled, revealing her long fangs.

"Not helpful," Peño said. He jumped up and down on his toes, trying to pump himself up. "Get the ball, get your hand," he said. "Easy-peasy. No problem. I got it. I'm the man. The—"

"Just go," Vin said, groaning.

Peño tried a classic double fake—right, left, right—but Kallo wasn't fooled. He felt something collide with him and was soon staring up at an awful lot of teeth. He closed his eyes, but all he felt was a tongue wash over his face, coarse and prickly, and then Kallo stepped off.

"Am I dead?" he whispered.

"Not yet," Rolabi said, which was no consolation at all.

His brother went next, and when Lab got his own victorious lick across the forehead, Peño laughed at his obvious disgust. It served him right for being so cranky lately.

"Like you did any better," Lab snarled.

"I did," Peño said. "And I wasn't shaking like a leaf either."

"Leaves don't shake," Lab said, folding his arms.

Peño scowled. "It's a common expression."

"You're a common expression," Lab snapped.

"Grow up."

"Why, so I can be a washout like you?" Lab said.

"I'm literally one year older than you."

"And three years worse at ball," Lab replied.

That one hurt. Peño shot him a dark look and turned away, feeling his cheeks burning. They could joke about those things, but it was different when Lab meant it. Especially since it was true. Lab was the better prospect. Peño could talk a big game, but Lab was taller and more athletic and had a real shot at playing at the next level. Peño was facing much longer odds, and that fact kept him up at night.

Kallo kept knocking down Badger after Badger. When it was Big John's turn to face her, he shook his head. Despite the urging of the team, he folded his arms and refused. And then Twig decided to get involved, which was a really, really bad idea.

"I'm just trying to help—" Twig said.

Peño rubbed his forehead. *Now* Twig decided to speak? He could already see Big John tensing up—his left hand clenched into a fist, his chest swelling up. There was trouble brewing.

"Easy, man," Peño said. "You guys are on the same team, remember?"

"You think you're a big tough guy now, or what?" Big John asked.

"I didn't mean anything by it," Twig said. "You looked like you could use a hand."

That did it. Big John shoved Twig and sent him toppling backward. Big John stepped forward, clearly about to start pummeling him into sawdust. Peño froze for a moment. He was the smallest player on the team and probably the least equipped to jump in. But Rolabi had told him to help the other players, and he suspected that having Twig become a fleshy paste was not what he had in mind. So he took a breath and flung himself onto Big John's back, linking his arms and legs around him like a chain. He winced as Big John kept going, straining to hold him.

"Down, boy!" Peño shouted.

A-Wall and Jerome each grabbed one of Big John's arms—Peño was just along for the ride. Big John's rage made his whole body shake and spittle fly out like a sprinkler. Peño tried to squeeze harder, but he had been reduced to little more than a backpack.

"You know where I go after practice?" Big John said. "To *work*. Two jobs. And we still can't pay all the bills. You ever spent a week in the dark 'cause you can't pay for no lights?"

Peño frowned. He didn't know that either. Most of the guys on the team dealt with poverty, but he thought only A-Wall was working. And for all their issues, his dad had never let the lights go off. He had thought he and Lab had it as bad as anyone. Clearly he had been wrong.

"I—"Twig said.

"This is all I got!" Big John screamed. "And you took it from me!"

It sounded like Big John was crying. Peño had never seen him cry before.

"Freddy decided on who starts,"Twig said. "It's just a strategy thing—"

Big John charged, and Peño knew he couldn't stop him, not even with A-Wall and Jerome's help.

"Twig, run!" he said.

Big John started to close the distance—Peño still strapped to him like a backpack, and A-Wall and Jerome holding his arms—and then their forward progress was abruptly halted. A massive hand grabbed Big John's shoulder and proceeded to lift all four of them off the ground with the ease of an industrial crane. A-Wall and Jerome dropped off right away, but Peño was so stunned that he held on, his eyes widening as Rolabi spun both Peño and Big John around to face him.

"Do you know why you are angry?" Rolabi asked.

Big John struggled for a moment, but it was useless.

"Do you?" Rolabi asked.

"Because he got into my business!" Big John said.

"Because you are afraid."

He lowered Big John to the ground, and Peño hopped off, relieved. He dusted his shoulders off and puffed his chest, eliciting a few snickers from the others.

"You're an idiot," Lab whispered.

"You mean hero?" he said.

"Fear is the root of anger and violence," Rolabi said. "It has made your choice for you. Fear of not being enough. Blame for the causes. But I value honesty. I will forgive the violence *once*."

"I'm done here," Big John snarled. "I'm done with this stupid training."

"You know the consequences of leaving."

Big John started for his bag. "I don't care."

"Ten minutes in the locker room."

Big John hesitated, and then looked back at Rolabi. "What?"

"Go look at your reflection for ten minutes. Ask yourself carefully if you want to leave the team. Then decide."

Big John looked for a moment like he might argue. Then he stormed into the locker room and slammed the door so hard, the walls shook. The door was having a really bad day.

Peño stared at it for a moment, ignoring the ensuing conversations. He hadn't known about the two jobs, or the lights, or anything about Big John really. He just assumed he was a loudmouth. But he had heard the cracks in his voice. Felt the tremors as he held on to his body. He had said, "You took it from me." Peño felt a pang of sympathy. Of course. Big John came from the worst neighborhood in the Bottom. His family was broken. He obviously thought he could get his family out of the Bottom with ball, and then Twig came along and took his starting spot. That's why he hated him. Peño rubbed his forehead. What else had he been missing?

Keep breaking down the wall.

Peño looked down. His hand was back, and he cradled it to his chest.

The gym filled with cheers, and he turned and high-fived Vin before hugging his hand once again.

"Sweet, sweet right hand," he said. "Never leave me again."

"Why couldn't you get past her?" Rolabi asked the team.

"Because she's a tiger," Peño muttered. He flexed his fingers, meeting Lab's eyes across the group. Lab instantly turned away.

Rolabi said something about reflexes and flicked a button off Twig's forehead.

"Reflexes are natural," Peño said. "You're born with them."

"We are also born with legs, but we must learn how to run," Rolabi replied, turning to him. "Your reflexes can be honed. They are a direct, unthinking connection to your brain. A measure of nerves and awareness and *alertness*. Train them. Training tells your brain to stay prepared."

"My brain is always prepared," Peño said. "I'm more worried about them." He nodded toward his teammates.

He vaguely saw Rolabi's finger move before a second button bounced between his own eyes.

Peño paused. "I would like to retract my statement."

"What is that?" Jerome asked suddenly.

Peño followed his gaze and stiffened. All of his blood ran cold. A black ball was floating in the middle of the gym. It kept shifting as he watched, like a glob of oil suspended in water.

"What . . . what is it?" Peño murmured.

"That is something you all will want to catch," Rolabi said. "No, it is something you all *must* catch. We can call it the orb for reference. Whoever catches it will become a far better player. But it won't last forever. If no one catches it, we run laps." He nodded to the orb. "Go!"

Peño joined the pursuit. The orb pinged around between the players, always just out of reach. Twice Peño almost had it, and twice it whizzed away before he could close his fingers. As they scrambled and tripped and shouted in frustration, Kallo jumped up like a missile and swallowed it whole, smiling again as she sat down.

"A true defender," Rolabi said. "Get some water. Laps and free throws."

Peño sighed. "My favorite."

The laps started again, with the floor shifting at every turn. Peño missed his free throw, jerking when a cruel voice in his ear said, "Remember Peño? Whatever happened to that kid?" They kept running for an exhausting forty-five laps until Twig hit a free throw and ended the drill.

Peño doubled over. "This is not cool," he managed, hands on his knees.

"It's a start," Rolabi said.

"A start?" Lab asked incredulously. "I'm about to keel over."

"Tomorrow we will work on team defense," Rolabi said. "Get some rest tonight."

With that, he headed for the front doors with Kallo.

Peño watched them, frowning. "Are . . . are you taking the tiger?"

As usual, Rolabi ignored him. The front doors swung open, accompanied by a blast of frigid winter wind, and the two of them walked out into the sunshine. If Peño didn't know better, he could have sworn that they were talking.

"He should really learn how to say goodbye," Peño grumbled.

He made his way to the bench and sat down with a sickly, squishy plop. He felt like a dirty dishrag. As he unlaced his shoes, thankfully with both hands, he shook his head.

"We practiced with a tiger today," he said.

Jerome was the first to laugh. It spread from there, and soon the whole team was roaring, Peño included. His sides ached. Their training was so ridiculous and impossible and strange that it seemed like he couldn't do anything else. He glanced at Lab, but his brother was scowling.

"Drop some lines, Peño," Jerome said.

Peño scratched his neck, trying to think.

Just don't use Badgers, he reminded himself, and launched into a verse.

> "We came to play ball
> but that ain't all
> we got a coach who's crazy
> don't know this team is lazy
> Big John don't run laps
> now he's about to collapse
> We got tigers chilling
> Twig's the villain
> and through it all
> Peño the man keeps his eye on the north wall."

He finished by pointing to the banners, flexing with his free arm, and the team folded into laughter.

Peño was putting his shoes in his bag when his brother got up and headed for the door. Peño stiffened. In all their years of ball, they had *never* walked home separately. It seemed almost unthinkable. Peño was stunned. Clearly this wasn't one of their usual, everyday fights.

But why? Because Peño had called him a complainer? It didn't make any sense.

As he pushed open the doors, Lab glanced back. Peño didn't bother to hide his dismay, and still his brother walked out. The doors slammed shut behind him, and Peño sat there, deeply troubled. For some reason, he pictured the still lake and the small sinking rowboat.

"Lab?" he whispered.

⑤
THE WAY TO LOSE

If you want to succeed,
start by turning your weaknesses into strengths.
❖ WIZENARD ⑪ PROVERB ❖

THE NEXT MORNING, Peño looked back at his brother, who was walking about ten steps behind him and wearing a very sour expression. They hadn't spoken to each other since yesterday, which wasn't easy, since they shared a tiny bedroom. Peño had thought about apologizing, and thought about the boat, but it was hard when Lab was constantly shooting him dirty looks or making comments under his breath:

" . . . fade isn't even cool."

" . . . nice 'stache . . ."

" . . . freestyling . . . awful . . . snored all night long . . ."

Peño had given up. He hadn't woken up Lab as he had every morning for the last three years, and Lab had barely gotten up in time for practice. He had missed his breakfast and the short, cold shower allowed by their water tank, and he looked exhausted. His hair was in a messy Mohawk.

It's what he deserves, Peño thought. *Maybe he will appreciate what I do for him.*

Somehow, he doubted that was what Lab was thinking. It looked more like he was considering tripping Peño when he wasn't looking.

Peño walked into the gym and let the doors close behind him out of spite. They swung shut, clattering against the loose door frame, and Peño realized Fairwood was empty. Sort of.

There was a castle sitting on the court.

It was gray, like weathered stone, and wrapped with ten-foot walls. Ramps opened at each corner, each leading up to an open level. A final ramp reached from that level to a tower in the center. And there, sitting grandly atop the whole structure, was the Elite Youth League national championship trophy. Peño stiffened. He knew that trophy well. He stared at a photo of it every single night. He had ripped it out of a magazine years earlier, and he still kept it beside his bed.

"What is basketball to you, Peño?"

Peño yelped and spun around. Rolabi was standing beside the doors.

"Oh man . . . you scared me. Where is everyone? Why is that castle there?"

"What is basketball to you?" Rolabi repeated. "The sport itself. What is it to you?"

Peño looked up at him, thinking. "It's everything."

"Why?"

"I . . . I don't know. I love it. I always have."

"What is your favorite part?"

Peño paused. For some reason, he felt his gaze drift to the bench, and he realized how strange and empty it felt without his teammates. Just like that, the question was answered.

"The friendships," he said softly.

Rolabi followed his gaze. "A fine reason. Remind your teammates of it if the road should change."

"What road?" Peño asked, frowning.

"The one you are on. But if you are to walk it, you must find your strength."

"I am strong," Peño said.

"No," Rolabi replied, "you are forgetting what the strongest must always remember."

"What?"

"That sometimes it is okay to be weak."

Peño caught a flicker of movement and spotted Reggie. "Where is my brother?"

"He is next."

Peño shook his head and went to join Reggie. What was Rolabi talking about this time? Why would a strong person ever be weak? It didn't make any sense. If he let his guard down, he might let his brother down, and his dad, and his mom from wherever she was watching. He had to always be strong.

Sure enough, Lab walked in soon after, and he too spoke with the professor. Peño looked at him questioningly, but his brother turned away. Peño still had no idea why he was so mad. Why should Peño apologize, anyway? *He* was the older brother. He did everything for Lab.

When the entire team had arrived, Rolabi summoned them over to the castle.

"Today we are working on team defense."

"Like . . . zone defense?" Peño asked curiously, his gaze fixed on the trophy.

It was beautiful—black granite inlaid with gold trim—and stood nearly three feet tall. The names of championship teams were engraved on the sides. Not one said *West Bottom Badgers*.

"In time," he said. "First you have to learn the fundamentals."

"Like how to pillage a castle?" Peño asked.

Rolabi lifted his purse and abruptly turned it upside down. Equipment began to stream out—helmets and pads. Half the items were red, half blue.

"Take one of each, please," Rolabi said. "Fasten the helmets tightly."

Peño scooped up a random blue helmet. He noticed Lab quickly pick up a red helmet, scowling at him. Clearly, the game was on. Peño grabbed a blue pad, holding Lab's sullen gaze. The pad was heavy and stiff, and he envisioned himself clobbering his little brother.

Maybe I can knock some sense back into him, he thought.

His smile slipped away when he saw Devon pick up a red pad. Now the red team had Devon, A-Wall, Reggie, and Vin—a good-size team, apart from Vin, and even Vin was bigger than Peño. The blue team was definitely outmatched in size: Rain and Jerome were both thin, and Twig was, well, a twig. Their only imposing player was Big John, but even he was not exactly a pillar of balance. That said, Devon had seemed reluctant to use his strength during the scrimmage. Peño was hoping he would come around . . . just not today. He made a mental note to talk to the big lug again later.

"The game is simple," Rolabi said. "One team will attack, and the other will defend. The team to get the trophy in the least amount of time wins. The losing team will run laps while the winners shoot around."

"How did you get the national championship trophy?" Peño asked. His fingers twitched, desperate to touch the black granite.

"I borrowed it," Rolabi said, as if the answer were obvious. "Blue team will defend first."

"So . . . like . . . we just push each other with these pads?" Lab asked. "Won't the strongest team win no matter what?"

"A fine question," Rolabi said, nodding. "You have two minutes to plan."

Rain led them up the nearest ramp, and Peño examined the fortress as they formed a huddle—the walls were high and smooth, so the only way to the trophy was through the ramps.

He listened as Rain outlined the plans, trying to envision the drill.

"What happens if they start switching and I get Devon or something?" he asked.

Rain waved him away. "We got to talk."

Peño nodded, though something was still nagging him.

"I don't feel like running laps for another two hours, so let's win this," Rain said.

Peño definitely didn't feel like running either. "Let's rock it, boys!"

Peño hurried down one of the ramps, rolling his shoulders. He heard steps and saw that Rain was close behind him. It seemed Rain was going to back him up first—probably because Peño was the smallest one on the team.

He saw Lab and the red team standing in a line now, facing them like an advancing army.

"This is going to be madness," Peño said. "But it's kind of awesome."

"Agreed," Rain said. "We're defending a castle."

"We just need some armor and this will be really legit," Peño mused.

"Begin!" Rolabi said.

Peño gasped as the ramp beneath him turned to real creaking wood. The floor around the fortress caved in and filled with water, creating a swamp-like moat. The hardwood on either side of the moat molded and stretched into four bridges that led to each ramp, which were now bordered by walls of coarse, true stone. Blue flags appeared overhead on each corner, fluttering in an unfelt wind, and even Peño's clothes changed into gleaming steel armor with blue trim. He looked down at himself in amazement.

"Peño . . ." Rain said.

"Yeah . . . I see it," Peño replied numbly. "I had to open my big mouth."

"Charge!" Lab screamed, extending his arm like a medieval general.

The red team split up as expected, and Vin sprinted headlong into Peño and Rain, his armored boots thudding over the bridge. Peño crouched down just as Vin slammed into him. He slid back a few inches but held his ground, using his squat legs like twin support struts. Peño was short, but he was also strong, particularly in his legs, and he knew he could hold Vin by himself.

"Good luck!" Rain said, clearly thinking the same thing.

Vin narrowed his eyes and pushed harder, and the two point guards remained locked in an almost perfectly even match of strength. Peño looked up over his pad, shooting Vin a smile.

"You're never getting through me, man," he said.

Vin smirked. "Never say never."

Vin drove forward again. Peño could hear shouting all around him, but he was focused on defending his own ramp. He just had to hope the others were doing their jobs. Footsteps approached, and Peño looked up to see Reggie charging across the wooden bridge, ready to join Vin.

"Uh-oh," Peño mumbled.

Reggie pushed hard into Vin's back and started to drive Peño up the ramp.

"I got two!" he shouted, fighting to stop the advance.

His steel boots didn't have much grip, and he slid backward rapidly, straining with everything he had to hold his position. His heartbeat hammered in his ears. Rain arrived just before Peño was pushed clean off the ramp, and once again, the attackers' forward momentum stopped.

"Push!" Rain shouted, driving hard into Peño's back to help him defend the ramp.

They began to drive Vin and Reggie back down, and Peño grinned as the attackers lost all their progress. He could easily hold the ramp with the high ground. The attackers had no chance.

"A-Wall just took off!" someone shouted.

"So did Lab!" another called.

Peño suspected that was bad even before Reggie stood back and smiled.

"Guys . . ." Jerome called weakly.

Peño turned as Rain sprinted up the ramp and slid to a halt, eyes wide.

"Uh-oh," Rain murmured.

Peño didn't even have a chance to move. Rain was knocked flying by the combined charge of Devon, A-Wall, and Lab. At the same time, Reggie and Vin attacked again and sent Peño crashing onto his back. They stepped over him and followed the others up the final ramp to the trophy.

Peño lay on the ground, exhausted. He had been worried about this exact scenario—the red team had joined up and overwhelmed one defender. It was a fairly obvious strategy, and yet the blue team hadn't been ready for it at all. He sighed and slowly got to his feet.

"One minute and forty-seven seconds," Rolabi said, his voice still carrying over the gym as if from loudspeakers. "Blue team, you will now attack. You have two minutes to prepare."

"Let's go," Rain said, marching over the nearest bridge toward the benches.

Peño followed him, taking an uneasy look into the water. Yellow eyes stared back at him.

"Try not to go swimming," he muttered to Big John.

"You don't got to tell me," Big John said.

They formed a huddle and made a quick plan. This drill was incredibly easy for the attackers.

Peño chuckled. "We'll have it in thirty seconds!"

He would soon be holding the trophy. The thought made him giddy.

"Blue on three," he said, sticking his hand out. "One . . . two . . . three . . . Blue!"

The team threw their hands up and spread out into an attacking line. Peño shifted in his armored boots. Apparently, Lab had been afraid to take on his older brother, but Peño had no such reservations. He was going to charge Lab's ramp head-on and send him flying.

But as the blue team approached the castle, no defenders appeared at the ramps.

"They can't even figure out who to put where!" Peño said, laughing.

"Begin," Rolabi said.

"They're not set up yet!" Rain said. "Follow me in!"

Peño fell in behind Rain as they sprinted up the closest ramp. Peño was opening his mouth to announce their win when Rain stopped. Peño ran into him, smashing his nose on Rain's back plate. His eyes flooded with tears as he looked up to see Devon standing at the mouth of the ramp, pad ready. The rest of the red team was lined up behind him—all the way up to the trophy.

"What the—" Peño said, his voice coming out a bit wheezy.

With a sinking feeling in his stomach, he realized what they were doing. The red team was protecting the final ramp.

"Push!" Rain shouted.

Peño and his teammates drove again and again into the pads, but it was futile. Peño was squeezed between the defenders and his own team shoving behind him. Minutes seemed to go by without a single step gained. Rain wouldn't stop the battle, even as Peño felt crushed.

Finally, Devon pushed forward and sent the whole blue team flying. Rain landed on Peño's stomach, knocking the wind out of him. Someone's knee dug into his thigh. He lay there, breathing heavily. Spots appeared in his vision like miniature suns. Another hard loss.

"The time is beat," Rolabi said. "The red team wins."

Lab picked up the trophy and held it over his head in triumph. Peño climbed to his feet, watching his brother celebrate. It was *Peño's* dream to hold that trophy—how many nights had he fallen asleep imagining that exact moment? But there was his brother instead, living Peño's dream. Peño sensed that he might very well be glimpsing the future. Peño would never hold that trophy. He was too short. Too slow. His shot wasn't good enough. *He* wasn't good enough.

The thought settled in like a thick fog, and Peño traipsed down the ramp, dejected.

"The red team may grab some balls and shoot around," Rolabi said. "Blue team, laps."

As Peño stepped over the bridge, the moat drained and the ground rose and leveled into a flat surface again, reforming into dusty hardwood planks. Peño cast his pad and helmet onto the floor in disgust and started running. It was nearly an hour before anyone hit a free throw, and when they finally did, he almost collapsed onto the bench, trying to rub the sting from his eyes.

"What was this drill about?" Rolabi asked.

"Team defense," Peño muttered.

"Yes. They played as a team. You did not."

Peño wiped his face again and took another gulp of his water. He and Lab filled their bottles from the kitchen tap at home. The water came out yellow and smelled like rotten eggs, but it was the best they had. Fairwood wasn't any better—most of the Bottom seemed to have the same issues. He drained the last drop as Rolabi plucked a small black cap from the side of the fortress. Air began to whoosh out as the entire structure collapsed in on itself. Peño nearly choked on his water. The castle was *inflated?*

In moments the structure was the size of a basketball, nothing but folds of gray rubber, and Rolabi picked it up and dropped it into his bag.

"What must a defender always be?" the professor asked, turning to them.

"*Ready*," Reggie said.

"The same goes for the entire team. If you are not ready, we are wasting our time."

Rolabi started for the doors.

"Are we done for today?" Peño asked. He was exhausted, but it wasn't even noon yet.

"That is up to you," Rolabi said.

He strode through the open doors, and they slammed shut behind him, shaking the gym. Rain suggested a scrimmage, but shouts abruptly filled the room. The orb had returned, and Peño could already feel the chill seeping into his bones.

"What do we do?" Peño whispered.

"Rolabi said we had to catch it," A-Wall said. "He said we would be better basketball players if we did, remember?"

That was all it took. Twig charged, and the team went after him. Despite their best efforts, the orb eluded them again. At one point, Peño slammed into Lab, and their shoulders clapped together with a painful whack. They both spun and landed on their butts, groaning.

"Watch out!" Lab shouted.

"You watch it!" Peño said.

He climbed back to his feet just as the orb zoomed toward the wall and vanished.

"Still up for that scrimmage?" Peño asked Rain dryly, rubbing his sore shoulder.

Rain scowled. "Nah. Let's just get out of here."

Peño didn't argue. He sat down and started to slip off his shoes. The others launched into conversation, but he didn't pay much attention. He had failed to catch the orb. Failed to get to the trophy. Failed to win the first scrimmage. Rolabi wanted him to lead, but he could barely do anything right. How could he lead? Rain was way better than him. Lab too. Maybe even Vin.

He was going to be left behind. Just like he had always suspected.

He threw on his outdoor shoes, zipped up his ratty old bag, and walked out alone. He was halfway across the parking lot when he heard the doors open again. Lab appeared beside him, falling into step.

"What do you want?" Peño said, scowling.

"Why are you so upset?" Lab demanded. "I thought that wasn't allowed?"

Peño bristled and turned to him. "This is different. You've been sad for *three years*."

"And why do you think that is, genius?"

"I lost her too," Peño said, taking a step toward him. "She was my mom too."

He emphasized the word, knowing it would get to Lab, not caring. Their eyes met. Peño could see the color flooding into Lab's face. This time he held his brother's gaze. Why should Lab have all the pain? Why should he get to be sad? Why did Peño have to take care of the house and take care of him and always be the strong one? It wasn't fair.

"You moved on," Lab said. "You cared more about basketball—"

Peño shoved him, hard, and Lab stumbled back, barely catching his footing. The moment he recovered, he launched himself at Peño, sending them both to the pavement. Peño felt the air whoosh out of him, gasped, and then rolled to get Lab off him. Everything was a flurry of grabbing arms and kicking legs, and he felt trash beneath him—squishy and stinky and it didn't matter.

"You don't . . . think . . . I . . . miss her?" Peño said, trying to get Lab into a headlock.

Lab kneed him in the stomach and almost weaseled out of the move. "You . . . don't . . . get sad," he managed, his voice a wheeze. "It's . . . all . . . good. Stop it! You . . . I'll kick your . . . Stop!"

They rolled again, and this time Peño used his strength to get on top of Lab and pin him. He was sweating and flushed, but he held both of Lab's hands down against the concrete for the victory.

"I miss her every second of the day," Peño said. "You're blind if you don't see that."

Lab tried to wrestle his way free, but he was stuck. "Get off me!"

"Did you ever think I don't show it because of *you*?" Peño said. "That maybe I don't want to remind you or Dad? Did that cross your thick, stupid skull? And maybe I do all the chores to make it easier for you too? Did you think about that?"

He was screaming now, and Lab stopped squirming, staring up at him.

"Sometimes it feels like I can't breathe," Peño whispered. "Like I'm gonna die. But you didn't notice that either, did you? At least you get to have hope. I don't even get that."

"What are you talking about—"

"You get a shot!" Peño shouted. "I don't. I get to be strong and watch everyone else go on without me."

He let go of Lab, roughly wiped his eyes, and stood up.

"I should teach you a lesson," Peño said quietly. "But I won't . . . because of her."

He stormed off. As he turned the corner, he glanced back. Lab was still lying in the parking lot. He thought about going back to see if he was okay. He was the older brother. The strong one. He was supposed to take care of him. But he didn't feel strong, and he was tired of trying to keep Lab and his dad up when nobody did the same for him.

He turned away and left him there.

NO SIGHT

Your story will be much happier
if the writer likes their protagonist.
✦ WIZENARD ㉖ PROVERB ✦

PEÑO RAN BACK to the bench for a quick drink of water. He was warming up hard today, and though he was trying not to make it too obvious, he was working mostly on his left hand. He had promised himself he wouldn't be humiliated by its ineffectiveness ever again. As a result, he was chasing rim-outs and wild air balls with alarming regularity, and he was already dripping sweat.

Last night had been . . . unpleasant. Lab and Peño were not talking or looking in each other's direction. Basically they were avoiding breathing near each other. Peño had cooked dinner—some chickpeas and stringy chicken in corn tortillas—but Lab had gone without.

Peño didn't exactly blame him for not eating. It wasn't easy to make anything too wholesome, since they shopped at an old warehouse called the Last Stop that stocked castoffs from the rest of Dren, but Peño tried to make the best of it. His mom had worked full-time *and* cooked *and* raised them both, so he couldn't exactly complain. Only now that she was gone did he realize how hard that must have been for her, especially considering she had been sick and hiding it from them until the final months.

He felt another pang of sadness but pushed it away—he had cried enough yesterday. He chugged some water and glanced upward, wiping his mouth with his sleeve.

"I'm doing my best, Mom," he said. "I don't know what to do about Lab, though."

He spoke to her often—whenever Lab was out of earshot. He spoke to her while he did his chores and before bed and when he was reading. He asked her how she was feeling. Told her he missed her. Asked her what to do with Lab. Sometimes it was prayer-like, other times conversational, but he needed those talks. They made him feel less alone.

He took another swig and was preparing to head back out when he noticed Big John getting changed alone at the end of the bench. He was putting his shoes on with exaggerated slowness, and he looked sort of . . . haggard. His eyes were puffy and ringed with dark circles.

"Hey, dude," Peño said.

"Yo," Big John replied.

"You good?"

Big John glanced up at him, and for just a second, Peño thought he saw Big John's upper lip quiver. But Big John caught himself and forced a lopsided smile.

"Yeah. Tired is all."

"I . . . uh . . . didn't know about the two jobs."

Big John shifted. "Catching some overtime is all. Got home late."

"Your mom don't mind?"

Big John laced up his shoes and stood up. "She asked me to. Lost her job."

"Oh."

Peño knew that Big John had two little sisters as well. His dad had died years ago, his older brother not long after. One to sickness, the other to violence.

"Yeah," Big John said gruffly. "She'll get another one. Just got to fill in for now."

"Sorry, man—"

"I don't need pity," he said. "It's fine. That's why I'm here. I got to get to college, man."

Big John hurried onto the court, and Peño watched him, troubled. For all his and Lab's problems, Big John had it worse. He'd lost two people instead of one, and he was stuck trying to keep his family afloat now.

Peño looked around the gym. They weren't all going to make the DBL. Rain could, maybe. The rest were long shots. Nearly impossible odds. Even, or especially, him. He knew it, much as he didn't want to admit it. It wasn't just his height—his shot wasn't reliable, and it was tough to get anywhere without a steady jumper. He played against scoring point guards better than himself all the time.

But what else could they all hope for? There was no future in the Bottom. If Peño didn't make the DBL, he was stuck here—working the same kind of backbreaking jobs as his dad, *if* he was lucky enough to get one. How could he face that? He *had* to make it. They all did, despite the odds. For now, he just had to leave it at that.

Peño headed back to the court—pointedly staying on the opposite end from Lab. He worked there until Rolabi showed up and called them in. Peño noticed belatedly that while he was avoiding Lab, everyone else seemed to be avoiding Rain. He looked around, confused. What did he miss?

"Today we are going to work on offense," Rolabi said. "We'll start with passing."

Peño perked up. He had always prided himself on his passing.

"The foundation of all offense," Rolabi continued. "What do all the great passers have?"

"Vision," Peño said immediately.

He knew what it took . . . He watched any DBL games he could get on their stations, studying the moves through the static and playing them again and again in his mind later. Sometimes he wrote down notes while he watched, much to Lab's amusement, or sat so close, he could trace his fingers from one play to another.

"Very good. A great passer must be quick and agile and bold. But mostly, they must have vision. Both of what is and what will soon come. They must see *everything* on the floor."

"So, we just have to practice seeing more . . . ?" Lab trailed off.

"Yes," Rolabi said simply. "And the best way to start is by seeing nothing at all."

Peño probably should have expected something weird. It was the sixth day, and strange things happened when Rolabi gave them a lesson. But Peño wasn't ready for sudden blindness. He cried out and waved his hands, rubbing his eyes to clear them. But the darkness was impenetrable.

Peño felt someone trod on his shoe and yelped. "Hey, watch it! That's my toe!"

"Well, how do you want me to avoid it when I can't see anything?" Big John said.

"How about you try not moving? You're like an elephant."

"Is that a crack about my weight?" Big John snarled.

"Well, it ain't about your memory."

Peño raised his arms to ward off any blows, but he couldn't tell where the voice was coming from. Everything was a jumbled mess of shouts and heavy breathing and curses.

"How is this helping us with vision?" Lab yelled over the other voices.

"*Vision* is an interesting term for it," Rolabi said. His voice seemed to fill the darkness. "In this case, it isn't only reliant on eyes. We can hear what is happening. We can feel it. We can predict it. If you can do that, your eyes are a bonus."

Someone began to dribble. Peño tried to focus on the sound, feeling the familiar vibrations beneath his feet. He loved that sound. It calmed him a little, and he breathed deeply, taking in the humid, sharp musk. This was Fairwood. Even in the darkness, he knew this place.

"The game is simple. The attacking team will start on one end of the floor. The other team will wait for them in the middle. The attacking team will pass the ball up the court. They cannot dribble—only pass. If they get to the far side, they win. If they lose the ball, then the other team gets a turn. We will go until one team wins. The losing team will run."

"We can't see anything," Peño said, waving his hands around. "This is impossible."

"You are all very focused on what is impossible," Rolabi said.

Peño felt something hard and rubbery bounce right off his forehead.

"Not cool, Professor," he grumbled. "You could have hit my nose. That would have been the end of my modeling career. My family would have been devastated, man."

"What are you modeling, baby clothes?" Big John said. "Doll shoes?"

"Clearly, it's how not to grow facial hair," Vin said.

Peño rubbed his upper lip self-consciously. "Everyone is a comedian in the dark."

"Starters versus last year's bench," Rolabi said. "Starters will go first. Find the ball."

Peño sighed. That meant him. He set out after the ball, shuffling and constantly feeling his way to avoid running into anything. It only half worked, and his knee collided with the wall.

"There goes my career," he said, rubbing the sore spot.

He continued the search, jerking every time he touched something. Lab finally managed to scoop up the ball and get it to Peño, and after another few minutes, they formed what was hopefully a line under the net. The defenders were supposed to be waiting for them at half, but Peño had no idea if they were all set up correctly or not. Rolabi refused to offer any guidance.

"Okay, I'm going!" Peño announced.

"We don't even know where you are, stupid," Lab said.

"I think that's the point, idiot," Peño said.

"This should be fun," Twig muttered.

"Here!" Rain shouted.

Peño took a few steps toward the voice and then bounce-passed it, hoping the noise would help Rain locate the ball in the dark. It bounced only once, so he must have caught it.

"Who's next?" Rain asked.

"Here. Pass it!" Lab called, and Peño heard squeaking shoes closing in.

There was a bounce, a pained groan, another bounce, and then silence.

"A little higher," Lab managed, his voice unusually high-pitched. "Keep moving!"

They slowly worked their way down the court—or so he hoped—and Peño tried to facilitate things as best he could. If they moved slowly enough and used very short bounce passes, the drill seemed easy enough. But when they made it farther up the court, the sounds of his team began to intermingle with the defenders. All of a sudden, the air was full of shouts and warnings and squeaking shoes. Peño froze with the ball, trying to decipher the voices.

Finally, he picked out Lab's voice and tossed it to him. He must have missed, because he heard a clanging like an old pinball machine. The ball was bouncing around under the bleachers.

"Oops," he said.

"Switch," Rolabi said.

It took the bench team even longer to find the ball and get started, and then they promptly lost it. Peño was secretly pleased—he couldn't have Vin performing better than him at these drills. He had to start proving why he was the starter.

And why is that? a deep voice seemed to whisper in his ear.

Peño nearly toppled over, surprised by the voice in the dark. "Who said that?"

"Who said what?" Lab asked. "Everyone's talking, Peanut. You got the ball?"

"I'm over here!" A-Wall shouted.

"I said *ball*," Lab snarled, "not A-Wall."

"Hmm," Rolabi said. "Perhaps we will work up to complete darkness."

An orange light appeared, like a perfectly spherical bonfire. As Peño approached it, he realized that the basketball was glowing with an internal light. He gingerly picked it up, but there was no heat. Stranger still, the light didn't radiate from the ball—not even to his fingers.

"This is weird," Peño said, bouncing the ball back and forth between his hands.

He followed his teammates' voices until he felt the wall and then turned to face what he assumed were the defenders. It was a lot of guesswork. He had never experienced *full* darkness before. Even at night in his room, some light always snuck in from the moon or streetlights, and always from Lab's small night-light.

This was something else entirely. The team was trying to *function* in the darkness. Move around and pass and play. It seemed ridiculous . . . and yet he had to admit that it was interesting to use his other senses. He never really thought about them on the court. It was a visual game.

"You guys ready?" Peño said. "Go!"

It was definitely easier with the lit-up ball. The problem was, it was also easier for the other team to find it . . . which they soon did when someone picked off one of Peño's errant passes.

"Stolen!" Jerome announced—clearly the thief.

"Nice pass, Peño," Lab said.

Peño scowled. "I can't see who I'm passing to. What do you want from me?"

"Vision," Lab muttered.

"I'm going to pass it into the side of your head next time," Peño said.

"You couldn't hit the side of a barn."

"Well, luckily your head is bigger than that," Peño said.

He lifted his fists, pretending to box with him, and connected with something soft.

"Ow!" Vin said. "Who did that?"

Peño bit his lip and quickly scurried away.

As the drill continued, Peño began to take control. He was a vocal player at the best of times, and in the darkness, he was the clear leader on the court. He called out everything and demanded that others do the same. Before long even Twig was shouting out what he was doing. It was a nice change, and Peño wondered if the talking would continue when then the lights came on.

Finally, after Rain managed to break through the line of defenders and receive a pass, Peño sprinted down the court as fast as he dared, waving his hands and shouting for the ball.

"I'm open!"

The pass came sailing through the air like a meteorite through the atmosphere, and Peño snatched it, preparing to turn and pass it to the next player. Instead, the dusty lights flicked back on, and he realized he was standing on the far baseline. They had made it across the gym.

"The starting team wins," Rolabi said. "Water break."

"Yeah boy!" Peño said, walking around and high-fiving his team—minus Lab, who was still avoiding Peño, and Rain, who had stormed off to the bench by himself.

"What's up with that?" Peño asked A-Wall, gesturing to Rain.

A-Wall shrugged. "He said he was the team yesterday."

"Oh," Peño said. "Perfect."

It seemed the team was getting *more* disconnected with every day of training camp. As they downed their water, Rolabi asked that each player say something honest, and they began to roll through one player at a time. Most of the statements were pretty standard: things to improve, goals for the season, bench players saying they wanted to start.

When it came to Peño, he strutted right up to the front and turned to the team.

"This year we are going to win the national championship, baby. Mark my words."

"How?" Rolabi asked.

Peño frowned. "By . . . winning all the games?"

"Interesting," Rolabi replied, though it didn't sound like he was interested at all.

Peño returned to the bench, feeling a bit deflated. He suspected Rolabi wanted him to dig a little deeper, but he just wanted to play. Winning meant more games. More travel. More *ball.* That was what he really cared about. The more they won, the more they played. He didn't really care about the glory or the fame or any of that. For him, the EYL trophy symbolized a long playoff run and, importantly, more basketball. If he could play ball every day, he'd be thrilled.

Rain was the last to go and apologized. The team just stared at him. No one moved.

A leader always has to take the first step.

Peño sighed inwardly, and then stepped up and gave Rain props. "We're good."

Everyone seemed to murmur their assent.

"Let's scrimmage for an hour," Rolabi said.

"No tricks?" Peño asked suspiciously.

"Just working on our vision. Rain, Vin, Lab, A-Wall, and Devon versus the rest."

Peño froze. He wasn't playing with Rain or Lab? They *always* played starters versus bench; it was ingrained into their practices. Were these the new starters: Vin instead of Peño and Devon over Twig? Was Peño being relegated to the bench? What had he done wrong? He looked at the professor, but when he caught those flashing emerald eyes, Rolabi said nothing.

Don't put me on the bench, Peño thought desperately. *Please don't leave me behind.*

Rolabi took a ball out. "We focus on one actor and miss the others in the background. We watch one card as the dealer palms a second. We watch the ball but miss the game."

He held the ball out for the jump, and Twig and Devon hurried to either side. With Big John on the same team as Twig, it seemed Big John would slot in as a power forward and let Twig have the center spot. Peño reluctantly fell in behind them, wondering how he could get himself back into favor. Was he being skipped over because of his height? His issues with his left hand? He knew he wasn't as in shape as he should have been. He held his round stomach. Maybe he could get a jog in after practice. Run home, maybe. He had to try and earn his spot back, starting now.

"We can see so much, and yet, we choose not to," Rolabi said. "It is an odd decision."

And then Peño went blind again. No, not blind. A strange blockage appeared in front of his eyes, leaving only his peripheral vision on either side. He felt like the whole world had been split in half. Peño tried not to panic. It was just another test. He had to try and get better at these. He turned his head around experimentally, trying to regain his bearings. It was incredibly disorienting, but he could still see a little. He just had to keep his head on a swivel.

He could do this.

"I can't see!" Big John said. "Well . . . sort of!"

"Ready to play?" Rolabi asked.

"Just to be clear," Peño said, "does everyone feel like they're talking to the hand?"

"Yeah," Jerome murmured.

So everyone had the same thing. That made it easier to plan. Peño kept his head sideways and peeked at the ball from the corner of his eye. Rolabi wanted him to push against the current. Well, it was time to swim.

The ball went up, passing out of his vision again, and the scrimmage began with Twig slapping Devon in the leg and the ball finding its way to Vin. Vin scooped it up, turning his head like a leery rooster. As he dribbled down the court, Peño hounded him, constantly moving his head back and forth to keep Vin in sight. He used his hands for guidance too.

"Call for screens!" Peño shouted. "Tell us who's around you!"

Vin tried to fake left, but Peño followed—hearing the squeak of his shoes and the shift of the ball even before he saw anything. He even felt Vin's dipping shoulder with his outstretched fingers. Blocked from the net, Vin passed the ball to Rain on the wing.

"You're alone!" Peño called, letting Reggie know there weren't any screens coming.

Rain went for the drive, gaining the corner on Reggie and heading directly for the net. But then he did something very unexpected—he passed the ball to an open Lab in the corner.

"Cover the wing!" Peño said, looking for Jerome.

He was too late. Lab caught the pass, lined up the shot, and hit it.

"I can see!" Lab shouted. "Nice pass, Rain!"

Peño frowned as Lab ran by. "Like . . . fully see?"

"Not anymore," Lab muttered. "Just when I was shooting."

Peño couldn't make sense of that, so he put it out of his mind. They were already losing to the new starters. He got an inbound pass from Twig and started up the court, realizing he could at least go right this time—no more invisible wall. Turning his head constantly, Peño watched the others form up and made mental notes of their positions. He felt like an army general carefully marking his troops out on a map. His stopped at the top of the circle and hit Jerome on a sharp cut.

"I can see too!" Jerome shouted, and then proceeded to miss the layup. "Never mind."

Peño cursed as they ran back on defense again, but before they could even get organized, A-Wall hit a layup. Peño bit his lip. They were falling behind. *He* was falling behind.

Peño worked even harder. He fought for every ball. He put a hand on everyone who passed him, he talked relentlessly, and he listened with a studious ear . . . marking the positions of his team. He couldn't see, so he had to visualize the game. It wasn't perfect, but in time the game began to grow around him like a spiderweb. There were tendrils connecting each player. A movement on one end of the court created a ripple of reactions, and he had to track each one back to the center of the game.

He soon realized that open shots were rewarded with restored vision. Contested shots were half-blind and mostly missed, so he had to find guys who were truly open. If he moved the ball fast enough, he could almost always find a good option. He had to seek out the true openings.

"Water break," Rolabi called.

Peño shuffled over and gulped his water back.

"Having fun yet?" Vin asked.

"It's not too bad," he replied. "Dancing around you gets tiring, though."

Vin laughed. "How do you like my bench mob?"

"They must be the starters now," Peño said with false bravado. "Since I'm on their side."

The drill resumed, and Peño finished strong. He scored only a few baskets, but he guided the bench players to a fairly even scrimmage. He talked and directed and encouraged them through the little moments. Peño started to think that it wasn't about winning the game—they had to win every single possession. Every second. And that was what he loved. Not the outcome.

The fight.

That is how you will lead them.

"That will do," Rolabi said. "Grab your bottles and join me in the center."

Peño's vision returned to normal. He shook his head, spraying sweat everywhere.

"Who won?" Peño asked. "I kind of lost track."

"Neither," Rolabi said with something like approval, though it was always hard to decipher emotion in his baritone voice. "And both. Was that how you normally play?"

Lab laughed. "Of course not. We were moving in slow motion."

"Speed is relative. To the fastest, everyone moves in slow motion. What else?"

"We . . . we talked a lot. More than ever," Twig said.

Rolabi nodded. "True. Anything else?"

"We spread the floor on offense," Peño said, thinking back to the scrimmage. The outside options were always the clearest, so they were forced to spread the ball and not repeatedly attack the same direct lane to the hoop. "More passes around the lane. Kick outs and stuff."

"A natural choice when one cannot see his own path," Rolabi said. "And lastly?"

After a pause, Rain spoke. "We had to think about where everyone would be . . . and should be. We had to predict the game."

"Indeed," Rolabi said. "We had to see more than our eyes allow. Now, I am owed some laps."

Peño grinned as the bench players took off, Vin in the lead. He had gotten the better of his backup in one of the drills, at least. But it wasn't much of a punishment—they hit their first free-throw attempt and were back in the circle almost immediately. Peño scowled at Vin.

"Lucky," he muttered.

"All skill," Vin replied, grinning.

Rolabi opened his bag. "You all have your full eyesight again. But are you really looking? We must relearn to see." He withdrew the daisy from his bag and set it down in front of them.

"Not again," Peño said.

"Many times more," Rolabi said. "If you wish to win, you must slow down time. Begin."

He started for the doors, and Peño glanced between the professor and the potted daisy, confused.

"Where are you going?" Peño asked.

"You will take the daisy home tonight, Peño. Be careful with it, please. Water it."

Peño gulped and stared at the daisy. He had to take care of it? It would probably try to eat him in the middle of the night. He decided to lock it in their closet when he got home . . . though he made a mental note to water it *very* thoroughly first. Rolabi seemed fond of the flower.

The doors crashed open, letting wind roar inside.

"How long do you want us to stare at it?" Rain shouted.

Rolabi didn't turn back. "Until you see something new."

With that, he vanished into the afternoon.

"Do you think that was, like . . . literal?" Peño asked.

"Who knows?" Vin said. "At least I don't have to take it home."

"Thanks," Peño said.

Big John stood and stomped toward the bench. "Where you going?" Jerome called after him.

"I'm not staring at a stupid flower if I don't have to," Big John said. "I'm out."

"Everything all right with you?" Peño asked.

Big John walked to the doors without answering, pushed one open, and then seemed to reconsider. "No, Peño. This is the Bottom. Things aren't just *all right*. You can go along with that weirdo all you want and play his games. But it's not a game out there. Remember where you are. I'm going to catch some extra time at work."

With that, he stormed out. A moody silence descended on the gym.

Rain went for his ball, abandoning the flower drill. Peño hesitated for a moment. Despite Rolabi's lessons seeming a bit more logical today, the flower still didn't make any sense. They couldn't slow time, but they could definitely waste it. Peño went to go shoot around too.

Not everyone followed. Devon, Twig, and Reggie stayed, staring at the flower.

"I wonder if we are ever going to—" Lab started, and then fell silent.

Peño felt a familiar chill creep up his arms. He didn't even need to turn to know what was causing it. The strange orb had returned . . . and this time it was hovering directly over Devon's head. Despite that, Devon didn't move. He just sat there, his dark eyes fixated on the flower.

Peño felt like he should warn him, but the words caught in his throat. Everyone was staring at the orb now. Devon had to know it was there, right? And still he stayed motionless.

Time seemed to stretch.

Then, without any warning, Devon shot his arm upward and caught the orb in one strong hand. He broke into a triumphant grin, the viscous black matter seeping through his fingers . . . and then he disappeared. Peño stared at the empty spot where Devon had been sitting.

"That's not good," Peño whispered.

Things seemed to speed up. There was shouting and people heading for the door, and as Peño watched it all unfold, his eyes fell on the flower. He remembered that he was supposed to take it home. His eyes lingered on it. Peño barely heard the others. And, for a moment, the flower wavered.

There is always time.

He thought about his rushed shots. He thought about his fears of his talent and his size. He thought about his deeper, darker fears. Weren't they all about time? Devon reappeared, but even that didn't break Peño's concentration. He slowly approached the flower, picked it up, and felt something come over him. A flood of tingling down his arms and legs. Then he saw *more.*

Silvery white light in his hands, the flower, the gym.

"What is happening?" he asked no one in particular.

Are you ready to use your grana, Peño?

He stared down at the flower, tucked the pot beneath his arm, and looked around in wonder.

"Yes," he whispered.

And what do the strongest remember?

Peño glanced at his brother. "That sometimes we are weak."

MAN ON A MOUNTAIN

You may tire on the road. It may grow dark.
Rest if you must, but never give up.
Walk until the darkness is a memory and
you become the sun on the next traveler's horizon.

❖ WIZENARD 50 PROVERB ❖

PEÑO SLID HIS hands under the tap and ran them over his face, relishing the cool streams of water. He stared at himself in the mirror, hearing the first rhythmic thudding of balls on the gym floor outside the locker room door.

Peño had managed to get the flower home in one piece. He had placed it on the windowsill, watered it carefully, and ignored all of Lab's snide remarks. It reminded him of his mom's garden box, except that it stayed green. It was healthy.

She would have loved it.

It hadn't been a great night apart from that. Peño had slept little, listening to Lab toss and turn, and he felt odd today. Worn down. Tired. He had never fought with Lab for this long before. Three days of awkward silence. And what for? Because his brother was better than him?

Where are they all going in such a rush?

Peño spun around the bathroom, roughly wiping his face with his arm. "Who said that?" he demanded.

It is strange when we desperately wish to follow others, though we say we want to lead.

I just want the tools, Peño thought. *I need something to work with.*

You have all you need.

For what? he thought. *To live in the Bottom for the rest of my life?*

There was no response. Peño sighed and gripped the sink. This had to stop. He didn't do self-pity. If he did, everything would fall apart. Maybe some people could afford weakness. But not him.

"Just play your game today," he whispered.

Peño hurried out of the locker room. He had only put up a few shots before Rolabi appeared on the sideline—this time in a wobble of air like baked concrete on a scorching summer day. It seemed no one else had noticed him yet, and his piercing eyes flashed to Peño, holding his gaze.

Peño saw something in the distance behind him: a clear lake and a wooden rowboat.

It was still sinking.

"He won't talk to me," Peño muttered.

Then speak without words.

Rolabi walked onto the court. "Gather around. Today we work on your shots."

Peño quickly grabbed the flower—which was still sitting on the bench—and brought it over. Rolabi tucked it into his bag, again placing it as if in some familiar spot, and looked at him.

"Better than when I left it."

Peño hesitated. "Do you think . . . I could take it home sometimes?"

"Here." He withdrew something from his breast pocket and held it out—a blue-green, round seed. "Plant this. Water it. Tend it. These seeds will grow anywhere. Even in the Bottom."

Peño took it, his hands shaking. "Thank you," he said. "She . . . My mom."

"Will watch it, and you, grow," Rolabi said.

Peño smiled, then ran to put it in his bag as the others gathered around

Rolabi. He tucked it gingerly into his spare towel, then ran back to join them, all seemingly unnoticed by the others.

"Hmm," Rolabi said, "this will be fascinating."

He tossed a ball to Devon, and the second it touched his fingers, the gym was replaced by open, azure sky dotted with a tapestry of stars. Peño looked around. The players were standing on top of a tall mountain unlike anything he had ever seen, even in photos. The plateau where they stood—the summit of the mountain—was a flat shelf of stone, not much bigger than the main floor of Peño's row house, its edges jagged. The cliffside around it plunged down into clouds.

Peño quickly backed away, his head swimming.

He was not a fan of heights, and this mountain didn't look very sturdy. In fact, it seemed impossible that something so tall and narrow could remain upright for long. He spotted a second jagged mountain beside their own, capped by a lone basketball net like a climber's flag.

"What is this?" Lab whispered. The soft question echoed a hundred times beneath them.

"A mountain, I guess," Peño said, hugging himself.

There was no wind, but it was cold—bitingly so.

"Thanks," Lab said, giving him a dirty look.

Peño had a mad urge to step closer to the edge, even though he only wanted to get farther away from the abyss. The ground seemed to tip toward it, and he felt his breakfast threatening to come up again.

"What do we do?" Jerome asked. "Climb down?"

"Are you serious?" Vin said. "We're like a mile up."

Peño began to tremble. He gasped against the thin air.

Find your center.

The words resonated in his mind, and Peño focused on them. His breathing calmed.

The eagle doesn't worry about the fall, the voice said.

"This is too much," Lab said.

"You said that last time," Peño replied.

"And you didn't listen!"

A crack split the air. It sounded like it was coming from below them, *inside* the mountain. The ground vibrated, confirming Peño's theory. Just then, a chunk of rock fell away behind the team, as big as a car, and tumbled off toward the clouds. It was swallowed in the gloom.

"We need to do something," Twig said, sounding far calmer than Peño felt.

"Like what?" Vin asked.

"We're supposed to be practicing shooting, right?" Twig said. "Maybe we need to shoot the ball."

There was another crack, and a second car-size boulder split away.

"Take the shot, Rain," Reggie urged.

There was another crack, and Peño grabbed his brother's wrist. For once, he didn't think about acting tough or even that *he* was the older brother. He just wanted to make sure they weren't separated, no matter what. Another boulder split off, smashing the cliffside on the way.

The summit was shrinking fast. Peño gulped and turned back to Rain.

He was hoping they only needed to make one shot, but he didn't get the chance to find out. Rain was shaking from the moment he caught the ball, and his shot bounced once off the rim and then tumbled over the side of the mountain.

"So much for that plan," Peño muttered.

Then the ball came rocketing back up again, arching well overhead before landing in Vin's hands. Peño wondered if there was some significance in that.

"Keep shooting," Twig said.

It didn't go well. One player after another missed. Twig finally hit one, but the ball flew back up anyway. It seemed they would all have to make a shot. The ball came to Peño last of all, and he looked at it, frowning.

He knew he should step closer to the net—the gap was about ten feet—but he didn't want to go anywhere near the splintering edges, so he took a long three instead and missed everything.

"Oh, great shot," Peño muttered to himself, watching the ball sail overhead. "Faster!"

"Don't rush the shots!" Vin said.

Peño bristled at the challenge, but Vin was right. They needed to take their time.

Rain promptly missed again, overtaken by more trembling. Vin made his attempt, and then so did Jerome, while Lab airballed his shot. Peño missed again, as well, this time off the back rim. He bit his fingernails. What if he was the only one that couldn't hit it? What if the team failed and it was his fault?

"Try to focus!" Jerome said, the panic creeping into his voice.

Rain missed again, still trembling uncontrollably.

"Come on, Rain!" Vin said.

Lab's shot fell short, and Peño could feel the ground shaking as the ball came back to him. They were running out of time. He stepped forward, coming within a few feet of the edge. His head swam when he peeked over, so instead he focused on the hoop and locked on to that alone.

The eagle sees only the prey.

Peño took a deep breath. He dribbled the ball on the uneven surface, letting the vibrations move through him. They were calming somehow. He tried to listen for the beat. *Boom, boom, boom . . .* He started whispering some lines:

> "Peño the bird of prey
> Taking flight to say—"

"You're freestyling now?" Lab hissed.

"A mountain can fall
But Peño's here to stay!"

His eyes never once left the hoop. He took the shot and swished it.

"Yes!" he shouted, pumping his fist.

But his elation was short-lived. Rain missed again, and Devon right after. Lab was next. Despite their fight, Peño couldn't resist a bit of coaching advice. On the mountain, it seemed silly not to talk. Their argument would mean nothing if they fell.

"You got this," Peño whispered. "Just relax. Regular old free throw."

Lab glanced at him as if to say something mean, took a moment, and then turned back. His shoulders visibly relaxed, his fingers calmed. Then he hit his shot. There was another crack. The summit was the size of Peño's kitchen now and shrinking fast. Soon the entire mountain would sway and collapse, bringing the Badgers with it. Peño's stomach turned— it would be a very, very long fall. He looked over the edge at death waiting below them. He had seen it once before.

He remembered sitting by her bed that night. She was so skinny. Her honey-brown skin had faded to beige. Nearly gray. The cancer had swallowed her up. He remembered her cold fingers in his.

"Promise me you'll take care of your brother," she'd said.

"I promise," Peño had whispered.

I won't let anything happen to him, he thought. *I promised you.*

Devon was the next to hit his shot, pumping a massive fist. Only Rain was left now. Another piece of the mountain fell away, and the team huddled closer together, standing shoulder to shoulder. Peño could hear their low, ragged breathing. There was nowhere left to go. The next break in the rock would cut the team in half at best—and bring them all down at worst.

"We're dead," Vin murmured.

"Just one more," Lab said.

The ball flew up and landed in Rain's shaking hands.

"Make it, Rain!" Peño said.

He had said it a thousand times. It echoed that many times and more around them. Another awful crack thundered beneath them. Without thinking, Peño squeezed his brother's arm. Lab said nothing.

"Hurry!" Vin said desperately.

Peño felt the ground shift beneath him. He exchanged a terrified look with his brother.

"Just hold on," Peño murmured. "We'll be fine."

"Shoot it!" A-Wall screamed.

The ball flew and the mountain fell. There was an inexorable pull backward, and Peño heard his teammates screaming. He slipped off the plateau, one hand still locked around his brother's wrist. That connection at least gave him comfort. He watched, unable even to scream, as the ball spiraled slowly through the air.

The ball swished through the hoop, and the mountain was gone. Peño looked down and saw the worn hardwood of Fairwood Community Center. He fell onto his knees and kissed the floor, ignoring decades of dirt and sweat and spit.

"It's so disgusting, yet so beautiful," he said.

Rolabi was watching them. Peño knew he should be angry with him—that the grana had almost killed them this time. But at the moment he felt only relief, and somewhere under that, a realization that they had just done something important. They had hit a shot because they had to. They had all taken the last buzzer-beater.

And they were alive.

Lab turned to Peño, and they met eyes for a moment. Neither spoke. But Peño had felt the fall, and in the moment, he really didn't care what Lab had said, or what they were fighting about, or who was more scared, who was mourning correctly. He just cared about his brother.

"Basketball is about confronting fear," Rolabi was saying. "If you won't face it, you will lose. We will practice a thousand shots. Ten thousand. Twenty. If you take them *all* from a crumbling mountain, you will become great shooters."

Peño thought about that. He was always rushing everything on the court. Why? Because he was afraid of being blocked and embarrassed. But humiliation meant nothing on a falling mountain.

"That will do for today," Rolabi said. "Tomorrow should be an interesting day."

"What was today?" Lab muttered. "Boring?"

Rolabi turned and walked toward the wall. There was another flash of light, and then he was gone, leaving nothing but yellowed cinder blocks in his wake. Peño reluctantly stood up.

"We almost died," Lab murmured.

"That was messed up," A-Wall said. "And tomorrow should be interesting. Ha!"

Peño frowned. "What are you doing, Rain?"

Rain had grabbed his ball from his bag and was heading for the free-throw line.

"Shooting," he said.

Peño smiled and shook his head. He knew Rain would shoot until he was *never* the last one to score again. For all his arrogance, Rain refused to be anything but the best player on the team. Peño decided to do the same. He grabbed his own ball and started for the same net, stopping on the three-point line and taking a deep breath. For once, he didn't rush anything.

He pictured a tall mountain, and a long fall, and took the shot like it was his last.

The team shot for hours. When they were finally tired, Peño grabbed his bag and walked out alone—but not for long. Lab fell into step beside him, hands in his pockets, shoulder to shoulder.

"You walking with me today?" Peño asked.

"Well . . . it's not safe for you to walk home alone."

"Why not?" Peño asked, glancing at him.

"You're too short. People can't see you over the hood of their car."

Peño started to laugh. "Shut up."

"Who said that?" Lab asked, trying to spot something down around his ankles.

Peño punched him in the arm and kept walking.

"Do you really . . . have trouble breathing sometimes?" Lab asked.

Peño hesitated. He had forgotten he had mentioned that. He had never told anyone about that before . . . not Lab, not his dad, not anyone. It felt like his chest tightened up, and he got dizzy, and all his breath stole away like he'd fallen into cold water. But it was his secret. His weakness.

He remembered Rolabi's words about leadership.

"Yeah," Peño said. "I guess . . . it's anxiety or something."

Lab nodded as they turned onto the street. "I get that sometimes too," he murmured.

"You can tell me when it happens," Peño said.

"You too," Lab replied.

Peño gave him a little clap on the shoulder. "We're gonna make it, bro."

"I know. Now, we gonna talk about that mountain or what?"

Peño laughed. They talked about Rain, and trophies, and strange castles appearing in the gym. Neither said sorry for their fight, and neither had to. For once, they had both said enough.

⑧
ALONE

If you don't like being alone,
you must learn to like yourself.
◆ WIZENARD ◇ PROVERB ◆

THE NEXT DAY, Peño and Lab were crossing the parking lot, sneakers falling on cracked pavement and faded white lines. The July heat wave was in full effect, and smog was encroaching from the old mining quarter. Soon it would blanket the sky, but for now, the sun was bright and brilliant.

Peño felt better today. He had put some soil into an old mug, planted the seed, then set it on the windowsill in his bedroom. He and Lab then shot against the brick wall at home for nearly three hours, releasing all the fear and doubt and relief of their experience on the mountain. He had cooked a big dinner, and he and Lab had both stayed up to eat with their dad. No fighting. No memories. Just laughter. Of course, that couldn't last forever.

"No girls like you, Peño," Lab said, rolling his eyes.

"None that I tell you about."

"So tell me."

"Mind your own business," Peño said.

"Your sorry excuse for a social life *is* my business."

Peño turned back. "You aren't really going there, are you? You have no social life."

"I have friends," Lab replied, his ears reddening. "And you know the girls love me."

Peño laughed. "Which girls?"

"Too many to name," Lab said.

"Characters in books don't count."

Peño pulled the front doors open. Reggie, A-Wall, and Twig were already there.

"You haven't gone outside on a weekend once this summer," Peño pointed out.

"I've been busy."

"Doing what? Face it, Lab: you're a hermit."

Lab scowled. "I like to be alone sometimes. Sue me."

"For what . . . cheese snacks?"

"Hilarious."

They sat down and stripped off their outdoor shoes. Peño yawned and stretched.

"Is that Peño yawning?" Reggie asked, raising an eyebrow. "That's new."

"We stayed up late," Peño said. "Dinner with the pops."

"What you eat?"

"Peño's usual cooking: cardboard meat and stale rice," Lab said.

Peño glared at him. "Actually, it was a delicious pork, rice, and bean combo. Yes, the pork was a bit . . . tough. And the rice was a little stale. Never mind the beans. But with a bit of sauce—I made my own—and a bit of love, they all came together. Pops said it was inspired."

"He'd been working for sixteen hours before that, mind you," Lab said. "So his judgment was a little off."

Peño let out an exaggerated sigh. "You can see what I have to deal with."

Reggie laughed and went to shoot around. Peño soon followed, switching between threes, elbow jumpers, and layups. Rain was last to arrive, and he burst through the doors breathlessly.

"Sleep in?" Peño asked.

"How'd you guess?" Rain said sarcastically.

Rain had just finished lacing up his shoes when the doors billowed open. But this time it wasn't just wind. A full blast of snow raced inside and swirled along the hardwood, forming shapes and faces and players running down the court. When it reached half, the snowy front cycled into a funnel and then erupted, spraying snowflakes that melted and disappeared before they ever reached the ground. A stunned silence greeted Rolabi as he walked inside.

"I really need to work on my entrances," Peño muttered.

"Am I still dreaming?" Lab said from beside him.

Rolabi stopped at center court. "Dreams are fleeting. A wisp of smoke and they're gone."

"It's too early for the philosophy, Coach," Big John said.

"I got dreams," Peño said. "You need dreams. They keep you going sometimes."

"A dream is nothing without vision," Rolabi countered. "Don't dream. Aspire. Find the rungs of the ladder and climb. And choose correctly. If a dream can be achieved without work, without sacrifice, then it is meaningless. It will bring you no joy. You didn't earn it, and so you do not own it. Don't wish for fleeting dreams. The road to your dreams is paved with hardship."

"I'm ready," Peño whispered.

Not yet.

"Line up facing me," Rolabi said. "Three of you have caught the orb so far."

Three? Peño glanced at Lab, but his brother gave his head a little shake.

"It is good to recognize who is defending us at all times," Rolabi continued, his eyes on the ceiling now. "To use size and speed advantages. But before that, we must understand what it means to attack as a team. And so we remove those advantages and create fully equal defenders."

Half the fluorescent lights flicked off. The ones *behind* the team had gone dark, leaving only a dim, eerie glow from the remaining bulbs, like a fading spotlight shining in their eyes.

"We will learn to attack as one. But first, we need defenders."

Rain cried out a warning, and Peño spun around. His shadow, which had taken form in the uneven lights, was pushing itself up to its feet. It twiddled its fingers and bounced on its toes. Peño realized it was an exact three-dimensional copy of himself—the same size, the same shape. His shadow faced him, as if equally surprised to see *him*.

"Not cool," Peño said.

"Meet today's defenders," Rolabi said. "You should know them well."

Peño's shadow stepped forward with its hand out, and Peño took a big step away from it. The shadow shook its hand impatiently and tapped an invisible watch. Peño tentatively stuck out his hand for the shake, and the shadow squeezed, sending tingles up his arm.

"Easy, bro," Peño said. "Don't make me get a flashlight."

"Into position, defenders," Rolabi said.

Five shadows hurried into position on defense while the rest stepped aside to wait.

"I think it's obvious who will be guarding you," Rolabi continued. "But it won't be a scrimmage—we will just be working on our offense. You will sub in as we go. Let's try a few as usual. Starters go first."

Rolabi tossed Peño a ball. Despite being thrilled that he was still a starter, at least for the moment, Peño wouldn't really have minded if Vin had to face the freaky shadow defenders first.

Peño sighed deeply. "Line it up."

He dribbled the ball at the point, and his shadow replica got low, spreading its hands and shuffling with short, strong jab steps. It was identical to the way Peño played defense—his positioning was something he prided himself on. It seemed his shadow was going to do the same.

"Can you, like, talk?" Peño asked.

The shadow shook its head.

"Right, no mouth," Peño said. "Rain!"

The Badgers' offense was pretty simple. Peño would pass Rain the ball on the right wing, and then he would either shoot a three or cut to the net. If by chance he was blocked from doing either of those things, they would reset again—but that was a distant second option. Most of their additional scoring came through rebounds and second-chance points from any of Rain's missed shots.

Rain took the pass and cut . . . but his shadow was right on him, dogging him the whole way. Rain tried to fake and drop back for a jumper, but his shadow stepped in, arm up. Rain was stifled, and he passed the ball back to Peño, scowling. Peño swung it to Lab, who was equally stumped.

It wasn't just that the defenders were evenly matched in size and strength—they also knew exactly what their creators liked to do on offense. It removed the element of surprise.

"Try the post," Lab shouted, throwing it back to Peño.

Peño caught the pass and shielded it, taking a hard bump from his opponent.

"Watch it!" Peño hissed.

The shadow gave him a little shrug and played even harder. Peño had to fake it twice just to get the ball down to Twig, who, to his credit, went in for the layup . . . and was horribly stuffed.

"I think our shadows are better at D than we are," Lab said as the bench players took their turn.

"They like to foul too," Peño muttered.

His shadow started to play a small, invisible violin.

The bench players were also shut out, and the starters took the court again.

Peño tried to get the ball to Rain, but Peño's shadow was ready for the pass this time. It picked the ball off easily, high-fived Rain's shadow, then strutted over to Peño like a peacock.

"It was one steal," Peño growled. "Get over it."

His shadow nodded, as if apologizing, and reached out for a handshake. But when Peño reached to reciprocate, his shadow swiftly pulled its hand away and ran it through its invisible hair.

Rain's shadow mimed laughter and patted Peño's shadow on the back.

"That shadow just threw some shade on you," Jerome said from the sideline.

"Very punny," Peño replied.

They went back and forth for an hour, and it didn't get any better. Peño had the ball stolen six times and was stuffed twice. His shadow bumped and grabbed and played the hardest defense Peño had ever faced. Every rejected shot led to a celebration—struts, moonwalks, hand gestures. His shadow had it all covered.

"Our shadows are annoying," Peño said, watching as it chest-bumped Lab's.

"I've noticed," Lab muttered.

"Take a break," Rolabi said, a definite hint of amusement in his voice.

Peño downed his water. He had been working as hard as he could, but it was no use. His shadow was too good on defense . . . he couldn't get past himself. It seemed oddly ironic.

"Why are you losing?" Rolabi asked, walking over to them.

Peño snorted. "Because we're playing magical shadows."

"You're playing yourselves," Rolabi said. "Just more focused."

Peño flushed at that one.

"We're all playing one-on-one," Rain said. "I guess I never really thought of it, but it's obvious. Our whole plan is to get it to the guy who has the best chance to score, but that's it. And it's tough because those . . . things know how we like to play."

"Precisely," Rolabi said, nodding at him in approval.

"But that's how you play basketball," Peño said. "You can pass and screen, but at the end of the day you are just giving the ball to one person who has to shoot it. That's basketball. Even the pros."

"That is often true. But are we really no more than five solo players attacking five others? If that's the case, then why don't we all practice separately? Why even practice together at all?"

Peño thought about that. "Well, we still need to pass to each other and stuff . . ."

"The way you play offense is the way most people play offense. It is effective right until it is not. For the most skilled player in the world, and for him alone, there is always an advantage. For all the rest, they must create the advantage for themselves. And that can only be done with the help of their team."

"But—" Peño said.

"If we play defense as a team, we play offense as a team. We talk. We plan. We see the floor."

"But—" Peño tried again.

"We attack as one. And that starts with a simple spotlight. Into your positions, please."

Peño sighed and went to the point. His shadow crouched down again, waving him on.

"You know, you're kind of a jerk," Peño said.

But who cast the shadow?

Peño scowled at Rolabi. As he did, he noticed the remaining lights were growing dimmer. There were only three rows of bulbs left, and even they seemed to be losing power fast.

"Peño, pass the ball to Rain," Rolabi said.

Peño hesitated. "I can barely see him. Can we turn some more lights on?"

"That is the hope. Pass the ball."

Peño passed the ball to Rain, already squinting in the darkness. A pool of light spilled around Rain, and his shadow stepped back, giving him room. But as Rain began to dribble, the darkness overtook him again.

"What's going on here?" Rain asked, looking around warily.

Peño was wondering the same thing. He noticed his shadow was growing larger.

"Oh, that's perfect," he muttered.

"Twig!" Rain shouted, and then lobbed a pass down to the center.

Twig was suddenly illuminated by a brilliant white glow. "The passing," he said. "It lights us up!"

"Options light up the court," Rolabi agreed. "When everyone moves, the darkness lifts."

Options, Peño thought. *That means anyone who gets open.*

Peño cut for the ball, and the spotlight shifted to him, causing his shadow to shrink back to a normal size. He got the pass, Rain cut across the zone, and Peño hit him, still illuminated. But as soon as Peño stopped in his usual position at the top to wait for the ball, the space around him grew darker again.

They can't see me when I stand still, he realized. *And I can't see them.*

A-Wall was fading fast on the low post.

"We have to keep moving!" Peño shouted.

And so he did. Peño had never done so much cutting in his life. He found himself on the wing, in the corner, and even crashing the boards— anything to keep the lights on and his shadow in check. He had always been so stuck to the point position that he had almost felt that he couldn't leave the top of the key. Now he had no choice but to venture off and get involved. He was soon boxing out down low, driving shadows back with his squat legs.

The Spotlight Offense soon became obvious. The best options were always the brightest, which made choosing passes simple—Peño just had to follow the light. He realized that the post players were open a lot more than he had ever realized, as long as he kept his head up. Usually if he drove to the net, the defense would close in on him, and he got lost in the trees. Now A-Wall and Twig lit up *behind* the closing players, and he hit them on bounce passes for easy layups.

He was also using the others to his advantage. He rubbed off screens and faked passes. His shadow ran into Twig and A-Wall constantly, and it was getting annoyed—stomping around and waving its hands at its shadow teammates. But the real difference was the *talking*.

Peño had never heard the Badgers talk so much—at least not with the lights on. Even Twig was calling out screens and moving and making shots. The whole game became audible.

Finally, Rolabi stepped forward with the flower.

"That's enough for today," he said. "Sit and watch. Thank you, gentlemen."

Peño sat down in front of the flower, focusing on it, and for once he didn't feel the need to move or fidget. He was engrossed, but he did notice when the room fell into an even deeper silence, and he looked up and saw that the orb was back, floating only ten feet away. Peño shifted warily.

"Here we go again," Lab muttered.

Vin went first, then Lab, and Peño raced after them. He tried to snag the orb on his first pass and missed badly, nearly falling from the over-reach. He turned back, noticing that Devon, Twig, and Jerome were all still seated around the daisy, legs crossed beneath them.

Those are the three who already caught it, he realized.

He lunged wildly at the orb and ended up face-first on the hardwood. "Ow," he muttered.

The orb stopped in front of Rain, and Peño rolled over onto his stomach, watching the confrontation. Rain approached it slowly. Then, when the orb launched into a sudden switch of direction, he pivoted on one heel and caught it with his right hand. Rain grinned and was gone.

Peño caught Devon heading for the bench. Peño and Lab had been discussing the burly new recruit last night . . . and they had made a couple of bets. He figured now was as good a time as any to resolve them.

"Lab and I have a bet," he said, walking over to Devon. "Why do you do homeschool?"

Devon shifted. "I . . . I like it better."

"Oh," Peño said, slumping. "I was betting your parents made you. How long you been doing that? Don't know anyone who is homeschooled, you know? Seems kinda cool."

"This is the fourth year," Devon said, still not making eye contact.

"So you used to go to regular school?"

"Yeah."

Okay, Peño thought, *I can still win the second bet.*

"Why'd you leave?"

Devon fidgeted. "I . . . didn't fit in."

"Oh," Peño said, disappointed. "I bet that you were expelled. No offense."

Devon loomed over Peño, standing a head taller and half again as wide. He didn't seem to have an ounce of fat on him.

"Man, I wish I looked like you," Peño said. "Your arms are thicker than my waist."

Devon rubbed his arm. "Sometimes I feel a bit . . . too big."

Peño laughed. "Too big? Own it, big man. You know what people call me?"

"Umm, no," he said.

"Shrimp, lil'boy, baby mustache . . ."

Devon let out a chuckle, and Peño smiled.

"Yeah, I guess that last one isn't about my height," he said. "The point is, I don't let that get me down. So what? I'm short and I'll still outplay them all. You're a beast, bro. Throw it down. Use it. And if people call you names, smile and ball 'em."

Devon forced a smile. "Yeah, you're right."

"Of course I'm right! You'll figure that out soon—"

Peño stopped midsentence. No wonder Devon wasn't talking—Peño hadn't initiated him yet.

"Hey, you don't have a nickname!"

"I . . . well, no. Not yet."

"I've been neglecting my duties."

"Don't worry about it."

Peño waved him away, thinking. He needed something good. Something to get Devon fired up. He was clearly shy, so maybe something that had a bit of a bite. Something with attitude. He talked while he was thinking, listing all the other nicknames he'd invented, hoping one of them would spark an idea. "And you . . . well, you're just huge. A brute. Beast. The Bull?"

Devon's smile flickered, and Peño held his hand up, seeing his discomfort.

"Skip that." He paused. "Big D?"

Devon looked even more downcast.

Nothing about size, you dimwit, Peño reprimanded himself. *He needs confidence.*

Then it hit him.

"Tell you what . . . let's give you one you're going to have to *earn*."

"Like what?"

"Cash Money," he said proudly. "Cash for short. Like every time you get the ball down low, you can just cash it in 'cause nobody can stop the big man."

Devon laughed at that one . . . a deep, booming rumble.

"Cash it is!" Peño said. "Let's get it, boy! Cash coming for the title!"

He gave him props and then headed for Rain, who had just popped back into Fairwood. He wanted to get some information out of him about the orb. About where it had taken him.

Peño heard a quiet voice behind him.

"Cash . . . yeah . . . that works for me."

Peño smiled. He hoped that Cash would start feeling a little more at home with the Badgers. Now he just had to get him to throw down on the block and be the beast he was clearly meant to be. Peño could do that with time. He considered himself a fairly talented motivator.

"You all right?" he asked Rain.

Rain hesitated. "Yeah. I'm all right."

Rain walked to the bench, looking a bit dazed, and Peño decided not to pester him. Maybe he wasn't supposed to know.

He sighed and decided to go cheer up Rain.

"Rain the baller
the big shot caller
he may be down
Slouching round town
but when the game is on
and time is almost gone
he'll hit the winner
Rain serves buckets for dinner"

Rain laughed and shook his head.

"You sure you're good?" Peño said, putting his fist up.

Rain gave him props. "You know it."

As Peño slipped on his shoes, quiet words played in his mind: *In the place you are most afraid to be.* He had no idea what that meant, but he suspected he wasn't going to like it.

THE
BOOST

We need not fear what we cannot control,
but we can learn to control our fear.
✦ WIZENARD (49) PROVERB ✦

PEÑO DIDN'T SLEEP well. He kept dreaming of sinking boats, roads slipping into fog, and falling mountains. Maybe dinner disagreed with him. He had conjured up such a lackluster pasta that even Lab didn't have the heart to insult it. Later, when he couldn't sleep, Peño read his old books and spun his ball on his finger. He felt like he was missing something. He awoke late—Lab woke *him* up for the first time ever—and they hurried to practice.

When he got there, Peño decided to work on Cash's game with him. The big kid was down on the post now, and Peño lobbed the ball to him. Cash turned sharply and laid it in with a grin.

"That's it, my brother!" Peño said, opening an imaginary register. "Cash it in!"

Devon threw the ball back to Peño, who lifted a hand, freestyling:

"Cash is a beast
down low he will feast
he may be schooled at home,
but on the court, he's the..."

Peño blanked, scratching at the back of his neck. He could still save it.

"He's schooled at home,
but on the court he will roam
he's the kid with the muscles
he must eat his brussels...
Sprouts?"

Peño frowned. "Definitely not my best work."

"That's an understatement," Lab said. "But wait . . . do you have any best work?"

"Shut up."

Peño dribbled to the sideline, imagining full bleachers. He couldn't wait for actual games. The thrill of stepping out onto the court, the opposing team across the line. The shouts and applause. His pops cheering them on, when he could. Peño closed his eyes. He could almost hear the voices.

"We have two days left of our training camp," Rolabi said, walking onto the court. "And two left to catch the orb."

But after just a few more words, he headed for the doors again, leaving the confused team at center court.

"There's no practice today?" Peño asked.

"Oh yes. You just don't need me," the professor said.

"What should we do?" Rain called after him.

Rolabi glanced back. "I leave that to you."

The front doors burst open, and Rolabi walked outside. When the doors slammed shut again, they dissolved into the cinder-block wall. Peño stared at the blank wall apprehensively. The only entrance and exit in Fairwood Community Center had vanished. The team was trapped inside.

"Perfect," Peño said. "I guess he's making sure we don't go home early."

"I wouldn't be so sure," Twig said.

As soon as Twig said it, a terrible grinding filled the air. Peño covered his ears and watched in horror as the two walls that ran the length of the court began to push forward.

"Impossible," Vin breathed.

"Possibility is subjective," Lab muttered. "Any ideas?"

Peño dropped his ball, watching as one wall began to push the bleachers forward.

"Maybe we need to score the ball again?" Vin suggested.

They grabbed their balls and started shooting. Peño hit a free throw and even a three—though with the noise and the encroaching walls, it took several attempts. They all seemed to make at least one basket. And still the two walls continued on, getting closer and closer now.

"This is useless," Lab said. "We did shooting two days ago. He wouldn't repeat it."

Peño tried to think. What else did they need? What else was there? Cash sprinted for the bleachers and grabbed one end, trying to heave it off the wall.

"Help!" he shouted.

The team scrambled into action, and it took all of them together to swing the bleachers out. Peño's dad had once told him that they were welded together *inside* the gym, and judging by the deep ruts in the hardwood, they had probably never moved since. When the bleachers were far enough off the wall, Peño ran to the other side and pushed, driving his legs forward like tank treads.

"Turn it sideways!" Rain shouted. "On three. One . . . two . . . pull!"

They were just in time. They slid the bleachers between the two walls, and Peño slumped, exhausted. No one spoke as the walls steadily closed in on the bleachers like huge, gaping jaws.

The bleachers are made of solid steel, he thought. *It could work.*

Once again, he was wrong. With an awful screech of metal, the bleachers began to fold under the pressure—driving the ends downward and buckling the middle into an inverted U.

Peño's heart raced. He ran to where the front doors once stood, feeling desperately to see if they were just invisible. But he felt only the dappled surface of the concrete.

He beat his fists against the wall.

"Rolabi!" he cried. "Help us! Someone!"

No one answered.

"Look!" Cash shouted.

Peño turned and saw the orb floating twenty or thirty feet overhead, as if mocking them. He could feel the chill in his bones that the orb always brought, but today it was too late, too far away.

"Great timing," Peño said.

"Someone can get out of here!" Twig said. "You vanish, remember?"

"Only for people that haven't gotten the orb yet," Reggie said. "It will only work for them."

Peño knew that was him and Lab, and, without thinking, he turned to his little brother. Lab stared back at him numbly. What if only one of them could escape? Peño narrowed his eyes.

It was going to be Lab.

"Get up on the bleachers!" Lab said.

There was nothing else to do. Peño scrambled onto the bleachers, pulling himself up the folding steel toward the arch-shaped bend that was being pushed steadily upward by the walls. The steel was sticky with old soda stains, and Peño grabbed and pulled and pushed the players ahead of him to help them up. When he reached the top of the buckling steel structure, Lab stretched for the orb.

They were still well short—it was some fifteen or twenty feet overhead.

Peño turned to the walls. They signified the end of the Badgers, and they were coming quickly. He started shaking. It had all been for nothing.

The mountain. The shadows. They had worked so hard, and, in the end, it was just to be killed. He felt defeated, and he turned to Lab.

Their eyes met, but they said nothing.

Then Devon made one last move. He dropped onto all fours, bracing his feet against a buckling steel bench and gripping another bench with his strong fingers.

"Come on!" he shouted. "Make a pyramid!"

There was no time to argue. Twig, A-Wall, Big John, and Reggie dropped down beside him, forming an uneven base. Rain, Jerome, and Vin climbed on next, wavering and clutching onto shoulders. Only Lab and Peño were left, and they climbed to the top, grabbing each other's hands from either side to pull themselves up. Peño dug his sneakers into the backs of his teammates, having no other choice, but no one cried out or even complained. Peño and Lab finally reached the top, holding on to each other's arms for balance.

Their eyes met again, and they both looked up at the orb. It was still ten feet up. Even Lab couldn't reach it—at least, not without a little help. Luckily, his big brother was there.

Peño crouched and linked his hands for a foothold. "On my count."

Lab scowled. "Peño, we didn't even talk about it—"

Peño shook his head. "Don't argue with me. Don't even think for a moment I'm leaving you. Now . . ."

Lab's eyes filled with tears. Peño wanted to hug him. But there was no time. Whatever else happened now, he was going to save his little brother.

"I can't just leave you either," Lab choked out.

"I'll be fine! Now, use those extra three inches and jump!"

"Peño—"

"One . . . two . . . three!" Peño shouted. "Go!"

Lab put his shoe on Peño's hands and jumped. Peño pushed through his knees with all his strength, straightening his legs and heaving his brother into the air. Time seemed to slow again. Then Lab's fingers closed on the orb, and he was gone. Peño smiled, not even looking around. The walls didn't matter now. At least Lab was safe. And with that, the walls began to slide backward.

"Badgerssssss!" Peño cried, pumping his fist overhead.

"Badgers!" the others shouted with him.

Peño climbed off and helped the others up. Laughs and cheers rose from the group as the walls pushed back, revealing the devastation they had wrought. But Fairwood wasn't devastated for long.

The bleachers straightened back in place. The shattered backboards reformed in brilliant swirls of glass like little galaxies. The pulp that was the two benches became whole again, as did the tattered banners, and even the team's bags. The gym wasn't just remade. It was all new. Polished. Fresh.

It was like the Fairwood of old, the one he imagined, when West Bottom teams weren't stuck in disrepair. He wondered if they could fill this gym with new banners. He imagined putting one on the north wall and smiled.

"Nice toss," Rain said, walking over.

Peño gave him props. "It's the giant muscles. Where do you think my bro is?"

Just then Lab reappeared, and Peño checked him over and wrapped him in a hug.

"What did you see?" Rain asked.

Lab glanced at him. "The future."

"And?" Peño asked quietly.

"We'll face it together," Lab whispered.

Peño hugged him again, and he felt his eyes well with unexpected tears. The orb returned, smaller now, waiting for one more. Peño finally pulled back, gripping his little brother's face.

"Is the boat floating?" he asked.

Lab's eyes widened. Then he just nodded. "It's floating."

Peño felt a great weight lifting . . . one he hadn't even known was there.

Now you are ready. The road awaits.

The road to what? he thought.

Does it matter?

Peño thought about that. "No," he murmured. "I guess it doesn't."

THE DARK ROOM

*To find the real leader,
search where the fight is hardest.*

WIZENARD ⟨3⟩ PROVERB

PEÑO TOOK OUT his ball the next morning, staring at it thoughtfully.
He was sitting on the home bench with Lab, watching Reggie and Twig
warm up. No one else had arrived at practice yet.

"Last one," Peño said, strangely sad to realize his morning routine was
about to change. "Been a nutty ten days."

"Went by fast," Lab agreed.

Peño tried to remember the first day, before Rolabi had walked in.
"Everything seemed a lot simpler ten days ago."

"Yeah. But I don't miss it," Lab said.

Peño glanced at his little brother. He had decided not to press him
on anything else. He simply told Lab that he was available to talk anytime—no judgments, no consequences. But Lab had helped with dinner
last night for the first time ever, and Peño had caught him holding their
mother's photo by the mantel. Something had changed for him. A wall
had come down.

"I miss Mama," Lab said suddenly.

Peño smiled. "You said the word."

"Yeah. Think it's about time. What do you think she'd say about all this?" Lab gestured vaguely to the gym.

Peño thought about that. "She'd say we should go out and kick some butt this year."

"That doesn't sound like her at all," Lab said.

"I know. But that's what I'm saying. And I'm the boss now."

Lab laughed and pushed him, and Peño tousled his hair and stood up, stretching.

"You gonna start cooking more often?" Peño asked.

Lab snorted. "If we want to live through the season, I better."

They went to warm up together. Peño had changed his routine. He used to shoot from the top of the key and work on driving solely from there. But he saw now that he had been limiting himself. So he took corner threes, and worked on posting up, and cut in and out before shooting to free up space. His shots didn't all go in. Most missed. But he returned to the same spots to try again.

Even as he worked, Peño saw Lab hitting his shots with regularity. He saw Rain come in and throw down a dunk. He knew that they were pulling ahead of him. For all his efforts, for all his growth, Peño was still being left behind. He felt a chill settle over him again. A hard truth.

"Gather round." Rolabi had arrived. "All but one of you have caught the orb. Why?"

Peño shifted. He was the last one, and everyone knew it. But somehow, he didn't feel that it was a race. He didn't regret his decision yesterday one bit. He was strangely fine being the last.

"Because . . . you told us to?" Vin said as they formed a semicircle.

Rolabi turned to him. "But why? What did you find?"

"Our fears," Reggie murmured.

Rolabi nodded, turning to the row of banners that hung on the north wall. "If one thing will stop you in life, it is that. To win, we must defeat our fears. For basketball . . . for everything."

"But . . . we did, right?" Big John asked.

"Fear is not so easily beaten," Rolabi said. "It will return. You must be ready. We have much to work on before the season begins. For today, we will review what we have learned so far."

There was a sudden scratching.

"Twig, you know the drill," Rolabi said, reaching into his bag.

He began to set up another obstacle course. Kallo returned. So did the shadows. Rolabi dumped out pads and helmets. Reminders of the whole training camp soon collected on the hardwood.

"In a line, please," Rolabi said. "We'll start with the free-throw circuit. We will run laps until someone hits. Once through that, we will watch the daisy for movement. We'll work on getting past Kallo and then strap up the pads for a defensive drill. After that, we will run the Spotlight Offense in the dark with a glowing ball, and then against our shadow defenders. Following that, we will run a circuit with our weaker hands. Finally, we will shoot to end the day and solve another little puzzle."

"Is there going to be weird stuff happening?" Vin asked.

Rolabi looked at him. "Weird stuff?"

"Never mind," Vin muttered.

Peño started the drill. It was harder than anything he had done so far—the challenges from previous practices all came back. He tried to work with a missing hand, crawled out from beneath Kallo, fought with his annoying shadow, missed shot after shot after shot. He poured sweat. His legs burned. He pushed and pushed and finally slid to a halt. The orb was floating in front of him. Peño took a deep breath.

"Just you and me, huh?" he said.

"Get it, Peño!" Vin called.

Peño made his move. But it wasn't random this time—he predicted the orb's reactions. He used his surroundings. He cornered it and closed in on it, and finally, with a burst of effort, he pounced on it in midair, clutching the seeping black liquid to his chest like a trophy. And then Fairwood vanished.

He was standing on a concrete floor. Everything else was open.

"Hello?" he called. "Professor Rolabi?"

He turned in a slow circle. There were no walls, no ceiling, just darkness on all sides, and a chill in the air—one he knew well.

"Peño?" a familiar voice asked.

He whirled around and saw Rain. Sort of. Rain was older—maybe in his twenties. He was dressed in expensive clothing, with a diamond earring, gold chain, expensive watch.

Rain lowered a cell phone from his ear. "Is that you?"

"Yeah, of course," Peño said, running over. "How did you get here? You look older."

Rain snorted. "Me? Man, I barely recognized you. How are things?"

Peño looked down at himself. He was dressed in plain khakis and a green golf shirt, and he had a paunch sticking out over his belt. His shoes were dirty and scuffed, his watch cracked. He felt his face and found a thick mustache, a heavy brow, and bags under his eyes.

"What do you mean?" Peño whispered. "We . . . how long has it been?"

"Must be ten years," Rain said, shooting him a lopsided grin. "Been crazy. Two titles, as you know. Lots going on. It's good to pop home for a bit . . . I guess." He laughed. "Place is still a dump. No wonder Lab won't come back here."

"Lab . . ." Peño said.

Scenes started to play behind Rain as though projected on a giant screen. Lab was older too, and playing in the DBL. Peño saw him hoisting the championship trophy. He saw screaming fans. He saw his father, stooped but beaming, watching from the bleachers. Rain was there too; he and Lab were on the same team. Peño slowly backed away.

"I wanted to play . . ." he whispered.

"Nah," Rain said. "You wanted to keep up. You just didn't have it, man. We can't all get it, right? You knew that. But we'll see you around. Come to a game sometime. I can get you tickets." His phone rang, and he picked it up and laughed. "What's it like? Same old. Sad."

And then Rain vanished. The whole team was around him now. His family too. His mom was standing there, looking healthy again. Happy. His eyes welled. But whenever Peño moved toward them, they all slid away. Peño fell on his knees, tears streaming now.

"Please, come back," he whispered.

"You aren't pushing them away, you know."

Peño looked behind him and spotted Rolabi standing outside the circle of family and teammates. "Let me out of here. Please," said Peño.

"You brought us here," Rolabi said calmly. "Not me. You brought them all here."

"I wish I didn't. Now, how do I leave?"

"Do you know where you are?" Rolabi asked.

Peño looked around. He felt the chill in the air. He saw the waiting faces.

"My fears."

"Very good. Your deepest fears. In this room, everything else is seeded and grown."

"But I don't understand."

"What is your deepest fear, Carlos Juarez? Why are these people here?"

Peño looked around at his mom and his brother and the team. He thought of them fading into the distance every time he moved toward them. He thought of saying goodbye to his mom.

"I can't keep up with them," he whispered.

"But why are you afraid?"

Peño hesitated. "I . . . I'm afraid of being left behind."

The words echoed through the room and lingered. The people around him nodded, as if confirming the theory. He wasn't good enough for any of them. He was going to be left behind.

"She seemed like a wonderful lady. We all process loss differently."

"My brother . . ."

"Lab hid from his sadness, so it began to consume him. It changed his sense of his own value. He felt worthless. He felt like he would let people down."

Peño nodded. "I know."

"And you?"

Peño stared at the ghostly image of his mother. "That was the first time someone left me. I tried to make up for it. But I felt like it would always happen. Like I would always be left behind."

"And you might be."

"But I thought you said I was a leader," Peño whispered.

"You are a leader, Peño. But that doesn't mean you must lead from the front."

"I want to be a pro," Peño managed. "I want to go with Rain and Lab."

"They might make it; they might not. You might make it; you might not. That isn't the point."

"What is?" Peño asked.

"Wherever you go, there you are. Your path is your own. If you race the world, you will lose. If you race your brother, you will let him down— and yourself. The same goes for Rain. Look."

Peño turned around. A thousand images flashed around him. He saw Rain staring at a crumpled note, tears leaking onto the paper. He saw Twig slouched in front of the bathroom mirror, dejected, and Reggie looking at old photos in the darkness of his bedroom. He saw Big John crying in his room, afraid, and Vin covering a fresh bruise with makeup, and A-Wall sleeping on the bare floor in a run-down house. He saw . . . pain.

"If you build people up so high that you cannot see their faults, then you cannot help them."

Rolabi laid a hand on his shoulder.

"Stop running after everyone, Peño. You are a leader. If you help the others get to the finish line, you won't care if you are with them. Then, and only then, will you win your race."

Peño felt his eyes well up with new tears. "I won't play in the DBL, will I?"

"I don't know. But if that is your only goal in life, then you have forgotten to live." Rolabi turned Peño to face him. "Be a great baller, Peño," he said quietly. "Be a better person."

Peño nodded. "I think we can go."

"I agree."

Peño was suddenly back in the gym, surrounded by his teammates. The obstacle course was gone, and Rolabi was standing in front of them.

Lab stepped over and gave Peño props. "Good, bro?"

"All good, man."

"So the building is alive . . ." Reggie was saying.

Twig grinned. "I don't know. It did try to eat us."

The team burst into laughter.

"Twig telling jokes," Peño said, shaking his head. "What's next?"

He started beatboxing.

"Camp is almost done
We probably still got to run
Putting Champs on a banner
The quiet over clamor
Peño waits to watch
Cheers and stops
He wanted rhymes with 'Badger'
But the words didn't matter

Ball is roads and ramps
No more time for lusses
Only time for champs."

Everyone cheered and closed in on Peño, shaking his shoulders and jumping madly.

Rolabi picked up his purse and headed for the doors.

"I thought you said we still have a puzzle to solve?" Rain called after him.

"You do," Rolabi said. "One for each of you. And by the way, welcome to the Badgers."

While everyone cheered, Peño thought about the puzzle as he went to change his shoes. What else was there? Around him, players fell into easy conversation, and Peño noticed that Cash was talking, and that Twig and Reggie were together on the far bench. For once, the Badgers looked like a real team.

He couldn't wait for the season to start.

As they each finished getting changed, the players waited for one another. Peño sat on the bench until his brother was done—unsurprisingly, Lab was last to be ready—and then they all stood up together and started for the doors.

A question of Rolabi's arose in Peño's mind: Where was the place he was most afraid to be? Peño knew the answer now: *Last.* Exactly where he had been, the last one to catch the orb. The place where he could easily be left behind.

But maybe Rolabi was right. Last was where Peño was supposed to be. He could lead the team from there. After all, someone had to *push.*

As the team came to the doors, Rain stepped out first and held one open. Peño waited, letting everyone else go through. He checked over Fairwood, smiled, and flicked off the lights.

He walked out last of all—only when he was sure that no one was left behind.

BOOK FIVE

LAB

LAZY DOG

There is only one critic who matters.

✧ WIZENARD ◇33◇ PROVERB ✧

LAB STOOD ON the threshold for a moment, uncertain. He sensed something in there. A feeling. He had been in Fairwood a million times, of course. He knew every inch, every stain and dent and stink. But this was different. A shift in the air. Salt instead of sour. Crisp cold instead of humid must.

Lab's eyes adjusted to the lighting, and the gym took form. Waiting nets. The silhouette of his brother breathing it in with arms splayed. Lab scanned the gym, looking for changes, but other than Reggie and Twig, it was empty. He was imagining things, or daydreaming, maybe. Of course he was; it was early, and he was tired, and he hadn't slept much last night, as usual.

Lab sighed and followed his brother inside. "It's so early," he said, rubbing his sleep-crusted eyes.

Lab wasn't a morning person. That had always been Peño's specialty— he woke Lab up; he packed his duffel bag; he made his breakfast. He basically did everything that *she* used to do. *She.* Even the pronoun made his stomach turn. It was all he could manage even in the privacy of his own thoughts. No name. No relation. Just a *she*. The word brought flashes. Smells. Soil from her attempted gardens. Her cinnamon candles burning from the living room—she made them herself to "sweeten up the place." He pushed them away. He did that daily—compacting and hiding the memories. Hourly. Sometimes by the minute. He pushed the memories back and back, and where they went, he didn't know and didn't care. Lab just hoped he never found them again.

"It's ball time," Peño said, basically skipping to the bench. "It's never too early."

"Debatable," Lab said.

"It's going to be a big year, Lab. Things are going to change."

"You mean you're going to grow?" Lab asked.

"Shut up."

They plopped onto the home bench, and Lab glanced at Reggie and Twig. They were *always* the first ones to arrive in the morning: a bench player and a bust.

"Reggie," Peño said, giving him props. "What up, brother?"

"Ready to go," Reggie said. "Same old."

Same old is right, Lab mused. He stared miserably at the scratched, worn-out court. He'd shoveled down some cornmeal mush that morning, and it was sitting in his stomach like a brick.

He pulled out his kicks. They smelled worse than Fairwood. He'd left his bag in the closet since last season ended, and something was growing in there. Peño looked at them, and his fingers twitched.

"Don't touch my shoes," Lab said.

"Dad saved up for like six months to get us those—"

"They still work fine."

Peño scowled. "They smell like two dead cats."

"You got problems."

Lab laced them up, yawning and stretching out his calves. His dad *had* worked a long time for the shoes. He worked a long time for everything, made little, and didn't complain. His dad was a digger at a sprawling gravel pit in the south end—the former industrial district. He had always worked long hours, but now that *she* was gone, his shifts were longer. Twelve hours . . . fourteen . . . twenty. Sometimes he barely slept.

Lab watched his dad sometimes when he passed out on the couch. He looked a lot like Peño—short and strong—but with cheeks leathered by the sun and hard, calloused hands. It made Lab's heart ache, watching as he slept with his clothes on, still dirty, and then woke and went back to work. All that, and still the family struggled. Lab looked down at his own hands. Soft and slender and barely worked.

I could be helping, he thought with a familiar pang of guilt.

His dad would never allow it. Peño and Lab had almost flunked out of school—and in the Bottom, there were no second chances. Their dad had been enraged. Lab had never seen him so furious. He said that he worked so they could go to school and play ball and leave this place.

And then take him with me, Lab thought. *He deserves that. He deserves everything.*

The gym doors swung open, and Lab looked up and sighed. Jerome and Big John strolled in, which meant it was about to get loud. Big John was the noisiest person Lab had ever met: he was like an obnoxious radio DJ who never took a break.

"What up, boys!" he called, his voice echoing around Fairwood like a foghorn.

The doors opened again, and sunlight burst through. A billion specks of dust spiraled in the glare. It was like sitting in a snow globe or beneath a clear night sky. Lab watched the sparkles dance around, smiling despite himself at the Bottom's only true star-scape.

"The Rain Maker!" Big John called, putting a pudgy hand to his mouth.

Peño grabbed his ball and stepped out on the court, dribbling through his legs with dizzying speed. Lab's brother had good handles, there was no doubt, but his shot was a different story.

"You got a rhyme for the season yet?" Jerome asked.

Lab groaned. Peño considered himself an amateur rapper, but he was awful. Deep down, Lab knew it was probably more than that. Peño had taken the habit up after *it* had happened. She used to sing every day, leaving for work, gathered around the table, putting them both to bed. Maybe Peño thought the house was too quiet. Maybe he really did just take to music like she did.

But for Lab, it was only another reminder. He couldn't bring himself to cheer Peño on.

"You ain't ready for it," Peño said.

"No, we aren't," Lab said.

"Pugh, pugh, che," Big John said, "pugh, pugh, che, pugh, che, pugh, che—"

"Stop," Lab moaned.

Jerome started dribbling, trying to stay in rhythm with Big John's beat.

Lab rubbed his temples. "I should have stayed in bed."

Peño just grinned and started rapping, throwing out yet another subpar verse—including a flubbed rhyme for *Badgers*. Lab snorted and shook his head. Peño had been working on that word for two years to no avail.

"Another classic," he called after him.

A tinge of guilt arrived. He didn't need to be a jerk about it. Why did it make him angry sometimes—just because of the memories? A small part of him wondered if it was jealousy.

Peño got her love for music. He got a part of her. What did Lab get?

Lab stood up, swinging his arms to loosen up, chasing the thoughts away. Now that he was here and sort of awake, he was ready for some ball. There was no better sound in the world than the swish of the net. Peño threw him a pass, and Lab took a quick jumper. *Clank.*

"You shoot like Grandma," Peño said.

"You look like Grandma," Lab retorted. "Except I think she's taller."

"Mom said I would be the tallest eventually," Peño said. "I'm just a slow starter."

Lab felt the word wash over him. Freeze his muscles. Turn his stomach. *Mom. Mama.* It was like dunking his head in ice water every time, stabbing and harsh and still raw.

"Yeah," he whispered.

He moved to the hoop, trying to put it from his mind. He always attacked easily—Freddy called him a "downhill scorer." Lab was the second-highest scorer on the team and the best corner three-point shooter. If he could only get more of the ball, he knew he could do more—but that was tough with Rain on the team. Lab hoped the new coach was going to mix up their offense. The Badgers needed more movement. More sharing. It couldn't be all Rain.

Freddy arrived last with the new kid . . . though *kid* was a real stretch.

The guy was jacked. For once, Freddy hadn't been exaggerating when he said he'd found something promising. As long as this kid Devon wasn't secretly thirty, he could be a real find. Lab wandered over to introduce himself.

Lab could immediately sense that he was nervous. Devon had pale brown skin, like blond oak, and a shaved head, his lip marked by a scar. His eyes were dark umber brown, big and glassy, and fixed on his shoes.

"Where you from?" Lab asked. "I never seen you at school before. Hard to miss."

Devon hesitated. "Homeschooled."

"Homeschooled!" Peño said. "Crazy. My pops barely wants me there *after* school."

Lab snorted. That was true enough. He usually told them to go do extra schoolwork or help seniors or do anything but sit around. The man didn't know what it meant to rest. Peño was just like him, always cooking or cleaning or shooting around out back. Lab was the outlier now.

Lab tried to push the thought away, but he was too late. A memory blossomed—Lab tucked into the nook of her arm as she sung to him. He remembered pieces of the song: teachers on an island, a cup of pure gold. She ran her fingers through his long hair, pulling out a twig.

"My little wild boy," she whispered.

Lab felt the pressure behind his eyes and drove it back. He pushed the memory down and down until he felt nothing. Why did he have to keep seeing her? Why couldn't he just forget her? How did Peño do it? How did he and their dad keep going as though everything were fine? Did they care less? *Love* her less?

He was yanked back to the present as the lights crackled violently and went out. The doors erupted inward under a powerful gust of wind, and the gym filled with angry howling. The draft tore at his baggy shirt and shorts and sent his overlong hair pounding into his eyes. He whirled away from the blast, wondering how a storm could have descended so quickly.

At last, the wind settled, and Lab turned back to the doorway. A shadow was blotting out the light. It wasn't touching the doors, and yet they remained wide-open even in the still air. The shadow ducked under the door frame and walked inside, straightening as soon as it was through and revealing itself as a man—the new coach, Lab assumed. He was tall, smartly dressed, and perhaps in his sixties, judging by his salt-and-pepper hair. Wrinkles and scars lined the warm brown skin on his face, but all his features paled beneath two radiant eyes, greener than anything Lab had ever seen. The man looked at him.

Where did you put all those memories?

Lab saw something flash in the coach's eyes—a still lake. A boat. Lab blinked, and the image was gone, lost in that brilliant green. He swallowed, fighting back the nervousness in his belly. He was daydreaming again, clearly.

Freddy hurried out, leaving the team alone with the new coach, who introduced himself as Professor Rolabi. His eyes darted from one face to the next like he was reading something on their foreheads. Lab had never heard such an enveloping silence.

Finally, Rolabi reached into his jacket and pulled out a piece of folded paper. "I will need everyone to sign this before we can proceed," he said.

When the contract came to Lab, he took it and frowned.

I, JAVI "LAB" JUAREZ, HEREBY AGREE TO LEARN FROM PROFESSOR ROLABI WIZENARD THE NATURE OF ALL THINGS.

BOUND BY THE LAWS THAT GOVERN THE KINGDOM OF GRANITY · THIS CONTRACT IS

SIGN HERE

"The Kingdom of Granity?" he whispered.

Something nagged at him about that name, but he couldn't place it, so he just signed and passed the document to his brother. Belatedly, Lab realized that there had been no other signatures. In fact, only his name was written on the contract, even though he had clearly seen multiple others sign it before him. He glanced over Peño's shoulder. The agreement now read: *I, Carlos "Peño" Juarez . . .*

Something clicked, like a puzzle piece rotating and locking into place. Their new coach was a street magician. Lab hadn't truly seen an image in his eyes—it was just hypnotism. Street magic was far from popular in Dren, but some poorer Bottom residents used illusions and tricky props to pick up extra pennies. Rolabi was just really good at it. Lab almost laughed.

He must have been tired; he had been about ready to believe in actual *magic*, of all things.

Twig signed last, and when he handed the contract back to Rolabi, the paper vanished. Lab snorted. Rolabi was certainly dedicated to his act. But why would Freddy hire a magician as their coach?

Because Rolabi tricked him too, he realized.

Lab would have to keep his guard up.

"What . . . Where did . . . ?" Twig managed.

"Gullible, right?" Lab said to Peño.

His brother was staring, slack-jawed.

And so are you, Lab thought, sighing inwardly.

Rolabi reached into his small medicine bag—right past his elbow. Lab had to admit: it was a good one. The paper trick had been clever too, not to mention the phony wind. But so what? He could afford good props. Lab folded his arms and smirked. At least *he* was too clever to be fooled by all this.

Then, without saying anything, Rolabi took out a basketball and threw it directly at Big John's head. The next ball flew toward Peño, who just barely managed to catch it. His brother straightened, staring at nothing, and Lab waved a hand in front of him. He didn't even flinch.

"Peño?" Lab whispered.

Something orange flashed in the corner of his eye, and Lab stuck his hands up just in time to catch his own ball, which was emblazoned with a blue *W*. He gasped. Fairwood had changed. The bleachers were now crammed with spectators—Lab saw his dad, and his teammates' families as well. Even his classmates from school were there. He scanned over the bleachers, waving awkwardly, confused. Then his hand paused in midair, fell to his side, trembled. There, right at the front of the bleachers, was Lab's mom. She had her favorite scarf on . . . a flowery, silken one her grandmother had left to her. It was tied loose as always and fell down over her shoulders with her dark hair. His breath caught at the sight of it. Her hair was full and thick again. It had grown back. Her eyes twinkled, no longer clouded and sunken.

Lab's knees buckled so suddenly that he fell into a crouch, catching himself with one hand and clinging to his ball with the other. He managed to stand and started toward her, dazed, reaching out for her. It was impossible for her to be here. She was gone.

"Ma . . . Mama?" he said, finding his voice. "Mama?"

She was standing up now, along with the crowd. As one, the rows of spectators turned and stared at the giant clock on the wall. Lab kept walking, ignoring everything else, even as players took shape around him like apparitions coming to life. He didn't care about them. He had to talk to her.

"Mama . . . how can you . . . how . . . ?" he whispered.

"Shoot it!" someone shouted.

His mother looked directly at him and screamed: "Take the shot!"

Lab glanced at the ball in his hand, bewildered. He turned to the clock: 3 . . . 2 . . .

He was surrounded by defenders. He looked frantically for someone to pass to, but he had no teammates. The spectators kept screaming. He whirled back to his mother, panicked.

"No, Mama, I can't—"

1 . . .

"Shoot!" she said.

Lab turned to the hoop, lifted the ball, and froze. He couldn't shoot.

His muscles seized at the pressure. His eyes welled with tears, knowing he had failed even before the buzzer sounded. Then, as one voice, the spectators started booing. Lab's teammates gathered around him, jeering along with the crowd. His dad was booing. His mom—booing him. It was too much. He turned helplessly in a circle, tears streaming down his cheeks.

Peño was the closest to him. "You blew it," Peño said. "You're a failure, Lab."

The booing grew louder, and Lab jumped back as a drink came splashing on the court.

"I didn't do anything," Lab protested. "I never said I was going to do anything. Mama!"

"You're a bust," Rain said, walking toward him. "We all saw it. You let us all down."

"But . . ." Lab said, trying to reach around his brother for his mom. "Wait!"

She was fading into mist.

"Mama!" he screamed.

"Just get out of here," Peño said. "We don't have room on this team for a failure. I don't need one as a brother either. Why don't you hit the road? We're better off without you, *bro*."

Lab felt tears dripping off his chin. He hadn't asked for the pressure of the last shot. He had worked so hard to *avoid* it. This moment was why. He knew he would choke. Then he noticed someone standing behind the team, watching silently, unaffected by the roaring wave of boos and hisses: Rolabi Wizenard.

"Interesting," he said. "That will be all today. I will see you here tomorrow."

The crowd vanished, and Lab was standing among his teammates, who all seemed lost in their thoughts.

Lab scanned the empty corners of the gym. "Mama . . ." he whispered.

"What time?" Peño called to the professor.

Rolabi headed for the doors, which crashed inward with another freezing gust of wind. Rolabi strolled right through them, and they abruptly slammed shut.

Peño ran after the coach. He pushed the doors open, hurrying out into the morning sun.

"Do we keep the balls?" he shouted. "What . . . Professor?"

Rolabi was already gone.

TRICKS OF THE TRADE

2

Winning is an empty cup.
Fill it with work, struggle, and compassion.

WIZENARD 21 PROVERB

THE NEXT MORNING, Lab watched his brother pause in front of Fairwood's doors, shifting uneasily, clearly nervous to go inside. He held back as well. He was exhausted. Even now, he kept seeing her every time he closed his eyes. The buzzer kept sounding, and he watched her boo and jeer.

He had let her down again. Of course he had.

Sitting outside the room, white walls, hushed voices. What was happening? Should he go in? No . . . he needed to stay in the hall, where everything was easier. He needed to pretend it was all right. That everything was normal. Why didn't he say goodbye?

Mama . . .

Lab shoved it all away, piling the memories even deeper than before, pushing them back and back and trying to think of anything else but her. Whatever Rolabi had done to him yesterday, it was a cruel trick. Lab had barely been able to eat last night, and he was still sitting on the couch when his father had come home around midnight. He had laid a calloused hand on Lab's shoulder, and the dust had left an imprint on his T-shirt, gray and ghostlike.

"You okay?" he asked.

"Yeah," Lab whispered, like the liar he was.

If he just kept saying he was okay, maybe he would believe it too.

Lab pulled his hands down his face, trying to come back to the present. He needed to play some ball. Peño was still staring at the green double doors.

"What are you doing?" Lab asked finally.

He wanted Peño to say something about yesterday. *He* wanted to say something—to tell Peño about the vision. But it was all too ridiculous. It was just a trick. A daydream. A stray memory that kept sneaking back in. Lab had no idea why Freddy had hired a magician to be their coach, but he wasn't going to fall for the hoax.

Still, it would have been nice if Peño admitted that he had seen something.

"Nothing," Peño said defensively.

"Well, you're not going inside," Lab said. "Are you afraid?"

Peño turned to him, furrowing his thick black eyebrows. They looked like the scrunchies she used to wear to work. Lab was sure his brother wanted to say something. He could read the doubt in his eyes. He had heard him starting constantly in his sleep, and even a croaking, whispered "I'm here . . ."

They launched into an argument. Sometimes it felt like they had been fighting since the day they could both talk—arguing over chores and bedtimes and school and just about everything imaginable. Peño was as stubborn as a brick wall.

"Okay, then go ahead," Peño said finally, gesturing to the door.

Lab grabbed a handle. "Fine. Coward."

Peño predictably flushed and took the other one. "We'll do it at the same time, then, if it makes you feel better."

"Fine. But I'll walk in by myself. I don't need you."

"On three?" Peño said.

Lab sighed. "On three."

"One . . . two . . . three!"

They simultaneously pulled open the double doors and stepped back. After a moment, they glanced at each other and peered inside. Reggie stood beside the bench, stretching alone. He looked at the brothers with a raised eyebrow. Immediately, Peño and Lab both straightened up and raced to the bench.

Lab plunked himself down and opened his bag. As always, Peño had packed him a water bottle and a granola bar, as well as a fresh towel—though their few remaining ones were getting threadbare and worn. Lab's shoes also looked suspiciously polished, and he caught a whiff of green apple and sighed. Peño must have cleaned them first thing in the morning.

He took them out, and the new basketball stared back at him. Lab eyed it suspiciously, then scowled. The ball wasn't magic. There was no such thing as *magic*. Peño and Lab had seen a lot of things in their lives, and none of it had been magical. They had seen her die. They had seen their dad work nonstop every day since. They had seen neighbors lost to violence—Elvin down the road had been killed just a few months ago. They saw their last grandparent, Grandma Juarez, growing sicker by the day in the squalor of a local nursing home. None of it was pleasant. None of it was hopeful.

With a hardening feeling in his stomach, Lab realized why Rolabi Wizenard made him so angry. If there was any magic in the world, it certainly didn't exist in the Bottom. He scooped up the ball, and nothing happened.

"Naturally," he muttered.

As he had guessed, yesterday had been a fluke. A trick.

He joined Peño, stopping on the corner of the three-point line. Lab had a somewhat unusual shooting form that Freddy had once tried to correct—his hands and feet were lined up almost parallel—but it worked for him, so Freddy had eventually given up. Well, it usually worked.

The shot clanged out, bouncing toward the bleachers, and Lab hurried after it.

Lab glanced under the bleachers as he scooped up the ball. Dust bunnies had multiplied into a carpet, building up in some spots like anchored clouds. Moldy popcorn lay sprinkled in their midst, along with soda cans, granola bar wrappers, and an assortment of other garbage that had fallen from above. The steel benches themselves were rusting from the spilled drinks—showing spots of flaking auburn.

"They need to burn this place down," Lab said, shaking his head in disgust.

"I guess this Rolabi guy isn't worried about being on time," Rain said.

"Maybe he isn't coming," Lab said, rejoining the team and firing another three.

"Or maybe he's already here."

Lab lurched as he came back down again. The voice had cut through the air from behind him, and Lab slowly turned around. Rolabi Wizenard was sitting on the bleachers. But that was impossible. Lab had just been there. He knew they had been empty.

It's just a trick, Lab reminded himself. *He's trying to scare you.*

"Put the balls away," Rolabi said.

It took the coach five steps to reach center court, and Lab noticed that the guys were racing back to their bags. He pointedly walked, not joining the flat-out sprint that his older brother had suddenly adopted. Lab was not going to be intimidated by magic tricks, and he returned to the group last of all, hovering at the edge and folding his arms. Rolabi's piercing eyes fell on him.

Where are all those memories going?

Stay out of my head, he thought, closing his eyes. *This isn't real!*

The voice fell silent.

I guess I told him, Lab thought smugly.

But when he opened his eyes, Lab was alone in a long white corridor.

He knew the place. He knew the yellowed wallpaper peeling where it met the ceiling. The annoyingly cheerful oil paintings of flowers and grassy hills. The worn tiled floor that smelled like bleach.

There were some old metal chairs in the hallway. He knew them. He hated them.

"No," he whispered.

A door flew open beside him, and he turned to see a crisp white bed. A woman lying there.

"Let me out of here!" he shrieked. "Rolabi!"

He stepped back and found himself standing in a wooden rowboat. Water splashed through the hospital, and the walls receded until the boat was outdoors, floating on a still turquoise lake ringed by mountains. Lab stumbled and fell, landing hard in a shallow puddle at the base of the boat. He looked around and tried to steady his breathing.

The boat was slowly filling with water.

Lab cried out and tried to find the leak, hands scrambling and splashing through the cold water. But he couldn't find the source, and the water continued to trickle inside. He leaned back, on his knees now, and felt the water pool around him with icy fingers.

You are the one who made the leak.

The voice seemed to come from everywhere and nowhere.

"Where am I?" Lab whispered.

You tell me. You are the one making this place. Yours is strong.

"My what?"

There was no response.

"What!" he shouted.

Lab blinked. The gym had returned. He gasped, realizing that the team had split up on either side of a jump ball. The starters were all behind Twig, waiting for the tip.

"Where . . . How—" he said.

"You playing?" Jerome asked, giving him a strange look.

Lab hesitated, then nodded, trying to regain his bearings. "Yeah."

He lined up next to Jerome, who played small forward behind him during the season. Jerome was quick and about the same height as Lab— maybe an inch taller with his 'fro. He also had an overlarge forehead that was dangerous for head butts. Lab had accidentally collided with him once and seen stars for days.

"You look a little pale," Jerome said.

"Didn't sleep much," Lab muttered.

Jerome nodded. "I hear you. Everything's crazy, man."

"Have you seen something?" Lab asked.

"I seen lots of things."

Big John won the tip, and Lab jogged back on defense, trailing Jerome.

"What did you see?" Lab asked.

Jerome glanced back at him. "Things I hoped I wouldn't have to see again."

Lab sensed a finality to the conversation. Jerome didn't want to talk about the details, and why should he? Lab didn't want to talk about what he had seen either. He loosely tracked Jerome with a free hand, keeping an eye on the ball. Jerome did a little fake to the corner and back, but Lab wasn't playing tight, so the quick move accomplished nothing, and they settled in to wait for the ball.

Vin went the other way instead, passing to Reggie. Predictably, Rain got the steal and sprinted down the court alone. The rest of the team chased, but Lab didn't bother. He let Jerome go and waited on defense, still eyeing Rolabi. Lab had seen the hospital bed. The awful, unforgettable chairs. How could those be tricks? How could Rolabi even know about those things?

Now you are asking the right questions, the deep voice said.

Lab thought about that. The only one who remembered those chairs vividly enough to re-create them in such brutal detail was him. Not even Peño could do that. Had Lab somehow summoned that image for himself?

Lab got into position as the bench team attacked again, and soon he surrendered a layup to Jerome. He scowled. He had guessed wrong on the drive, overstretching, and been beaten cleanly to the middle. Lab ran up the court, then realized that Peño was struggling against a one-man press. It was like he had forgotten how to dribble. Lab watched as he barely made it past half and then drove directly into Vin's chest. Vin proceeded to strip the ball and score an easy layup.

"What are you doing, Peño?" Lab asked.

"Nothing," he said. "Just lost the ball. Get back and set a pick, why don't you?"

"I thought you had mad handles?" Lab said. "You look like Twig dribbling."

"Thanks," Twig said.

Lab sighed. Just what Twig needed: another shot to his confidence.

Peño made it up the court, though just barely, and Lab decided to make his move. He faked the cut to the net, causing Jerome to lose his balance, and then called for the pass. Rain was still looking lost on the far side, so Peño whipped the ball to Lab, who turned for the three.

"I thought you were supposed to be good," someone said.

Lab hesitated. An older man with closely cropped white hair and hard eyes was standing next to him, holding a clipboard. He was wearing a green bomber jacket embroidered with the logo of a college team that Lab liked. He scribbled a note on his clipboard.

"Who are you?" Lab said, frowning.

"Javi 'Lab' Juarez," the man said, continuing to write. "A lesser Rain Adams. Going nowhere."

Lab flushed. "But I haven't—"

"A waste of potential." The man flipped a page as though he had made a decision. "Disappointing."

Lab felt his cheeks burning. Did no one else see this man? Was this another illusion?

Jerome closed in on Lab, putting his hand up to block the shot, and the man turned to Jerome, apparently far more interested in Lab's backup. Flustered, Lab passed the ball back to his brother, and the man promptly vanished. Lab rubbed his eyes. He was seeing things. He had to be.

But more scouts appeared every time he touched the ball. They sighed or wrote notes or shook their heads. One scout called Lab "another Bottom Beggar." Lab took a few more shots, but he always missed badly and soon avoided the ball altogether. Still the scouts kept coming.

"Worse than his brother."

"His dad must be ashamed."

"Should get a job."

"Nothing good comes from the Bottom."

Finally, the professor strode onto the court. "That will be all for today."

"We aren't going to do any drills?" Peño asked.

Lab snorted. Only Peño would ask about drills after a scrimmage like that.

Rolabi put the ball away and proceeded to the bleachers, taking a seat on the lowest bench and checking his watch. Just then, the locker room door was torn open by a fearsome gust of wind. Lab stared at it, trying to think of something, *anything*, that could explain wind erupting from that windowless room. But he was running out of excuses, and he knew it. When he turned back, Rolabi was gone, the locker room door slammed shut, and silence descended.

"So . . . we're pretty set on our coach being a witch, right?" Big John said.

Lab rubbed his forehead. It was too much. It couldn't be real. It *couldn't*.

How long can you lie to yourself? a voice asked him.

This time the voice sounded suspiciously like his own.

"What are you, six?" Lab said, glaring at Big John. "There's no such thing as witches."

"Says who?" Big John said.

"Says everyone. Says physics and logic. I know they aren't your strong suit."

"Didn't you fail—" Vin started.

Lab scowled. "Does Peño tell everyone my business?"

He followed his brother to the bench, plunking himself down and chugging his last few drops of water—sour, brown, and smelling of sulfur. The white corridor flashed across his mind again. The stiff metal chairs. Why was he seeing them after so long? He had been trying to forget about them, about all of it, for three years now. Why wouldn't the memories fade?

He threw his shoes into his bag and zipped it up, barely listening to the others.

"This Rolabi dude is messed up, huh?" Jerome said to Lab, climbing to his feet.

"Yeah," Lab muttered. "He ain't the only one."

3

THE
LAST STRAW

Anger is just your mind telling you
to step away and breathe.

❖ WIZENARD ⟨15⟩ PROVERB ❖

LAB WISHED HE were still in bed. Peño had dragged him out that morning, even using the dreaded ear-pull at one point. It had been yet another long, restless night of questions Lab didn't want to answer. Why didn't he go into the room? Why did she have to leave them? Why did nothing feel the same since? The unanswered questions made the night feel heavy, the morning worse.

In his heart, Lab knew the visions weren't some magician's trickery. Perhaps they weren't even Rolabi's doing. Whatever they were, they were real, and tangible. And that made him even angrier. If magic was real, then it was useless. Why couldn't magic get his dad a better job? Help them eat better? Why couldn't it have saved *her*? Lab looked around at the dull cityscape packed with hovels, the factories spewing dead air beyond them. Why couldn't magic fix this place? If it existed, it was a cruel thing. And if it was in him, then wasn't he cruel too?

The morning was hot already, like most July days in the Bottom, and a sticky breeze swept across the parking lot. Lab was sick of it. The choking smog. The people wandering the streets fighting for scraps from dumpsters. He was sick of the fact that his own future was written all around him.

Why don't you fix that, Rolabi? Lab thought angrily. He kicked through a stray paper cup and grimaced as coffee spilled on his shoes.

Peño's mood this morning was just as sour. He and Lab had argued about magic and Rolabi and everything else for half the night. Peño believed the visions and the magic were real, same as Lab. But Lab refused to say so aloud—was perhaps unable to—and that seemed to drive Peño mad. He was still pestering him now.

"What is your problem?" Peño asked. "Why can't you admit that something is off?"

Lab gritted his teeth. Why couldn't Peño just drop it?

"Because that's not how the world works," Lab snapped. "It ain't magical, Peño. Sorry."

Lab grabbed the door. He needed to stop thinking about it—the visions and the memories and what they all meant. He just needed to get in there and play ball. That was why he was here—to get *away* from all that.

Peño grabbed his arm. "Is this about Mom?"

Lab flinched at the word. She had been *Mom* to Peño. *Mama* to Lab. He had said it as a baby and never lost the habit. The question made him even angrier. Of course it was about Mama. Everything was. Didn't Peño get that? Didn't he feel the same loss? He yanked his arm away.

"It's not about anything," he snarled.

"I miss her too—"

He couldn't, though. Not like Lab. Not every minute. Every second.

"And you saw her dying just like I did," Lab said hoarsely. "Wasn't it *magical?*"

He stormed inside, heading for the bench. Tears were threatening, and he preemptively wiped his face with his arm. The pain was still so fresh. It turned his stomach and sent bile creeping up his throat. Why did Peño have to bring it up? Why couldn't everyone just leave it?

Without pain, we cannot grow.

Go away! he thought.

Lab dropped onto the bench, ignoring everyone and pulling out his shoes. Distantly, he heard them talking about the phone number Rolabi had given, and their parents calling in. The conversation only made him feel worse. His dad couldn't have called—he had gotten home after midnight again, staggering with fatigue, his teeth stained black from the swirling dust in the gravel pits. Lab quickly tied his shoes and zipped up his bag.

Then he looked up and froze. "Not again," he murmured.

The gym was empty. A white screen stretched in front of him—the old kind, perched on a three-legged metal stand. On the bench beside Lab sat an ancient film projector, like the one his school used for presentations. He stared at it, confused. There was no film reel in it. No power cord. Lab looked around and yelped when he saw Rolabi sitting nearby, hands folded in his lap.

"Why do you have to do that?" Lab snapped.

"Do what?"

Lab scowled. "What is this? Another vision? Another annoying lesson?"

"Which teammate of yours do you think has the best life? Who is the happiest?"

"What?"

"Think about it. You don't seem to like yourself, so whose life would you prefer to take?"

Lab glared at him. Maybe if he played along, Rolabi would take him back to practice. He thought about his teammates. There were different options. Better talent. Better size. But then Lab considered what it'd be like to have money. Money for a cell phone and those self-tying shoes and a nice house with a real hoop outside.

Money for a doctor. Money to give his dad a break.

"Twig, I guess," Lab said. "His family does pretty well."

Rolabi nodded and fished a film reel out of his pocket. *Twig* was written on the side.

"Put it on," Rolabi instructed, pointing. "Just slide it there and press that white button."

Lab frowned and did as he was told. After he had attached the reel, he pressed the button, and the projector turned on, humming and vibrating and spinning. A grainy image appeared.

"What is this—"

"What you wanted," Rolabi said calmly. "Your pick for best life on the team."

Twig appeared in front of a mirror. The room was unfamiliar—it must have been his bathroom at home. Unstained counters, new sink. It was just what Lab had figured. But Twig was crying. Tears streamed down his face. His fingers went to his cheeks, first rubbing, then pinching, pulling.

"What . . ." Lab whispered. "What's he doing?"

"Watch."

Lab watched for a few minutes. He saw skin picked until it bled and more tears. The scene changed, and he saw Twig's father screaming at him, lecturing him, making the kid walk past shelf after shelf of polished trophies. He saw Twig crying alone in his darkened bedroom, slender hands over his cheeks, tears and blood and snot intermingled. He saw *pain*. Lab turned away, stomach roiling.

"How did you get that footage?" he whispered. "How can you know all that?"

"We all have a story, if you take the time to look."

"I . . . I didn't know."

"You didn't look."

Lab scowled. "But that's just one guy. Give me Vin, then. His dad runs a pawnshop."

Rolabi handed Lab another film reel, and Lab reluctantly popped it in. A second film started, just as grainy as the first. Rapid-fire images flashed by: Vin being pushed around in an empty classroom at school. Vin at a park at dusk, getting beaten up by an older boy, then hiding the bruises. Vin throwing up his dinner. Vin pacing, waiting up for his brothers. Vin stealing a cell phone from his father's store—

"Turn it off!" Lab demanded. "Why are you showing me this?"

"Because you felt alone."

Lab snorted. "So we're all miserable. Great. I feel much better now."

"Don't wish for other people's lives," Rolabi said. "Everyone has their struggles."

"What are you . . . a walking de-motivational poster?"

To Lab's surprise, Rolabi laughed. "I have heard something to that effect before."

"How are you doing this?" Lab asked, gesturing to the screen and the empty gym. "How does this work?"

"You brought us here. Your grana."

"Grana?"

"An energy. It arises from emotions, from the private experiences that make us human. It needs only an opportunity to be released, and then it can show us precisely what we need to see."

"I'm pretty sure you just made that word up."

"And yet you knew you created that white corridor. You created your own fears."

Lab looked away. He had suspected that, yes. Had he really been using something called grana?

"It still sounds made-up."

Rolabi smiled. "I suppose you would prefer if I called it magic?"

"There's no such thing as magic," Lab snapped.

He was suddenly back in the gym, and the whole team was staring at him.

"Is that so?" a deep voice asked.

Lab spun around to the source of the voice so quickly that he toppled off the bench. The rest of the team went along with him, collapsing into a pile of limbs and groans and complaints.

"If you don't believe in magic," Rolabi said, walking around the bench, "you need to get out more." His eyes fell on Lab, and there was a noticeable twinkle. "We will start with laps."

Lab scowled and shuffled into line.

"We will take free throws, one at a time," Rolabi said. "As soon as someone scores, you will stop running for the day. If you miss, the team runs five more laps."

They ran the five laps, and Peño stepped out of line, huffing like he was trying to blow up a balloon.

"I got this," Peño said.

Lab didn't argue. He could already feel the sweat beading on his forehead. Clearly, they all needed some cardio work. He looked up just as Peño was taking his free throw—and watched in disbelief as Peño heaved the ball right *over* the backboard. He had missed by ten feet at least.

"What kind of a shot was that?" Lab said.

Peño slowly turned back to the group. "I . . . I don't know."

"Five more laps," Rolabi said.

Lab frowned. Peño wasn't exactly the best free-throw shooter on the team, but he was far from the worst. And nobody was *that* bad. Peño must have seen something. Did that mean he could use grana too? He wondered if everyone was having visions and what they were about.

His eyes wandered to Twig and Vin. He could guess at theirs, at least.

"Umm . . ." A-Wall said.

Lab turned and froze. The team wasn't running, and it didn't take long to see why—the whole gym had leapt up on one side, bending and warping until the floor rose at a nearly 45-degree angle. Lab felt himself slipping back and grabbed on to A-Wall for support.

"It's . . . impossible," he breathed.

He wasn't alone this time. The whole team was scrambling and scraping as they tried not to fall backward.

Rolabi stood with his feet firmly planted right at center court, sharing the slope. "Begin," he said.

They started running. Lab felt his entire world, his understanding of it, changing with every twist of the gym. Valleys, staircases, and hurdles materialized from nothing. Every time Lab turned a corner, he was greeted with the impossible. He ran and climbed and jumped, and his legs burned, but he felt like it was his mind that was working.

Walls could change. Floors could warp. Everything around him was not stagnant.

This was proof of what Lab had suspected earlier, and it made him angrier still. If grana could change things so easily, even buildings, then why did the Bottom look the way it did? Why did people live in squalor? Why did people *die*?

Lab took another step and felt the floor dissolve beneath his feet. He tumbled into darkness and cried out, spinning, screaming all the while, and then he abruptly stopped, just barely keeping his footing.

"I used to ask myself those questions," Rolabi said, walking out of the darkness. There seemed to be no floors or ceiling or walls, yet both of them were standing. "When I was younger, I knew about grana. But I saw places like the Bottom and I wondered why they existed."

Lab bent over, feeling his breakfast coming up. "Not . . . cool . . ."

Rolabi gestured to the blackness around them, and buildings started popping up like mushroom caps. The ground beneath Lab's feet turned gray, then cracked, and garbage rolled in from the darkness like a pestilent flood. Rusted cars appeared, choking the streets. A sky formed—gray and dark and polluted. People too. They began to shuffle amid the growing city. They lay on the ground on street corners. They huddled in dank alleyways. Lab knew it well.

"My neighborhood—" he said.

"Look at your hands," Rolabi instructed.

Lab did. Silver light was coursing through them. He yelped and stepped back, watching as the light streamed through his body. It moved like blood, splitting and fragmenting and meeting in great arterial streams. There was darkness too, right at his core, black as night.

"Grana doesn't exist in buildings, Lab. Or cars. It lives in people." Rolabi turned to the cityscape. The cars and the buildings dulled, becoming shadows, but the people themselves grew brighter. Each became a silvery spot of light in the gloom. "It is inside them," he said quietly.

"What are you saying?" Lab asked, holding up a silvery hand.

"People die because they must. But they live the way they do because *humans* have distorted their own grana. The rich betray the poor. The strong, the weak. But they all have the power for more. They could change this. This is what they chose. They built it." He turned to Lab, pointing at the dark core. "I told you: Grana originates with your emotions. When they sour, so does the grana."

Rolabi took a step toward him. His eyes were blazing like flickering green fire.

"If you don't like what you see out there, *change it*. If we change our perspective, our emotional landscape, then the real world may just change with it. That is how we fix all this."

Lab cowered under the force of his gaze. "I'm a kid. I can't do anything."

"We will see about that."

Lab found himself back in line, his team around him, huffing and gasping for air.

"You gonna shoot, Lab?" A-Wall asked, prodding him with a finger.

Lab looked around and checked his hands for silver light. They were back to normal: walnut skin, freckles on the back, fingers soft and unworked. He cleared his throat and straightened, nodding.

"Yeah," he managed. "Sure."

Lab accepted the pass from Rolabi and walked slowly toward the net, trying to catch his breath. He kept seeing the silver pulses and those fiery eyes. Rolabi's words reverberated in his head.

Change it.

Lab pushed the thought away. Before anything else, he needed to make this shot. He dribbled and looked up at the rim, almost nervously. There was a plain hoop staring back at him. Taking another deep breath, Lab lifted the ball to shoot. Then a man appeared in front of him.

He had a thick beard spotted with scraps of food, including part of a chicken bone. His hair was long and tangled; his clothes, tattered. A round belly stuck out over his pants, which were held up with a frayed rope. The man smiled, and his teeth were like kernels of corn, yellow and spotted with brown. His eyes were the same, though. Lab knew them well. They were his own.

"You ain't ever gonna make it," the filthy man said, still wearing that crooked smile that Lab knew he gave Peño sometimes. "You gonna let them all down. You *belong* in the Bottom."

Lab yelped and shot the ball out of reflex. It rebounded off the back iron and bounced away, and the man was gone. No, not the man. Lab in the future: homeless and alone.

You could get your wish. No one to let down.

Lab stood at the free-throw line, shaking. He walked back to the team in silence, trying to clear the man's weathered face from his mind. The group started running again, and Lab pushed his feet to move, trying to leave the vision behind him.

Vin, Big John, and Twig missed shots one after another. Each time, the team had to run again, making their way through the bizarre obstacles. Lab was barely able to keep upright—his legs had grown leaden, and his head was swimming. Finally, Reggie managed to hit a free throw, and the team mumbled a feeble cheer.

"Water break," Rolabi said. "Bring your bottles over here."

Lab grabbed his bottle and joined the seated circle, his mind still on the vision. If he was creating them as Rolabi claimed, why couldn't he make nice ones? Where were the visions of glory and trophies and his father lounging in a hammock on a beach somewhere? How could Lab make those?

The grana flows from your fears. Your needs. You must face the darkness before you can hope to understand it.

I don't want to! Lab thought.

So you choose what seems easy.

Lab rubbed his forehead. It was a strange sensation to speak through thought: he had to focus and verbalize and quiet all the noise that usually rampaged around his brain. He was amazed he could do it so easily. Was it true? Was there . . . *grana* coursing through him? Through all of them? And if it was, why find out about it now? How had Rolabi unlocked that potential?

You will learn.

Rolabi pulled a potted daisy out of his bag and stared at it thoughtfully.

With a flower? Lab thought, frowning.

I can think of nothing better.

Lab sighed and settled in. He let his mind wander. That was easy for him, at least. Peño couldn't sit still for more than a few minutes—he was already fidgeting—but Lab didn't mind silence. Most nights he lay in his bed and stared at the stucco ceiling, making shadow shapes with his hands in the glow of his night-light, while Peño snored across the room.

Twice, his father had removed the night-light, and twice Lab had panicked in the blackness.

"What's to be scared of in the dark?" his dad had said. "It's the best time of day."

"You can't see anything," Lab had replied.

"So?"

"So you don't know what's coming."

His dad had snorted. "So you're scared of life. That's a bigger problem."

Still, when Lab went to his room that night, the night-light was back in its usual spot, and his dad never tried to take it away again.

Even with the comfort of the night-light, staying still and thinking wasn't always easy. Sometimes at night, Lab's mind went places he didn't want to go, and he relived memories that were better left in the past. They started to appear now, and Lab tried to focus on basketball.

Lab goes to the outside, gets the ball, the buzzer goes down . . . shoot it . . . shoot it . . . The ball sticks to his hands. He can't take the shot. The fans are going wild. Shoot it . . . shoot it . . . shoot it!

He blinked the image away. The silence dragged on, and soon Lab grew uncomfortable. Peño looked ready to explode. His fingers were twitching.

"What part of the body moves first?" Rolabi asked, breaking the silence.

What does this have to with the flower? Lab thought testily.

It has to do with time.

We're wasting time, Lab thought.

Oh, no. We are building more of it.

Lab scowled and folded his arms. He was talking in his head. He was staring at a flower. He was doing everything Rolabi asked of him, and all he got were cryptic half answers and judgments and lectures. It wasn't fair.

Then change the rules.

Stop that! he thought, and even in his mind, his voice sounded shrill.

"And how are we supposed to get more time?" Rain asked.

"By watching the flower grow. Water bottles away. We have one more lesson today."

Rolabi began to walk in a circle around the gym, reaching into his bag and tossing out random items. It was enough stuff to fill the bed of a truck. In moments, an entire obstacle course had taken shape around the gym. Lab had never seen so much equipment—all brand-new.

He wondered for a moment where Rolabi came from, where he went after practice.

The Kingdom of Granity, he recalled, thinking back to the contract.

The name stirred something again. That half-remembered song from his mother. He tried to think. There had been a place called Granity. And the cup—it had the power to fix something. He looked away, mouthing the words. *So they came from away, and for peace, they all played . . .*

The voice rose up in him, soft and lilting, and he pushed it away as his eyes burned.

Rolabi gave instructions for completing the circuit and told the team to begin.

Rain reached down to pick up a ball, grabbed his right wrist, and started to scream. Like dominoes, one player after another looked down and shrieked along with him. Lab looked down as well, almost reluctantly. His right hand, his *good* hand, was gone.

"What is this?" Big John shouted, his eyes bulging.

"An exercise in balance," Rolabi said with infuriating calm. "Proceed."

Everything seemed to collide at once. The gym and the grana and the visions—it had been pushing Lab toward an edge he hadn't seen. And now his hand was gone. Rolabi had taken a piece of him, and he didn't have much to spare. Lab marched out of line, temper boiling over.

"No!" he said. "This is too much. The other stuff . . . fine . . . but this is messed up!" He started for the bench and then whirled back, gripping his wrist. "And give me back my hand, you wack job!"

"If anyone leaves the practice without cause, they are off the team permanently."

Rolabi's tone of voice was the same as ever: even and calm. But the words hung in the air, and Lab paused, hearing the threat even through the pounding in his ears. Not even a threat—a certainty. He turned back.

Peño would come with him, surely.

"I can see your hand," Peño said. "It's right there."

Lab looked down. "No, it isn't. I'm the only one who lost it!"

And that was true. Everyone else still had their hands. They were all gripping their wrists, cradling them to their chests, but the hands were there. Lab paused, taking in the scene. Of course they couldn't see their own hands. They had been screaming. And they could see his. The missing hands were just another illusion.

Lab felt dizzy, trying to process. They were doing this to themselves—that's what Rolabi had said. Which meant . . . they needed to lose their hands? Why on earth would that be?

"This isn't possible," he said, feeling his knees wobble.

Why? Why would *he* need to lose a hand?

You are finally starting to see.

"Possibility is notoriously subjective," Rolabi replied. "Shall we begin?"

"Just come play," Peño said, looking straight at Lab.

Lab stood there, his eyes flicking from one player to another, and then to Rolabi.

If you quit, everything stays the same.

I'm fine with that— Lab thought.

Are you?

Lab turned away. He thought of his father and their run-down house. Of the hollow feeling in his stomach. Grasping for happiness that wasn't there. Stuck in memories that wouldn't fade. Wondering sometimes, most of the time, if it was worth pushing through at all. The coldness intensified. His skin prickled.

It would be easier to give up, he thought.

Yes, the voice agreed. *And that's how you know it would be wrong.*

Lab blinked back sudden tears. He looked at his one remaining hand. He wanted to play ball. He *needed* to play. It was the last thing that made sense. He walked back into the line.

And so the road begins.

Lab was the last to start the circuit, and by the time he dribbled toward the first hoop, shouts, falls, and frustration were everywhere. He didn't fare much better than his teammates. His left hand was uncoordinated, though stronger than Peño's. He botched layups, lost the ball through cones, missed passes, and airballed shots. He figured it was just a bad start, but the next round was the same. So were the third and fourth. Lab managed to plunk A-Wall in the side of the head with a wayward pass. The drill was a complete disaster. When it finally ended, Lab doubled over, wiping his sopping face. He was drenched, and he could taste the acrid salt.

"Can we have our hands back now?" Rain asked hopefully.

"Tomorrow we will be working on our defense. They will be helpful then," said Rolabi.

Lab turned to him. "Wait . . . we don't get them back tonight? Professor?"

Rolabi was heading for the nearest cinder-block wall, though there wasn't a door within fifty feet. Lab was about to say something when the lights flashed and then switched off. Wind roared in from nowhere, and Lab stared at the impassable wall as the fluorescent lights flicked on again. Rolabi had vanished, and silence descended on the gym.

"Okay," Peño said, "I think maybe we should talk to Freddy. Rain?"

Rain nodded. "It's time to fire Rolabi."

Lab looked between them, surprised. Fire Rolabi? It was what he had wanted . . . wasn't it? If they got rid of Rolabi, this grana business might go too. Things would return to normal, which was exactly what Lab had asked for. He looked around the gym. Old and run-down and fading.

For a second, he saw silver light coursing through his teammates again, feeding into the place, connecting with one another like bursts of static electricity. He blinked and the image was gone.

Lab went to the bench and ran his left hand through his hair. It had gotten long again, and now it was soaked, and he knew it was probably standing on end, making him look almost as crazy as he felt. He stared down at his flat wrist. There was silver light there too, forming a perfect hand. Lab sighed and awkwardly kicked his sweaty shoes off.

"Still think this ain't magic?" Vin asked, plunking down beside him.

Lab glanced at him and recalled the grainy video he had seen in another vision. The bullies and the nervousness for his brothers and the stealing from his father's store. Vin had issues too—in fact, Lab wasn't sure he would make that trade after all. With Vin or Twig.

"It's magic, all right," Lab said. He paused. "Listen, uh, if you ever have stuff going on, you know we're here, right? Like, you can talk to me and Peño. Or anyone."

Vin frowned. "Yeah . . . sure. I know. Why?"

"Just in general. And no, a missing hand doesn't count."

Vin laughed, and a voice spoke in Lab's head, nearly at a whisper.

And in the gloom, a distant light appears.

4

THE ORB

When you are in a hole, help everyone else first.
By the time you are done, the hole will no longer exist.
◆ WIZENARD ⒁ PROVERB ◆

LAB SAT DEJECTEDLY on the home bench, staring at the empty space where his right hand used to be. He still couldn't get used to the sight. By now he'd confirmed that everyone else could see it but him, even his dad. Lab had waited up for him—he got home after midnight again—and shared some leftover casserole, pointedly using his left hand to dig out an awkward scoop and sticking his right wrist out on the table. His dad never mentioned it. He just shoveled the food down like a starving man and asked about their training.

"Great," Lab muttered. "I think the other guys want to fire Rolabi, though."

"Why?" his dad asked, fork paused midway to his mouth.

Lab wanted to tell him everything. But how? His dad was about as likely to believe in magic as Lab had been. He would probably just tell Lab to get more sleep, or eat better, or do more homework. Homework was his usual answer for everything—even during summer break.

"Personality conflicts," Lab murmured.

"Personality?" his dad said. "What does that have to do with basketball?"

Lab rolled his eyes. "It helps if people get along."

"It helps if people do their jobs," his dad replied. "Getting along can come later."

They finished and went to bed, and Lab lay there most of the night. When he finally did sleep, it felt like he had just closed his eyes when sunlight was streaming in and Peño was yanking him out of bed by his ear. Lab stumbled up and brushed his teeth with one hand. Got dressed with one hand. Ate some stale oatmeal with one hand. It was difficult, awkward, and annoying—especially with Peño there. He almost seemed to enjoy it. He kept saying it was a challenge and a chance to strengthen their weaker sides and a bunch of other peppy nonsense. It reminded Lab of the fact that he might very well be doing this to himself, which made the frustration even worse.

The two of them were sitting on the end of the bench now. Another attempt at a knot slipped out of Lab's shoelaces. He leaned back and sighed.

"I don't like you right now," Lab murmured, glaring at his brother.

Peño was trying to tie his shoes as well, and making a complete mess of it. "We'll get them back today."

"How do you know that?"

"Because he said we would."

"Peño, we are talking about a crazy person."

"I'm not so sure he's crazy. Just magical. Besides, Freddy is coming today."

"Are you not hearing yourself? You want to fire the dude that has our hands?"

"When he leaves, the hands will come back."

"How are you so okay with this?" Lab demanded.

Peño sighed and turned to him. "What do you want me to do, Lab? It's magic."

"Magic isn't supposed to exist. Remember?"

"Well, it does. And I think that's kind of cool—missing hands aside. Don't you?"

Cool? Obviously, Peño hadn't experienced the same visions. He hadn't seen her. He hadn't been on a sinking boat. Lab was being subjected to the real grana—the one Rolabi seemed to be describing. The fear and the questions and the darkness. That's what this "magic" was for.

"You sound like a child," Lab said.

"And you sound like a whiny old man," Peño snapped. "All you do is complain. You complain about getting up. You mope around at home. You don't eat my cooking. You don't come play at Hyde anymore, and you barely seem to want to play ball. What is wrong with you?"

Lab stared at him. He and his brother exchanged quips and jokes all the time, but it was never like *that.* Clearly, Peño had been holding his thoughts in for a while. It was true, maybe. Sometimes he felt weighed down.

Did Peño think he *wanted* that? Did Peño forget that *she* had died? Did he forget where they lived? For a dangerous moment, Lab felt his eyes well up. Then his temper won out instead.

"Nothing is wrong with me, except that my older brother is an idiot. Stay away from me."

"No problem!" Peño said.

Peño pointedly slid down the bench, and Lab returned to his sneakers, fumbling with the laces. It was hard enough with only one hand, but now that hand was shaking with anger.

Peño finished tying his shoes and stalked away. Clearly everything was easier for him. He could move on. He could pretend it was okay. Lab couldn't. Maybe he never would. Maybe it would always hurt.

Where are you putting all the pain?

Lab turned toward the back wall, hiding his watering eyes from the team. He closed them, feeling the tears threatening to fall, and when he opened them, he was sitting in the rowboat again. Sinking as before. Lab looked around, disoriented. The water had risen since the last time. It was seeping over the tops of his shoes, still cold as ice. There was a bucket, but he didn't even bother with it. What was the point? The water would keep coming. He couldn't find the leak. Lab just sat there, watching the water rise to his shins, his whole body trembling. A flicker of movement caught his eye. Way out on the shore, standing right by the water, someone was watching him. Someone familiar.

"Peño . . ." he whispered.

"The water is cold."

He turned and saw Rolabi sitting behind him in the old rowboat.

"Yeah," Lab said softly.

"I suppose it doesn't matter. Somehow I don't think you plan on swimming."

"The shore is a long way away," he muttered.

"You built the lake," Rolabi said. "The boat. The leak. You built it all."

Lab stared down at the water. It was clear but faded far below into nothing.

"I sort of figured that out by now. But I didn't have a choice. I was dropped in this boat when she died. I've been bailing it out since. I've been going to school. Coming to ball. I tried."

"It's strange," Rolabi said. "You were the most resistant to grana at first. The angriest one. Yours is the deepest darkness. And yet you keep coming back to it. You create these worlds again and again." The professor's eyes searched Lab's face. "What does it feel like? Why do you want to give up?"

"Heavy," Lab whispered. "It all feels so heavy."

"And so sinks the boat," Rolabi said, nodding. "It's not going to get easier."

"What's not going to get easier?"

"Your road. It will be hard. Harder even than before."

Lab snorted. "Is this supposed to cheer me up?"

Rolabi leaned in, eyes blazing. "No. I'm telling you to find the leak."

"How?"

"By finding the hiding place."

The lake disappeared. Lab was back on the bench, the team around him, and Freddy and Rolabi were staring at each other, hands clasped. Lab frowned. He hadn't seen Freddy come in.

"Rolabi will remain the coach," Freddy whispered, pulling his hand away. He was trembling. "I . . . I look forward to the season."

He left without another word, walking into the morning sunlight.

"So much for that firing," Vin muttered.

Rolabi faced the team. "Today we will be working on defense. Before I can teach you proper zones and strategies, I must teach each of you how to be a defender. They are not the same lessons."

A scratching sound interrupted the lecture. It made the wispy hairs on Lab's arms stand on end.

"What must a defender always be?" Rolabi asked.

Lab was barely listening. He kept expecting something to burst out at them from the walls. He looked around nervously, ready to bolt. The lake and Peño and everything else was forgotten, for the moment. If this was grana . . . was Lab creating it again? He tried to think of something nice, like fans cheering on the sideline, but the scratching continued. It didn't make anything better. Lab still didn't understand how any of this worked.

Rolabi abruptly turned to him. "Do you want to see more?"

Lab opened his mouth, looked around, and saw that he was alone. "Yes."

The gym melted into darkness. Lab found himself standing at the base of a mountain that soared above him, rising into clouds. The salty ocean air was laced with the fresh scent of pine trees. Lab turned slowly, eyes wide, catching a glimpse of a castle on one of the lower slopes. He remembered more of the song. A place of sand and snow. He could almost hear her voice in the distance.

"The Kingdom of Granity," he whispered.

"Remembered in Dren only in book and song," Rolabi agreed, stepping up beside him. "The home of the last Wizenards."

Lab glanced at him. "So that's not your name—it's what you are."

"Correct. Long banned from Dren."

"Why?"

"Because of grana."

Rolabi snapped a finger, and he and Lab were suddenly standing in a cavern. Heat pressed in on Lab's cheeks. A river of molten lava was flowing past. Lab had seen pictures of volcanoes in books, but nothing could have prepared him for the sight of liquid rock. Crimson and orange, fire moving like water.

"Where—"

"Grana is tied to our emotions. Our feelings. Our morality. It is capable of the greatest change. It can carve like water, build like stone. All of us have it equally. All have the same potential."

"And . . . Dren doesn't like that?" Lab guessed.

"No. Many nations don't, and your government forbade all mention of it. Before you were born, President Talin expelled the Wizenards. Clamped down on this nation and stripped its freedoms. But he does not understand grana. Let me ask you: If you wanted to move this magma, to divert the flow, how would you go about it?"

Lab stared at the magma and felt the terrible heat of it on his face. He looked around for inspiration. The cavern was large and vaulted, with stalactites hanging down like jagged teeth. It was empty otherwise, apart from scattered boulders and rocks that lay piled near the steep walls.

He tried to think. He couldn't touch the magma. Somehow, he didn't think politely asking it to flow elsewhere would work either. But, if he started piling rocks, he could create a channel. There were probably enough, though it would take him hours of backbreaking work.

"Well done," Rolabi said, as if Lab had been speaking aloud and not just following a train of thought. "It is the only way. To channel that energy to the direction you need to go, you must build a step-by-step pathway. If you leave cracks, the magma will flow out. If you flag, you will not reach the goal."

Lab frowned. "So grana . . . just flows. You need to redirect it?"

"Yes. With work. With little steps. Only when you have built an emotional landscape without cracks will it flow."

"And what are my cracks?"

"Fear. Fear of what, you yourself must find."

Lab looked out over the river of magma, considering. "Does President Talin know you're in Dren?"

Rolabi smiled grimly. "Not yet."

With that, the gym reappeared, just in time for Lab to see an enormous tiger stroll out of the locker room. Lab stumbled in shock, but the tiger just walked right past him and sat down.

"Meet Kallo. She has graciously volunteered to help us today."

The tiger looked over the group, almost regal with her raised chin.

Who is making this one? Lab thought nervously.

No one. I simply brought a friend.

"Rain," Rolabi said loudly. "Step forward."

Rain didn't move. He kept looking between Rolabi, the tiger, and the front doors. Lab almost assumed he would walk out, but to his surprise, Rain took a small, slow step forward.

"Yes?" he murmured.

Rolabi rolled a ball to center court.

"The drill is simple," Rolabi said. "Get the ball. Kallo will play defense. We will take turns and go one at a time. I want everyone to watch and take note of what happens."

Lab looked at the professor in disbelief. They were supposed to get around the tiger? Kallo started to pace, protruding claws clacking on the hardwood. They looked razor sharp. He glanced at his brother. Lab was still angry, but he didn't exactly want to see Peño get eaten by a tiger either. He wondered if Peño knew that Rolabi was a Wizenard and was banned from Dren.

The thought triggered questions: If Rolabi was banned, why had he come back just to coach the Badgers? And why was a Wizenard coaching them, period? What would President Talin do if he found out?

"The first one to get the ball gets their hand back," Rolabi was saying.

That caught Lab's attention. "Are you saying the rest of us don't?" he asked.

Have you earned it?

Well, I was born with it, Lab thought sourly.

So, no.

Rain hesitated and then reluctantly stepped forward. He faked to the left and went right, dropping his shoulders and moving fast enough that 99 percent of defenders would have been left grasping at thin air. But Kallo was not remotely fooled. She hit him directly in the chest, bringing him down. Rain stared up in disbelief as Kallo bared her deadly, inch-long fangs.

"What do we do?" A-Wall whispered.

"Get ready to squeal and run away," Vin said.

But she licked Rain across the face and stepped off.

"Devon," Rolabi said.

Devon didn't fare any better. Lab went fifth, and he stepped forward without hesitation, not wanting to look like a coward now. Peño had already gone and been knocked flying—much to Lab's amusement—and his brother would have a field day if Lab didn't even try. Kallo tracked his movements, flashing him a lopsided grin. He had the distinct feeling she was mocking him.

"What is the point of this again?" Lab said.

"There are so many," Rolabi replied. "I suspect the answer might be different for everyone."

"That was a rhetorical question."

"And so you received a rhetorical answer," Rolabi said with a shadow of a smile.

Lab tried a double fake: left, right, and then left again, moving low to make himself a smaller target. It didn't work. Before he knew it, Kallo was pinning him with a paw across his chest. Her breath washed over him, hot and sticky. Then she licked his cheek with a coarse, grating tongue and walked away to wait for the next attempt. Peño snorted with laughter.

"Like you did any better," Lab said, climbing to his feet.

"I did," he replied. "And I wasn't shaking like a leaf either."

"Leaves don't shake."

"It's a common expression."

"You're a common expression," Lab said. It didn't make any sense, but he was angry.

Peño rolled his eyes. "Grow up."

Lab hated when Peño said that—like he was so much older and wiser. "Why . . . so I can be a washout like you?"

"I'm literally one year older than you," Peño said.

"And three years worse at ball," Lab snapped.

Peño turned away, and Lab sighed, dejected. He didn't feel any better.

After everyone went—except Big John, who refused, then tried to beat up Twig, fight half the team, and argue with Rolabi before being sent to the locker room—Kallo sauntered back over to Rolabi and sat down.

"None of you got the ball," Rolabi said, giving Kallo an affectionate pat. "But you all showed real courage. That is a good start."

"Yes!" A-Wall cried out.

Lab's right hand tingled. It was back. He hugged it to his chest.

Courage always yields rewards.

Lab looked at Rolabi, scowling. *I don't need courage*, he thought. *I just want to forget.*

Then you seek weakness.

Lab thought about that. It seemed to resonate for some reason. Was weakness what he was after? And if it was, why was he so surprised that he felt *weak*?

Cold suddenly flooded his body. A deeper cold than he had ever felt in his life. Goose bumps trailed up his arms like the pebbling on a new basketball.

"What is that?" Jerome asked, pointing with a shaking finger.

Lab followed his gaze to an orb floating at center court. Instantly, he knew it was the source of the cold. It was black as space and rolling and fluctuating in midair. Somehow, he knew that there was something deeply wrong about that orb, yet also familiar.

"Ah," Rolabi said, turning to face it. "Just in time."

"What . . . what is it?" Peño asked nervously.

"That is something you all will want to catch," Rolabi said. "No, it is something you all *must* catch. We can call it the orb for reference. Whoever catches it will become a far better player. But it won't last forever. If no one catches it, we run laps." He nodded to the orb. "Go!"

His voice cracked across the room like a starting gun. Without even wanting to start running, Lab was suddenly in the chase. It felt like he was being pulled along on a string—but not by anyone else. He wanted it, deep down. There was something tantalizing about the dark shape.

But the orb was not easily caught.

It zoomed out of reach, bouncing between players like a ping-pong ball. Lab swiped at it and missed, though he wasn't sure if he was disappointed or relieved. It seemed that everyone was caught up in the thrill of the hunt. They jumped and dove and crashed into one another. Lab watched in disbelief as the orb managed to slip through every outstretched hand. It was uncatchable—at least, for them.

At one point, it wandered just a bit too close to Kallo, and she erupted like a geyser and swallowed it in one snapping bite before settling back on her haunches and shooting the team a grin.

"A true defender," Rolabi said. "Get some water. Laps and free throws."

That was met by a chorus of groans.

Lab's stomach felt queasy. Why had he chased that orb? There was something off about it—something bad. And yet he had raced after it like a bloodhound. He sighed and sat down on the bench.

After a short water break, Lab felt a little better, and the team took off again, scaling hills and stairs and sliding down valleys. Lab was soaked by the time Twig hit a shot—forty-five laps in. Lab had already missed his own attempt after glimpsing a distant sinking boat.

"It's a start," Rolabi said to Kallo.

"A start?" Lab said, shaking his head like a wet dog. "I'm about to keel over."

"Tomorrow we will work on team defense," Rolabi said. "Get some rest tonight."

With that, he headed for the doors, Kallo walking along beside him.

"Are . . . are you taking the tiger?" Peño asked.

The doors burst open, hit by howling, icy wind, and the professor and the tiger walked outside.

Lab plopped onto the bench, rubbing his burning thighs. He was exhausted, and he wasn't the only one. Big John was patting his face with a towel, seemingly unable to speak.

"We practiced with a tiger today," Peño said.

There was silence for a moment, and then Jerome started to laugh. It spread rapidly. Soon everyone seemed to be laughing, though Lab refused to join in on principle.

Now that practice was over, Peño's angry words came back to him once again. So Lab was sad. Wasn't he supposed to be? If anything, Lab was angry that Peño had just moved on. Why did Lab have to be the only broken one? It wasn't fair that Peño could be happy again when no one in their family should be. And yet . . . Lab wanted Peño and his dad to be happy, of course. It was confusing. Nonsensical. Lab wondered whether he would feel guilty either way—whether what was left of his family was happy or miserable forever.

"Drop some lines, Peño," Jerome said.

Peño began to bob to some unheard music. Lab changed out of his wet shirt and started for the doors. For the first time in eight years of playing basketball together, he left Peño behind. He pushed open the doors and glanced back. Peño looked hurt, and for a moment, Lab considered waiting for him.

But then he remembered that Peño was mad at *him* for being sad. For mourning too long. If Peño wanted to forget things, if he wanted to pretend life was great, then he could do it alone.

Lab narrowed his eyes and walked out, letting the rusty old doors slam behind him.

BABY BROTHER

*Every grudge is a new weight you
must drag along behind you.*

◆ WIZENARD ⑩ PROVERB ◆

THE NEXT MORNING, Lab and Peño walked apart the entire way to Fairwood. They hadn't spoken all night. When you shared a room, and ate dinner together, and had only one TV with four grainy channels, that took some doing . . . and lots of glares, mutters, and awkward silence.

For the fourth straight night, Lab had barely slept. The nightmares were bad before, but they were even worse now—had been since he saw *her.* That encounter in the gym had been far worse than the picture that Peño still kept on the mantel, the one Lab ignored when he walked past.

In the vision, he could have touched her, spoken to her, and he didn't get the chance. That nagged at him. He wanted to talk to Peño about it, but he was still too angry. His brother was supposed to be on his side. Lab didn't talk to his dad either. He was busy. Tired. He didn't need a reminder. And so Lab was alone, which was nothing new. He felt alone even around other people.

Peño hadn't woken him up that morning, and he'd just barely gotten up in time for practice. He hadn't even had a minute to brush his teeth. He felt like he had cotton balls crammed in there that smelled conspicuously like last night's spaghetti. Peño hadn't prepacked Lab's bag either, so he had no water bottles, no towel, and no granola bar. His duffel smelled like Fairwood on a particularly hot day. Peño was walking ahead of him, and he stormed inside, letting the doors slam in Lab's face. *So immature*, Lab thought sourly.

He walked in after his brother and froze. Peño wasn't there. No one was. The gym was completely empty apart from, well, a castle.

"What is basketball to you, Lab?" a familiar voice asked.

He jumped about a foot in the air and whirled around to find Rolabi leaning against the wall. Lab scowled. He was tired and miserable, and he knew Rolabi was the cause of all of it.

"What did you say?" Lab muttered. "And where is my brother?"

"What is basketball to you?"

Lab rubbed his eyes. "Can we stop with these stupid questions?"

"Only if you quit."

Lab glared at him. "What was the question?"

"Why do you play the game?"

"I don't know," Lab said, shifting uncomfortably. "I like it."

"Why?"

Lab felt his temperature rising. "I just do. What do you want from me?"

"Truth."

Lab tried to think. Why did he play basketball? Did he even know? It wasn't just because Peño did it. He would have played whether Peño came or not. And it wasn't even because he thought it was his ticket out of the Bottom. He knew in his heart that the odds were never great.

"I play because . . . because I feel better out there."

Rolabi nodded. "What does it make you feel like?"

"Free," Lab whispered, looking out at the court. "Or lighter maybe. I don't know."

Even Lab wasn't exactly sure what he meant, but Rolabi seemed to understand.

"A place where we can leave our darkness at the door," Rolabi said softly.

"It was important . . . after."

"I imagine so. And it remains. But why leave our darkness at the door? It will simply be waiting for us when we are finished. Why not destroy the darkness and come and go in peace?"

Lab turned away. "Where's my brother?"

"It looks like he is getting his shoes on."

Lab spotted Peño sitting on the bench, along with Reggie and Twig. They hadn't been there a moment ago.

"Sometimes you just have to live with the darkness," Lab said quietly.

"Only if you choose that fate."

Lab shook his head and went to join the others. Peño looked up, clearly wanting to ask him something, but then seemed to remember they were fighting and turned away. Lab put his shoes on in silence, wondering at his own answer. Did he really feel *lighter* playing ball? He'd never thought about it that way before. But it was true: He needed to move. Run. He needed the freedom of a simple goal. He needed to be a member of a team and not just broken Javi Juarez.

When everyone had arrived, they gathered in front of the fortress.

"Today we are working on team defense," Rolabi said.

He tipped his bag upside down, and a mound of red and blue equipment spilled onto the hardwood: a jumble of helmets and pads.

"Take one of each, please," Rolabi said, gesturing to the equipment.

Lab waited until Peño had picked a blue helmet and then grabbed a red one. He wasn't sure what the drill was, but he felt like it might be a good chance to clobber his brother. He scooped up a matching pad and examined his team approvingly. They had a definite advantage. He had Reggie and Vin, plus two heavy hitters in A-Wall and the abnormally muscular Devon.

"The game is simple. One team will attack, and the other will defend.

The team to get the trophy in the least amount of time wins. The losing team will run laps while the winners shoot around."

Lab looked up at the castle. "So we just push each other with these pads? Won't the strongest team win no matter what?"

"A fine question," Rolabi said. "You have two minutes to plan."

Lab joined the rest of the red team in a huddle by the benches, then glanced back at the fortress, eager to get started. This was already his favorite drill, and they hadn't started yet. Peño's favorite books were always about animals, but Lab loved the fantasy and adventure stories. Knights, battles, heroes . . . he read those ones again and again, or used to. She used to read them to him mostly, and it was hard to go back to the stories. Still, he had some tucked beneath his bed—the only place in the house he had some private storage. Beyond the books, he had only three other things under there: a photo, a mostly empty bottle of perfume, and a shoelace.

He stared at the castle, only half listening to the plan. Did Peño even remember that day? It didn't matter. This fight was his fault. He had come after Lab; he had called him *whiny*.

"We'll push through and get to the trophy with Devon at the lead," Reggie finished.

"Gonna smash my bro," Lab said excitedly.

He put his hand in first for a cheer—which was not like him. "Red on three. One, two, three . . . *Red*!"

The team threw their hands up and shouted with him.

"Begin!" Rolabi said.

His voice triggered something beneath their feet, and a tremor moved through the gym. Lab watched in amazement as the floors around the castle caved into a trench. Water came flooding in from all sides until a moat rose against the base of the castle. Narrow planks appeared over the water, leading to each ramp. The castle itself changed from smooth rubber to stone, while flags fluttered from the parapets.

Lab looked down and realized he was even dressed like an actual knight in polished silver armor with red trim, while his pad was a thick, heavy leather with a Badgers crest on it.

For the moment, everything was forgotten. He broke into a wild grin.

"Charge!" he shouted, pumping his fist like a medieval commander.

Lab considered going after his brother, but Vin had already targeted Peño, so Lab rounded the fortress and saw Twig guarding a ramp by himself, shifting nervously. The perfect target. Lab slammed into him, and their leather pads collided with a breathless thud.

Lab hadn't even noticed that Reggie was following him, but he soon felt another pad driving into his back, adding to their momentum. Twig gulped as he started to slide up the ramp.

"He's finished," Reggie grunted.

"Surrender the keep!" Lab said.

But just when they were about to push through into the open level beyond the ramp, Rain rushed to help Twig, using the higher ground to push them down again. Lab gritted his teeth.

They were losing!

"See you later," Reggie said, and then he took off for another ramp.

"Keep pushing, Twig!" Rain shouted as he disappeared back into the castle.

Lab used Twig's distraction to surge forward again. "Give up, Twig!"

"You give up!" Twig retorted.

"You can't hold me, Stick Man."

Twig cringed, just visible over the pad. "I'm doing . . . fine . . ."

"You sound tired," Lab pointed out, though his own legs were ablaze.

"Nope . . ." Twig managed.

Lab knew by now that he wasn't going to be able to get through—Twig was doing just enough to hold his ground. But it didn't matter—there were other spots to attack. Lab broke off and retreated across the bridge. He spotted Devon driving Jerome up his own ramp and A-Wall running to back him up. Lab grinned. The blue team was finished.

He joined the attack and drove his pad into Devon's back. Jerome went airborne. Devon, Lab, and A-Wall sprinted into the castle. Rain appeared in front of them and slumped.

"Help!" Rain called.

The three boys charged, and Rain soon met the same fate as Jerome. Lab and the others ran up the final ramp, where Devon scooped up the granite trophy with one hand and hoisted it triumphantly. The gold accents glittered in the light.

"Red team!" Lab shouted.

He was pleased to see Peño looking up at them from well below, scowling.

"One minute and forty-seven seconds," Rolabi said. "Blue team, you will now attack. You have two minutes to prepare."

As the blue team went to form an attack plan, Lab's team gathered into another huddle. Lab looked up at the tower. How could they prevent the same thing from happening to them?

"We need a plan," he said.

Vin nodded. "It's tough on D. Lab, you and Reggie—"

"No," Reggie said suddenly, laughing.

"What's funny?" Vin said.

"It's actually pretty simple," Reggie replied. "The other ramps are just distractions."

Lab frowned. "What are you talking about?"

"All we have to do is protect the trophy," Reggie said. "So we only need to block the *last* ramp."

"Of course," Lab said, whistling. He looked at the trophy. Reggie was right—the only way to get to the trophy was up the final ramp. If they just protected that one, and held the attackers there, then the blue team couldn't reach it. They assembled into a reinforced line on the ramp, and

Lab found himself standing right behind Devon, who was guarding the entrance like a grim sentry. Lab could practically feel his blood pumping as he waited for the attack. He couldn't remember the last time he had been so energized. It had been so long ago, but the memories were still there. Good ones. Excitement for holidays. For weekends when his mom and dad used to get a day off. They would play cards and cook big dinners, and his dad would even sit down for a few hours to watch television with them.

It struck him how long it had been since he had felt *excited*, and the thought disturbed him.

"Begin!" Rolabi said.

Lab heard shouts and pounding footsteps on the ramps and focused on the present. He set his legs and waited as the blue team stampeded up the fortress, Rain at the lead. They rounded the corner at a sprint, then slid to an abrupt halt. Realization dawned on their faces.

"Push!" Rain screamed.

The blue team charged, but they had no chance fighting uphill— particularly against Devon. Lab leaned into his back, feet wide, arms tensed and locked. The two teams pushed against each other for a solid minute at least, everyone straining and grunting and shouting:

"You're going down!"

"Come on—push!"

"It's not working!"

Finally, the pressure eased, and Lab felt relief flood his body as his muscles relaxed. The attackers were getting tired. Devon obviously sensed it too. Without warning, he drove forward and pushed with all his strength, and the blue team spilled down the ramp into a heap.

"The time is beat," Rolabi said. "The red team wins."

The red team cheered again. Lab tried to pick up the trophy with one hand, found it way too heavy, and dropped his pad to lift it with both. He shook it over his head, cheering and laughing, and then noticed

Peño looking up at him. His brother almost seemed near tears.

Lab lowered the trophy, suddenly feeling guilty, and passed it off to Reggie. Peño had already started for the benches, shuffling and slouched. Lab had never seen him look so depressed.

"The red team may grab some balls and shoot around," Rolabi said. "Blue team, laps."

The victorious red team exited the fortress, casting their helmets and pads aside. Lab tried to catch his brother's eye, but Peño refused to look at him. His own temper came back. So now Peño got to be upset? Lab thought that wasn't allowed. And what was his sadness for—a loss at a drill? So that was okay, but not actual grief?

Lab stewed on that as he shot around, watching with satisfaction as Peño and the blue team jogged lap after lap, running for almost an hour before someone finally hit a free throw.

Finally, both teams gathered at the bench for a drink. Lab didn't have one today, of course, so he just watched thirstily. Lab glanced down at Peño, who had his eyes on his shoes. Despite himself, Lab couldn't help but wonder why he was so upset. Why was he taking the loss so personally? It wasn't even a real basketball game. Peño still looked near tears.

Rolabi walked over to the castle and plucked a black cap from the side. The whole structure softened, then folded in on itself like an old grape. Lab wasn't even surprised anymore.

"What must a defender always be?" Rolabi asked.

"*Ready*," Reggie replied.

"The same goes for the entire team. If you are not ready, we are wasting our time."

He started for the doors. At some point he must have put the discarded helmets and pads back in his medicine bag, though Lab hadn't seen him do it. He wondered if Rolabi truly went back to the Kingdom of Granity every night.

"Are we done for today?" Peño called.

"That is up to you," Rolabi replied.

The doors slammed shut behind him, and the orb simultaneously appeared in the middle of the court. Once again, Lab felt goose bumps trail up his arms.

A hush fell over the gym. No one moved.

"What do we do?" Peño asked quietly.

"Rolabi said we had to catch it," A-Wall pointed out. "He said we would be better basketball players if we did, remember?"

That was enough for Twig, apparently. He took off after it, and the rest followed—Lab last of all. Once again, he was torn between his fear of the orb and his inexplicable desire to catch it. His desire won out. And again, it was useless. The orb was simply too fast. It was like chasing a shadow with a flashlight. Lab and Peño even collided at one point, which resulted in a bruised tailbone and more glaring. Finally, the orb flew into a wall and vanished, and Lab sighed.

They would never catch that thing.

"Still up for that scrimmage?" Peño asked.

"Nah," Rain said, obviously annoyed. "Let's just get out of here."

Everyone headed for the bench, and Lab took a seat, exhausted. But soon an argument formed—Rain and Reggie, which was a surprise. Rain clearly hadn't enjoyed the drill.

"It was a stupid game," Rain snapped. "You play D by stopping the ball. And you *win* by scoring." He climbed to his feet, shaking, he was so enraged. "By *me* scoring. And we aren't getting any closer to winning by me not working on my shot. This is a big year for me."

"You mean for *us*," Lab said.

Rain headed for the doors. "Yeah . . . Rain Adams and the West Bottom Badgers."

He let the doors slam behind him. Lab shook his head. Rain was so arrogant. It was always his team, his offense. Lab could score just as much if he got the opportunity. But the thought soon evaporated as he saw Peño walk out in silence. Lab's temper flared.

Lab finished changing his shirt and hurried after him.

"What do you want?" Peño snarled.

"Why are you so upset? I thought that wasn't allowed?" His voice almost cracked without warning. He felt a ball forming in his throat and was near tears. His big brother was supposed to understand him.

"This is different," Peño said. "You've been sad for *three years*."

Three years. Impossible but true.

"And why do you think that is, genius?"

"I lost her too. She was my *mom* too."

Lab clenched his fists. Why did Peño have to say that? His brother knew how much that word pained him. He was trying to hurt him now, to dig deep, to stab and twist. Tears stung Lab's eyes—tears of anger, guilt, betrayal.

He went for a deep cut himself.

"You moved on," Lab said coldly. "You cared more about basketball—"

He wasn't ready. Peño drove his hands into Lab's chest, and Lab barely stayed up, fighting for balance, and then reached for Peño and tackled him back. The brothers fell together and hit the pavement hard, Peño cushioning most of the blow. Lab felt the air rush out of Peño as he squeezed Peño's torso. But Peño was strong, and in seconds they were rolling. Lab smelled rot, and something jabbed him in the back, but he didn't care. He fought madly, trying to punch and kick his way free. Peño wrapped him up, locking an arm around his throat.

"Let go!" Lab shouted.

He threw himself out of Peño's grip and into another roll, but Peño was faster. He grabbed Lab again and pinned him down. Lab twisted violently, but Peño had his hands, and all Lab could do was writhe and struggle.

"I miss her every second of the day," Peño said. "You're blind if you don't see that."

"Get off me!"

"Did you ever think I don't show it because of *you*?" Peño screamed. That question struck Lab into stillness; Peño rarely screamed, rarely broke his composure. "That maybe I don't want to remind you or Dad? Did that cross your thick, stupid skull? And maybe I do all the chores to make it easier for you too? Did you think about that?"

Lab stared at him, motionless, stunned.

"Sometimes it feels like I can't breathe," Peño whispered. "Like I'm gonna die. But you didn't notice that either, did you? At least you get to have hope. I don't even get that."

Lab frowned. "What are you talking about—"

"You get a shot! I don't. I get to be strong and watch everyone else go on without me."

Peño climbed to his feet, leaving Lab to stare up at him. What was he talking about? A shot at ball? What did that have to do with anything? And why couldn't he breathe? From grief? Anxiety? None of it made any sense. Peño was strong. Everything just rolled off him, always had. But Lab could see him quivering and the tears spilling out. He was telling the truth.

"I should teach you a lesson," Peño said quietly. "But I won't . . . because of her."

He stormed away. Lab lay on the filthy pavement, still too stunned to move. Yellowed clouds floated overhead, tinged with smoke, and he watched them, reeling. Peño was suffering after all.

And he had never noticed. Never asked. Never cared. The anger cooled, and guilt remained.

"Strange place to have a snooze," Reggie said, stepping over Lab.

He stuck out his hand and pulled Lab to his feet. Reggie looked him over.

"You and Peño get in a fight?" he asked, raising an eyebrow.

Lab nodded and started for the road, embarrassed.

"I have a lot of bad days too," Reggie said quietly. "Thinking of my parents."

Lab stopped and looked back at him. He knew both of Reggie's parents had passed in an accident many years ago, and he had been raised by his grandma. But Reggie had never spoken of it to him before.

"What do you do those days?" Lab asked.

Reggie smiled thinly, staring up at the yellow sky. "I talk to them. Look at pictures. Sometimes I imagine they're in another room. Mostly I think that I want to make them proud."

Lab's eyes watered. "Doesn't it hurt to think of them?"

"Yeah," Reggie said. "But it would hurt more to forget."

Lab stared at him, then nodded and started for the road again. "Maybe you're right."

"Lab?"

"Yeah?" he said, turning back.

"Don't let it go too far with Peño. You're gonna have to stick together. We all are."

There was something in his voice. A warning. "Why?"

Reggie sighed and started for home, heading in the other direction. "Because everything is going to change."

Lab watched him walk away, wondering what Reggie knew.

THE
DARKNESS INSIDE

You do not jump for the summit.
You take hundreds of small, imperceptible steps.
❖ WIZENARD (48) PROVERB ❖

LAB HELD THE ball up by his shoulders, faked left, and then spun right for an elbow jumper. He leapt with his legs extended and his toes aligned with the target—straight up and down. He knew as soon as the ball left his flicking fingers that it was going in, and it swished through the hoop.

He waited a beat, expecting a whoop or compliment. But none came. Of course. He still wasn't talking to Peño. He glanced at the other end of the court, where Peño was shooting around with Twig and Reggie. Lab had gone home yesterday thinking he would take Reggie's advice, especially after Peño's admission that he too was hurting. It made Lab want to apologize. To talk about what they were feeling. But as soon as he saw his brother, he thought back to the fight and his humiliation at being pinned. He thought about the fact that Peño had hid his feelings from him for so long and tried to act tough and made Lab feel weak. He thought of all that, and he had decided to say nothing. This morning, Lab had gotten himself out of bed and packed his own bag. He and Peño had walked to practice separately again.

Lab scooped up the ball. But how could they fix it? Were they supposed to apologize to each other for mourning in different ways? He sighed and spun for another jumper. Nothing made much sense anymore. He was just about to release the ball when a voice announced:

"Gather around. Put the balls away."

Lab jerked, and the ball rolled off his fingers and missed well wide. He grimaced at Rolabi, who was now standing at center court. Lab put his ball away and joined the group, keeping his distance from both Peño *and* Rain. He hadn't forgotten what Rain had said. It was no surprise, but Rain had never actually come out and said it before: that he was separate from the team. He was so full of himself, and Lab was sick of playing second best to him, getting no attention. So he hung back at the edge of the group, sour, lonely, and watched Peño do the same.

"Today we are going to work on offense," Rolabi said.

"Finally," Rain said, smirking.

Lab glanced at him. Rain didn't even seem the least bit embarrassed about yesterday. Maybe they really should let him play alone—just stop passing him the ball and rebounding and setting those picks.

Rain wouldn't be such a star then, Lab thought darkly.

Why do you turn back to comparisons?

He glanced at Rolabi. *What do you mean?* he thought.

Who is richer. Who is faster. Who is the best. Always about someone else.

Lab scowled. *Some people just have it better*, he thought. *That's not my fault.*

You don't have time to live anyone else's life but your own.

Lab looked away. He remembered the films, of course. And maybe it was true that everyone had problems. But he didn't want *their* lives. He just wanted his to be better. Happier.

Then look to yourself.

"What do all the great passers have?" Rolabi asked.

"Vision," Peño said confidently.

"Very good. A great passer must be quick and agile and bold. But mostly, they must have vision. Both of what is and what will soon come. They must see *everything* on the floor."

Lab wasn't following again. "So . . . we just have to practice seeing more . . . ?"

"Yes," Rolabi said. "And the best way to start is by seeing nothing at all."

And then Lab went blind. He closed his eyes, and nothing changed. He rubbed them, feeling his breath quickening. Lab had never liked the dark. For Lab, darkness meant bad dreams. Flashing memories.

Sweat beaded on his forehead. His chest felt leaden. He could hear the others panicking and talking, and he whirled around. A million unseen threats took form in the black expanse around him.

"How is this helping us with vision?" Lab asked shrilly.

The voices seemed to fade. He felt the air grow colder, and a shiver ran down his back. Soon all he could hear was his own rapid breathing. He stuck his hands out, searching.

"Peño?" he whispered.

"To be a Wizenard, one must spend an entire day in pitch-blackness."

Lab whirled to the source of the voice. "Rolabi, where am I? Turn a light on!"

His skin grew hot. His breathing felt more difficult now—shallow and short.

"Our minds shape the darkness. When we see nothing, we choose our surroundings."

"Rolabi—"

"Many of us choose fear. Doubt. But if we can move about comfortably in darkness, if we can find peace there, then imagine how well we can move in the light. Why do you see only dangers?"

Lab focused on where he thought the voice was coming from. "I . . . I don't."

"You do. And if you see fears in the dark, they stay with you in the light as well. They affect your decisions. They make you afraid to be what you are."

"And what is that?" Lab asked sharply.

"Whatever you choose."

Lab tried to relax. He forced longer, slower breaths. "Am I making this again?"

"You are making it a frightening experience. Make it an illuminating one."

The voices of the team suddenly returned, and Lab heard Peño and the others searching for a ball. He hesitated, and then started after them, moving slowly, carefully. He held his arms out in front of him, constantly wincing like he was about to hit a wall. A part of him wanted to curl up and lie on the floor. But he thought back to Rolabi's words and kept searching.

"There it is!" Twig shouted. "I just kicked it!"

Lab heard a ball bouncing close to him. "I'm on it!" He followed the noise, moving a bit faster, and then crouched down and laid a hand on familiar rubber pebbling. "Got it!"

"Now into position," Rolabi instructed. "Line up beneath the net."

That wasn't any easier. When Lab and his teammates finally got into what they hoped was a line under one net, the defenders shouted that they in turn were "probably" lined up at half.

"Okay, I'm going!" Peño said.

"Here!" Rain called. "Who's next?"

Lab hurried toward his voice. "Here. Pass it!"

He vainly waved for the ball just in time to receive it in a very sensitive area. He groaned and doubled over, gasping for air, though he did manage to scoop up the ball on the second bounce.

"A little higher," he managed weakly. "Keep moving!"

They progressed slowly but without further incident. Lab was just starting to think the drill wasn't too hard, when they got to half-court, and everything went to pieces. The defenders were waiting there, trying to pick off the ball. The voices intermingled, as did the squeaking shoes, and Lab lost track of everything. When Peño tried to throw him a pass, Lab missed it completely. The ball went bouncing off like a fading drumbeat.

"Switch," Rolabi said.

Lab turned, waiting for the bench team to find the ball and take their turn. He was already starting to feel a little less vulnerable in the dark. He could hear and feel and smell the other players, and he began to create an image of the court around him. He could sense A-Wall shifting beside him, and he heard Rain shouting orders, Peño's heavy breathing, and even Twig chewing his nails. The bench team took their turn and lost it in about twenty seconds.

"Hmm," Rolabi said thoughtfully. "Perhaps we will work up to complete darkness."

The ball lit up. It was a strange, fiery color, like it had been set ablaze from the inside. Someone picked it up, and Lab watched in amazement as it floated across the gym.

"This is weird," Peño said. "You guys ready? Go!"

The illuminated ball made a big difference. Lab could catch it more reliably and didn't take any more unfortunate passes in unfortunate areas. But they still couldn't get past the row of defenders. Peño shouted that he was making the pass before promptly throwing it to the other team.

"Stolen!" Jerome shouted.

"Nice pass, Peño," Lab muttered.

They technically still weren't talking, but it felt a little easier in the darkness.

"I can't see who I'm passing to," Peño replied. "What do you want from me?"

"Vision," Lab said sarcastically.

"I'm going to pass it into the side of your head next time," Peño snarled.

There was just a little hint of amusement in his voice—like one of their usual fights.

"You couldn't hit the side of a barn," Lab said, smiling.

"Well, luckily your head is bigger than that."

Lab bit back a laugh. It felt good to talk normally again. He wondered if it would continue when the lights came on.

They repeated the drill again and again, and Lab became more attuned to the darkness with every round. Hours might have gone by. He took a few elbows and body checks, but for now, he saw no more monsters.

It was Rain who finally broke through the defenders. He sprinted down the court, got the ball from Lab, and then threw it down to a shouting Peño. The ball stopped four feet above the ground, and the lights flicked on. Peño was standing on the far baseline beneath the hoop.

"The starting team wins," Rolabi said. "Water break."

The starters celebrated with high fives and props, though Peño didn't come over to Lab. Obviously it wasn't going to be that easy. Lab sighed inwardly and walked to the bench alone, where he downed most of his water bottle in one gulp and gobbled half a granola bar too. He had managed to pack himself something that morning—it had been a long, thirsty practice yesterday.

"The losing team will run at the end of practice," Rolabi said. "The winning team can decide then if they want to join them. So, clearly, on offense we must learn to listen. What else?"

What did you see in the darkness?

Nothing, Lab thought dryly.

Are you sure?

Lab thought about that. *I . . . I guess I saw that it wasn't as scary as I thought.*

It usually isn't.

"Twig, come up here, please," Rolabi said.

Twig slowly made his way to the professor, looking concerned.

"I want you to tell the team one thing you would like to say to them. One *honest* thing."

"What sort of thing?" Twig asked.

"It could be anything. If you cannot be honest with each other, you cannot be a team."

Twig hesitated, scratching his arm. It reminded Lab of Twig's film reel. The skin picking—which explained the pockmarks on his cheeks. His dad screaming. Pressuring him.

"Okay, well, I have been working really hard," Twig said softly. "You know, in the off-season. And I am trying really hard to be better. I know maybe you guys didn't want me back this season, but I really am trying to help the team. I want you guys to know that."

Lab felt his insides twist. Had he ever told Twig he'd played a good game? Had he ever asked him if he was all right? Or even how was he doing? Not once. In the midst of all the loneliness he'd felt, Lab hadn't even noticed that Twig felt the same. How many others?

"Jerome," Rolabi said.

They went one-by-one, and it soon came to Lab. He walked up beside Rolabi, trying to think. He didn't really have anything—nothing he wanted to share with the team, anyway.

Think of your game, then. Small steps.

"Umm . . . well . . . I hope we win it all?"

"Is that a question?" Rolabi asked.

"No," Lab said, fidgeting. "Okay . . . well . . . I am going to work on my D a little this year. I know you guys all think I suck at it. Going to work harder on that end. That's how I'll improve."

"Good," Rolabi said, nodding.

Work. That is how you keep moving.

Rain was last, and he walked up and fidgeted. Lab glared at him.

"I'm sorry," Rain said, still shifting uncomfortably, hands searching for nonexistent pockets. "About yesterday. I shouldn't have said I was the team like that."

"Do you believe it?" Vin asked.

Lab was wondering the same thing. It sounded like a pretty insincere apology. In fact, as he watched Rain protest with the other players, he felt his temper rising. Rain didn't even care.

"I do push you to be better," Rain said.

"No," Lab cut in. "You just try to score enough to pull us along with you."

Rain glanced at him, and Lab held his eyes, not backing down.

"Well, what do you want from me?" Rain asked.

"To be a part of the Badgers," Lab said coolly. "Not Rain Adams and the Badgers."

Rain sighed. "I will be. For real. Are we good?"

Peño was the first to step forward and accept Rain's apology, and slowly the team murmured their assent. Lab was reluctant, but he nodded too. A small part of him knew his resentment was jealousy, and that in turn was embarrassing. He wanted some of that attention. The showy isolation plays. The scouts and the hype and all of it.

Lab got nothing. Second best on the Badgers might as well have been worst.

But will you take the last shot?

Lab looked away from the team. It was true. How could a star avoid the last shot?

"Let's scrimmage for an hour," Rolabi said.

"No tricks?" Peño asked.

"Just working on our vision. Rain, Vin, Lab, A-Wall, and Devon versus the rest."

Lab looked at his new team—they *always* practiced starters versus the bench. But the starters had just been mixed up. Rain couldn't be benched. Did that mean Peño had been demoted? He could see his brother considering that possibility with an expression of real concern. Peño lived for the Badgers. If Peño got benched, he would be devastated. The thought made Lab's stomach turn. He couldn't imagine starting a game while his big brother watched from the sideline.

Rolabi held a ball out for the jump. "We focus on one actor and miss the others in the background. We watch one card as the dealer palms a second. We watch the ball but miss the game."

Twig and Devon stepped up for the jump ball.

What is he talking about now? Lab thought, growing increasingly concerned.

It sounded like something magical was going to happen, and he peered around warily. Would it be his grana again? Or was a tiger going to jump on his head? His whole body tensed.

"We can see so much and yet choose not to," Rolabi said. "It is an odd decision."

There was no tiger. And the lights didn't turn off either, though that might have been better than what happened: Lab's vision split into two pieces. Now he could see only a narrow sliver on either side—his farthest peripheral vision. It was like a curtain had been hung over the rest, and though he rubbed his eyes frantically, the blockage didn't budge.

Rolabi tossed the ball up.

"I can't do this," Lab shouted.

If that is what you believe, then you are correct.

Lab tried to calm down again. It was just grana. His grana. He thought back to the river of magma and how he could divert it. He was in control. He just had to stay calm and direct the flow.

He spotted his new point guard, Vin, with the ball, so Lab jogged to the hoop, moving his head back and forth to see the floor. He found his way to the corner and stopped there, realizing he was open. Everyone was moving very slowly. Rain caught a pass and cut to the net but slowed down as the post players collapsed in. He would usually drive right through them and force up the shot, but today he kicked the ball back out to Lab in the corner. Jerome had cheated inside, so Lab was all alone. To his relief, the blockage in his vision suddenly vanished.

"I can see!" he shouted. He lined up the shot and drained it. "Nice pass, Rain!"

The blockage in his vision returned.

"Like . . . fully see?" Peño asked.

"Not anymore," Lab said, frustrated. "Just when I was shooting."

Lab ran back on defense, getting there well before Jerome. When it was fully dark, Lab had focused on the voices to get a sense of positioning. Now he did that as well, but he also paid attention to what was happening *around* him, as opposed to what was in *front* of him, as usual. He found himself unusually aware of what everyone else was doing, where they were going, and who was the most open. They were moving slowly—very slowly—but they were playing smart.

Whenever he was open, his vision would clear again. The same didn't apply for forced shots, so Lab found himself constantly moving to space. The scrimmage continued until they were all drenched in sweat, and Lab's shirt was clinging to him like a second skin. It could have been hours.

"That will do," Rolabi said. "Grab your bottles and join me in the center."

The blockage in his vision lifted, and Lab went to grab a drink. After a quick discussion of the drill, Rolabi sent the bench team on a run. Lab wondered if any of the starters might take up his offer and join them—maybe Rain after yesterday's incident. But Rain stayed put, and so did the rest of them, just watching the losing team run. When the bench team rejoined the group after a made free throw, Rolabi took the potted flower out of his bag and set it down. Lab groaned.

"Not again," Peño said, clearly of the same opinion.

"Many times more," Rolabi said. "If you wish to win, you *must* slow down time. Begin."

He turned and headed for the doors.

"Where are you going?" Peño asked indignantly.

"You will take the daisy home tonight, Peño. Be careful with it, please. Water it."

Lab turned to the flower. They had to bring one of Rolabi's . . . *things* home? He exchanged a concerned look with his brother, their fight momentarily forgotten, as the front doors crashed open with the wind. But Peño turned away again, scowling, and Lab did the same.

"How long do you want us to stare at it?" Rain shouted.

Rolabi kept walking. "Until you see something new."

The doors slammed shut, shaking the gym and dropping dust onto their heads like snow.

"Do you think that was, like . . . literal?" Peño asked, frowning.

Vin sighed. "Who knows? At least I don't have to take it home."

"Thanks," Peño said.

"Where you going?" Jerome asked.

Lab turned and saw that Big John was heading for his duffel bag.

"I'm not staring at a stupid flower if I don't have to," Big John said. "I'm out."

"Everything all right with you?" Peño asked.

Big John turned back. "No, Peño. This is the Bottom. Things aren't just *all right*. You can go along with that weirdo all you want and play his games. But it's not a game out there. Remember where you are. I'm going to catch some extra time at work."

He left, and Lab glanced at his brother. Big John was right about one thing—they didn't need to stare at the daisy if Rolabi wasn't there. Lab went to grab his ball to work on his shot. Something important. Most of the other players followed, but Devon, Reggie, and Twig just stared at the flower.

From somewhere outside himself, Lab felt a flicker of disappointment.

I thought you wanted to learn about grana.

I want to learn about ball too, he thought.

They are one and the same.

Lab scowled and went to shoot, working again and again on his corner three-pointer.

"I wonder if we are ever going to—" he started.

"Look!" Peño said.

Lab followed his gaze and saw that the orb was hovering over Devon's head. Lab froze, feeling the familiar chill. Devon didn't move, and no one warned him. Somehow, Lab could tell he already knew it was there. After what seemed like hours, in a flash Devon shot his hand up and snatched the orb out of midair. The black liquid oozed through his fingers, and then he disappeared entirely. Lab stepped back. Devon was gone.

Where is he? Lab thought.

The same place you must go, when you are ready.

Where? he thought nervously.

The hiding place.

THE BIG SHOT

If you chase happiness, you will never let
yourself suffer. Chase purpose instead.
◆ WIZENARD 16 PROVERB ◆

LAB WATCHED AS Devon took another shot from the elbow—
missing as he had for the last twenty or so attempts. Every time, he
simply retrieved the ball, went back to the same spot, and shot again.

He had reappeared yesterday a minute or so after his disappearance.
Ever since, Lab had been wondering where he'd gone, or more accurately,
what his hiding place was like. What did the new kid put down there?
And did Lab really have to go to his place as well? That frightened him
more than anything he could think of. He didn't even know how many
memories he had stuffed down there in the last three years, and what they
had become.

All he knew was that everything kept feeling heavier and heavier.
Getting up in the morning was a struggle, and falling asleep was even
harder.

Lab had been sitting on the couch last night when his dad shuffled in.
He had plunked down beside Lab, face crusted with dirt and sweat.

"Not sleeping much lately, huh?" he said.

"No."

His dad nodded, slipped his boots off, and put his feet up on the table. "Been thinking about her?"

Lab kept his eyes away from the photo on the mantel. She was smiling back at them, healthy, happy . . . not knowing what was coming. Lab wanted to take it down, but Peño refused.

"Yeah," Lab said.

His dad sighed and wiped his face, leaving streaks in the dust there. "She wouldn't want this."

"She wouldn't want to be dead either."

They had both sat in silence.

"Hits me too," his dad said.

"What do you do when that happens?"

His dad glanced at him. "I remember the good times, and I keep moving."

"And what if I can't keep moving?"

"You got no choice," he said. "It happened whether you face it or not." He stood up and clapped Lab on the shoulder. "Your mom wanted the best for you. Go get it. Make her proud."

The word hung with him. Proud? How could he do that when even the thought of her hurt so badly?

"Gather around," Rolabi said, shattering Lab's memory. "Today we work on your shots."

Lab flinched, dropping the ball. As usual, he hadn't seen the professor come in. He scooped up his ball and put it away.

Rolabi's eyes went to Devon. "Hmm," he said, "this will be fascinating."

Just as Lab was joining the huddle in front of the professor, Rolabi threw a ball to Devon, and Fairwood vanished. The hardwood turned to stone. The walls fell away into open air, stretching in all directions and carpeted by a brooding cloudscape. The team was standing on a mountain—

though it was so narrow that it was more like a great stone tree trunk. A second tower rose only ten feet away from it, and atop that one was a basketball net. Both sun and stars shone in the thin atmosphere. They were a mile up. Maybe even more.

Lab turned to his brother, who was trembling.

"What is this?" Lab asked softly, his breath coming in clouds.

"A mountain, I guess," Peño managed through chattering teeth.

Lab knew that his brother was not a big fan of heights. Peño's gaze was flicking rapidly from one cliff edge to another, and he looked even smaller than usual, like he had drawn himself in.

Jerome peeked over the edge. "What do we do . . . climb down?"

The cold air was creeping beneath Lab's shirt. Grana had caused this, he was sure of it. But was it his, or Devon's? This mountaintop didn't mean anything to Lab . . . did it? He glanced over the cliffs at the clouds below. At the fall into nothingness. Wasn't that what he was facing?

A bone-grinding crack traveled through the ground. Lab cried out as a massive boulder splintered and fell away behind the team, bouncing once off the cliffside before disappearing into the clouds.

As it vanished into the swirls, more cracks spread out across the summit.

"Maybe we need to shoot the ball?" Twig was saying.

Another boulder fell away. Lab turned to Peño, huddling next to him. Boats sinking. Mountains crumbling. Why was everything falling apart? Was this because of his fears?

Everything you see is framed by your mind.

He considered that. He thought of the Bottom itself, and how often he felt frustrated by its poverty. Its trash. Its relentless disintegration. His thoughts were never about fixing the problems; they were always about wishing he were somewhere else. But was the Bottom even as bad as he thought? Was he seeing the bad parts because . . . he wanted to?

Your dark room approaches.

I don't want it! Lab shouted silently.

Rain missed the first shot, and the ball came rocketing back up to Vin. Lab felt sweat beading on his forehead. Heat built up beneath his shirt, even in the thin mountain air. Questions roiled in his mind. How much of the darkness around him had *he* built? The mountain split again.

Rolabi, get us out of here! he thought.

Why don't you?

"Keep shooting!" Twig urged.

By the time the ball came to Lab, only Twig had scored. Lab took a deep breath . . . or tried to. It caught in his throat, and when he looked at the gap between him and the hoop, his head spun. He steadied himself, flinching at another crack, and took the shot. The ball hit the rim and plummeted toward the distant clouds. Lab wondered numbly if he would be following it soon.

Only if you choose to fall.

Time seemed to speed up. Lab's eyes kept darting from shot to falling boulder to Peño to his own shaking hands, even as he missed yet another attempt. Reggie hit. Peño missed again. Rain missed for a third time. Devon missed. Lab missed and nearly screamed in frustration. His mind filled with new voices:

"You're going to let them down."

"You are the disappointment."

"It's going to be your fault!"

Why are you afraid of the pressure? Rolabi asked.

I don't know!

Peño managed to quell his shaking long enough to hit his shot and pumped his fist. Rain and Devon missed again. The ball came flying back to Lab. "You got this," his brother said. Lab saw the desperation and fear in his eyes.

Take off the weight.

Lab flinched as the deeper voice rose over the others. The image of the sinking boat flashed through his mind, as clear as the water that streamed over the planks. He knew he was weighing himself down with the *fear* of missing. The fear of disappointing his teammates. His brother. The fear of letting them down—it shackled his limbs.

Breathe. Cast them off.

How? he thought weakly.

Focus on the details. The stone. The net. Your lungs, moving in and out.

Lab allowed himself to breathe deeply. His heartbeat slowed, and he stepped closer to the edge. He focused on the hoop, on evenly aligning his toes, and on his fingertips shifting and gripping the rubber ball. For a peaceful moment, all was quiet. Then Lab released the ball and hit the shot.

And that is why we stare at the flower.

Lab stood at the cliff edge, breathing heavily.

There was another crack, and then Devon hit his shot. The team pressed closer together.

"Just one more," Lab whispered, glancing at Rain.

The ball landed in Rain's hands. His whole body trembled.

"Make it, Rain!" Peño shouted.

The ground beneath their feet cracked and shifted ominously. They had no more room.

"Hurry!" Vin shrieked.

The mountain teetered. It was all going to fall this time.

"Just hold on. We'll be fine," Peño murmured.

"Shoot it!" A-Wall said.

The ground gave way just as Rain released the ball. The mountain swung backward, away from the net, and Lab felt gravity seize his limbs. Peño clutched Lab's wrist, his nails digging into his skin, but Lab just watched the ball fly. It moved impossibly slowly.

Just as Lab started to feel like he was flying too, the ball dropped through the hoop.

Gone was the mountain and the basket alone on its rock and the cold air. The Badgers were back in Fairwood, and Lab doubled over while Peño dropped to his hands and knees and kissed the hardwood planks.

"You are gross," Lab said, fighting back a laugh.

He remembered Peño's hand on his arm. His brother's first instinct. Protect Lab. Always.

"Welcome back," Rolabi said. "What makes a great shooter?"

Vin scowled. "You almost killed us!"

Lab met Rolabi's eyes. His pupils grew large, showing a true mountain, broad and full.

It has been rebuilt. You are almost ready for the room.

What will I find there? Lab thought.

Only you can know that.

"Think about the *heart* of a great shooter. What does he lack?" Rolabi asked the team.

"Fear," Devon said after a long pause. "He lacks fear."

"All great shooters are fearless. If they fear missing, or being blocked, or losing, then they will not shoot. Even if they do, they will rush it. They will allow fear to move their elbows or turn their fingers to stone. They will never be great. And how do we get rid of our fears?"

"We face them," Devon said.

"Yes, and one thing we all fear is letting down our friends," Rolabi said.

Lab looked at Rolabi, feeling the weight of that statement. He could almost hear the buzzer counting down . . .

"That will do for today," Rolabi said. "Tomorrow should be an interesting day."

"What was today?" Lab said. "Boring?"

Rolabi turned and headed for the nearest wall. Once again, he was nowhere near the doors, and once again, the lights flashed and died, and he was gone when they blinked back on.

"What are you doing, Rain?" Peño asked.

Rain was heading for the free-throw line with a ball. "Shooting," he said.

They all hesitated and then went to grab their balls as well, forming two free-throw lines on either end of the court. Lab shot again and again, retrieving the ball and lining up until his arms and legs were tired and the whole world was just a ball, a hoop, and a straight black line, and it made sense, and it was enough. The team shot for hours. Finally, they called it and went to change. As Lab was putting on his street shoes, Peño left alone again, though he glanced back as the doors closed. Lab hurried after him. He was tired of fighting with his brother—it didn't seem to matter much when you were falling off a mountain. In that moment, Peño had moved on too.

As Peño stormed across the parking lot, Lab fell into step with him. He considered blurting out an apology, or saying thank you for the mountain, but none of that really felt right.

"You walking with me today?" Peño asked.

They were brothers, and Lab just wanted things to be normal again.

"Well, it's not safe for you to walk home alone," Lab said.

"Why not?"

"You're too short. People can't see you over the hood of their car."

Peño flushed and then burst into laughter. "Shut up."

"Who said that?" Lab asked, peering at the ground.

They walked in silence for a moment. A car rolled past, spewing exhaust into the sky. Lab thought back to their fight, and to what Peño had said. The difficulty breathing. The moments alone. It occurred to him he hadn't been there for his brother. But that could change.

"Do you really . . . have trouble breathing sometimes?" Lab asked.

"Yeah," Peño said. "I guess . . . it's anxiety or something."

"I get that sometimes too."

"You can tell me when it happens," Peño said.

Lab fought back a sudden rush of tears. This was what he'd been waiting for. Someone to tell him he wasn't alone. Someone to talk to. It had been right in front of him the entire time.

"You too," Lab said.

They said nothing more about it. They didn't need to—not right away. But Lab knew he could, and that made all the difference.

8

THE
REAL ENEMY

When we are struggling,
we are learning the tools to help others.

◆ WIZENARD ◆28◆ PROVERB ◆

SNOW ROARED INTO the gym, crashing and frothing and streaming toward center court. Lab stared in wonder as flurries swirled around him, and players made of snowflakes dribbled past. Fans cheered, and shots flew through the air. The snow wasn't cold at all, and it finally gathered at center court and erupted into a plume of white before disappearing altogether. Not a single flake hit the floor.

"Am I still dreaming?" Lab whispered.

Rolabi strolled into the silent gym and stopped at center court, hands clasped. Lab was so entranced, he didn't even register Rolabi's reply.

"Line up facing me," Rolabi said, snapping Lab back to attention. "Three of you have caught the orb so far. I can see some changes. The rest must stay vigilant. They must be ready when the moment comes."

Three? Lab wondered, exchanging a glance with his brother. Who else caught it?

He looked around the team, and wondered again if they all actually had something to hide. Did everyone? How could every person have a secret? How could they *all* be afraid?

Because they are human.

"Today we will be focusing on team offense," Rolabi continued. "You have worked on your passing and vision. You have worked on your shot. But this is not a game of one. It is a game of many. Even the greatest players cannot win this game alone."

He looked up at the rafters, and Lab followed his gaze, confused. The ceiling looked much different than he remembered. The rafters had been freshly stained, and the fluorescent panels were no longer dusty and flickering. Lab turned. Even the bleachers seemed like they had been newly polished. Had Freddy hired someone to come fix the place up?

Half the lights blinked off, and Lab snorted. Never mind. Fairwood was just as ratty as ever. He noticed that all the lights facing the team remained on, and even brightened. Lab blinked against the sudden glare.

"We will learn to attack as one," Rolabi said. "But first, we need defenders."

Someone yelped, and Lab spun around to find that the team's shadows were picking themselves up off the floor. Lab stepped back in horror as his shadow climbed to its feet and shook its limbs out, jumping on the spot. It was Lab's identical silhouette, and it turned to him as it warmed up, faceless and terrifying.

"Not cool," Peño whispered.

"Meet today's defenders. You should know them well."

Lab's shadow stuck its hand out. Lab didn't move, and the shadow stepped closer, insisting. Lab gulped and shook its hand, and his shadow nodded before resuming its warm-up.

"This is the weirdest one yet," Peño said.

Lab nodded. "I think I miss the tiger."

"Into position, defenders," Rolabi said, and the shadows jogged onto the court.

Lab rubbed his eyes. He had seen plenty of strange things in the last eight days, but this one had them beat. It was like perfect cutouts of the team running around, stretching, jumping.

"Line it up," Peño said reluctantly.

Lab walked to the left wing, and the shadow version of himself moved to stay in front of him, sliding along the floor. It stayed low and compact, with one hand stretched out to track him.

"Relax, will you?" Lab said. "We haven't even started yet."

The shadow shook its head.

"I guess you don't talk much?" Lab said.

Another shake. Lab realized he was talking to his own shadow and rubbed his temples.

"Rain!" Peño said, passing him the ball like he did at the start of every offensive possession.

As usual, Rain tried to fake and cut to the basket—but his shadow blocked him perfectly. The ball came to Lab instead, and he tried a quick step to free up some space, but his shadow didn't go for the fake. It was right on him, jockeying and keeping a free hand up for the block in case he tried a sudden jumper. Lab shielded the ball from the aggressive reaching and scowled.

"Try the post," he called, getting the ball back to his brother.

Peño managed to get it to Twig, who went for a rare layup . . . and was promptly stuffed.

"Switch it up," Rolabi said.

"I think our shadows are better at D than we are," Lab muttered.

His shadow nodded in agreement, and Lab gave it an exasperated look.

The starters went back on after the bench players were shut out.

This time the ball was stolen almost immediately. Two of the shadows exchanged high fives, and Lab's shadow even reached over and mussed up his hair.

"Hey!" Lab said. "Not cool, shadow me."

They went back and forth between the starters and the bench. Lab managed to hit a quick shot, but he was stuffed six times and had the ball stolen three more. Lab's shadow seemed to get more and more arrogant with every defensive stop, and at one point it did a chest bump with Peño's.

"Our shadows are annoying," Peño muttered.

"I've noticed," Lab said.

As the starters were gulping down their water on a break, Rolabi walked over to join them.

"How is your defense, Lab?"

Lab looked around and realized he was standing alone on the court. He shifted uneasily.

"Not bad—"

"I've heard differently."

Lab glowered. "I just like to play my own style. I like man defense."

"Ah," Rolabi said. "I see. But you don't play man defense. You play *my man* defense."

"What's the difference?" Lab asked, frowning.

"You think stopping your man is all you have to do. 'My man didn't score.' 'My man didn't rebound.' True man defense means *nobody* scores on you."

Rolabi took a step toward him.

"If you want to be a starter on this team, you must play defense like a tiger."

Lab shrunk away. "I . . . I'll try . . ."

"Good. For now, let's get back to offense. Into your positions, please."

Lab blinked, and the team was back again, the shadows waiting for the starters in a loose zone. Lab walked to the wing, and his shadow stepped out to meet him. The gym grew darker.

"Peño, pass the ball to Rain," Rolabi said.

Lab's shadow continued to jostle closer, keeping its arms up. Lab stepped back, annoyed, but it followed, keeping less than a foot between them.

"Chill," Lab said.

But the shadow just shifted, blocking the angle from Peño—making the pass difficult.

"He said Rain," Lab muttered. "I ain't getting the pass."

Peño did as he was told, and immediately, a white light fell on Rain. His shadow moved again, this time blocking him from both Rain and a cut to the net. Cold fingers brushed his arm.

You created the shadow.

So? Lab thought, glancing at Rolabi.

So you know how to play defense. You just hold back.

Lab scowled and turned back to his shadow. It was true. He didn't play defense like this . . . but wasn't it a waste of energy for offense? Wasn't it more important to hit corner threes?

As if to answer the question, his shadow stepped closer still.

"We'll see what you got, then," Lab said.

He had figured out that a spotlight seemed to fall on a player who got open, so he made a quick fake down low and then stepped back again, raising his hand for the skip pass. It was his favorite play, usually. A spotlight did fall on him, but it was far dimmer than the others.

I'm not a good enough option, he realized.

Lab cut for the corner and called for the pass, his shadow racing to catch up. This time the spotlight on him was blazing.

Rain threw him the ball, and Lab dribbled only once before throwing it to A-Wall down low. Lab stopped in the corner, but as A-Wall turned away from him, trying to post up, the light around him grew dim again. A-Wall couldn't see him, and the defender was in the way of a pass.

Normally, Lab would wait there anyway. But there was no time.

He cut back toward the top of the arc, getting into A-Wall's line of sight, and received another pass. His shadow closed in fast, growing bigger as he delayed, so Lab threw the ball to the point and cut again. He started running from the point to the wing to the corner in a loose triangle. It was more than an issue of spacing—he had to help his teammates too. When Lab passed Twig the ball down low, Lab cut immediately to give him an option to pass it back. When Lab ran to the corner, he used a big man as a screen and rubbed the defender to free up his own shot, creating wide-open looks. He hit five corner threes in an hour, and his shadow wasn't chest-bumping anymore.

"What now, Shadow Lab?" Lab asked, slapping his chest.

His shadow stared back at him facelessly, and Lab stopped talking.

After Rain hit another open layup, Rolabi stepped forward with the daisy.

"That's enough for today," he said. "Sit and watch. Thank you, gentlemen."

The lights all turned back on, and the shadows disappeared instantly. Lab grabbed his water bottle and then sat cross-legged in front of the daisy, happy for the break. He had been so consumed with the drill, he'd barely realized how tired he was. It occurred to him that maybe he had been spending a little too much time hanging back from the play, wanting the ball more.

Had he ever gone to *get it*?

"If you use the Spotlight Offense, you will be more effective," Rolabi said. "Follow the light, invite it to yourself, and you will conquer any darkness."

"Pretty heavy for basketball," Big John said.

"And perfect for life," Rolabi said. "Why not live every part of it with the same values?"

With that, he turned to the flower. Lab still had no idea how they were supposed to see it grow. But he was also exhausted, so he drank his water and enjoyed the break. Then the gym grew still and tense . . . like no one was breathing anymore. Lab knew the orb had arrived before he looked.

"Here we go again," he muttered.

Vin was first to move, and Lab scrambled to his feet and sprinted after him. As he did, he noticed Twig, Devon, and Jerome stayed behind—clearly, they were the three who had already caught it. They had all faced the hiding place. What was in their rooms? What were they hiding?

As he closed in, Lab waited for the orb to make its move. "Split up!" he shouted.

Lab snatched at the orb and missed, flinching as it zoomed right past his face. Rain lunged for it and missed, wildly swinging his arms and smacking Vin in the chest. Lab watched as Peño made another desperate swipe, and then the black shape slowed, facing off with a prowling Rain.

Rain was ready. He faked and pivoted, snagging the orb and disappearing instantly.

"The fat kid is clearly at a disadvantage here," Big John said.

"I thought it was Bad Man Blubber?" Peño said.

"It's still blubber," he said.

Lab rubbed his hamstring—he felt like he'd pulled it during the chase. He shuffled to the bench for water, only belatedly thinking to look for Rolabi. But the professor was already gone. He sighed and dropped onto the bench, massaging his legs. Vin sat down beside him, scowling.

"I'm getting sick of that orb," Vin said.

"Same," Lab said, watching as Rain reappeared.

They stripped their shoes off and sat there for a moment, catching their breath.

"Hey," Vin said quietly. "You know what you said the other day? About you being around if I needed anything?"

"Yeah."

Vin scratched the back of his neck, looking uncomfortable. "Well, I was wondering if you, and Peño if he wanted, would come play ball with me at the park sometime this summer."

"By your place?" Lab asked, raising an eyebrow. "Why not play here?"

"Well, I go there, and there's these kids giving me a tough time. Stupid stuff and—"

"I'll be there," Lab cut in immediately. "Peño too. Anytime you want."

Vin looked at him, obviously surprised. He cleared his throat and nodded. "Thanks."

Vin started to pack up, and Lab thought he saw him wipe his eyes with a quick shoulder.

The ones that hurt the most always have the most to give.

Lab felt a lump form in his throat. *How come no one is helping me?* he thought.

Because you have decided you aren't worth helping.

Lab closed his eyes. He was ready for the dark room.

THE
DARK ROOM

*If you bring too much with you,
how will you help others with their bags?*
✧ WIZENARD (42) PROVERB ✧

LAB HUNCHED OVER on the sideline, panting. His sides burned with cramps, his hair draped over his forehead like an oil spill. He had been warming up hard . . . almost manic. Shoot, rebound, shoot, rebound. He had worked until even Peño had asked if he was feeling all right.

He wasn't. He hadn't slept well. That was nothing new, but last night he'd barely gotten a wink. It was fear over his hiding place. Fear of what he might find down there. Maybe everyone had something they were hiding, but he was the one who didn't sleep and felt sick all the time and hated himself. It was the last admission that had surprised him. He hated who he had become.

And now he was trying to sweat it out, to push all that pain away and be ready.

But was he? How could he ever be ready to face those memories again?

"We have two days left of our training camp," Rolabi said, walking past him onto the court. He had seemingly emerged from thin air. "And two left to catch the orb."

Lab stiffened. *Two?* When had all the others caught it? He looked at Peño and saw the same confusion on his brother's face. They were the only ones left. Was that significant?

Was it because they had the most issues to face?

Rolabi continued. "From there we will return to three evening practices a week until the start of the season. We will practice everything we have discussed here again and again until it becomes second nature. In your free time, you will focus on your mind. Read. Study. Learn to see. The mind and body are intertwined; if you neglect one, the other will fail. Never stop."

"It's summer break," A-Wall said. "We're not supposed to be studying."

"No break is needed, or wanted, for the tenacious mind," Rolabi replied, starting for the doors. "I will see you tomorrow."

"There's no practice today?" Peño asked.

"Oh yes," Rolabi said on his way to the door. "You just don't need me."

"What should we do?" Rain asked.

Rolabi glanced over his shoulder. "I leave that to you."

He walked through the front doors, and they promptly disappeared, trapping the team inside. The only exit from the building was gone, and Lab looked around the gym nervously.

"Perfect," Peño said. "I guess he's making sure we don't go home early."

"I wouldn't be so sure," Twig murmured.

He was right. Something began to churn and grind, growing so loud that Lab covered his ears. As the noise intensified, the gym's two longer walls suddenly shook and pushed forward, closing in on the team like an enormous vise. They slid over the floors, inching toward the trapped team.

"Impossible," Vin said.

"Possibility is subjective," Lab muttered. "Any ideas?"

"The locker room!" Rain shouted. He ran for the door, but it vanished before he could reach it. He slapped the wall in frustration. "Now what?"

"Maybe we need to score the ball again?" Vin said.

It was as good an idea as any. But nothing worked. Lab hit threes and layups. They all did. They shot again and again until they were sweating profusely and the walls had driven the lumbering steel bleachers almost onto the court. The whole gym was forming a sort of corridor—something he remembered well. Even the walls were white, and he looked around in horror as it all seemed to shrink back toward that day. His breath caught in his throat.

It felt like that memory was finally going to crush him alive, just as it had been threatening for the last three years.

"This is useless," Lab said. "We did shooting two days ago. He wouldn't repeat it."

"So what's left?" A-Wall said. "We've done defense and offense now!"

Lab looked around the gym. He had no idea. There was nothing left.

"We need to stop the walls," Devon said suddenly. He hurried over to the bleachers and began to heave vainly on one side. "Help!"

Lab ran over to join him. The bleachers were one giant structure of welded steel, and they were incredibly heavy. Lab tugged until his entire body was on fire.

"Turn it sideways!" Rain shouted. "On three. One . . . two . . . pull!"

They turned the bleachers with inches to spare. The walls pushed on, and Lab watched, biting his lip. But even the steel behemoth was no match for the walls. The metal screeched, folding like paper.

"It's not working!" Peño screamed.

Lab looked back and forth. It was nearly a true hallway now. He half expected to see metal chairs propped against the cinder blocks and smell the sharp acrid sanitizers and hear the noises of crying and shouts and beeping. He thrust his hands over his ears without thinking.

He didn't believe it—he *couldn't* believe it—but what were they missing? Rolabi said they were creating their own grana. But why would the team do this to themselves? Was he doing it—was he creating this hallway again? What was the point? He crouched down, hands still over his ears. There had to be a meaning to it. A purpose to the destruction. What was it?

"Look!" Devon shouted, pointing upward.

Lab didn't have to look . . . he could *feel* the orb. A flash of hope returned to him: maybe Peño could catch it and still escape in time. But when Lab turned to the orb, dropping his hands and standing up, his hope dissipated once again. It was floating twenty feet in the air, at least. They would never be able to reach it.

"Someone can get out of here!" Twig shouted. "You vanish, remember?"

"Only for people that haven't gotten the orb yet," Reggie said. "It will only work for them."

Lab and Peño stared at each other, and Lab turned to the folding bleachers. The middle was being driven up like an archway, and it was heading steadily upward—toward the black orb.

"Get up on the bleachers!" Lab said.

They all climbed, using each other to pull and push themselves up onto the peak of the steel archway, slippery though it was. The climb was precarious, but the bend was still large and flat enough that they were all able to get on top of it, though they struggled to keep their balance.

Lab reached wildly for the orb, desperate to escape the corridor, but it was no use. Even from there the orb was still too high, and they were running out of time. Lab exchanged a desperate look with his brother. He could see the fear in Peño's eyes.

Lab glanced between the walls and the orb. Even with the extra height they would get as the bleachers were bent further, it wouldn't be enough. They would be crushed by the folding steel first. After everything, they were going to fail. Whatever the lesson was, they had missed it.

And then Devon crouched down, bracing his hands and knees against the bending metal.

"Come on!" he shouted. "Make a pyramid!"

The largest players got down beside him, and then Rain, Jerome, and Vin climbed on, managing to balance on the shaking, swaying backs beneath them. Lab and Peño scrambled up last of all from either side.

It was a difficult climb, but finally he and Peño reached out across the top and pulled each other up, standing mere inches apart. Lab knew instantly that neither intended to take the orb. Maybe if someone got it, they would all be spared. Or maybe it would just be one of them.

How could he take that risk?

"Hurry!" Rain shouted. "Get it!"

Peño instantly linked his hands into a foothold. "On my count."

"Peño . . ." Lab said furiously. "We didn't even talk about it—"

Peño glared at him. Lab knew that look. That stubborn, obstinate glare.

"Don't argue with me."

"But—"

"Don't even think for a moment I'm leaving you. Now . . ."

Lab stared at him. He knew Peño would never reach for the orb first. He would never leave him behind.

"I can't just leave you either," Lab said, tasting tears and sweat.

"I'll be fine!" Peño said. "Now use those extra three inches and jump!"

Lab looked to his right. The wall was so close, he could almost touch it. "Peño . . ."

"One . . . two . . . three!" Peño shouted. "Go!"

Lab stepped onto Peño's hands and leapt with everything he had, tears streaming down his face. He felt Peño drive him upward as well, and he flew dangerously over the wreckage of steel, knowing that a miss would kill them all. For a moment, he thought he wouldn't make it.

And then his fingers closed on the orb, and he was gone.

Lab was now standing in an empty room. The plain concrete floor stretched off in all directions until it was swallowed by darkness. He looked around warily. Somehow, it almost seemed . . . familiar here. He knew this place, but he wasn't sure how. He started walking, and a spot-light moved with him, though it seemed to have no source. Finally, he heard an urgent voice.

"Get your stuff on, Lab—"

"What is it?" a groggy voice asked.

"Your mother—hurry up."

Images appeared in the darkness. Two boys and their father getting into their rusty car. Speeding through the night. Hurrying down a white corridor like the one he'd just escaped. There was commotion. Someone crying. The image suddenly became clear. A younger Lab sitting on those metal chairs while Peño and their father waited by the bedside. Her bed-side. Mama. Mama was in there.

Lab peeked through the open door. Peño had his hands wrapped around hers, even as the nurses were working frantically. His mama lay still, head to the side, eyes closed. There was no heartbeat. Peño was sobbing.

The younger Lab in the hallway finally stood up and walked into the room.

"Mama," he said, eyes flooding with tears.

He hadn't been there for her when she died. He had stayed in the hall, unable to face her pain. He had let her down, right in the end. His mama.

The younger Lab threw himself over his mama's legs, and his dad was grabbing him and Peño too. Lab fell on his knees as he watched. The hospital faded to dark and a million images went by, like photographs floating through the blackness. Every second he'd had with his mama. The singing and the stories and walking down the street behind her while her scarf fluttered in the wind. The photos swirled around him like flakes in a snow globe, and he screamed and covered his ears. It was too much. This was the place. This was where he had been hiding it.

The floor began to vibrate, and the flakes vanished, and he was inside his memories again. Lab saw himself sitting alone on his bed, staring at his

hands. He saw himself avoiding his friends. Picking at his food and excus-
ing himself from dinner. Smelling the last bit of her perfume when no one
was around. Distant words emerged with his voice: *I let them all down.*

Cold water spilled over the floor, rising past his legs.

He had been dreading coming here, but he realized it was all so familiar. He had been in this place for three years. Lab lived in this hiding
place. So many mornings he felt sick to his stomach and didn't want to get
out of bed. So many nights he just wanted to sleep because it was a break
from his mind. His energy had faded away. His smile had faded away. He
was watching it happen one quiet scene at a time.

"I want it to end," he whispered.

"No," a voice said. "You want the pain to end. That is different."

"What am I supposed to do?"

"You choose to live here," Rolabi said. "Why?"

Lab thought about that. "Because . . . because of my mom."

"That was the start. The loss of a loved one is a powerful catalyst—for
good or ill. But you created the dark room for a reason. You are hiding
things here. *You* are hiding here. Why?"

More scenes rolled by. More days and nights alone. More guilt and
more . . . shame.

"Because I couldn't handle the memories."

"No, deeper than that. Why won't you take the last shot, Lab?"

Lab looked at him, frowning. "What does that have to do with—"

"When the buzzer sounds, you don't want to shoot. Why?"

Lab thought back to the vision he'd had the first day of training. The
ball in his hands, his mother telling him to shoot, the rage of the crowd
when he failed. It was true. He was petrified of the final shot.

"Because I started to feel like I was letting everyone down," he murmured. "My mama . . . we were so close. She needed me. But I wasn't
there." He was racked by a sob. "She died, and I wasn't there."

"When we are in pain, we want to take the blame. We want to take back control."

"I let her down!" Lab shouted. "You saw it, didn't you? She—"

"Knew you loved her. You were all with her, inside the room or not. You remain so."

Lab broke down, burying his face in his hands.

"What is the heart of this place?" Rolabi said gently. "What do you fear?"

Lab was quiet for a moment. "That . . . that I will always let people down."

"That is how fear works," Rolabi said. "It grows constantly if not confronted. That which you push away comes back when you are not ready. You relinquish control of your fears."

Lab wiped his nose. "How I am supposed to change—"

"Take small steps forward. Do not wake up expecting happiness every day. Wake up expecting your fears to return. Accept that they are part of you, and in time, they will lose their power to harm you. Take the harder road."

He laid a hand on Lab's shoulder.

"Everyone needs help. Bear no guilt, Lab. No shame. All that weight is sinking you."

Lab started to sob. Rolabi put a firm hand on his back, waiting patiently for him to stop.

Lab's whole body convulsed. Tears spilled out.

"What did you see in all these moments?" Rolabi asked. "Who are you truly letting down?"

Lab lowered his hands. One of his memories had frozen, like he had pressed pause.

He saw himself lying in bed, staring at the ceiling. He saw himself watching Peño with his friends from their bedroom window, wondering why he didn't want to join them. He passed away the last shots. Walked on defense to avoid being beaten.

"Myself," he whispered.

"When we live in the dark room, there can be no other way," Rolabi said. "You are not alone, Lab. I am here. Your father is here. Your teammates. Your brother." He turned Lab toward him. "It's a long road back. But you can start walking now."

Lab wiped his eyes. He had built this place to be alone. To hide in. The problem was that it was working too well. He was sinking inside of it. He was *becoming* his fear. Lab wasn't sure he could leave it forever. Destroy his hiding spot. But for the moment, he was sick of this place.

"We can go," Lab said.

The dark room vanished, and Lab was standing back in Fairwood. Peño rushed over and wrapped him in a hug, then pulled back, looking Lab over. He frowned at Lab's tears.

"You all right?"

"Yeah," Lab said. "I think I am."

"What did you see?" Rain asked.

Lab glanced at him. He thought of the memories. The photos flying around him, reminders of all the pain and guilt and everything he had lost. But that was not all he saw.

He had also seen a way to move past them. And it started with leaving that dark room.

He turned to Rain. "The future."

THE WAY FORWARD

The road is all that matters.

WIZENARD ❶ PROVERB

LAB STOOD IN front of the mirror. His hair was slicked back with water, falling halfway down his neck, beads dribbling down his face. He was thinking about last night. He had helped Peño with dinner. He'd organized his duffel bag and made his bed. They were little things, really, but they felt . . . different. Small steps that led somewhere. Somewhere *he* controlled.

But mostly, he stared at her picture. It had always been on the mantel—but ignored. Avoided. Last night Lab had held it. Stared at it. Remembered.

He had found more photos tucked away in drawers or closets. He put the one under his bed—the picture of his mama holding him as a toddler—on the nightstand. Another in his duffel bag. He fell asleep with yet another in his hands. He had let the memories flood over him until he felt like he would be carried away . . . but he wasn't. All the guilt and pain remained, but he didn't try to push them away. He saw now that he had been lying to himself when he pretended he could.

He didn't have the power to forget those things, and he didn't even want to anymore.

Lab ran his fingers over his face. He had the same high cheekbones as her. The same almond-colored eyes. Lab knew the pain was never going to leave. But he knew it wasn't about that. It was what he did with it. It had been hard, but he wanted to see what came out of the fire.

As he turned to the door, he saw something written on the wall in silver ink.

What is the first thing you do when you climb out of a hole?

Lab stared at it, thinking. He knew what the hole was, but what was he supposed to do now? Was it a riddle? As he watched, the question faded back into the paint, and he put it aside for later. He wasn't sure, but maybe the answer would reveal itself today. He knew he had time.

When he reached the home bench, Lab plunked down next to Peño. They talked and joked as they put on their shoes and then went to warm up. As Lab shot around, he looked down and saw the silvery light coursing through his veins, pulsating. He stared at his glowing hands in wonder.

You have taken another step, a deep voice said.

What was it?

Vulnerability. When our fears are released, and faced, the grana comes with it.

What do I do now? Lab thought.

You prepare for the road ahead.

"Gather round," Rolabi said, appearing at center court.

Lab put his ball away and hurried over, joining the group.

"All but one of you have caught the orb. Why?"

Lab glanced at his older brother—the last one to catch it. He wondered what Peño would face. What had the loss of their mother done to him? What did he have in his secret hiding place?

Vin frowned. "Because . . . you told us to?"

"But why?" Rolabi asked. "What did you find?"

"Our fears," Reggie murmured.

Rolabi nodded and turned to the banners. "If one thing will stop you in life, it is that. To win, we must defeat our fears. For basketball . . . for everything."

"But . . . we did, right?" Big John said.

"Fear is not so easily beaten," Rolabi said. "It will return. You must be ready." He opened his bag. "We have much to work on before the season. For today, we will review what we have learned so far."

Lab heard a sudden scratching behind him.

"Twig, you know the drill," Rolabi said.

He began to set up another obstacle course. He threw cones into different patterns, tossed out slender poles, and dumped more helmets and pads onto either side of the halfway line. He placed a ball at the top of either key, and Lab thought he saw a flash of clouds behind the net, like the ones that had hung above the tall, crumbling mountain. The lights flickered, and the team's shadows rose up from the floor.

Lab watched, remembering when he had not so long ago refused to believe in magic. Now he grinned as the shadows started stretching, and as Kallo paced around the gym, and as one item after another came flying out of the bag and fell into perfect lines. He wondered what else grana could do.

They will come to find out.

Who? Lab said.

The room darkened. The other players fell into gray, and soon it was only Lab standing in a dull spotlight at center court and the shadows in the corners. One of the shadows stirred. A shape appeared, gray in the black, and strode out in the light. The sharp lines of his face took form, almost skull-like, and the sunken eyes remained shadowy. But Lab knew the face well.

Everyone in Dren did.

"There is no place for grana here," President Talin said, his voice low and gravelly.

His dark eyes fell on Lab, freezing him in place.

"Take them!" he shouted.

The shadows closed in from all sides, and Lab was about to scream when the gym lights flared again, banishing all the shadows. He stood there, panting, looking warily around Fairwood. He thought back to Rolabi's story about the Wizenards, and how they had been banned from Dren. President Talin. He didn't want grana here. And the Badgers were using it.

He looked at Rolabi. The big man held his eyes.

No. But it must return anyway. And you must be the bearers.

Why? Lab thought.

Because you can. And you are going to change everything.

Lab glanced at his brother. He was afraid. Desperately so.

But he was also ready to change things.

"In a line," Rolabi said.

It was the hardest drill of Lab's life. It took five attempts before they hit a free throw, which meant they had run twenty-five laps before they even started. The floors shifted at every turn. Kallo pounced on them. The shadows challenged every shot. Lab met his own personal challenges: disappointed voices, flashing memories of the last few years, a crowd chanting that he was a failure. He pushed on, and the crowd began to quiet.

At one point, he came to the jump shot. The gym cleared instantly. It was him and the hoop and voices from all sides. Spectators counting down the clock. *Three . . . two . . .*

He felt the familiar pressure. The thought that he would let them down. That he could only let people down. But then he breathed. He had only a second. He slowed it in his mind. He felt his breath, and the ball in his hand, and he thought of nothing but the shot. The voices faded away.

The shooter who masters time does not fear the moment.

Lab took the shot and hit it, and the gym returned again. He stood there, panting, feeling like he had won a playoff game. The others were running around, facing their own challenges, and from the corner of his eye, he saw Peño pounce onto the black orb and disappear.

Rolabi called the drill to a halt, and the team launched into discussion. Lab was only half listening—he was wondering what was in Peño's room. Whatever it was, Lab would be there to talk, if Peño wanted.

Almost on cue, Peño popped back into the gym.

"Good, bro?" Lab said, relieved.

"All good, man," Peño said, giving him props.

The team suddenly burst into laughter, and Lab joined in. He hadn't even heard the joke, but for some reason he laughed anyway, and kept laughing, hard enough that his sides hurt. He felt like the whole experience, all the ridiculous, impossible things, were all pouring out of him.

"Twig telling jokes," Peño said. "What's next?"

Peño started beatboxing, clearly preparing himself for a freestyle.

Lab rubbed his forehead. "Not again."

"Camp is almost done
We probably still got to run
Putting Champs on a banner
The quiet over clamor
Peño waits to watch
Cheers and stops
He wanted rhymes with 'Badger'
But the words didn't matter
Ball is roads and ramps

No more time for losses
Only time for champs."

Lab stared at his brother in amazement.

And then chaos broke loose as everyone crowded around Peño. Lab jumped in, and he grabbed Peño's shoulders and shook him, laughing wildly.

"You aren't the world's worst freestyler anymore!" he shouted.

"Hey!" Peño said.

Rolabi picked up his medicine bag and headed for the doors.

"I thought you said we still have a puzzle to solve?" Rain called after him.

"You do," Rolabi said. "One for each of you. And by the way, welcome to the Badgers."

He walked out to an uproarious cheer, and then the Badgers headed for the benches. Lab sat down and slipped off his shoes. He thought back to the words on the bathroom door. The riddle. Rolabi's last puzzle for him:

What is the first thing you do when you climb out of a hole?

Lab slowly put his shoes away. Stretch? Look for food? Enjoy the sunshine? None of it felt right.

He looked at his teammates again. He thought of Vin asking if he would come to the park and help him with some bullies. He thought of Big John struggling with two jobs. He thought of Peño, and how Lab hadn't even known that his own brother was hurting. He had been weighing himself down so far, isolating himself so much, that he couldn't see what they were all going through.

Lab knew the place below sadness. He had been living there for ages. He had been in the hole. And just like that, he knew the answer to the silvery question on the wall.

The first thing to do was turn back and help the next person climb out.

Lab smiled. He could do that. He could take the next step on his road.

When the team had finished changing their clothes and zipping their bags, they all stood up together and headed for the doors. Rain was first, holding the door, while Peño let everyone else go ahead. The afternoon sunshine grew brilliant, the door wide, and Lab walked through, smiling. He knew there was trouble coming. He knew that this would not be a normal season.

But he was with the team, and the light was back again, and he was ready for anything.

THE END OF THE BEGINNING

NO ONE WAS talking. Reggie felt the sweat beading on his forehead.

The last two months had flown by in a haze of sweat. They had faced many challenges, real and magical, and now the season had come. A Friday night in Fairwood Community Center, and it was packed. Every spot in the bleachers was full. More spectators were standing along the walls.

Rolabi walked into the locker room. "Full house tonight."

"We noticed," Jerome said, rolling his sweaty hands in his lap.

"Why are there so many people?" Twig asked.

"The Bottom has been a difficult place lately," Rolabi said. "They need some basketball."

Reggie nodded. Everything had changed. The government had come back for them.

"You have worked hard," Rolabi said. "I ask that you do the same tonight. The road to the championship is paved with sweat and pain and fear. Tonight, you start walking that road."

Reggie looked down at his shaking hands. He wondered if the

others knew that this season was going to be different. If they knew that the road would be harder than they imagined.

"The time has come," Rolabi said. "Everything we have learned, everything we have practiced . . . it comes out tonight. It starts here. And now I must ask you . . . are you truly ready?"

Reggie closed his hands into fists. He was ready. He had never felt more *ready*.

Rain stood up and put his hand in the middle of the room, and soon ten trembling hands were overlapping. Reggie took a deep breath. He had been dreaming of this day for months now.

"Badgers on three," Rain said. "One . . . two . . . three . . . *Badgers!*"

Rolabi started outside, and the cheers erupted immediately. Reggie saw his gran and sister shouting and waving from the bleachers. He smiled, but he felt the flicker of concern.

Above all else, he had to protect them.

"Reggie," Rolabi said quietly. "Hang back."

He frowned and let the others go ahead. "Yeah, Coach?"

"You will be playing big minutes tonight. You are our first sub for the backcourt."

"But Vin and Jerome . . ."

"I've already talked to them. They agree you can play any spot back there."

Reggie was speechless. "I . . . Thank you."

"You earned it."

Reggie grinned and turned to go, but he felt an enormous hand on his shoulder.

"You know what this means, don't you? You know where this road is leading."

"Yes," Reggie said softly. "I think so."

"And you still have chosen to take it. Your parents would be proud."

Reggie felt tears in his eyes, but he just nodded and sat at the end of the bench.

Twig stepped into the circle for the tip. Reggie chewed his nails, his heart racing.

The ref blew the whistle and threw the ball up. Twig and the other center jumped, desperately reaching, and the ball spun in midair as two hands closed in. But Twig was faster.

The ball flew back toward Peño. The game was on.

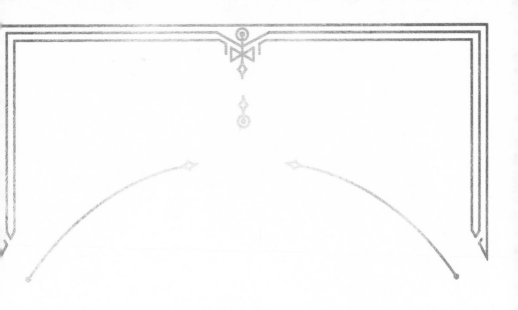

TO BE CONTINUED WITH REGGIE . . .

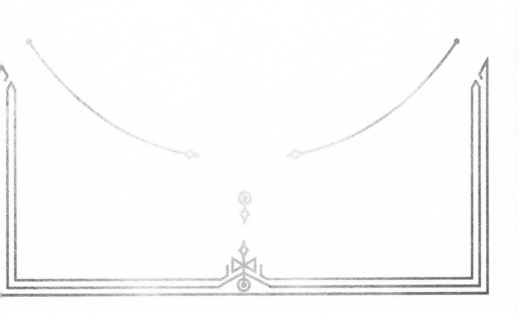

WIZENARD PROVERBS

The road is all that matters.

Give your fear a face or you will see it everywhere.

To find the real leader, search where the fight is hardest.

If you don't like being alone, you must learn to like yourself.

Never let your identity be written by another.

Victory happens in the mind first.

Suffering is our greatest chance for strength.

A true leader stands at the bottom, pushing his team up.

No one wins alone. Those that forget this do not win.

Every grudge is a new weight you must drag along behind you.

If you want to succeed, start by turning your weaknesses into strengths.

Everyone has a choice every moment of the day. Look, or look away.

A person is the same as a tree. Without a strong foundation, they cannot grow.

When you are in a hole, help everyone else first. By the time you are done, the hole will no longer exist.

Anger is just your mind telling you to step away and breathe.

If you chase happiness, you will never let yourself suffer. Chase purpose instead.

You know nothing of your strength until you have felt truly weak.

If your nights feel empty, then your day can still be filled.

We fear what is different only because we think it makes us less.

If you rise above the conflict, you can see who needs your help.

Winning is an empty cup. Fill it with work, struggle, and compassion.

Courage is understanding that it is okay to be afraid, and then to walk on regardless.

If you are afraid of loneliness, spend more time alone.

Even the loudest voices cannot fell a tree.

There is always a deeper darkness. Find it, face it, and know the night will pass.

Your story will be much happier if the writer likes their protagonist.

Complacency guarantees failure.

When we are struggling, we are learning the tools to help others.

If you can't read minds, put yourself in others and open your eyes.

If you assume someone is perfect, you miss the opportunity to help them.

The past is a gift. It reminds you there is a future.

If you worry about what others think of you, you don't think enough of yourself.

There is only one critic who matters.

The lone wolf will soon starve.

Never let your desire for more supersede your gratitude for any.

Stare at the sky and choose if you will be a mouse or a mountain. Either way, you are right.

If your road is easy, use the time wisely. Grow strong. There are hills over the horizon.

If you are unsure of your destination, you might as well keep walking.

When we dwell on regret, we make the past our future.

Wake up with a purpose or risk going to sleep without one.

A champion is like the tide. Controlled, powerful, and most of all, consistent.

If you bring too much with you, how will you help others with their bags?

If you want to be stronger, lift the ones who need to be carried.

Spectators can applaud or jeer. Does it matter? Either way, the track remains.

You are stardust and light. If they cannot see that, then you have chosen to hide it.

What you see in the mirror comes from the mind, not the body.

We are made of a million questions that only one person can answer.

You do not jump for the summit. You take hundreds of small, imperceptible steps.

We need not fear what we cannot control, but we can learn to control our fear.

You may tire on the road. It may grow dark. Rest if you must, but never give up. Walk until the darkness is a memory and you become the sun on the next traveler's horizon.

KOBE BRYANT is an Academy Award winner, a *New York Times* best-selling author, and the CEO of Granity Studios, a multimedia content creation company. He spends every day focused on creating stories that inspire the next generation of athletes to be the best versions of themselves. In a previous life, Kobe was a five-time NBA champion, two-time NBA Finals MVP, NBA MVP, and two-time Olympic gold medalist. He hopes to share what he's learned with young athletes around the world.

WESLEY KING is the award-winning author of eight novels. His works include *OCDaniel*, *The Vindico*, and 2018's *A World Below*. His books have accumulated more than ten literary awards and multiple Junior Library Guild Selections and have been optioned for film and television and translated for release worldwide. When he is not writing, Wesley travels extensively around the world and gives workshops and presentations for thousands of students annually. Wesley is also known for his height (6'7") and his fondness for all things *Star Wars* and sports.

GRANITY STUDIOS, LLC
GRANITYSTUDIOS.COM

Library of Congress Control Number: 2018964205
ISBN (hardcover): 9781949520019
ISBN (eBook): 9781949520026

Printed in the United States of America
1 3 5 7 9 10 8 6 4 2

Book design by Karina Granda
Cover and art direction by Jeff Toye and Spandana Myneni